THE MURDER AWARDS

AN AMY ROWLINGS MYSTERY.

T.A BELSHAW

SPELLBOUND
BOOKS

My Ruddington Village Readers

CHAPTER
ONE

Spinton Town Hall was built in 1910 in the popular Edwardian baroque style and consists of several large meeting rooms, a council chamber, complete with a huge, colourful coat of arms above the mayor's chair, and a nicely appointed Assembly Room which was the biggest space in the building and boasted a vaulted ceiling, oak panelled walls and a diamond patterned parquet floor. It was lit by two rows of low hanging crystal, waterfall, chandeliers with pairs of fan-shaped sconces set at intervals along the walls.

Amy Rowlings stood alongside a hungry and impatient, Detective Inspector Bodkin in the mostly well-behaved queue for the buffet which had been set out on a series of tables that took up almost the entire length of the room.

Amy was an attractive, twenty-one-year-old woman with a slim, but shapely figure. Her flaxen hair was cut to shoulder length and swept back at the sides, held in place by two, cobalt coloured hair clips. She was wearing a blue, thin strapped, calf length, bias cut dress with a plunging V back. She had finally bought it from Brigden's nearly new fashion shop in the town after being tempted by it for weeks. It had taken a month to save the twenty-five shillings the dress had cost. Bodkin was dressed in his spare, navy blue, work suit with a white shirt and blue tie. Bodkin could never look smart; no matter how well his clothing was pressed, it seemed to hang on him as though it was at least two sizes too big. Amy did her best to keep him on his feet, knowing that once he'd sat down for more than five minutes, his trousers would begin to rumple and look like he'd been wearing them for a week.

The policeman looked longingly at the rows of plated up sandwiches, sausage rolls, quiches and cheese and pineapple speared sticks.

'My stomach thinks my throat's been cut,' he said.

'Bodkin, you were offered a sandwich before we left home, it's your own fault.'

'I wasn't hungry then,' he replied, sticking his neck out so he could look along the queue.

'Bodkin?' The detective inspector swivelled around to find himself face to face with his old boss, Acting Superintendent Laws who had recently taken up a temporary post down in Maidstone.

'This is a ... erm, pleasant surprise, sir. I wasn't expecting to see you here tonight.'

'I thought I'd do my bit, Bodkin. Chief Superintendent Grayson has been my superior for twenty odd years. It would have been churlish of me not to come and see him receive his public service award.' He closed one eye as he thought. 'What are you doing here though, that's the question?'

Laws suddenly spotted Amy who was doing her best to hide behind a large woman just ahead of her in the queue. 'And you have Miss Rowlings with you as usual. You two seem inseparable, even when you're supposed to be at work.'

'I was asked to stand in for Chief Inspector Harris, sir. He had to withdraw at the last minute, something to do with the case he's working on.'

'Hmm, well, you could have dressed for the occasion man. That looks suspiciously like your work suit.'

'It is my work suit, sir. I only have two.'

Laws leaned forwards. 'You could have hired appropriate clothing for the night, Bodkin. You're not even wearing a bow tie, let alone white gloves.'

'I couldn't get hold of a pair of white gloves, sir. As I said, it was late notice, I wasn't aware that I was coming until this afternoon.'

'Your girlfr... erm Miss Rowlings seems to have got the dress code message.' He held out his gloved hand to Amy. 'You look very nice, my dear.'

Amy took his hand and shook it gently as she waited for Laws to return to type and berate her for involving herself in Bodkin's cases. Instead, he smiled at her. 'My erm, my wife couldn't make it tonight, sadly. So, I brought my former secretary with me... where is the woman?' Laws scanned the area looking for his guest. Ah, here she is.' He put a podgy hand on the blonde woman's back. 'Bodkin, you already know Trixie, don't you? Trixie, this is Miss Rowlings.' Laws turned away as he spotted a waiter with a tray of drinks.

Amy's heart sank. Trixie was a secretary at Spinton police station and lived in a flat on the floor below Bodkin's at Bluecoat House. They had got off on the wrong foot and their relationship hadn't improved since.

'Oh, we've met, actually,' Trixie said, pinching up her face she looked Amy up and down. 'You're a machinist at the Mill, aren't you? Did you make that dress yourself? You're very clever.'

Amy glared back at the blonde bombshell. Trixie was a platinum blonde with bright, oval shaped, blue eyes and lips that looked like they had been inflated with a bicycle pump. She wore a glittering, white and silver, full length, off the shoulder gown, which showed off of her fulsome breasts to their best advantage.

Amy tipped her head slightly and examined Trixie's dress carefully. 'I actually bought mine, Trixie, but I think I might have run yours up at the factory. We do a lot of good quality dresses for the lower end of the market.'

As Trixie's mouth dropped open, Bodkin took hold of Amy's arm and hurried her away from the queue.

'Don't you dare tell me to calm down, Bodkin,' Amy said, narrowing her eyes at the inspector. 'I'm perfectly calm.'

'What is it with you two? Can't you at least be civil to each other?'

'Civil...? She doesn't know the meaning of the word. Anyway, she started it, as usual.'

'But couldn't you have ignored her, just this once?'

Amy's eyes opened wide. 'You are joking aren't you, Bodkin? If you think I'd let that... CREATURE, get the better of me then you really don't know me as well as you think you do.'

Bodkin sighed. 'It was a spiteful thing to say. I can see why you reacted.' He took a pace back and admired her. 'You look fabulous.'

'Thank you, Bodkin. You look quite presentable too, very handsome, but please, I'm begging you, don't sit down until you get home.'

When the fifty or so guests had finished their buffet meal, long-serving councillor Ray Dimple walked onto the stage and tapped the microphone twice to check it was working. Then, pulling out a typed sheet of paper from his inside pocket and after tapping the microphone once more, either for luck or reassurance, he cleared his throat and addressed the crowd.

Dimple was a fat man with button eyes, a turned-up nose and

a huge flap of sagging skin that hung over his collar almost hiding his black bow tie.

'Ladies and gentlemen,' he said in his flat, almost emotionless voice. 'Tonight, we gather here to show our appreciation to some of the stalwarts of our community...'

Dimple droned on for a further five minutes, noting the achievements of Basil Thornalley, the outgoing mayor before wishing the newly appointed mayor, the 'best of British luck' for his tenure. The new mayor, councillor Robert McKenzie, climbed the three steps to the stage to polite applause and made a short speech, assuring the guests that he would do his best to live up to the standards set by his predecessor before handing over a silver plate, engraved with the town's coat of arms to the former holder of the office.

As McKenzie left the stage, Dimple stepped up to the microphone again, and in his monotonous tone, announced that the Spinton Council, long service shield, would go to John Anthony, the clerk to the council, who was reluctantly retiring in two weeks' time.

Dimple's voice droned on as he presented awards to retiring or long serving council staff and Bodkin was beginning to find it harder and harder to stay awake. His head began to nod and he was only saved from falling asleep by a dig in the ribs from Amy's elbow.

'Uh, what...?'

'Grayson's up,' Amy hissed.

Bodkin shook his head to clear it and tried to concentrate on the ceremony.

'... since the reorganisation of the Kent region police force and the building of the new police station, Spinton has seen a noticeable fall in crime...'

Bodkin almost choked. 'What? We could do with building another cell block, we fill them up so quickly,' he muttered.

'… the man who has brought two evil murderers to justice this year alone, the man who keeps our streets safe for our families, Chief Superintendent Stuart Grayson!'

Bodkin and Amy got to their feet and applauded politely as Grayson took to the stage. Amy liked the man, he was so much friendlier than his underling, Laws, and had given permission for Amy's one-woman band, investigations agency, ARIA to be given police accreditation.

'You should be getting that award, Bodkin,' she said in a stage whisper. 'You caught the murderers, not him.'

'They also serve who only stand and wait,' the policeman replied.

'You see, you should be up there, you can quote John Milton. You really are full of surprises, Bodkin,' Amy said, her eyes shining.

'Your detective work helped solve both those cases, Amy. I might well have got there in the end but it was your knack of spotting a well-hidden clue that brought both cases to a speedy conclusion.'

Amy squeezed Bodkin's arm and smiled up at him. 'It's nice to be appreciated,' she whispered.

The Man of the Year Award went to a local businessman, Nelson Kelly. Dimple took a step back and applauded as the recipient climbed the steps to the stage.

Kelly was a handsome man who looked a few years younger than the forty summers he had actually been on the earth. His mop of unruly, straw-coloured hair flopped over one eye and had to be occasionally brushed back with a sweep of his white gloved hand. His company, Kelly Construction and Development Limited had become very influential in the town over the last ten years and had been responsible for building not only the new police station and the apartment buildings that went with it, but had also set out a five-year plan for the development of the land on which a swathe of dilapidated Victorian houses stood. Kelly intended to build a new armaments factory on the site, a proposal that was backed by the government which had suddenly found itself years behind Nazi Germany in building up the country's outdated military.

After a rousing speech promising modernisation and prosperity for all, Kelly stepped down to a mixture of cheers, a few loud mutterings and the pop of a flashgun. His plans were not universally accepted in the town. A compulsory purchase order had recently been issued to allow the land to be acquired and more than a few owners of the ill maintained Victorian terraces felt they had lost out financially on the deal.

As Kelly stood, surrounded by back slapping well-wishers at the foot of the stage, a female cloak room attendant scurried in from the corridor on the right-hand side of the Assembly Room. She stood patiently for a full minute before announcing in a loud voice that there was a telephone call for Mr Kelly. She held out her arm before leading him down the passage to the telephone that was situated on the wall opposite the cloakroom.

A few minutes later, Grayson approached Bodkin with Laws and Trixie in tow. After congratulating his superior officer on his award, Bodkin introduced Amy.

'You know Miss Rowlings of course. She's the—'

'ARIA investigations,' Grayson said, enthusiastically. 'Of course, how could I possibly forget.' He beamed at Amy as he held out his gloved hand. 'That was a fine piece of investigative work you carried out in the Villiers case, my dear. I only wish some of my officers possessed the same intelligence.' He gave Bodkin a quick nod. 'Present company excepted of course.'

Just then, a woman screamed, her voice carrying above the hum of twenty or so conversations.

Bodkin was first to react and hurried across the parquet floor towards the sound of the horrified scream. Amy weaved amongst the crowd behind him, trying not to trip as her two and a half-inch heel clicked staccato-like across the wood block floor.

She reached the wide, airy corridor only a few yards behind the inspector who, after taking in the scene for a few seconds, suddenly turned and held out his arms, trying to block the view of any onlookers.

'Please, go back, stay in the Assembly Room,' he said.

Amy took a pace to the side so that she could see what the sobbing woman had witnessed but she was soon caught up in a rush of bodies as the people behind her pushed forwards, eager to get a better view.

On the floor in the centre of the corridor lay the prone figure of a fair-haired man. He was lying on his back, his eyes and mouth wide open. His once, white shirt now covered in blood. Sticking out from beneath his sternum was the bone handle of a cook's knife. The front of the woman's cream dress was covered in the man's blood, as were her elbow-length white gloves. The fire exit door at the end of the passageway was wide open. On the left, the double swing doors that led into the kitchen were wedged apart. A caterer's trolley, stacked with plates and cutlery had been parked up against the wall. At the side of the kitchen ran a short corridor that led to a wide, blue painted door.

'It's Kelly.' The word spread quickly through the circling crowd as they craned their necks to see the horror that lay just behind Bodkin. Suddenly there was a loud pop and a bright flash as the newspaperman got off a quick shot.

'Keep control here, Bodkin, I'll ring for a bit of back up,' Grayson said as he pushed his way through the crowd to get to the telephone.

Acting Superintendent Laws began to usher the horrified guests back into the Assembly Room. 'Back off, please, there's nothing to see here,' he said.

Trixie put a hand to her mouth and then swooned into the

arms of a tall, dark-haired businessman, who half led, half carried her to a nearby table, sat her down and began to fan her with an elegantly folded table napkin.

Amy stepped forward as the kneeling woman continued to sob uncontrollably. Crouching at her side, she put an arm carefully around her shoulders.

'Shh, shh, help is on its way,' she said soothingly.

The woman lifted her head and looked tearfully at Amy, the area under her eyes were smudged with black mascara.

'Poor Nelson,' she sobbed. 'Who would do such a thing?'

CHAPTER
TWO

'What's your name, Miss?' the uniformed policeman asked as Amy let go of the sobbing woman's hand and stepped back to allow the officer to get closer to the body of the dead man.

'Lorna,' the woman said between sobs. 'Lorna Wetherby.'

'Well, let's get you away from here, Miss Wetherby,' said the officer, gently. 'Come on, we'll find you a quiet spot in the Assembly Room.'

Amy looked around for Bodkin and spotted him walking towards the open fire exit. She hurried after him, and caught up just as he stepped onto the pathway that ran between the Town Hall and the library, which was about ten feet away.

Bodkin looked right and left before walking towards the front of the building. Next to the public telephone box was a bus stop where a young courting couple were wrapped in each other's arms. His attention was dragged away from them when a taxi pulled up at the kerb about twenty feet away and the figure of a black-suited man wearing a dark hat, climbed in. The taxi drove off as Bodkin stepped towards it.

'Adam's Cabs. Just in case you didn't spot it,' Amy said as she came up behind.

'How could you tell?' Bodkin asked. 'They all look the same to me.'

'It wasn't black,' Amy replied. 'All the rest are.'

'Well spotted,' Bodkin replied, pulling out his notebook and jotting down the information and the time. He turned back to the courting couple who were still lost in each other.

'Excuse me?'

The couple carried on kissing.

'Excuse me,' Bodkin said, louder, tapping the young man on the back.

They parted reluctantly.

'What?' snapped the young man, obviously annoyed.

'Did you see anyone coming out from the side of the Town Hall a few minutes ago?' Bodkin asked.

'I didn't see a thing, mate. I kiss with my eyes closed.'

'Sorry,' the girl put in. 'We were... otherwise engaged.'

As Bodkin turned away, the couple resumed their embrace.

'They wouldn't have noticed a bomb going off,' Bodkin said as he began to retrace his steps. 'Let's have a look around the back.'

He hurried towards the rear of the Town Hall where there was a narrow, paved area between the back wall of the building and a five-foot wooden fence that marked the tree-lined boundary of Russell Park, a favourite spot for dog walkers and family picnics.

A row of seven dustbins lined the fence, the third in line lay on its side, the lid turned upside down on the tarmacked surface. The bin had a deep dent about half way down its length.

On the back wall of the Town Hall, a row of three windows looked out over the park. In between the left-hand window and the larger, centre one, was a solid-looking, blue-painted door. Bodkin tried the handle and pushed it open. It led into a short corridor with a stack of empty cardboard boxes which the caterers had used to transport the evening's buffet, piled haphazardly against one wall. After pulling the door shut and holding his hand over his eyes to stop any reflection, he peered into the larger of the windows.

'That's the kitchen, I can picture where we are in relation to the corpse now.'

With Amy in tow, Bodkin walked the full width of the building until they came to a narrow pathway that ran between the Town Hall and the Register Office. He looked up towards the main road, then over to the Register Office where a light shone through a half glass door on the side of the building.

'So, our murderer either used the bin to scale the fence, or jumped into that taxi,' Amy said as they walked back around to the fire exit.

Bodkin shrugged. 'Both are strong possibilities. But there are other options.'

'You mean the killer might still be inside?'

Bodkin led Amy back to the fire escape and looked over to the library where a chink of light was showing through a small gap in the window blind.

'Cleaners probably,' he said, turning back towards the fire exit.

Inside, an ambulance crew had arrived, along with Doctor Mortensen who was the police doctor on call and three uniformed officers, one of which was female.

'Anything immediate to report?' Bodkin asked.

'Apart from the fact that he's dead? No, it's far too early for that, Inspector,' Mortensen replied a little testily.

Bodkin nodded.

'I'll ask the pathologist to put him on the table first thing tomorrow, but I doubt there'll be any surprises,' the doctor said.

Bodkin took another long look at the victim, before turning away to face the cloakroom.

'Where's the girl who brought the message about the phone call?' he asked.

'She's back inside the cloakroom,' PC Fernley said. 'One of the catering girls is with her. She's a bit shaken up.'

Bodkin was about to enter the cloakroom when he heard Grayson's voice calling his name. He turned to see the Chief Superintendent beckoning him from the Assembly Room end of the corridor.

'Laws wants to send all the dignitaries home, and I tend to agree with him,' he said, as Bodkin frowned. 'None of these people could leave town without it being noticed, Bodkin. The mayor wants to get his wife home ASAP, she's rather upset,' he waved his arm in the general direction of the Assembly Room. 'They're all highly influential people and they want to go home and I don't want to spend the next week fending off complaints from the chief constable. Get uniform to take names and addresses, then let them go.'

'Everyone in the room will be upset sir,' Bodkin replied. 'If the killer is still inside, he'll be more than happy to be sent home.'

'I think it's pretty obvious that our man cleared off through the fire escape, Bodkin.'

The inspector pulled a face. 'Possibly,' he replied.

'Look, man. Sometimes the obvious line is the line to follow.' Grayson looked over his shoulder and motioned to his wife to stay where she was. 'This is your case, Bodkin. Chief Inspector Harris has enough on his plate and you were at the scene of the crime after all. It shouldn't be too difficult to track down the only man on the guest list who isn't still here. You could be back working on that plague of burglaries by next week.'

'I'd still like to ask a few questions of the guests, sir. While their memories are fresh. It shouldn't take that long, most of them are couples, I can question them together if it speeds things up.'

'All right, Bodkin. But the mayor, his lady wife and their

guests are going home. They were all in a group by the stage when the incident happened.'

'I'd prefer to talk to them now, sir, but if you insist, I'll drop my objection and question them later. How many people are we talking about?'

'A dozen or so, no more. Alderman Franklyn is kicking up a fuss. The official cars will be parked up waiting to take them home and Mrs Franklyn wants to powder her nose and pick up her fur coat. She's concerned that our murderer might be an opportunist thief who was caught in the act.'

'Just give me five minutes to question the cloak room girl, sir.'

Bodkin turned away with a thin smile on his face and called to one of the uniformed officers guarding the fire exit.

'Palmer. Sit yourself down at that side table near the front entrance and take down the names and addresses of everyone in the mayor's party. If anyone refuses to give you their details, arrest them and I don't give a damn if they claim to be the mayor or the king of Siam.' He turned to another officer who was standing by the fire exit. 'Spencer, set something up to screen off the body will you,' he pointed to four, tall, brass based standard lamps that were laid out at ten-foot intervals along the wall of the corridor. 'Use those.'

'They won't hide much, sir,' Spencer replied, with a puzzled look on his face.

'Position them around the body, cover them with tablecloths to make a screen, there are plenty in the Assembly Room. Didn't you ever make an indoor tent when you were a child, man?'

Debbie Vallance sat on the stool behind the counter in the cloakroom, drumming her fingers on the marble top. If she was upset, she had a very strange way of showing it. On the other side of the counter was a teary-eyed woman wearing the uniform of the catering company that had provided the buffet for the evening. She looked up with red eyes as Amy and Bodkin walked in.

Debbie was a slender girl, about twenty years of age with short, loosely curled chestnut hair, green eyes and a full-lipped, friendly smile. She was eager to tell her story to the policeman.

'Now, Debbie, there's no reason to be nervous. I just want you to answer my questions as truthfully as possible. Give me the facts as you remember them. All right?'

'Oh, I'm not nervous, this is probably the most exciting night of my life, even better than when my Colin proposed.'

Bodkin gave her a short smile. 'You gave Mr Kelly the message telling him he had a telephone call, is that correct?'

'Yes, sir. I was just sitting here reading my copy of Peg's Paper, there was a really good story in it about—'

'Never mind the story, Miss Vallance. Tell me about when you heard the telephone.'

'Oh, right. Well, as I said I was sitting here reading my magazine when I heard the telephone ringing in the corridor. It's my job to answer it if it rings, I wasn't being nosy or anything. Anyway, there's a woman's voice on the line and she wants to speak to Nelson Kelly.'

'What exactly did she say?' Bodkin asked. 'Word for word.'

'Blimey... erm,' Debbie closed her eyes as she thought. 'She said, I want to speak to Nelson, tell him it's urgent.'

'Nelson? Not Mr Kelly, not Nelson Kelly, just Nelson?'

'That's right.'

'And?'

Debbie giggled.

'Oh yes, well, I told her I had no idea who he was, but then she got a bit iffy with me and said, "It's Nelson Kelly, he's receiving an award tonight, he'll be in the main hall, just go and get him." So, I did.'

'What did the woman sound like? What sort of accent?'

'Posh, definitely posh.'

'And you're sure she didn't give her name?'

'Positive,' Debbie looked puzzled by the question. 'I'd have said, wouldn't I?'

'Eventually,' said Bodkin.

The inspector flashed Amy a look and rolled his eyes heavenwards.

'So, you run into the Assembly Room... what then?'

'Oh, I didn't run. We're not allowed to run, it's in the rules.' Debbie held Bodkin's stern look. 'Well, we can't run, it's a fact. You said you wanted all the facts.'

Bodkin ran his hand over his forehead.

'You gave Mr Kelly the message, then what?'

'He followed me along the corridor and picked up the phone, I'd left it sitting on the shelf on top of the phone book.'

'Was the fire exit door open or closed when you came back?'

'Oh, erm... it must have been closed or I'd have noticed it, wouldn't I?'

'And what did you do then?'

'I came back in here, picked up my Peg's Paper but before I could find my place in the story, I heard a scream. I looked out of the door and saw a woman crouching down next to Mr Kelly. He had a knife in his chest and she was screaming like nobody's business... mind you, I'd have screamed as well. I nearly joined in with her when I saw him lying there. It was just like that film with—'

'Did anyone come in here around that time, to use the facilities perhaps?'

Bodkin nodded towards the two doors on the right-hand side of the cloakroom that led to the ladies and gentlemen's conveniences.

'The woman who discovered the body was in here not long before. And there was a man. I've no idea who he was.'

'Describe him?'

'Tall, dark haired, very handsome... I didn't see him leave... I was engrossed in my story.'

'Did he arrive before, or after the woman?'

'At the same time, really. I wondered if they were an item. He reminded me of the hero in my story, he—'

'Did you see the woman leave?'

Debbie hung her head as she shook it.

'I was reading...'

Bodkin sighed.

'Thank you, Debbie. Some of the guests will be through in a moment or two to gather their belongings so I'll leave you to it, but before you go home tonight, I want you to give your name and address to the constable at the front door.' He gave her a thin smile. 'Just your name and address, not your life story.'

Bodkin turned to the still shaking woman at the side of the counter.

'And you are?'

'Rosie Barret. I work for At Your Service Catering. I was on drinks tonight.'

'All right, Rosie, wait in the Assembly Room with the rest of the staff. We'd better get out of the way so that our elders and betters can get their coats.'

'I did hear a bit of an argument,' Debbie said suddenly. 'It didn't last long, less than thirty seconds.'

'Can you remember what was said?' Bodkin asked. 'Think hard, Debbie.'

Debbie closed her eyes and screwed up her face as she concentrated.

'There was a bit of conversation, I couldn't really hear, then a man's voice got a bit louder, "You've ruined me," he said. The other man's voice was a bit smoother... I'd pricked my ears up by then. He said, "It's just business, it's nothing personal." That was it. I didn't hear anything else until the woman screamed.' She paused. 'Oh, she was in here... she left thirty seconds or so after the argument. She smiled at me as she walked out. I remember now.'

Bodkin sighed. 'Is there anything else?'

The girl shook her head under Bodkin's steely gaze.

'Give your details to the policeman before you go home. Just in case anything else springs to mind, you can get me on this number.'

The inspector handed her a printed card. Debbie read it carefully, then tucked it into her magazine, sticking out of the top like a bookmark.

Bodkin opened the door to the corridor and allowed Amy and Rosie to walk out first, then, after holding the door for the first person in the queue, he followed the two women past the line of whispering guests and made his way back to the Assembly Room.

Walking up to the stage, he tapped the microphone before addressing the guests.

'Ladies and gentlemen. I am Acting Inspector Bodkin of Spinton police. I apologise for the inconvenience but I'm sure you'll understand that in the circumstances we will require you to hang around for a short time while we ask you a few questions. It won't take long, so please, bear with us. I'll talk to Miss Wetherby first because she really does need to get home to change as quickly as possible.'

Bodkin selected a table at the back of the room and dragged out a chair. Amy stood behind him trying to make herself look as inconspicuous as possible as the guests gathered in an irritable group in the centre of the room.

'Can we at least get a drink while we're waiting?' A short, grey-haired man called out.

Bodkin caught the eye of one of the waiters and lifted his hand to his mouth as if he was taking a drink, then motioned to a female police constable to bring Lorna Wetherby to the table.

Lorna Wetherby was of medium build with dark, almost black hair, cut in a bob. She was an attractive woman with sleepy green eyes, high cheek bones and full lips. Her makeup had run around her eyes but she had attempted to patch it up while she had been sitting at the table with the police woman. Bodkin gave her a reassuring smile.

'I'm sorry to inconvenience you like this, but these things have to be done. I believe you've been checked over by the ambulance crew and apart from...' Bodkin waved his hand in the direction of the woman's chest... 'the staining on your clothes, you are unhurt.'

Lorna nodded. 'I'm all right, it was just...'

'I completely understand, it must have been awful for you... Now, take your time if you need to but I'd like you to tell me exactly what happened when you discovered Mr Kelly's body. Why were you out in the corridor in the first place?'

'I went to... powder my nose. When I came out of the cloakroom, I saw Nels... Mr Kelly lying on the floor. He was still squirming about at that stage.' Lorna dropped her head into her hands. 'It was awful, his eyes were pleading, he just kept gurgling... help me... help me.' She dabbed at her eyes with a lace trimmed handkerchief.

'When you were in the cloakroom, did you see anyone else, apart from the girl reading behind the counter that is?'

'A man followed me in. I don't know him.'

'Can you point him out please?'

Lorna turned and scanned the room, before pointing to a dark-haired man who was sitting at a table on the right-hand side, sipping a glass of red wine.

'That's him, the man drinking wine at the table.'

'Thank you. Now, when you came out of the cloakroom, did you notice if the fire exit door was open?'

'It was, I remember because I felt a chill breeze on my back. I thought it was the shock at first.'

Bodkin leaned forwards and placed his hands palms down on the table.

'Did you see anyone else in the corridor, or anyone going into, or coming out of, the rooms that led off it? The kitchens for instance?'

Lorna looked up and to the left as she concentrated. 'No, the kitchen doors were wedged open but I didn't see anyone inside. There was no one in the corridor, just a pile of boxes, and I can't remember seeing anyone standing outside the fire exit.'

Bodkin smiled softly. 'Miss Wetherby, you might find the next question or two a little personal but I do have to ask them. Did you know Mr Kelly personally? Were you friends?'

Lorna looked down at her hands. 'We, erm. We were... good friends.'

'Very good friends? Lovers perhaps?'

'No... no... we were good friends, that's all. I'm a respectable woman, Mr Bodkin.'

'I'm sure you are, Miss Wetherby,' Bodkin smiled reassuringly. 'Now, forgive me for asking, but why are you here tonight?'

'I'm doing some publicity work for Mr Kelly. I was going to write up a press report on the event.'

'Do you work for a company, or is it your own business?'

Lorna fished about in her bag and pulled out a business card.

'I work for a public relations company called Pitch and Press. Mr Kelly was taking a bit of a battering in the local newspapers over his latest project, so he called us in to soften his public image.'

'How long have you been working with him?'

'About six months, on and off. It's been a lot more on than off just recently.'

'Do you know anyone else here tonight?'

'I know a few people by reputation or by having seen their pictures in the paper, but I don't think I've actually met anyone in person apart from Mr Kelly.' She hesitated. 'I've only been living in the area since I joined the company. I'm from Sittingbourne originally.'

'You say you wanted to soften Mr Kelly's reputation. Did he have any enemies?'

'Plenty in the business world I would imagine, and the press were on his back recently because of all the old houses he was about to purchase. They were all going to be demolished to make way for a factory and there were a lot of people upset about it. Not just the tenants, but the owners of the properties too. Some of them claimed that they had been swindled out of the true value of the houses.'

'Anyone in particular?'

'You'd have to ask the Post. They were getting their information from someone in the know.'

'They have a reporter here tonight; I'll have a chat with him soon. Thank you, Miss Wetherby.' Bodkin got to his feet and smiled down at the woman. 'You can go now. Constable Norris will see you get home.' He nodded to the female police officer. 'Get a taxi, and bring those stained clothes back to the station when she's changed out of them.'

Lorna got to her feet and the policewoman led her back to the cloakroom to pick up her jacket. Bodkin strolled across to the dark-haired man and motioned to him to get to his feet.

'Follow me please.'

The man picked up his wine glass and followed Bodkin back to his interview table. He was, as Debbie had said, a tall, handsome man. His dark wavy hair was cut neatly and parted on the right. He wore an evening suit with a starched shirt collar and a black, bow tie. As he sat down, he pulled out a silver case and lit a cigarette with a gold coloured, Ronson lighter. After taking a deep draw, he smiled up at Amy and began to fiddle with his signet ring.

Before Bodkin could sit down, Amy caught his eye. As he leaned towards her, she whispered.

'You're not the only one without white gloves, Bodkin. He's got the rest of the get up, why not the gloves?'

THREE

Bodkin placed his notebook on the table, pulled his pen out of his top pocket and smiled across at the man.

'Name please?'

'Drake, Francis Drake.'

Bodkin raised one eyebrow. Drake scratched his cheek with a manicured fingernail.

'Without the Sir in front.'

'So far we've got a Nelson and a Drake,' Bodkin grinned as he looked over the man's shoulder. 'I wonder which one of that lot is going to be Blackbeard.'

Drake pointed his elegant finger at Bodkin. 'Good one,' he said with a stuttering laugh.

Bodkin tapped his notebook with the tip of his pen. 'Right, to business. Why are you here tonight, Mr Drake?'

'I was invited. My company runs a few small to medium sized businesses around these parts and I'm a member of the local civic society. I am a bona fide guest, Inspector.'

'Can you tell me a little bit about your company?'

'It's a family run affair. I took hold of the reins about a year

23

ago now. We own a fair bit of property around the area and have the controlling interest in a construction company and the local cement works. We also dabble in housing rentals. They all fall under an umbrella company, The Drake Group.' He pulled a card from his wallet and tossed it across the table.

'Were you in direct competition with the late Mr Kelly?'

'In business? Of course. I was also in competition for tonight's award. I was shortlisted too. To be honest, I wasn't surprised I didn't get it, I don't think I offered a big enough donation to the Mayor's Fund.'

This time Bodkin raised both eyebrows. 'The Mayor's Fund? What's that when it's at home?'

Drake winked. 'You'll have to ask the mayor... or should I say, former mayor about that. It's his, ahem, personal project. I have no idea how the money is spent. I do know that if you wanted to get anywhere with a project of your own, or if you wanted a council awarded contract, a donation to the fund would help grease the wheels.'

'Are you saying the former mayor was taking backhanders?'

Drake winked again. 'Oh, I couldn't possibly comment on that. I was surprised I didn't get more support for my bid as it was almost identical to the Kelly proposal. Nelson's bid was for an enormous armaments factory, no housing included. God knows where the people on the street due to be demolished would have gone, there are nowhere near enough empty properties in Spinton to have rehoused them all.'

'You say you are surprised that Kelly won the race for the land. Didn't I read somewhere that the government were behind him?'

'Of course they were, and they were willing to back him with some soft loans. They're in a race against time, you see? War is on the not-too-distant horizon, Mr Bodkin. Thousands of factories will soon be turning out bombs and guns, when a few months before, they'd have been making pots and kettles.'

'Did the former mayor back Kelly too?'

'No, I don't think so... Not entirely anyway. For one thing, he would have had a huge homeless problem on his doorstep. Those evicted people would have to go somewhere. Blame wouldn't only have been placed on Nelson's shoulders. The mayor knew there would be a lot of muck thrown and he didn't want to be the one to catch most of it. I believe there was some friction between them. He tried to persuade Nelson to add a number of houses to his scheme and it would have sailed through the planning department on the nod because of the backing of the government. Nelson was having none of it though.'

'Were you surprised when the mayor stood down?'

Drake pulled out another cigarette and lit it. Taking a deep draw, he blew smoke across the table.

'He didn't stand down, Inspector. Councillors elect the mayor, not the public. He won the vote unanimously last time it was held, so something has happened for him to lose that much support in the space of two years, don't you think?'

Bodkin waved his hand in front of his face to dispel some of the smoke. 'Do you know which side of the fence the new mayor is on?'

'He was for Nelson's bid. I know that because he told me I couldn't count on his support.'

Bodkin made a few notes in his book, then scratched behind his ear with his pen. 'Back to tonight, Mr Drake. Can you tell me when and why you left the Assembly Room?'

'Nelson had finished his speech. He was getting pats on the back and warm words of support from a few of the guests, but I'd heard enough of his fake patriotism. He was in it for the money, not the good of the country. He would have made a fortune on government contracts and he knew it.' Drake took another long draw on his cigarette and flicked ash onto the floor. 'As for why, it was a simple call of nature, Inspector.' He looked up at Amy and grimaced. 'Sorry, my dear, but I just had to go.'

'Did you see anyone else in the corridor area while you were out there?'

'Nelson's... how shall I put it... lady friend come publicist, Lorna Wetherby. She came into the cloakroom more or less the same time as me. I didn't see her leave and she wasn't in the corridor when I came out but then, ladies take longer... I'm sorry, my dear.' Drake looked at Amy and once again pulled a face.

'Was anyone in the corridor when you came out of the cloakroom.'

'Nelson was speaking on the wall phone as I stepped out.'

'Did you hear any of the telephone conversation?'

'A bit. He sounded a little annoyed, he said something like, "It's not over until I say it is." That was about it, really.'

'Was the fire escape door open or closed?' Bodkin asked.

Drake looked at the ceiling as he thought and blew a plume of grey-blue smoke into the air.

'Closed. Yes, I'm sure it was closed.'

'I notice you aren't wearing gloves, Mr Drake,' Bodkin said, looking at the businessman's bare hands.

'No, I stupidly left them on the coffee table when the taxi arrived,' Drake replied. 'Poor form, I know, but it just wasn't worth the time and effort it would have taken to go back for them.' He looked at Bodkin's hands and nodded at them. 'I wasn't alone in my negligence though.'

'I didn't forget mine, Mr Drake,' Bodkin replied. 'I don't own any.'

Amy smiled to herself and surreptitiously patted Bodkin on the back.

'Is there anything else you can remember? Anything at all, even the smallest thing could help us,' Bodkin said, looking Drake directly in the eyes.

'Oh, and I saw the mayor... the former one that is, he was walking into the kitchen. I only saw the back of him, but I knew who it was. I'd recognise that combed over hair anywhere.'

FOUR

Before Bodkin could call up the elderly couple who were next in line for questioning, Chief Superintendent Grayson stepped up to his side.

'Bodkin, this is all taking a bit longer than you said it would. Is there anything we can do to speed things up a bit?'

'I won't need to ask too many questions of a lot of them, sir. Only the ones who left the room or saw someone else leave.'

'Look, I'll give you a hand, shall I?' He looked at the group of guests who were getting more and more agitated by the minute. 'I'll just send my wife home. She can get a cab with Laws and Trixie; you don't need to talk to her tonight, do you?'

'No, I can have a chat to her on Monday morning, sir.'

'Right, just give me a moment, then send the older couples to that table over there.' He pointed to an empty table on the other side of the room. 'We should get through them in no time between us.'

Bodkin did a quick head count. After discounting himself, Amy, the Graysons, Laws and Trixie there were twenty-four people left in the Assembly Room, not counting the six catering staff. As most of the guests were in pairs, he might only have to conduct another eight or so interviews himself.

He motioned to the elderly pair to wait at Grayson's table, then beckoned towards a forty something couple who were chatting amiably with the reporter from the Post.

Bodkin soon found that they could add nothing to the information he had already gathered and after only a few minutes questioning, he told them to pick up their coats and go home.

As the next couple stepped forward, Bodkin got up from his seat and waved to a plain clothes officer that had just arrived from Gillingham to help process the crime scene.

'One moment, please,' he said to the next couple as he strode quickly across the room. After a quick handshake, he led the man into the corridor to where the screened-off body of Nelson Kelly lay.

Amy smiled at the couple as they sat down. The woman wore her brown hair in a bob and looked to be in her late thirties, the man was grey haired and at least ten years older.

'Hello,' she said. 'I'm so sorry you have to be put through all of this. It's such a faff, isn't it?'

The woman smiled back as the man grunted. 'I've seen you in St John's church, haven't I?'

Amy nodded. 'Yes, I'm a regular. I go every week with my mum and dad.'

'Ah, yes, the Rowlings. I've met James and Elizabeth. Your father is an engineer at Dransfield's isn't he?'

'He is,' Amy replied looking closely at the woman. 'I can't quite place you, I'm sorry.'

'You wouldn't, my dear. We only moved to the area a couple of years ago. We still attend St Mary's church over at Pucklebury. We have to share a vicar so we only get a Sunday service once a month. We go to a couple of other churches in between.' She held out her hand to Amy. 'I'm Kristina Timms and this is my husband, Edgar.'

'Did you know, Nelson?' Amy asked, sitting down on Bodkin's chair.

'Yes, we know... knew, him quite well as it happens. Edgar was about to invest in his new venture but we don't know whether it's going ahead now. It depends who takes over the company and what their priorities are, I suppose.'

'It's all so sad, isn't it?' Amy said. 'He was a good-looking, successful businessman set to make a lot of money. He must have really upset someone for them to want to do this to him.'

'All businessmen have enemies,' Edgar put in. 'I've got a few of my own. I doubt they'd go to this length to get their revenge on me though.'

'The local paper was always slating him. Or at least that reporter was.' Kristina looked over her shoulder to the pressman who was writing in a thick notebook. 'We tried to keep things on a friendly level when we were talking to him just now. We wouldn't want Edgar to get the same treatment as Nelson got in the Post.'

'Did you see anything tonight?' Amy asked. 'I was in here; I didn't see a thing.'

'Who are you with?' Edgar asked, suddenly. 'How did you get an invitation? I hope I'm not being rude, but it was rather an exclusive guest list.'

'Oh, I'm with...' Amy hesitated for a second... 'Chief Superintendent Grayson's party. He was up for an award. I've done a bit of work for him recently so he very kindly invited me to come along.'

'What kind of work? Are you connected to the police in some way?'

Amy fished around in her bag and pulled out one of her pink business cards.

'ARIA Investigations. Agent, Amy Rowlings,' Kristina read aloud.

'Police accredited,' Amy said, pointing to the line underneath.

Kristina opened her bag and dropped the card inside.

'I know where to come if I suspect that Edgar is being unfaithful to me,' she said, giving her husband a sidelong glance.

'Perish the thought. I wouldn't dare, my darling,' Edgar replied with just the hint of a smile.

Kristina patted her bag and gave Amy a thumbs up.

'I love the pink card,' she said. 'Very swish.'

Just then Bodkin returned.

'Amy, you couldn't do me a huge favour could you? I'm absolutely parched. Could you get the caterers to conjure up a pot of tea? They must have the makings in the kitchen. The councillors drink gallons of it.'

Amy smiled at the Timms and walked across to the half-cleared buffet tables where the six-strong catering staff were sitting.

'Inspector Bodkin wondered if you could rustle him up a pot of tea from the kitchen,' she said.

A middle-aged man with steel grey hair and a five o'clock shadow on his jaw, nodded and turned to one of the young girls.

'Rosie. Off you go.'

'I'll give you a hand,' Amy said as the young girl got to her feet.

Rosie focussed hard on the left-hand wall as she walked quickly past the screen that was hiding the body from view. The plain clothes policeman was standing behind it, taking photographs of the corpse. Stepping aside to avoid the catering trolley that was parked up near the wedged-open swing doors, she stepped quickly through and made her way across the back of the kitchen. Picking up a box of matches she lit the gas hob, then shaking the kettle, she walked towards the window and filled it from a tap on the huge, white Belfast sink.

'The teapot is in the cupboard on your right,' she said. 'We generally make it in an urn when there's a function, but that's going a bit overboard, don't you think?'

Amy opened the cupboard door and pulled out a large, brown teapot. She placed in on the counter next to Rosie and opened up one of the bottom cupboards.

'Where's the tea, and more importantly, as it's Bodkin, where's the sugar?'

Rosie opened a cupboard door next to the cooker and pulled out a box of Lipton tea bags and a bowl of sugar.

'The milk is in the refrigerator over there,' she said, pointing across the room. 'I'd never seen a fridge before I did my first stint here. No expense spared for our councillors, eh?'

Amy, who had only ever seen even a picture of a refrigerator in a magazine, opened the white steel door of the box and looked inside at the shelves containing plates of sliced meat, racks of eggs and a whole trout. On the top shelf was a half-full bottle of milk. Amy sniffed at it suspiciously, then closed the fridge door and carried it across the room to Rosie who had just pulled a china milk jug from the cupboard. She poured a generous measure from the bottle, then carried it back to the fridge.

Amy had just loaded up two cups and saucers onto a tray when she heard raised voices coming from the corridor outside. Stepping out from the open double doors, she saw a uniformed officer standing by the fire exit, talking firmly to a handful of what looked to be cleaning staff. A man in his mid-forties with unruly salt and pepper hair, wearing a faded, blue jacket and baggy grey trousers, was holding the handle of a heavy looking vacuum cleaner; one of the three women directly behind him was holding an identical machine.

'When can we get in then? My staff only get paid until midnight and we've got the entire building to clean.'

PC Spencer spoke clearly but firmly. 'I'm sorry, sir, but as you can see, there has been an incident and no one from outside is allowed to enter the premises. Not by this route anyway. The Inspector might allow you to come in via the front door and work on the upstairs rooms, but I can't see him letting you get at anything down here until tomorrow afternoon at the earliest.'

'Can I have a word then? I'm contracted to clean this place and I won't be paid if we don't get the work done, and if I don't get paid, neither do my staff.'

'PC Spencer?' Amy called as she stepped into the wide corridor, doing her best to ignore the policeman who was still fussing over the body. 'I'll get Bodkin.'

Amy hurried past the tablecloth screen and made her way through the shrinking crowd of guests.

'Excuse me,' she said to the Timms who were just getting to their feet after concluding their interview. 'Bodkin. There's a team of cleaners at the fire escape door. They want to get in to start work. Spencer won't let them of course, but he wondered if you could have a word. Maybe allow them up to the first floor via the main entrance.'

Bodkin sighed. 'All right, I'm coming.'

He looked across to Grayson as he got to his feet. His boss seemed to be getting through his share of witnesses incredibly quickly. 'Would you like a cup of tea, sir?' he asked as he passed Grayson's table.

Grayson shook his head and held up a glass of white wine.

'I'm Inspector Bodkin, how can I be of assistance?'

'We'd like to get in so that we can start work,' said the man.

'And you are?'

'My name is Terrence Derby, I am the proprietor of Derby Cleaning Services, this,' he held out his arm to his colleagues, 'is my team of cleaners.'

Bodkin stepped outside and stood next to Terrence. Amy stayed just inside the building and listened intently as Bodkin spoke.

'If you go around to the front entrance, I'll allow you to get the upstairs areas cleaned. I assume that's the priority area.'

'It's all priority, Mr Bodkin. If we don't fulfil the whole contract, I don't get paid. We've already finished the Register Office and the Library so there's only this place to do and my staff won't work after midnight and I don't blame them. I wouldn't want to work beyond midnight either. Would you?'

'It's a regular occurrence in my job, Mr Derby,' Bodkin replied. He scratched his head. 'Look, I'll try to get cleared up down here by lunchtime tomorrow. Could your staff come in to finish off then? You can do the committee rooms, the offices and the council chamber tonight. I honestly can't let you clean on this floor until our investigation of the crime scene has been completed. You understand that, surely?'

Derby sighed. 'Can't we just do the kitchen and the Assembly Room?' He looked over Bodkin's shoulder to the ambulance crew who were laying a stretcher on the carpet. 'We'll stay out of the corridor.'

'No, it can't be done. The victim has a cook's knife in his chest, so the investigating team will have to do their stuff in the kitchen too. We can't risk contamination or vital clues being removed.'

Derby sighed again. 'All right, we'll do upstairs then come back tomorrow lunchtime.' He pointed towards the main street. 'Go in through the main entrance and get yourselves upstairs, girls, I'll catch you up in a minute.'

Derby pulled off a pair of thick, brown rubber gloves, rolled them up and stuffed them into his jacket pocket, then he pulled out a pack of cigarettes, offered it to Bodkin. When the inspector shook his head, he pulled one out himself and lit it with a match. Amy shuddered as she saw the red blotches and tight skin that stretched over his hands. Derby saw her looking at them and after taking a long drag on his cigarette, held them behind his back.

'They're not pretty are they, miss?' he said. 'I was in the merchant navy in 1917, we were torpedoed by a U-boat, the whole ship went up. I got into the water but not before my hands had been burned trying to get over the side.' Derby took another draw on his cigarette, then tossed it away and pulled on his gloves again.

'Who's dead anyway?' he asked, as the ambulance crew loaded Nelson onto the stretcher. He leaned into the doorway as Kelly's head flopped to one side showing his mop of straw-coloured hair.

'Is that the bloke I saw earlier?' he asked.

'What bloke? When?' Bodkin asked, eagerly.

'It was about nine, nine-fifteen, maybe. We had just walked around from the Register Office to unlock the library so that we could get started in there. I turned on all the lights for them, then walked back to the Register Office to check that all the work was up to standard and to lock up for the weekend. When I came back, I went into the library. There was a sack of rubbish by the back door, so I took it around to the bins at the rear. When I got back, I saw a man standing at the fire door with his back to me. He was in earnest conversation with someone, that unfortunate chap, I reckon.'

'You're sure?' Bodkin asked.

'Positive. You don't see too many with hair like that.'

'Who was he talking to? Can you describe the man at the door?'

'I only saw him from the back. He was wearing a dark suit, he was about five-foot-ten, eleven, light-ish hair. Not the same colour as that fellow, but not blond either.'

'How long where they talking for?'

'I have no idea; I went back into the library and got on with my work.'

'You work with the girls; you don't just run the business?'

'I can't afford not to, Inspector. I only got the contract by undercutting the people who had it before me, so I don't make a lot of money out of it. I run two teams. The day shift looks after our domestic clients. I don't get involved in any of that, but I do help out the evening shift. We clean all three of these council buildings every weeknight. On the odd occasion we come in on Sunday morning if there's been a wedding reception or something on the Saturday evening. I'd love to sit back and employ a cleaning foreman, but at the moment, I can't afford to. I save a wage by getting stuck in myself.'

'How long have you held the contract?'

'About ten months. I took it on when my mother died. She left me a bit of money; I bought into some property and started the cleaning business with it. The contract for this job had been put up for tender, and I had to go as low as I possibly could with the quote to make sure I won it. I also had to make a rather generous donation to the mayor's fund. There isn't a lot of profit in it, but I'm hoping to get more work from the council as other contracts come up.'

'It cost you money to get a contract? That's a bit strange, isn't it?'

'It cost me money to build up a workforce, Inspector, but yes, as it happens, I did have to contribute to the mayor's fund before he'd sign the deal. As for it being a bit strange, I have no idea, it's the first time I've had any dealings with the council.'

Bodkin shook his head. 'You're not the first person to mention the mayor's fund, Mr Derby.' He rubbed his chin as he thought.

'Okay, I'll let you get on, but I will almost certainly want to speak to you again about the man you saw. Could you give the constable on the front door your contact details?'

Derby nodded, then picking up his vacuum cleaner, he limped off towards the main road.

CHAPTER

FIVE

'IT'S ABOUT TIME WE GOT YOU HOME.'

Bodkin took hold of Amy's arm and began to lead her along the gap between the Town Hall and the library. 'I'll get you a taxi.'

Amy shook his hand off and turned back towards the fire escape. 'It's hardly late, Bodkin. Mum and Dad won't be expecting me yet.'

'It's after ten-thirty. They'll start to get worried soon.'

'I'm a big girl now, Bodkin. It's Saturday tomorrow so I don't have to get up for work.' She smiled at the tall officer. 'Anyway, they know I'm with you. I couldn't be in safer hands. You're a policeman after all.'

'They won't be happy knowing you were at the scene of a vicious murder and I let you hang around for hours. We can't even let them know you're safe and well because you're not on the phone network.'

'Blame my esteemed father for that, Bodkin. You know I've been nagging at him for months to get one put in. It's his own fault I can't let him know I'll be a bit late.'

Bodkin shook his head slowly.

'Amy, I'd much rather you went home. I'm going to be here for

38

most of the night, I don't want to...' he tailed off and grimaced, knowing she was about to react.

'You don't want to what, Bodkin? Worry about me getting in the way?'

'No, no... nothing like that, Amy. But I am concerned about what your mum and dad will think of me, allowing you to get involved in this... and for keeping you out 'til all hours.'

'I'm not Cinderella, Bodkin. I won't turn into a pumpkin at midnight you know.'

'Her coach turned into a pumpkin, not her,' Bodkin replied, then grimaced again.

Amy gave him a look. 'You know what I meant,' she said as she narrowed her eyes.

Bodkin sighed. 'I don't have time to argue, Amy. I've still got to work my way through what remains of the guest list. Then there's the catering staff... We need to question them before they can go home. It looks as if one of their knives was used to kill Mr Kelly.'

'Well, don't stand here wasting time arguing with me then, Bodkin. Come on.'

Amy turned and walked briskly back into the building. Bodkin hurried after her.

'You can't stay here all night, Amy. I'm serious. I value your assistance; you know that, but I'm honestly not happy thinking about your parents waiting up, and you know they will.'

Amy stopped, closed her eyes, then nodded. 'All right, but let me stay for another hour. I'll still be home before midnight and my lovely princess dress won't suddenly turn into rags.'

'An hour,' Bodkin replied. 'Then it's the taxi. We don't want to risk you losing a shoe.'

. . .

They returned to the Assembly Room to find that Chief Superintendent Grayson had interviewed three more elderly couples, leaving a much smaller group of annoyed people to glare at Bodkin as he walked to his interview table where one of the catering staff had placed a tea tray with two china cups and saucers. Bodkin filled the cups with tea, added a splash of milk, and handed one to Amy. She sipped at it, pulled a face, then put the cup back on the tray.

'Stewed,' she said.

'As long as it's still wet.' Bodkin tipped two spoons of sugar into his cup and added a little more milk. Lifting it to his lips he drained the lot in one big glug. 'Stewed,' he agreed.

Bodkin motioned to the reporter from the Post to step forward. The press man stopped jotting notes in his pad and moved towards them with his hand held out. Bodkin shook it and invited him to sit.

'I'm Detective Inspector Bodkin and this,' he looked sideways at Amy, 'is Miss Rowlings who is assisting us with our investigation.'

The man smiled at Amy, then began to write in his pad.

'Do the police employ female plain clothes officers now, or are you a female PC out of uniform?' he asked.

Amy produced a pink card from her bag and handed it to him across the table.

'ARIA Investigations,' he read aloud.

'Police accredited,' Amy pointed out.

'I'm Sandy Miles,' the reporter said, making another note. 'I'll tell you what. When this is all over, I'll do a feature on you if you like.' He looked to the ceiling for inspiration. 'Spinton's Super Sleuth with Sex Appeal. How would that do for a headline?'

Amy snatched the card from Sandy's fingers and stuffed it back into her bag.

'I like the pink card,' he said, looking into her eyes. 'Nice gimmick.'

Before Amy could retort, Bodkin held up his hand.

'Mr Miles. Did you observe anything tonight that could help with our investigation? You being a reporter, I assume you notice things that other people don't.'

'It's been an interesting evening,' Sandy replied. 'One or two things that I only suspected have proven to be true.'

'Such as?'

'The Wetherby Woman for a start. There's more to her than meets the eye, that's for certain.'

'In what way?' Bodkin frowned as he looked across the table.

'Well, she claims to be just a PR girl working with Kelly, but there's more to it than that. There have been rumours about them for a long time now.'

'And what did she do tonight that made you put two and two together?'

'Oh, it was just little things. The way she looked at him, the way he spoke to her, the way he smiled. If you studied body language, you'd spot it a mile off.'

Amy narrowed her eyes as she looked across at the reporter. 'They could be just good friends, Mr Miles, or are you saying there were problems with the Kelly's marriage? I read the gossip column in the Post regularly but I haven't seen anything to even hint at it.'

'There are rumours but...'

'But nothing with enough truth in them that you'd risk being sued if you printed the tittle tattle,' Amy replied, scornfully.

Sandy shrugged. 'A story is a story.'

'From what I've read, the Post... and you in particular, seem to have it in for Mr Kelly,' Bodkin said as he poured out another cup of cold tea.

'We report the news, Inspector. Mr Kelly upset a lot of people with his plans for that factory.'

'But wouldn't it have brought a lot of jobs to the area?' Bodkin asked.

'Jobs are no good if the workforce has nowhere to live,' Miles replied with a look of scorn on his face. 'Most of those jobs would have been filled by engineering workers from Gillingham.'

Amy pursed her lips. 'From what I know of the area, and I do know the town well having lived here all my life... unlike you, Mr Miles, the vast majority of those houses are derelict, rat-infested hovels. They have been earmarked for slum clearance for years.'

Miles rolled his head from side to side. 'Most of the inhabitants want to stay where they are. They like living on the estate.'

'How many is most?'

'I don't have the exact figure but there are quite a few. People will be breathing a sigh of relief in the morning.'

'Why is that?' Bodkin asked. 'Won't the company go ahead with the plans regardless?'

'Nope! It's dead in the water now. Horatio Kelly, Nelson's brother, was against the plans from the start. He almost resigned his directorship over the matter. He'll take over the business now, so that's the end of the factory scheme.'

'Horatio and Nelson? Good God...'

'Bodkin!' Amy gave him a stern look.

Bodkin held up both hands in submission. 'Sorry, Amy.'

'Ah, so you're a God botherer are you?' Miles asked with a grin across his face.

'I'm a churchgoer, Mr Miles, I don't "bother" God and I'm sure He's far too busy to notice even if I tried.' She stared hard at the reporter. 'I don't expect non-believers to understand, but I do expect them to show a little respect to those who do believe.'

It was Sandy's turn to raise his hands in the air, his palms aimed towards Amy.

'No offence. My mum is a Methodist and I wouldn't have used those words in front of her. I apologise.'

'Good,' Amy replied. 'Now, where were we?'

'Did you see Miss Wetherby leave the room, Mr Miles,' Bodkin asked.

'I did, I was watching the pair of them. She pretty much followed him out.'

'Did anyone else leave the room at the same time?'

'No... wait... Just before Nelson got the message about the phone call, Frank Drake left... Oh and the former mayor went out just before Drake.'

'Did any of them return before you heard Miss Wetherby scream?'

'I can't remember, sorry.'

Bodkin nodded slowly and Miles made a few more notes.

'Tell me one more thing, Mr Miles,' said Bodkin thoughtfully. 'Do you intend to carry on the campaign against Mr Kelly and his company?'

'It depends what I can dig up,' Sandy replied. 'A good story doesn't die with the victim. There's more to come out, believe me.'

'So, you're not concerned about his widow and how she will react to anything you publish?' Amy asked. 'Don't you think she'll have been through enough?'

Miles stared hard across the table at Amy. 'The truth will out, Miss Rowlings. The truth will out.'

'If you have any information that might be pertinent to this case, I expect you to reveal it,' Bodkin said, sternly.

Miles shrugged nonchalantly. 'I know nothing about what happened tonight, Inspector. But I warn you, please don't try to get me to reveal my sources for anything that I might have learned about Nelson's private life or business dealings. What I know is between me and my editor. The information is out there.

I found it, so you should be able to.' He looked around furtively, then turned back to Bodkin. 'Look, we can do each other a favour here. I'm willing to share what I find if you'll do the same for me. Exclusive inside information on the murder case. You know it would make sense.'

'Mr Miles,' said Bodkin angrily. 'When I see you next, I expect you to answer any questions I have, honestly and truthfully and... if I think you are holding out on me, I'll have you in the cells for obstructing a murder investigation. Do I make myself clear? Or do I have to have strong words with your newspaper's owner?'

'Don't threaten me, Mr Bodkin.' Miles got to his feet and glared at the policeman, but Amy noticed there was a look of uncertainty in his eyes.

'What a horrible man,' Amy said as she watched the reporter walk away. 'I have a feeling he knows more than he's letting on, and I don't just mean about Kelly's private and business dealings. I think he has an inkling about who hated Nelson enough to have murdered him.'

'We'll see,' Bodkin replied. 'Mr Sandy bloody Miles hasn't seen the last of me.'

SIX

By the time Bodkin had interviewed the last of his share of the guests it was eleven forty-five.

'Come on, Cinders,' he said, pointing at his watch. 'Your carriage awaits.'

Amy yawned and put the back of her hand in front of her mouth.

'It has been a long day,' she said. 'I was up at six this morning for work.'

Bodkin put his hand in the small of her back and led her across the Assembly Room, then down the ornately decorated entrance hall and out of the main doors. A taxi was parked at the side of the kerb right in front of the building. Bodkin opened the rear door to allow Amy to get in, then tapped on the driver's window.

'How much to Long Lane, just down from the Old Bull pub?' he asked.

'Two bob should do it,' replied the cabbie, 'it's not far.'

Bodkin stuck his hand in his pocket and pulled out a two-shilling piece and handed it to the driver, then he stuck his head in the back of the taxi where Amy was once again yawning.

'Thank you for a wonderful evening, Bodkin,' she said, leaning forward to kiss his cheek. 'You certainly know how to show a girl a good time.'

Bodkin laughed easily. 'Thank you for being such wonderful company, once again. Sleep well. Are we still on for the pictures tomorrow night?'

'Of course!' Amy replied seriously. 'It's the Sherlock Holmes story, The Hound of the Baskervilles with Basil Rathbone. It's only been out in America for a few weeks. How our little backwoods cinema has managed to get it this early I don't know. It's usually months before the latest movies arrive here.'

'I've read that book,' said Bodkin. 'It's a bit scary, isn't it?'

'It's just a big puppy dog, Bodkin. Don't be alarmed. I'll hold your hand if you get frightened.'

Bodkin laughed as he slammed the door, then waved after the cab as it drove off up the High Street.

'Did you have a good evening, Miss?' the cabbie asked, twisting his neck around to look into the back of the taxi. 'Oh, it's you, Amy, I didn't recognise you with your glad rags on. How are you? Are you still working at the Mill?'

The Mill was the name the town knew the Handsley garment factory by. The building had once been a cotton mill.

'Oh, hello, Rory. Yes, I'm still working there, for my sins. Someone has to keep the country in cheap frocks. How's you mum? I haven't seen her since she left the Mill, that must be six months ago now.'

'She's doing well now thanks, Amy. She'll never be the same as she was but the doctor managed to sort out some medication for her heart problems. It's called digi..dig.. something... It's made from foxgloves the doctor said.'

'Foxgloves? Aren't they poisonous?' Amy asked.

'Dunno,' replied Rory, 'but it works for Mum.'

They drove in silence for a while, then Rory looked over his shoulder again.

'How's Alice? I haven't seen her for a year or two now. Is she still on the farm?'

Alice was Amy's best friend and had taken over the running of Mollison Farm at the age of eighteen when both her parents died.

'She's fine. She actually runs the farm now.'

'Runs it? But she's a wom—'

'A woman? Well spotted, Rory. Do you think that only men are capable of running a farm?'

'No... well, yes... Oh, I don't know. It just seems like a lot of responsibility for a young girl. I mean, she must have a dozen farmhands to look after, don't they resent being ordered about by a woman?'

'They don't mind being paid by one, Rory.'

'No, I suppose not... Things are changing, aren't they? There's a woman pharmacist at the chemist shop now. She owns the place and there's a woman working as a doctor at the free hospital.'

'Scary isn't it?' Amy replied. 'We're taking over, Rory. You'd better watch out, there might be some female taxi drivers soon.'

'We've already got one,' Rory replied bitterly. 'She can only work school hours because of the kids. It's not fair on the rest of us really.'

Amy sighed.

'Anyway, regarding Alice, say hello from me the next time you see her. I've always fancied her. She looks just like that woman off the films... whassername? Rita something... Haywood? Gorgeous... Alice is a dead ringer for her.'

'It's Rita Hayworth and it has been mentioned a few times,' Amy replied. 'Alice has a daughter you know?'

'A daughter? She's only about nineteen, isn't she?'

'What's that got to do with anything? She's a mother and she runs a farm. I'd say that's an achievement for someone so young, wouldn't you?'

Rory turned off Middle Street onto the Gillingham Road.

'I don't know about that... nineteen... a mother... and unmarried...'

'You seem to be going off her, Rory. Shall I tell her you're not interested anymore?'

'Erm... it's just that I don't think I'm cut out for taking on someone else's kid, I mean... well...'

'That's a shame, I bet Alice will be devastated,' Amy replied.

If Rory had picked up on the derision in her voice, he didn't show it.

'What about you, Amy. Are you seeing anyone...? Ah... that bloke who paid for your taxi, you gave him a peck on the cheek. Isn't he a bit old for you? I could take you out for the night if you fancy it. I'm a bit more your age.'

Amy smiled to herself.

'Thank you for the kind offer but I'm not looking for anyone at the moment.'

'That's a shame. A nice-looking girl like you should have a bloke on her arm. I've got a good job, good prospects. Think about it at least.'

Rory turned right at the telephone box opposite the Old Bull pub. 'Who is that bloke anyway? I've seen him around town, I'm sure I have.'

'He's a policeman, Rory. A detective inspector.'

'And you and him are...? Whoops. I'd better watch my Ps and Qs in future, hadn't I?'

'I think that's a very good idea, Rory,' Amy said with a grin.

The car pulled up outside Amy's house where the lights were still on in the hall. Amy fished around in her purse and passed him a threepenny bit as a tip. She was about to open the door of the taxi when she had a thought.

'Have you been on duty all evening, Rory?' she asked.

'I've been on since nine this morning. I had an hour off, four until five but I've been hard at it ever since.'

'I don't suppose you picked up a posh looking man at about nine... nine-fifteen ... he was a fair-haired man wearing a black suit.'

Rory thought for a moment.

'Ah, the drunk with all the blood down the front of his shirt. Yes, I dropped him off at the Skelton Junction on the Gillingham Road.'

SEVEN

As Rory performed an untidy five-point manoeuvre to turn his car around, Amy hurried up the lane to the telephone box. Picking up the directory, she ran her finger down the columns looking for numbers for the council's civic buildings. There was a long list of them, but near the bottom of the page was an entry for, Assembly Room, Spinton Town Hall. After lifting the handset, she pushed two bronze pennies into the slot and dialled the number. It rang for a full three minutes before it was answered.

'Hello?' It was a man's voice.

'Hello, is that the Town Hall?'

'It is.'

'Who am I speaking to please?'

'Who is asking? That's more to the point.'

'I'm Amy Rowlings, I attended the event tonight as a guest of Inspector Bodkin. Do you think it would be possible to speak to him please? It is very important.'

'He's interviewing the catering staff at the moment, Miss, I don't really want to interrupt him.'

'Please!' Amy begged. 'It's VERY important. Tell him it's about the man in the taxi.'

'The man in the taxi? What about the man in the taxi?'

'Please,' Amy said. 'Honestly, it's to do with the...' Amy groaned as the pips beeped.

'Tell him the–'

Amy slammed the handset down in despair as the call was cut off. She fished around in her purse again but could only find two florins and a silver threepenny bit. She picked up the handset again and considered asking the operator to put through a reverse charge call but wasn't sure if anyone at the other end would accept it. Placing the handset back on the cradle she pushed open the door of the kiosk and walked back to her family cottage, hoping against hope that the person on the end of the line would take the call seriously and pass the message on to Bodkin.

As she pushed open the front door, she found her mother waiting for her in the hallway.

'Hello, love, you're late. We were beginning to get a bit concerned. Did you have a nice time?'

Amy took off her coat and hung it on the peg.

'It was very eventful; I'll tell you all about it in a minute. Is there any tea in the pot, Mum? I'm parched. The last drink I had was tepid and stewed.'

'Really?' her mother sounded shocked. 'You'd think they'd know how to serve a cup of tea at a posh do like that.'

Her father looked up from his book as Amy came into the sitting room. 'Look what the cat dragged in.' He smiled and looked at his watch without saying anything else.

Amy sat at the table and picked up the teapot and shook it.

'I'll make a fresh brew, Amy,' Mrs Rowlings said, taking the pot from her and walking out to the kitchen.

'How's Bodkin? Did he have a good time too?' she called.

Amy pushed a few strands of flax coloured hair away from her face and took a deep breath.

'Actually... I don't know how to put this...' she shrugged and then continued. 'Someone was killed tonight.'

'Oh my goodness. Was it a road accident?' Mrs Rowlings hurried back into the room. Mr Rowlings looked up from his book again.

'No... It was the man who won the businessman of the year award, Nelson Kelly, he was murdered in the corridor next to the Assembly Room. He was stabbed to death with a kitchen knife.'

Mrs Rowling's hands went to her open mouth. 'And you were there? You didn't see it happen I hope.'

'No, Mum, but I...' Amy decided to keep the fact that she had knelt down beside the body to herself. 'Chief Superintendent Grayson was there for an award. He put Bodkin in charge of the investigation.'

'Have they caught the person that did it?'

'No, they don't know who killed him yet, Mum. We've been interrogating the guests since nine-thirty and—'

'WE?' Mr Rowlings looked sternly at his daughter. 'Amy, please don't tell me you've been interfering in police business again.'

Amy grimaced. 'I was there, Dad. I was a witness of sorts, not to the murder but I did have some background information as to who was where when it happened. I wasn't allowed to leave, no one was... well, that's not strictly true, the mayor's party was allowed to go home but the rest of us had to stay behind.' She decided to keep the fact that she had been questioning witnesses to herself.

Mr Rowlings wiped a hand across his brow. 'And we have been sitting here in blissful ignorance while my only daughter was penned up in the same room as a murderer.'

'You wouldn't have been in blissful ignorance if we had a telephone, Dad. I'd have called you to let you know what was happening.'

Mr Rowlings shook his head. 'Whilst it obviously would have been handy on this one occasion to have been on the telephone network, the disadvantages still outweigh the advantages. If I've said it once, I've said it a hundred times. I will not be at the beck and call of my employers. I'd be on the train back to work ten minutes after I got home if they could get hold of me that easily.'

Mr Rowlings was an engineer at a large factory in Gillingham.

Mrs Rowlings placed the freshly brewed pot of tea on the table. 'Couldn't Bodkin have sent you home, Amy? He obviously knew it was nothing to do with you.'

Amy looked away. She hated lying to her parents but she knew they wouldn't react well if she admitted her involvement in the proceedings.

'Bodkin paid for a taxi to take me home,' she said, studying her nails.

'But why did he keep you there so long if—?'

She was interrupted by someone knocking at the front door.

'I'll get it.'

Amy got to her feet and rushed out into the hallway. When she opened the front door, she found Bodkin standing on the step, wearing his scruffy mac over what was now a very untidy-looking suit. His dark hair was tousled and he had a five o'clock shadow across the lower half of his face. He looked at her through tired eyes.

'I got your message, Amy, it was very cryptic though. Something to do with the taxi driver? You'd hung up by the time I got to the phone.'

Amy stepped outside and pulled the door closed behind her leaving her mother peering out from the sitting room.

'Rory, the taxi driver who drove me home, also picked up that man we saw getting into a taxi earlier tonight.'

'REALLY! That is a stroke of luck. Where did he take him, did he say?'

'Yes, he dropped him at the Skelton Junction. You know, that crossroads about a mile down the Gillingham Road?'

'Well done, Amy. Thanks so much for letting me know, I'll nip round to the taxi firm's offices and have a word with him in the morning. I assume he'll be at work on a Saturday.'

'That's not the best of it, Bodkin. Rory said the man was very drunk, and had blood all down the front of his shirt.'

Bodkin blew out his cheeks. 'In that case I think I'd better speak to this Rory fellow tonight. Do you know what time he finishes?'

'No, I don't, I didn't ask, but it didn't look like he was ready to go home. I think there are quite a few fares to be had from the taxi rank late on Friday night.'

Bodkin placed a soft hand on Amy's cheek.

'I'm sorry you got dragged into all this,' he said softly.

'I'm not!' Amy retorted. She treated Bodkin to a wide smile. 'I'm part of an official murder inquiry. The only thing I'm sorry about is the fact that the poor man died. Everything else is a bonus. I'm so excited, I doubt if I'll get any sleep tonight thinking about it all.'

Bodkin shook his head slowly.

'Why am I not surprised,' he said.

He turned to walk down the path to the picket gate.

'Bodkin... Aren't you forgetting something?'

The policeman stopped and turned with a puzzled look on his face only to find Amy standing in front of him. She put her arms around his neck, raised herself on her tiptoes and kissed him softly on the lips.

'That's your reward for a wonderful evening,' she whispered.

. . .

The following morning, Amy had a bit of a lie in and didn't go down for breakfast until just after eight o'clock. She tied her shoulder length, flaxen hair back with a scarlet-coloured ribbon as she walked into the sitting room. Mrs Rowlings was in the kitchen; Amy heard the fat sizzle as she dropped three rashers of bacon into the frying pan.

'Morning, dear, did you sleep well after all the excitement last night?' Her face appeared at the kitchen doorway. 'It's all over the news. Your father is just reading about it.'

Mr Rowlings held up his copy of the Morning Post. Across the front page was the headline. THE MURDER AWARDS! and underneath in smaller print. LOCAL BUSINESSMAN STABBED TO DEATH.

'This reporter...' he glanced quickly at the front page again... 'Sandy Miles, is a bit full of himself. Reading this you'd think he was in charge of the investigation.'

Amy poured herself a cup of tea and took a long sip. 'I met him last night. He's not a very nice person. He'd write any old lie if he thought he'd get a headline out of it.'

'He quotes Bodkin quite a lot.' He read on for a while... 'and what's this? Accompanied by the beautiful local gumshoe, Amy Rowlings... Gumshoe? What on earth is a gumshoe?'

Amy snatched the paper from her father's hands and quickly scanned the story which continued across pages two and three. She breathed a sigh of relief to find that her name was only mentioned the once.

'You look a little pale, Amy,' Mr Rowlings said as she passed him the paper.

'I was just a little concerned about what he might write about me,' Amy replied. 'He said he'd like to do a feature on me at some point. I didn't agree to it, but you know what the journalists at the Post are like. They'd just make any old thing up.'

Amy's mum came in from the kitchen with a plate of bacon

and eggs. She placed it on the table, then went back to the kitchen to get the toast.

'Why is he so interested in you, Amy? And what's all that about gumshoes? Does he mean gym shoes... plimsoles?'

'A gumshoe is a private detective, Mum. It's an American term but it's used over here now as well.'

'I see, but why is he calling you a gumshoe? You're not a private detective.'

Amy decided to come clean. She picked her bag up from the chair and pulled out one of her pink cards. Her mother read it out loud then passed it to her husband.

'ARIA INVESTIGATIONS. Agent Amy Rowlings.'

'Police accredited,' Amy added. She took another sip of tea, then continued. 'I had them done so that I was allowed to help out with the vicar's murder,' she said quickly. 'It was Chief Superintendent Grayson's idea. He wanted someone local as an advisor, someone who knew the people around the Reverend Villiers. As an accredited private detective, I was able to help Bodkin on the case without any questions being asked from higher up at police headquarters. It was all done by the book.'

Mr Rowlings flipped the card over, then handed it back to his wife.

'Isn't that Alice's telephone number?'

'Yes, it is. We don't have one of our own so—'

'Don't let's get into all that again, Amy. Does Alice know her number is being thrown around like confetti?'

'It isn't. I don't have enough cards to give them away willy-nilly. I'm not taking on any private cases or anything like that, and yes, actually. Alice suggested I use her phone number; it makes the card look more professional. She's hardly going to be inundated with calls from suspicious wives.'

'I'm pleased to hear it,' Mr Rowlings said. 'The last thing we need is for a member of this family to be associated with scandals like that.' He folded his paper, stood up and walked across to the table where he picked up the teapot and poured himself a cup.

'So, can I take it we aren't going to have lines of sobbing, angry housewives hammering on our front door begging for your services?' He winked at Amy and treated her to a broad grin.

Amy smiled back at him. 'Dad, I have no intention of taking on any private investigations of my own. This is solely for when Bodkin or Chief Superintendent Grayson ask for my help. There can be times when a woman can be of great assistance during an interview. Men can be so hard at times, and a softer, friendlier face can put a female witness at her ease.'

'Don't they have any women on the force that can do that?'

'They have one, but she's only there to make tea, really. I met her last night; she was horrified by the sight of... Anyway, apart from her there's only that floozy, Trixie, and she's only there for show... though I think she types a bit too.'

Mr Rowlings took his tea back to his chair and sat down. Balancing the saucer carefully on the chair arm he picked up his paper again and unfolded it.

'Let's just hope there aren't too many intimidated female witnesses who require your presence during an interrogation, dear,' he said.

Mrs Rowlings put the business card on the table and patted her daughter on the shoulder softly as Amy tucked into her breakfast.

'Good for you,' she whispered. 'I love the pink card. Very swish.'

CHAPTER
EIGHT

AT NINE-FIFTEEN, AMY CAUGHT THE BUS FROM THE STOP OUTSIDE THE
Old Bull and got off at the Flag pub on the High Street. Just
around the corner was her favourite shop, Brigden's Nearly New
Store.

The shop was set up like one of the up-market designer stores
in London and carried a plethora of 'labelled' items, many of
which had only been worn once or twice at most. Amy loved
browsing in the store even though a lot of the items were beyond
what she could afford to pay, despite their pre-owned status.
Some of the top-quality items were displayed in small, well-lit
niches, others were shown off to their best advantage on shiny-
faced, porcelain mannequins.

The usual focus of Amy's interest was the two, long, bargain
rails at the rear of the shop. The rails were hung with items of
clothing that were not in pristine condition, or were produced by
one of the minor labels, sometimes one of the big London department stores. Some of the items on the rails could be bought for as
little as seven and sixpence. If the buyer was lucky, they might
find a blouse and skirt combination for fifteen shillings or a neat,
out of season jacket for twelve and six.

As she walked into the store, she was greeted by Sharon, the sales assistant. She had begun working at Brigden's at more or less the same time as Amy had started shopping there and the two young women had become good friends.

'Hello, Amy. What a surprise.' She laughed. 'Why don't you just get a job here? You spend enough time in the place.'

Amy laughed too. 'I'd spend all my wages on clothes,' she said. She looked around the shop with a big smile on her face. 'Anything new that I might like?'

'There's a lot of stuff you might like but not quite as much that you can afford, dear,' Sharon replied. 'There are three or four dresses in your colours on the back bargain rail, and there's a lovely jacket, oh and a couple of blouses that would look great on you.'

As the store wasn't too busy, Amy took a leisurely stroll around the featured items before making her way towards the back of the store. On her way past a display of out of season winter coats she spotted a cornflower blue, full length, velvet coat with two, darker blue buttons at the waist, large lapels, and flap pockets. Amy looked eagerly across to Sharon and mimed trying it on. Sharon shook her head as she wandered across to her.

'It's eight pounds, Amy.'

'EIGHT! Wow. It is beautiful though. Why doesn't it have a price tag... Oh, wait, I know. It's Eileen's message to us all, isn't it? If you have to ask the price, you can't afford it.'

Sharon nodded. 'That's the one.'

Amy stroked the coat, then looked slowly away from it. 'If it ever hits the bargain rail, ring Alice straight away. She'll put the order in for me.'

Sharon laughed. 'If it gets anywhere near the bargain rail, Amy, I'll be wearing it before it's even been put on a hanger. Staff perks and all that.'

Amy took one last lingering look at the coat, then made her

way to the back of the shop. As Sharon had hinted, there were three dresses in her size, all in the red or green shades she favoured, but as she had bought similar items over the last few weeks, she left them on the hangers and walked around to the last rail where she found a silk, cream blouse with pearl buttons that would go well with the maroon, flared skirt she'd bought just before Christmas and hadn't worn yet. Taking the blouse from its hanger, she held it up in front of her, then turned it slowly, looking for any stains or blemishes. On the right-hand seam, near the bottom of the blouse, the stitching appeared to have worked loose. Amy put her hand behind the seam and held it up to the light. Sure enough she could see that about an inch of the stitching had begun to come away. She checked the price tag, then folding the garment carefully over the crook of her arm, she caried it across to the long table at the end of the centre aisle where the till was situated. She found Eileen, the manageress, writing out price tags for a stack of dresses that were piled on a chair at the side of her.

'Hello, Eileen. Could you have a look at this please?' Amy said, trying not to appear too eager.

'Sold as seen, Amy, you know that,' Eileen said as she studied the weak seam.

'But it's not worth ten shillings looking like that, is it?'

'It depends how badly someone wants it,' Eileen replied. 'It is pure silk you know?'

'Exactly,' Amy said. 'Silk is tricky stuff to work with. You'd have to know what you're doing to repair it properly.'

'And you, being a seamstress, could fix it in five minutes flat.'

'I'm a machinist, not a seamstress,' Amy reminded her. 'And whether it would take me five minutes or five hours is irrelevant, really. Seventy percent of potential buyers wouldn't have a clue how to make the repair.' Amy was sure Eileen knew nothing about dressmaking so she pressed a little harder. 'I might have to cut a tiny sliver of the material out, unpick the rest and make a new seam to ensure it's straight. You couldn't wear it without a jacket if you botched it.'

Eileen sighed. She was used to customers trying to barter, but Amy didn't usually try to get things cheaper than they had been valued at.

'How much are you offering then?' she asked.

'Five shillings,' Amy said.

'FIVE! I'm sorry, Amy but I can't possibly let it go for that.'

'Six then.'

'You can have it for eight shillings.'

Amy studied the garment again, then put her hand behind the damaged seam and held it up to the light so that Eileen could see the loose stitching more clearly.

'It could take up to an hour to fix this and that's assuming I've got the right shade of silk thread at home.'

'And have you got the right shade of silk thread at home?'

'Yes, but that's irrelevant. Ninety-five percent of your customers won't have.'

Eileen sighed. 'Seven and six, and that's my final offer.'

'SOLD!' yelled a delighted Amy. She handed the blouse over the counter, then turned and winked at a grinning Sharon.

Eileen folded the blouse carefully and slipped it into a brown paper carrier that sported the Brigden's logo, then she smiled softly at Amy as she counted out the three half crowns.

'Don't tell anyone you talked the price down, Amy. They'll think I've gone soft in my old age and everyone will be at it.'

Amy put a finger to her lips. 'Mum's the word,' she said.

After leaving Brigden's, Amy walked around to the Post Office where she deposited another five shillings into her savings account. Checking the total at the bottom of the page, she closed her savings book and slipped it into her bag. Usually, on a Saturday, she would have walked around the corner to her favourite café on the High Street and bought an espresso with a biscuit or a small slice of cake, but as she stepped out of the imposing front door of the Post Office, she was distracted by the sound of a loud sports car screeching to a halt on the opposite side of the road. Two old ladies, gave her dirty looks as they were forced to walk around her in order to get by.

Amy barely noticed them. Her eyes were fixed on the occupants of the sports car that had come to a halt outside the Westminster Bank. The hood was down and she had a clear view of the driver and his passenger. Seconds later, Francis Drake slipped out of the car, walked around the front and opened the passenger side door to allow Lorna Wetherby to slide gracefully from her seat. Laughing, she slipped her arm through his and the pair walked slowly along the pavement until they reached a stone-built office block. Francis held the door open to allow Lorna to walk through, then stepped inside himself and pulled the dark, wood panelled door closed behind him.

'Interesting,' Amy said to herself, then after looking both ways for traffic, she crossed the road and hurried along the street until she reached the building that she had seen the pair enter.

On the column at the side of the door was a brass plaque listing the names of the business that were hosted inside. Amy smiled to herself as she saw that the first floor was the home of The Drake Group.

Amy looked around her furtively, then pulled down the handle and pushed the door open a few inches. She found herself looking into a marble tiled entrance lobby. Sitting at the huge desk facing her was a woman, about thirty years old. Her hair was styled in a bob and she wore a white blouse under a thin checked jacket. She looked up as Amy stuck her head into the gap.

'Can I help you?' she asked.

Amy stepped smartly into the hall, thankfully there was no sign of Drake or Lorna.

'My, erm... My dad was thinking about investing in one of Mr Drake's businesses,' she said, thinking on her feet. 'Would you have a brochure or something like that?'

'Ah, yes, I've got something here that might help him decide.' She handed Amy a glossy brochure with a picture of a confident-looking Francis Drake on the front.

'Is he interested in Drake Construction or one of the other companies in the group?' she asked.

'Is there a difference?' Amy said. 'I'm afraid things like that go right over my head. I just enjoy the extra cash Daddy gives me when he gets his pay-out every year.'

'Dividend,' said the woman. 'It's called a dividend.'

'Ah,' Amy replied. 'I thought that was the Co-op.'

'What was the Co-op?' The woman looked confused.

'Dividend... Divi... you know?'

The woman shook her head. 'It's similar but not quite the same thing. Anyway, the brochure will tell your father all he needs to know about the group of companies.'

Amy rolled the brochure into a tube shape and waved it at the receptionist.

'Thank you, I'm sure Daddy will buy some dividends very soon.'

As the woman looked confused again, Amy turned towards the door but was stopped dead in her tracks when she heard laughter coming from the direction of the stairs. She shot a quick glance across the room to see Francis Drake and Lorna Wetherby walking slowly down the marble tiled steps.

CHAPTER
NINE

DROPPING HER BRIGDEN'S BAG, AMY QUICKLY UNROLLED THE LARGE, glossy brochure and held it in front of her face as she turned herself away from the couple coming down the stairs.

'Was there anything else?' the receptionist asked as Amy stood, facing a plain, off-white, painted wall.

'No, I'm fine,' Amy hissed as she heard two pairs of footsteps click across the marble floor. Thinking she must look odd with the brochure right in front of her face, she turned quickly towards the desk, smoothed the brochure out flat, then bent over so that her eyes were a mere two inches away from the pamphlet.

'Are you all right?' the receptionist asked as she stared at Amy.

'I'm a bit short-sighted,' Amy replied, softly. 'I was just checking... something.'

Amy straightened up as she heard the door to the lobby click shut. Blowing out her cheeks, she picked up her shopping and sliding the brochure from the highly polished counter, she turned away from the desk.

'I couldn't make head nor tale of it,' she said, fanning her flushed face with the pamphlet. 'Drake's have a director... Do they make films too?'

Waving in the general direction of the reception desk, Amy walked briskly across to the door and opened it, leaving a gap just big enough to be able to stick her head through, then, after seeing the sports car shoot past, leaving a thick, petrol smelling cloud of exhaust behind it, she stepped smartly out onto the pavement and made her way to the café for a much-needed espresso.

Thirty minutes later, feeling much more sure of herself, Amy walked slowly up the High Street until she got to the newsagents where she bought a copy of her favourite movie magazine Photoplay and a card for her mother, whose birthday was coming up the following week. The newsagent slipped the card into a brown paper bag and handed both items over to her with her change. Sliding the card and magazine carefully into the Brigden's bag she headed back down the hill and made her way to the bus stop opposite the Town Hall. Nodding to a couple of people she knew, Amy pulled out her magazine and began to read the contents page. She was just about to turn to a feature about one of her favourite actresses, Katharine Hepburn, when she heard her name being called. Looking across the street, she saw Bodkin standing at the taxi rank. He was waving to her.

'Do you fancy a taxi ride?' he shouted.

Amy stuffed the magazine into her bag, waited for a double decker bus heading for Gillingham to pass, and hurried across the street.

'I can get the bus, Bodkin,' she said. 'It's due in five minutes.'

'I'm not taking you home... at least, not yet. Come on, hop in, this is part of the investigation.' He opened the back door of the cab and waited until Amy had slid onto the seat, then he slammed it shut and made his way to the passenger side where he climbed into the front.

'Hello again, Amy,' Rory twisted to face her from the driver's seat.

'Long time, no see,' Amy replied. 'How are you, Rory?'

'I'm quite excited to be honest,' he said turning to Bodkin. 'It's like being in one of those films isn't it...? What is it the policeman shouts when he jumps into the taxi... Follow that car? Although I'm not following one... I'm... oh never mind, it's still exciting. I'm part of a murder investigation. Wait until Mum hears about it, she'll—'

'Can we just get going,' Bodkin said, irritably.

'Where are we off to?' Amy asked as the taxi pulled away from the kerb.

'Rory here is going to take us to the place where he dropped off our blood-covered mystery man last night,' Bodkin replied.

'He wasn't actually covered in it,' Rory said. 'He wasn't blood-soaked or anything like that.'

'He had a significant amount of blood on his shirt, that's what you told me,' Bodkin said, looking hard at the taxi driver.

'And it's true, he did. He had dried blood under his nose too, like I told you and he had some blood on his hands, I saw it when he handed me the fare. He looked like someone had given him a good right hook.'

They drove in silence until Rory turned onto the Gillingham Road. About a mile further on he pulled over at the side of a grass verge.

'This is it; this is where I dropped him.'

Bodkin looked around. 'It's in the middle of nowhere.' He got out of the taxi and walked around to the front of the cab. To his left was a shallow ditch in front of a hawthorn hedge. Beyond that was a long empty field. On the other side of the road was a small wooded area.

'Are you sure this is it?'

'Positive, if you look at the verge a few feet down you'll see my tyre tracks where my back wheels ran onto it as I turned around to go back to Spinton. I'm not very good at three-point turns,' he added.

Amy climbed out of the back seat and looked around herself. There were no houses that she could see.

'The nearest houses are at the crossroads,' she said. 'It's about four hundred yards further down the road.'

'That's what I was thinking.' Bodkin rubbed his chin as he mused. 'Come on, get back in. Rory can take us to the crossroads, there's no point in us walking.'

'But what if our man dropped something on the way,' Amy said. 'He was drunk... maybe he got out of the cab because he thought he was going to be sick... maybe it was an urgent call of nature.'

Bodkin grinned. 'We'll make a detective of you yet,' he said.

As Amy grabbed her bag from the back seat, Bodkin motioned for Rory to wind down his driver's window.

'We might need you to hang around and give us a lift back. You're absolutely positive that this is where you dropped the man off?'

'I'd swear on it. He gave me a ten-shilling note and the fare was only four bob, I'm hardly likely to forget a tip like that.'

Bodkin nodded. 'All right, wait for us at the crossroads.'

'Am I being paid for all this driving and hanging around?' Rory asked. 'I've got a living to make you know?'

'Drop in at the police station on Monday morning,' Bodkin replied. 'I'll get Constable Ferris to pay you out of the petty cash tin.'

As Rory began to wind up his window, Amy took hold of Bodkin's arm.

'We don't need a taxi back from here, Bodkin. I know a shortcut that will lead us across Russell Park. It's less than half a mile from the crossroads and it will take us past the back of the

Town Hall. There's an alley just beyond that, next to the big houses. It leads to the High Street.'

'It's very handy having someone like you around,' Bodkin said, nodding to Rory to give him permission to leave.

'What do you mean, "someone like me?" There's only one of me, Bodkin. You ought to know that by now.'

Amy and Bodkin watched Rory perform a very awkward seven-point turn, then with Bodkin asking a question about how he was allowed to drive the public around if he couldn't perform that simple feat, they turned towards the crossroads and looking down at the grass verge, began to walk.

'You stay on this side, Bodkin,' Amy said. 'I'll walk along the other side. You never know, he might have crossed the road to walk home. Especially if he lives on that side of the crossroads.'

'I was just about to suggest the same thing,' said Bodkin. 'I had thought of that you know.'

'Of course you had, Bodkin. You're a policeman.' Amy bit her lip as she waited for a small, green van to pass before she walked across to the verge on the other side of the road.

'What have you got on this afternoon, Bodkin?' she called as they began to walk.

'I'll be going through all the witness statements from last night. Which reminds me. I'll need a signed statement from you, as you were one of the invited guests.'

Amy grinned. 'OOH! I have to make a statement in a murder inquiry. Wait until Big Nose Beryl hears about this. It will keep her going for a month.'

Beryl was one of Amy's co-workers at the Mill. She didn't have a particularly big nose; she just couldn't resist sticking it into other people's business. She was the bestower of every tiny bit of gossip, no matter how trivial it was. She would even create something out of thin air if there was nothing new to talk about in the canteen on a Monday morning.

They walked on in silence for a while, then Amy suddenly stopped to look at something lying in the mud on the wall of the ditch.

'Bodkin,' she shouted excitedly. 'I think I've found something.'

Bodkin hurried across to where Amy was standing.

At her feet, was a white, blood splattered handkerchief. Bodkin pulled a pen out of his pocket, slipped it under the side of the hanky and lifted it up.

'It's monogrammed,' he said. 'That's a stroke of luck.'

He took the corner of the handkerchief between his finger and thumb and held it up for Amy to see.

'H.K.'

'That could be, Horatio Kelly!' shouted Amy. 'Nelson's brother.'

TEN

Bodkin patted his pockets with his free hand, then cursed.

'Sorry for the language, Amy. We're supposed to carry paper bags with us these days to collect bits of evidence like this, especially during murder investigations. It's to help stop cross contamination.'

'You're forgiven, just this once,' Amy replied with a smile. 'I take it you forgot to pick some up at the station?'

'They give us what they call a murder bag; it contains evidence bags, a pair of tweezers a magnifying glass, rubber gloves, that sort of thing.'

'A magnifying glass? That's very Sherlock Holmes. Where's yours?'

'Back at the High Street in the car,' Bodkin said with a sigh.

Amy laughed. 'Not to worry, I have just the thing.'

Amy stuck her hand in her bag and pulled out her mother's birthday card. She slipped it out of the paper bag the newsagent had given her, dropped the card back into the Brigden's bag and handed the small brown paper one to Bodkin.

'What would I do without you?' Bodkin said as he dropped

the bloody handkerchief into the bag. 'The force should employ you as my personal assistant.'

'You're right, they should,' Amy said, brightly.

After slipping the bag into his jacket pocket, Bodkin and Amy made their way to the crossroads on opposite sides of the road, but they found nothing else of interest along the way.

Skelton Junction sounded far grander than it actually was. The main Gillingham Road continued to the south but two, narrow roads, not much more than country tracks, fed off to the east and west.

Bodkin studied the wooden sign post that was situated on the east side of the junction. The white-painted sign had four wooden blades pointing to all four compass points. Skelton to the west, Spinton to the north, Gillingham to the south and Spinton (Via Russell Park) pointed east.

'Well, here's a conundrum,' Bodkin said. 'Where did our man go from here?'

'I think we can rule out north and south,' Amy said. 'It's just open countryside for at least two miles heading towards Gillingham, and why would he go back the way he came? That wouldn't make any sense.'

Bodkin looked around. 'So, it's either Skelton or...' he turned to look up the narrow country track that led to Russell Park ... 'back towards Spinton. Now, why would he do that?'

'There are about a dozen big houses up there, Bodkin,' Amy said. 'And, I mean, big.'

'What's over the road then?' Bodkin asked. 'I've only ever heard of Skelton Junction, not the actual village.'

'It's more of a hamlet,' Amy replied. 'A tiny one at that. I would say there are only about six or seven houses. There are a couple of small farms. Alice knows the tenants, one of them fancies her, he used to follow her around like a lost lamb at the young farmer's events. I went to what they laughingly called, a young farmer's ball in Skelton with Alice once. There were only eight of us there and six of them were needy men, none of them very young looking.'

Bodkin laughed. 'You weren't attracted to life on the farm then?'

'Not with any of that lot, besides, I can get as much farm life as I could ever need just by walking down the lane to Alice's place.'

Just then they heard the rattle of bicycle wheels on gravel; they turned to see a postman cycling towards them from the direction of Russell Park. The postman wobbled uncertainly as his bike slipped into the dried-out ruts left by a truck or tractor.

'Good morning,' Bodkin said, holding up his hand to the postman. 'Can you spare us a moment?'

The postman was about sixty years old with lank grey hair sticking out from beneath his dark navy cap. His brown delivery sack was slung over his shoulder. He took both feet off the pedals, dropped them to the floor and skidded to a halt at the side of the policeman.

'How can I help?' he asked.

'I'm Inspector Bodkin of Spinton police and this is Amy Rowlings. We were wondering if you could help us find someone who lives around here? They have the initials, H.K.'

Amy smiled to herself. She loved it when Bodkin introduced her to people as if she was part of the investigation.

The postman took off his cap and scratched his head.

'I'm not really the one to ask. You need to talk to Percy really... that's Percy Tanner. This is his round. I'm only standing in today because he's at a wedding. That's why I'm so late, I haven't covered this round before.'

Bodkin nodded in understanding. 'Ah well, never mind. We'll let you get on with your day.'

The postman put one foot onto a pedal and slapped the cap back onto his head.

'Hang on a minute. I've just delivered a couple of letters to a Mr Horatio Kelly. That's H.K. isn't it?'

'It is, whereabouts does he live?' Bodkin asked.

The postman twisted on his seat and pointed back up the track.

'It's up there on the right. Great big house it is... two huge gates, then a long drive leading up to it. We should be paid extra for delivering to places like that.'

The postman nodded to them and after checking the road for traffic, he pushed down on the pedals and began to ride over the junction. When he was half way across, he looked back and called to Bodkin.

'Oaklands, it's called. You can't miss it, there's a big, brass plate next to the gates.'

They found the entrance to Oaklands about two hundred yards along what was now a reasonably well maintained, single track, tarmacked road. The huge double, wrought-iron gates were set inside two stone pillars. The gates were closed, and locked with an enormous padlock. At the side of the right-hand column, set into a six-foot, stone wall, was a small wooden gate that had been left swinging open by the postman. Bodkin stepped through and looked into the grounds.

The house was well named. A wide, stone-chipped drive was lined on both sides by what were clearly, ancient oak trees. The house itself was situated behind a large, oval shaped courtyard on which was parked a highly polished, soft topped, Lagonda sports car.

'Wow,' Amy whispered. 'He's worth a few bob.'

'Not necessarily,' Bodkin replied huffily. 'A lot of these people are in huge amounts of debt but they refuse to give up their expensive lifestyles. It's all about show with most of them.'

'Ooh, Bodkin. I didn't have you down as the resentful type.'

'I'm not, Amy, honestly I'm not, but when you have to deal with these people... not all of them I admit... but, well, let's just say some of them think they are above the law, they think they are entitled, just because they have the trappings of wealth. If I had a penny for every time I've been told to back off because one of them has had a word with the chief constable at the golf club, I'd have—'

'Ninepence?' Amy interrupted.

Bodkin laughed. 'Yes, about that much.' He took her arm and led her back to the single-track road. 'Come on, let's get back to town. I'll give you a lift home seeing as I caused you to miss your bus.'

'Aren't you going to question him then, Bodkin?'

'Oh yes, I'll be having a word, more than one, but it will have to wait until early next week. I need to get through all of those witness statements this afternoon and I'll have to grab a quick word with the chief super before I go bothering Mister Kelly. Let someone else take the flak from the chief constable when old Horatio rings up to say he's being harassed.'

They walked along the tree lined avenue and past another four large houses. A hundred yards further on the ground opened out onto Russell Park, a favourite picnicking place for the town's population.

Amy and Bodkin walked along a well-trodden path that meandered between clumps of shrubs and bushes behind which grew a range of trees that included ash, beech, elder and silver birch. At the top of the park was a children's playground with a selection of rickety looking swing frames, a roundabout and a sheet-metal slide that had a gaping hole half way down its length. On the right-hand side was a tree-lined, high boundary wall which separated the park from the High Street. Amy pointed out the top floor of the Town Hall and the roof of the library next door.

A few yards further on was a line of pensioners' bungalows. At the gate of one of them sat an elderly man smoking a pipe as he watched his collie dog chase after the stick he had just thrown.

'Mornin,' he called as Bodkin and Amy approached. 'Nice day for it.'

'Good morning,' Amy called back as the man's dog ran up to her holding a thick stick. The collie dropped it at Amy's feet, then backed off, eyes bright, tongue lolling as it waited for her to throw it.

'Oh, I'm hopeless at throwing, sorry.' Amy pulled a sad face at the dog.

'Don't you worry,' said the old man, she'll bring it back here in a minute. She thinks everyone she meets has time to throw the stick for her. She tries it on everyone. No one can walk past here without being challenged. I sit out here from morn 'til dusk when the weather's fine, and the only time she'll stop running is when the missus puts her dinner out.'

Bodkin picked up the stick and hurled it as far as he could manage. The dog yapped excitedly and hared across to the boundary wall to retrieve it.

'You'd better make your escape while you can,' the old man advised.

Bodkin looked at Amy with a quizzical look on his face.

'How do we get back to the High Street from here?'

'There's an alleyway between the library and the first of the big houses,' she said. 'You can't see it from here, you have to walk between the last two bungalows to find it.'

Amy turned back to the old man and looked at him with a tilt of her head.

'Were you sitting out last night by any chance?' she asked. 'I'm Amy by the way.'

'I'm Pervis Drayman and yes, I was. It was a warm evening so I didn't go in until eleven.'

'I don't suppose you noticed anyone jumping over the fence behind the Town Hall, did you? It would have been nine-ish possibly, nine-fifteen.'

'No one came over that fence at any time yesterday. Meg would have barked non-stop if anyone had.'

Amy walked quickly towards the wall and began to search around the boggy ground for footprints but the only ones she found had obviously been left by the dog.

'He's right,' she said as she walked back towards Bodkin. 'No one jumped over that fence, not recently at least. The ground is still wet from all the rain we had in midweek, he would leave an imprint where he landed, that's for sure, but there's nothing but paw prints. I say he... I really can't see a woman in a dress clambering over that fence, it's a ten-foot drop.'

'I know,' said Bodkin with a sly grin. 'I had a look myself early this morning.'

Amy screwed her face up, then shook her head. 'You might have said.'

'It gets quiet on the park when the kids go home for their dinners,' Pervis said. 'No one came along here after about eight, apart from that posh woman.'

'Posh woman?' Bodkin's eyes flicked towards Pervis.

'Yeah, she walks past here two or three times a week. Goes down towards the crossroads between seven and eight and comes back between ten and eleven. Always walks with her head down and a scarf pulled across her face. Not sure what she's up to but she obviously doesn't want anyone to know who she is.' He pointed back along the line of bungalows. 'She disappears in the gap between the last two houses. She'll be heading for the High Street down the alley, I suppose.'

'What time did she walk past last night?' Bodkin asked.

'It was a bit early for her. It would have been about nine-thirty. She was in a hurry; I know that much. Fair ran past me she did, head down, scarf pulled across her face. I may be wrong, but I had the impression she was crying.'

CHAPTER
ELEVEN

AMY SLIPPED HER ARM THROUGH BODKIN'S AS THE PAIR WALKED ALONG TO the narrow footpath that ran between the last two sets of bungalows. She pointed to a gap between a high wall on the left side and the metal railings of the library on the right.

'Voila,' she said.

At the back of the last two pensioner bungalows was an overgrown hedge, behind which was hidden a six- foot, brick wall. Built into the wall was a sturdy-looking timber gate with an iron ringed handle. A barely used path, littered with broken stones and tall clumps of couch grass, led off up a slight incline to the back gardens of some of the larger houses in the town. The pair walked into the alley in silence, both thinking hard about who the mystery woman could be.

As they came out of the alley and onto the High Street, Bodkin led Amy to a side road where he had parked his car earlier in the day. Amy climbed into the passenger seat and placed the Brigden's bag carefully on her lap. After looking down into the footwell, then over her shoulder into the back seat, she turned towards Bodkin.

'Where's the murder kit? I was hoping to have a look at it.'

'It's in the boot,' Bodkin replied... 'Spread out over the carpet in the boot, actually. The bag burst and the contents are all over the place. I think I'd better get a new one.'

Amy put her palm to her forehead and shook her head slowly.

'You know, for a policeman, you're—'

'I know, hopeless.'

'I was going to say, very untidy,' Amy said with a short laugh.

'I can't argue with that observation,' Bodkin replied as he eased the car away from the kerb.

As they drove past the picture house on Middle Street, Amy waved to the cinema owner who was on the top step, about to open the doors for the Saturday afternoon matinee. A line of the town's kids queued along the pavement, eager to watch the next episode of Roy Rogers or Gene Autry, the singing cowboy.

'Oh, I know what I meant to ask you, Bodkin. Did you get anything out of the caterers last night? You didn't start interviewing them until I'd gone home.'

'I haven't got around to reading all the reports yet, Amy, I'll do that this afternoon, but I did talk to the foreman of the catering staff, and the girl who used the murder weapon to cut the slices of beef for the buffet. She said that the last time she saw the knife, it was lying on the trolley that was parked up at the end of the corridor that runs alongside the kitchen. The interesting bit is, she had washed the knife in very hot water before she used it to cut the beef, so, really, hers should be the only set of finger prints on the handle. If there is another set, they will probably belong to the murderer. The catering staff have all been at the station this morning having their fingerprints taken. I wish we could have managed to get the prints of everyone at the event. I'm still angry about the mayor and his party being allowed to leave. The former mayor had been outside the Assembly Room when the murder took place... or at least around that time.'

'Do you have a suspect in mind yet?' Amy asked, eagerly.

'No, there isn't enough evidence yet. At the moment I'd really like to know who had such an urgent need to speak to Nelson last night. They rang a pay phone; I wonder how they got hold of the number?'

When I rang last night, I got the number from the phone directory in the call box near the Old Bull. It was listed as, Spinton Town Hall, Assembly Room.'

'Ah, I see. So that phone is listed with all the other Council numbers,' Bodkin said, taking one hand off the steering wheel to stroke the dark stubble on his chin.

'Do you think the phone call could be someone's way of setting Nelson up?' Amy asked.

'I've been thinking about that,' Bodkin replied. 'Let's just assume for a moment that the caller, a woman, we know that much, telephoned at a prearranged time and that someone knew that call was coming and was waiting outside the emergency exit when it came through. Nelson answers the call but the woman hangs up, then, the person waiting at the door, knocks on it, shouting for help or something. Nelson opens it and allows whoever it is to enter. They have strong words, Nelson backs off into the corridor, it's only a few feet away from where the knife was sitting on the trolley, it gets a bit out of hand, the knife is picked up and it's curtains for Nelson Kelly.'

Amy thought about it for a moment.

'It's possible I suppose, but it does seem a little illogical, I mean... if they meant to do Nelson in from the get go, wouldn't they have brought a weapon with them, a gun for instance? And, they couldn't have been sure that Nelson would be the only person in the corridor when the door was opened. There were a lot of guests at the awards, the chances are pretty high that someone would have been on their way to, or coming back from the cloakroom. That scenario looks a little unlikely to me.'

'I agree,' Bodkin replied, 'but it's still a possibility. Of course, the phone call may have had absolutely nothing to do with the murder and it is highly probable that it was committed by someone invited to the event. Having said that, we do have a witness who states that he saw a man with fair hair, wearing a dark coloured suit, talking to Nelson at the fire escape door, and we did see someone fitting that description climbing into a taxi, someone with a heavily bloodstained shirt.'

Amy squirmed with excitement and reached out to squeeze Bodkin's arm.

'Ooh, I do like a good puzzle,' she said.

They passed the police station at the bottom of Middle Street, then Bodkin turned left and drove along the Gillingham Road until he reached the telephone box outside the Old Bull. As he turned right onto Long Lane, he looked back over his shoulder towards the pub.

'I'm really looking forward to tonight,' he said. 'I could murder a pint.'

'You've just missed Alice, dear. She hung on for a while because I was sure you'd be home earlier than this. She wanted to get what she called, "the nitty gritty on last night's do".' Mrs Rowlings got up from the sofa where she had been reading her copy of Woman's Own magazine.

'I'll nip down to see her after lunch. She'll be dying to hear all about it,' Amy replied. 'I met Bodkin in town. We went for a walk on Russell Park.'

'Oh, that's nice, dear. It's lovely there when the sun's out.' She walked into the kitchen and came back carrying a plate of egg and cress sandwiches. 'I've put the kettle on; tea won't be a minute.'

'Where's Dad?' Amy asked. She had expected to see him sitting in his chair listening to the radio.

'He's up at the church talking the vicar through tomorrow's sermon.'

'It must get pretty boring for Dad on a Sunday when the vicar reads it out, I mean, he spent all week, writing it for him.'

'Your father likes to hear others read out his words,' Mrs Rowlings said, placing the large, brown teapot in the middle of the table. 'Did you find anything nice at Brigden's?'

Amy nodded with her mouth full of egg and cress and pointed to the Brigden's bag. Suddenly realising that her mother's birthday card was lying on top of the blouse, she leapt to her feet and hurried across to the sofa, snatching the bag up before her mother could open it.

'Mmmnnff,' she spluttered, almost choking on the sandwich. She swallowed hard, then walked quickly back to the table, poured tea into a cup and drank it without adding milk and sugar.

'Ahem,' she said, clearing her throat. 'Sorry, Mum, there's something in there you can't see yet.'

Mrs Rowlings smiled as she walked back into the kitchen. 'I hope you haven't been wasting your money on me.'

'It wouldn't be wasted money, Mum, you're worth far more than I can afford to spend on you.'

At two o'clock, Amy made her way down to Mollison Farm to see her best friend, Alice. She found her in the yard, throwing scraps to the chickens as she lifted the latch and let herself through the wide, three-barred, back gate.

'Hello,' Alice called out as she turned at the sound of the gate opening. 'You've been having fun again I hear.'

Amy nodded, walked over and gave Alice a hug.

'I've been dying to hear all about it,' Alice said as she shook the last few scraps from the bowl she was carrying and led Amy up the three stone steps to the kitchen. Miriam, Alice's long-time friend and housekeeper, was just putting a blue-striped tea pot onto the huge, ancient, well-scrubbed, oak table.

'Perfect timing,' she said, giving Amy a big smile. 'A little bird told me that you've been having another adventure.' She patted a high backed, wooden chair. 'Come on, sit down and tell us all about it.'

'I hope that little bird isn't a noisy, squawking, parrot,' Amy said, pulling the chair out a little further before sitting down and reaching out for the mug of strong tea that Miriam had just poured for her.

Alice rinsed out the bowl she had used to feed the chickens and placed it upside down on the wooden draining board next to the white Belfast sink.

Amy smiled at her best friend as she turned to face her, noticing again the strong resemblance to the Hollywood starlet, Rita Hayworth. She even had the identical shade of auburn hair and the high cheekbones of the American beauty. The local cinema owner had asked Alice to parade up and down outside the theatre the last time one of Rita's films had been shown. Alice had declined, despite his offer of payment.

Alice was only nineteen, but more had happened in her short life than many women twice her age had experienced. After her mother had died young, her father had slipped into depression and had become an alcoholic. When he died, only a few months earlier, Alice had been left alone to run the farm at the tender age of eighteen. With the help of her trusted foreman, Barney and the loyalty of her workforce who had all known her since childhood, she had made a success of the business and was now turning over more money than her father had ever done. Alice's pride and joy were her pigs. She took sole responsibility for their welfare and could be found clearing out the sties at five o'clock every morning, whatever the weather.

Amy and Alice had been friends since their nursery days. Amy being a year older. They had been more like sisters through school and saw each other as often as they could, hardly ever missing their Saturday night at the movie theatre which would be followed by a few drinks at the Old Bull pub at the end of the lane.

Alice put a padded box on the table, opened it, took out a long needle and began to darn a large hole in a beige coloured, silk stocking.

'The hole is above the knee, thankfully, this is my last pair. I only noticed it this morning when I was putting my laundry away.'

'I've got a pair you can have in an emergency,' Amy replied. 'But then, your legs are a bit longer than mine, you need the next size up, really.'

'These will do for tonight,' Alice said, finishing off the darn and snapping the cotton thread with her teeth. She held the stocking up to the light. 'I might get another month out of this one.'

'I'll pick you a pair up next Saturday morning when I'm in town if you like?' Amy offered.

'It's all right. I have to go to the bank on Thursday to get the lads' wages. I'll grab a couple of pairs then.' Alice closed the lid of her sewing box, picked up her mug of tea and took a long sip.

'Did you find anything at Brigden's this morning?'

Amy nodded eagerly.

'I bought a lovely silk blouse. There is an issue with one seam, but I'm going to sort that out this afternoon. I might wear it tonight.'

'The Hound of the Baskervilles,' Alice said, giving a fake shudder. 'It's ages since we saw a scary film. Bela Lugosi was the last one... Son of Frankenstein, that gave me nightmares for a week. It was good though.'

Alice drained her mug and refilled it from the pot. Miriam sat down in her armchair by the fire and picked up her knitting.

'Now,' she said, after a quick look at the pattern. 'What's all this about Friday night?'

'So, Bodkin has no idea who the murderer is yet?' Alice asked as Amy finished reciting the events of the previous night.

'Nope, it could have been one of a number of people. I'm not sure about the man at the fire exit myself, but it is feasible. We should know a bit more after Bodkin interviews Nelson's brother next week.'

'Ah, yes, the mystery man with the bloody shirt who dropped a clue on the grass verge.' Alice rubbed her hands together. 'A proper mystery. It's just like the films.' She looked across the table at her best friend and winked. 'I love the way you use the word "we" when you talk about the investigation. You're in your element, aren't you?'

Amy grinned. 'I'm the leading actress in this movie. Isn't it fabulous?'

'Well, it seems to me that you're the one finding all the clues, Amy,' Miriam said, looking up from her knitting. 'Mind you, there's no big surprise there.'

Amy clasped her hands and looked into the distance, dreamily.

'I hope they let me get involved in the questioning. I was right in the middle of it after all.'

'Chief Superintendent Grayson might let you do a little bit to help,' Alice said. 'He seems a nice sort.'

'He's incredibly nice for a policeman, intelligent too, and that's a rarity. He can see a role for females in the force. There are a couple of women to interview, one of them a newly made widow, so they'll have to be a little softer with their questioning. That's exactly the sort of thing he thought I might be able to help with when he suggested I register ARIA Investigations with the police.'

Alice got up from the table when she heard Martha waking up from her nap. 'Just be careful, Amy,' she said over her shoulder as she walked through the open door into the parlour. 'We don't want whoever it was thinking you know too much about the incident.'

'That's why we have to glue Miriam's little parrot's beak shut,' Amy replied.

The friends sat chatting about general town gossip while Alice fed Martha a small bowl of crushed biscuits in evaporated milk. It seemed there was enough going on in the town to keep Big Nose Beryl happy for a month.

At three-thirty, Amy got up from the table, gave Martha a kiss on the forehead, then opened the back door.

'Right, I'll see you this evening, Alice, my darling. Six o'clock sharp.'

As Alice threw a mock salute, Amy stepped out of the door and made her way back home.

The faulty seam didn't turn out to be quite as bad as Amy thought it might be, and it took her less than fifteen minutes to unpick the threads and repair the damage. When she had finished, she took the blouse into the bathroom which was in an extension at the far end of the kitchen and hung it on the door knob on a wooden hanger while she ran a hot bath.

After she had bathed, she pulled on her favourite, flower patterned dressing gown, wrapped a towel around her hair and carried the damp blouse into the kitchen where she ran a medium hot iron over it. Satisfied with her efforts, she laid the garment over her arm and carried it upstairs to her bedroom where she hung it from the handle of the wardrobe door to dry.

Amy's pride and joy, was the radiogram she had saved up for, for over two years. She had finally been able to give her uncle the money to buy it the previous month. He was an importer of American records and sheet music and Amy had built up an impressive collection over the past few years.

She was listening to Bing Crosby singing, You Must Have Been A Beautiful Baby and letting her mind run over the events of the morning, when she had a thought about the monogramed handkerchief she had found. Maybe they were putting all their eggs in one basket when it came to Horatio Kelly. What if there was another man with the same initials living somewhere close to Skelton Junction? It wasn't too likely, was it? There were only about twenty households in the area after all. Then she suddenly had an idea how she could check. Every one of the big houses in that area would be on the telephone network and their numbers, along with their names and addresses, would all be listed in the local telephone directory.

Amy leapt up from her bed, threw off her dressing gown and after slipping into a pair of black slacks, she pulled a knitted jumper over her head, stepped into her soft shoes and hurried down the stairs.

'Back in two shakes, Mum,' she called as she ran out of the front door, leaving it swinging open behind her.

At the telephone kiosk, Amy yanked the door open and stepped inside, the directory was on a shelf next to the handset. She picked it up and turned the pages looking through the index for surnames beginning with K. *There couldn't be that many in a town the size of Spinton,* she thought.

Flicking through the pages that advertised everything from chicken feed to electric irons, Amy eventually found the listing she wanted. She had just begun to work her way down the column when she heard a tapping on the glass panel behind her. She turned to see a red-faced woman staring angrily at her.

'Are you going to use that telephone or just stand there reading the directory all day?' she asked.

'I won't be long,' Amy replied as nicely as she could manage. 'This is important.'

'So is my telephone call,' said the woman as she pulled open the door. 'Hurry up, my bus will be here any minute.'

'Do you need the directory?' Amy asked as she left the kiosk and was almost knocked over by the woman moving quickly into the space she had just vacated.

The woman ignored her, shoved two pennies into the box and picked up the handset.

Amy sat on the grass at the side of the kiosk and opened the phone book. After running her finger down the column of Ks and finding nothing but Horatio Kelly's name, she flicked onto the next page and shouted out loud as she spotted a listing at the very top of the left-hand page.

Kitson. Harold. Skelton Grange. Skelton. Kent.

'GOTCHA!' she whispered, giving herself a fist pump.

CHAPTER
TWELVE

ALICE ARRIVED JUST AS AMY WAS PUTTING THE FINISHING TOUCHES TO her make up.

'Ooh, I love that shade of red, do you think it would suit me?' she said as Amy pursed her lips and looked up from the mirror.

'It's Max Factor Vermillion. I saw it advertised in Photoplay, there was a coupon you could cut out to buy it from them by mail order. The parcel arrived in the week.' Amy held up her fingers. 'I got matching nail varnish too. You can borrow it next week if you like.'

'Is that the new blouse? It's lovely, Amy, it goes so well with the maroon skirt.'

Amy gave Alice a twirl. 'I'm taking a tan jacket just in case it gets chilly later, but I'm only going to carry it, it's warm enough without for now.'

She looked Alice up and down. She was wearing a v neck red dress with an olive-green shawl around her shoulders.

'Love that neckline, Alice, it really shows your bust off to perfection. Ferris won't be able to take his eyes off you.'

Alice laughed. 'Poor Ferris. I do like him but he's really not for me you know.'

Amy pulled a sad face. 'I know. Do you think he's got the message now?'

'I thought we'd sorted that out months ago,' Alice replied, 'but just recently his interest seems to have perked up again.' She took out her compact and studied herself in the tiny mirror. 'I'll let him down gently. He's still a kid really.'

'He's two years older than you, Alice,' Amy reminded her.

'Oh, I know, but he's still a kid, mentally. I go for a more mature sort of man... as you know.'

'He certainly has a mature singing voice. Has he got a spot at the Bell again tonight?'

'No, I think he's singing at the Milton Hotel this week. I'm sure that's what he said last Saturday, they're giving him a trial with their cocktail lounge band.'

'Wow!' Amy replied, mouth agape. 'It's very posh in there. How come I didn't know about this?'

'You were canoodling with Bodkin on the dance floor when he told me,' Alice said with a wink.

'I don't canoodle,' Amy said seriously. 'We were probably just having a very serious, whispered conversation.'

She took one last look in the mirror, then grabbed her bag and coat.

'Speaking of Bodkin, where is he? He's usually here by now.'

Alice slapped her forehead.

'Sorry, I meant to tell you. He rang about half an hour ago. He said, is it okay if he meets us outside the Roxy? He's been up to his neck in interview statements. He said he'll only just about have time to nip home and get changed.'

'I hope he has time to run an iron over his trousers,' Amy said, pulling a face.

The girls walked into the living room as Mrs Rowlings was clearing away the tea plates.

'Are you off, girls? Have a lovely time; I hope the film doesn't give you nightmares.'

'It's okay, Mum, we've both read the book so there shouldn't be too many surprises.'

Mr Rowlings looked up from his evening paper. 'Where's Bodkin? He's usually here by now, isn't he?'

'He's been stuck at work going through the witness statements,' Amy replied. 'He's meeting us at the Roxy.'

'I was going to ask him if he's seen the paper,' Rowlings said pointing at his copy of the Post. He held it up so that Amy could read the headline.

WAS THE MURDERER ON THE RED CARPET? Then underneath a smaller headline. MORE PICTURES INSIDE.

Amy took the paper from her father and quickly read the column. It was accompanied by a photograph of Nelson Kelly arriving for the presentation. Turning the page, she scanned the three extra photographs that were featured inside. One showed the mayor's party, another showed Francis Drake and a few of the other major dignitaries along with their wives, the last one showed Lorna Wetherby, arriving amidst a number of the other guests including Chief Superintendent Grayson and Chief Inspector Laws who was walking alongside a pouting Trixie.

'There's nothing we don't already know in this piece,' Amy said, handing the paper back to her father. 'That Miles chap is just speculating, as usual. He has no evidence.'

Amy gave her father a kiss on the cheek and her mother a big hug, then looking at the clock she took hold of Alice's hand and almost dragged her out of the room.

'We'd better hurry, the bus will be along any minute.'

'That was really good wasn't it. It was just like the book,' Alice said as she walked down the steps of the Roxy.

'It was very atmospheric,' Bodkin said. 'They did well with the special effects, those scenes on Dartmoor were done really well. The fog gave it a very creepy atmosphere.'

'That bit at the séance was creepy,' Amy added. 'When the beast howled as the medium was trying to get in touch with the dead Baskerville.' She looked up at Bodkin as they stepped down onto the pavement. 'Sorry about grabbing your arm when the hound was stalking Richard Green. It must have hurt.'

Bodkin shrugged. 'You didn't squeeze as hard as you did in the Boris Karloff film the other month.'

'Did you enjoy the film, Ferris?' Alice asked.

Ferris was walking just behind the others, a faraway look on his face. He didn't reply.

'Ferris?' Alice said, a little louder.

Ferris was a brown-haired man with boyish good looks and a slim frame. Unlike Bodkin he could look neat and tidy in the most casual of clothes. He was shy around women usually but his personality really came alive when he was standing in front of a microphone with a jazz band behind him.

'Sorry, Alice, I was just working my way through the songs I'm going to be singing tonight. There are a couple I haven't done before and I'm just making sure I know all the words.'

Alice slowed to allow him to catch up, then patted him on the arm.

'I'm sure you'll be fabulous,' she said softly.

'He always is,' Amy said, looking back over her shoulder. 'Are you doing Begin the Beguine tonight, Ferris?'

'I was going to do that as an encore, but I might put it in earlier as I'm not sure they'll ask me to sing one. It's a lot posher than the Bell. It's a different audience.' He was silent for a few moments, then he said. 'Are you coming to see me sing then? I thought you were off to the Old Bull.'

'Of course we are,' Amy called. 'We're coming to support you. We wouldn't miss it.'

'It's a bit expensive in there you know?' Ferris said.

'It can't be that much dearer than the Old Bull,' Amy replied. 'We'll be having the same drinks, won't we?'

'I don't think they sell beer, not in the cocktail bar anyway. There's a lounge bar where you can buy normal pub drinks but in there it's strictly cocktails.'

Bodkin sighed. 'I wonder if they'll let me buy a beer in the lounge and carry it through.'

Amy slapped his arm. 'Stop being mean, Bodkin. It's a one-off night and if it's too expensive we can always switch to drinking water.'

'I bet they even charge for that,' said Bodkin unhappily.

The Milton Hotel was an imposing Edwardian building that had been built in the early years of the century just off the Main Street in the town. The cocktail bar had a carpeted floor, chandelier lighting with sconces made to resemble candlelight on the floral papered walls. There were two highly polished bars with brass rails running along them on either side of the lounge. At the far end was a stage with a small dance floor in front of it. Guests were seated at many of the thirty, square tables, each covered by a white table-cloth and surrounded by four, well-padded, red leather chairs.

Amy and Alice picked out an empty table near the back of the room while Bodkin and Ferris walked to the bar. A waistcoated waiter with slicked back hair looked over the counter at them as they approached.

'It's table service, gentlemen. Just grab a seat and someone will be over to take your order.'

'Do you have a price list?' Bodkin asked.

'Sadly not, sir,' the waiter replied. 'The cost of the drinks are relative to the ambience and the atmosphere you will experience. I'm sure you will soon find that the entertainment and the refined nature of the clientele is well worth the little bit extra.' He returned to polishing the glass he was holding. 'So much better than the Lamb and Flag, sir.'

'Give me the Lamb and Flag any day of the week,' Bodkin muttered as the two policemen retraced their steps.

They had just sat down when a waiter approached carrying a stack of drinks menus. He handed one to each of them. Bodkin studied his worriedly.

'The Manhattan. That is a whisky-based drink, is it?'

'Bourbon based, sir, with vermouth and—'

'I'll have that. What about you, Ferris?'

'Same for me please, sir. If it's not too expensive, that is.'

'I have no idea how expensive it is, Ferris, they won't let us know that until we've got the drinks.' He gave the waiter a look, then turned to Amy and Alice. 'What would you like, ladies?'

'Could I have a Martini,' Alice said. 'I've had one before... when I was at the Café Blanc with my lawyer, Godfrey. I thought they were called Martina's so that's what I ordered. Made a right fool of myself.'

Amy laughed. 'I remember you telling me about that, Alice. So funny.' She grinned at her friend. 'I was going to have a Margarita, but I think I'll have the same as Alice.' She looked up at the waiter who was waiting to jot down their order on a pad. 'So, two Martina's please.' She winked at Alice. 'I've been dying to do that ever since you told me about it. They will always be Martina's to me.'

Amy and Alice chatted excitedly as Bodkin checked the contents of his wallet with his hands held below the level of the table. As Ferris wandered across the stage to have a chat with the band leader, the waiter returned with a silver tray. After handing out the drinks, he passed a slip of paper to Bodkin.

The inspector closed his eyes and gulped as he read the ticket. Taking a ten-shilling note from his pocket he dropped it on the tray.

'I want change, that's not a tip,' he growled.

Amy picked up a drink and took a sip.

'Ooh, that's gorgeous, thank you so much, Bodkin. I could get used to these.'

'Please, Amy... drink it slowly,' Bodkin pleaded.

When Ferris returned a couple of minutes later, he was full of nervous energy.

'I'm not on until ten,' he said. 'I've got a half hour slot to show them what I can do.'

'You'll be great, Ferris,' Amy said, taking a long sip of her cocktail. 'Ooh, this is really scrummy.'

'You'll get the next one for free,' Ferris said with a grin. 'I won't be paid for performing tonight, but I do get free drinks, and as you are my guests, that benefit is passed on to you... for one round anyway.'

'Fabulous,' said Amy as she downed her cocktail. She waved her glass at Bodkin. 'Come on, drink up, Mister Misery. Call that waiter across again.'

The band struck up a few practice notes, then the leader introduced Maddie York, a blonde woman of about thirty years of age. She walked onto the stage to a smattering of applause and began to sing the Adelaide Hall ballad, I Get Along Without You Very Well. Amy swayed side to side in her chair, taking quick sips from her newly arrived cocktail. Alice sang along quietly as Ferris watched the singer through wide eyes.

'Isn't she fabulous,' he whispered. 'I can't compete with that.'

'Is she doing a trial tonight too?' Amy asked.

'No, she's a lounge regular, they pay her to appear,' Ferris replied. 'She's worth every penny of what they give her too.'

By the time Maddie York had come to the end of her second song, A version of the Bebe Daniels hit, Until Love Comes Along, Amy had finished her second Martini. She turned to Bodkin who hadn't said a word since ordering their free drinks from the waiter.

'Are you ready for another, Bodkin. I'll get this one.'

'I'm fine with this, thank you.' He raised his glass then put it back on the table and leaned towards her. 'You can't afford to buy a round in this place, Amy. It's a day's wages for you. It's over three times what we pay for a round in the Old Bull.'

'You only live once, Bodkin,' Amy replied. 'Anyway, Alice will go halves with me.'

Alice emptied her own glass and stuck up her thumb.

'It's nice here, it won't hurt to splash out once in a while.'

'You won't have to pay for mine, so it will be a bit cheaper,' Ferris said, downing his Manhattan.

Bodkin gave in. 'All right, but please, take it easy. It's only a quarter to ten and we're staying until Ferris finishes his set.'

Amy reached across, patted his hand and smiled at him fondly. 'I do love that grumpy face of yours, Bodkin. You remind me of my dad.'

Amy and Alice counted out three shillings and sixpence each from their purses and Bodkin caught the eye of the waiter again. After explaining that Ferris's drinks were free, the inspector gave him the order. Five minutes later he returned and handed Bodkin a slip of paper.

'You can collect the tickets and pay at the end of the night if you wish, sir,' the waiter advised him.

'No, it's fine, we'll pay as we go,' Bodkin replied, tipping a handful of small change onto his tray. The waiter looked at it and rolled his eyes as through he'd never seen so many sixpences and one shilling pieces before.

'It's all legal currency,' Bodkin said, cheering up immediately.

Maddie York continued her set with a couple of upbeat numbers, then reverted to a ballad, Helen Morgan's When He Comes Home To Me, for her last number before taking a break.

Amy and Alice sang along quietly as they smiled at each other. When Maddie finished singing, they both got to their feet, applauding energetically. Amy looked around the room, eyes shining.

'I wish we could afford to come here every week,' she said, looking down at Bodkin who was clapping politely. 'Could we make it a once-a-month thing, I think we...' She broke off as she looked across to the entrance. A well-dressed woman and an impeccably dressed man had just walked into the room.

'Bodkin,' Amy hissed... 'Bodkin...' She nodded in the newcomer's direction as the policeman swung around in his seat.

'Well, well, well, if it isn't Francis Drake and Lorna Wetherby. I read his witness statement today. Now, this is interesting. He seemed to intimate that he didn't really know the lady. She was Nelson's PR woman, nothing to do with him.'

'Well, he was with her this morning in town,' Amy said.

'Really?' Bodkin turned back to look at her.

'They pulled up outside his office in a red sports car. They walked inside arm in arm.'

'Interesting,' Bodkin said again, narrowing his eyes as he shot another glance at the couple.

'They disappeared upstairs, then came back down a few minutes later, they were laughing and joking about something,' Amy said.

'Were they indeed? And only a few hours after the man she was representing was murdered.' Bodkin stroked his chin. 'Hang on!' he said suddenly. 'How do you know they went upstairs... or that they came back down laughing?'

Amy screwed her up her face and looked away from his stern eyes.

'I, erm... I went inside to see what they were up to... Don't look at me like that, Bodkin. It was something worth knowing, wasn't it?'

'Did they spot you?'

'No, I hid my face in a brochure. They were far too wrapped up in themselves to notice me.'

Bodkin shook his head slowly.

'That's something at least... Honestly, Amy, you really do have to stop putting yourself in danger like that. What if he... or she... is the killer? We have no idea yet.'

Amy put her finger to her lips and made a shushing sound, then she began to wave and call over to the couple.

'Ooh, Ooh, Mr Drake... Lorna, remember me? It's Amy Rowlings, we met last night.'

THIRTEEN

Francis's eyes hardened, and for a fleeting moment the smile left his face, then he recovered his composure, turned and walked across to Amy's table.

'Hello there, of course I remember you... and Inspector Bodkin of course,' he nodded to the policeman... 'but I don't think I've had the pleasure of meeting this lovely lady.' He bowed his head towards Alice. 'I'm pretty certain I'd have remembered.'

'This is my best friend, Alice,' Amy said as she shot a quick glance towards Lorna who was looking narrowed eyed at Alice.

Drake took Alice's hand and kissed it. 'Charmed,' he said.

'And this is Constable Ferris,' Bodkin put in.

Drake held out his hand. 'Drake.' The businessman introduced himself as he shook Ferris's hand firmly. 'And this, is Miss Wetherby... Look, can I buy you all a drink,' he turned towards the bar and clicked his fingers, a waiter picked up his pad and hurried across the room.

Bodkin shook his head. 'We're all right, thank y—'

'Oh, that's so kind of you,' Amy interrupted, giving Bodkin an almost imperceptible nod. 'I'll have a Martina please. Alice will have the same.'

'Martina?'

Amy grinned. 'It's a private joke. I mean Martini of course.'

When the waiter had taken their order, Drake clapped his hands together and treated them all to his best smile.

'Well, it's been lovely to meet you again. I'll just—'

'Join us please,' Amy said. 'Ferris is just about to sing. He's got a wonderful voice.'

'No, I don't think...'

'PLEASE!' Bodkin got to his feet and pulled across a leather chair from the next table along.

'Could you move along a bit, Amy, so Miss Wetherby can sit with Mr Drake?'

Ferris stood to allow Amy to take his seat, then he made his way towards the stage where the band leader was waving to him.

'And now, ladies and gentlemen, we have a new singer. Please put your hands together for Mister Orlando Ferris.'

'Orlando?' Bodkin put his head in his hands.

'Shh, it must be his stage name,' Amy hissed. She looked at Alice with wide eyes and mouthed, 'Orlando?'

Alice grinned. 'He didn't think Earnest was cool enough.'

Amy nodded. 'He's right,' she said.

Bodkin looked away from the stage and turned his attention to Francis Drake who was licking his lips and looking into his Daiquiri as if there was something wrong with the way it had been made.

'It doesn't take a genius to get this right,' he said to himself.

'I was a little surprised to see you walk in with Miss Wetherby,' Bodkin said smoothly. 'I got the impression you hardly knew her.'

'I don't, not really,' Drake replied. 'I met her outside; she was coming in anyway, so I asked her to join me.'

'That's very gallant of you,' Bodkin said, amiably. 'It's unusual to see a woman out drinking on her own, even in places like this.'

'She was waiting for a friend, but I believe she had let her down.'

'Oh, that's a shame,' Bodkin said. 'What happens if the friend turns up late?'

Drake's lips became tight. 'Then she can join us,' he said curtly.

Bodkin gave Drake his best smile. 'Again, that's very nice of you.' He took a sip of his drink, then put his glass down as Ferris began his first number, I'm In The Mood For Love.

'So,' he said, giving Drake a sidelong look. 'You didn't know Miss Wetherby before last night?' He shot her a glance. Her eyes were fixed on Ferris.

'I sort of knew her,' Drake replied. 'She worked for Nelson, I'd seen her about here and there.'

'But not to speak to, not well enough to invite out for drinks?'

Drake cleared his throat. 'No,' he said.

'Now that is odd, seeing as you were both seen getting out of your sports car earlier on today.'

Drake put his hand to his brow. 'All right, I bumped into her in town this morning and took her for lunch. She was a bit down after what had happened and I thought I'd try to cheer her up a bit.'

'Your generosity knows no bounds, Mr Drake.' Bodkin looked at him sternly. 'If she was feeling as unhappy as you claim, how come the pair of you were joking away and giggling like a pair of newlyweds inside your premises this morning.'

Drake blew out his cheeks and shook his head. Lorna's head snapped around and she placed her hand softly on top of Drake's. 'Tell him,' she said, softly.

'It's a fair cop,' Drake said, looking Bodkin in the face. 'We've been in a relationship for a few months.'

'While she was publicising Nelson Kelly, your fiercest business rival.'

'I wouldn't use the term fierce, more like, highly competitive,' he replied.

'Did she pass all his secrets on, Francis?' Bodkin asked.

'No, she's very professional. She wouldn't...'

'Pillow talk?' Bodkin mused, stroking his chin. 'It's surprising what comes out.'

'No,' Drake snapped. 'She was already working for Kelly when we met. As I said, she's a model professional.'

'You didn't think about using her to represent your company? I mean, if she's that good...'

'She was already working for Nelson, it would have looked bad... anyway, we already have an account with a PR company from Maidstone. We're very happy with them.'

'I see,' Bodkin mused. 'Is that why you weren't talking to each other last night? I find it odd that you didn't even bother to comfort her after what happened.'

'I did... later... I telephoned... I felt it was best... Look, I thought it might be best if we didn't let on we were an item. Especially with that Post reporter hanging around. He'd have had a field day.'

'Now that, I do understand,' Bodkin replied.

Amy who had been listening intently to the conversation, suddenly leaned forwards.

'While we're on the subject of the Post. I saw an article about Friday's presentation on the front page tonight. There were a few photographs. You were in one of them.'

Drake shook his head. 'They're always taking pictures of me. It's nothing special.'

'This one is very special,' Amy replied. 'It's only just registered. I knew there was something wrong but I couldn't put my finger on it until you began to talk about last night, then it came back to me.'

Drake took a sip of his drink, pulled a face, then motioned

towards the waiter who was hovering about ten feet away. He pointed to his glass, then made a circular motion with his hand so that the waiter would know it included everyone else in the round, then turned to face Amy.

'Really? And what was it that came back to you?'

'In the photo you were clearly wearing gloves, but you told us you'd forgotten them when you left home.'

Bodkin looked wide eyed at Amy, then turned his attention to Drake. 'Now then, that is a puzzle, isn't it? Do you have an explanation, Mr Drake?'

FOURTEEN

DRAKE DROPPED HIS HEAD TO HIS CHEST THEN SLOWLY BROUGHT IT BACK up again as he looked at the policeman. 'I... erm...'

Bodkin glanced at his watch. 'We don't have all night, Mr Drake. We can do this at the station if you prefer.'

Drake shook his head vigorously. 'No... no... that's the exact reason I lied about the gloves... I didn't want to spend a night at the police station.'

'Please explain.' Bodkin leaned back in his chair and took a sip of his drink, then held the glass between both hands next to his chest.

'Go on.'

'I spilled red wine on my gloves. It was when Lorna screamed, it made me jump. I knew she had gone to the cloakroom and I hadn't seen her come back.'

'And...'

'They were a mess so I took them off and stuffed them in my pocket.'

'I see, but why did you then tell us the lie about leaving them at home?'

'I was worried you'd think it was blood and send them off for testing. You wouldn't have let me go home if you suspected me. Can you even begin to imagine what something like that would do to my reputation. Especially with scum like that Miles character at the scene?'

Bodkin shook his head slowly as he looked at the businessman. 'Mr Drake. Ninety-nine percent of the population could easily tell the difference between a wine stain and a smear of blood. That is one of the flimsiest excuses I've ever heard. As for Mr Miles. Do you think he has it in for you?'

'I don't know about that. I don't get the same amount of bad press as Nelson did, but I wouldn't trust Miles as far as I can throw him.'

'Again, that's something we agree on, Mr Drake,' Bodkin replied. He put his drink back on the table and listened to Ferris singing the Bing Crosby classic, Brother Can You Spare A Dime for a few seconds, then he returned his attention to Drake.

'Did you speak to Miss Weatherby in the cloakroom? You were both in there at the same time.'

'No, there was a girl on the counter. She was watching us. I was hoping to snatch a word but it didn't seem to be the right time or place.'

Bodkin nodded as though accepting the explanation. 'Were you in competition with Kelly's company over the factory project?'

'Yes, as a matter of fact, I was.'

'And how did your plan differ from Nelson's? Was it a grander proposition? What was the difference?'

'Our plan wouldn't have meant knocking down so many houses. The factory was a tad smaller, not by much, but we planned to build it at a different angle meaning the houses on Ebenezer Street wouldn't have to be demolished.'

'From what I've heard, demolition would have been the best thing that could happen to them.'

'They're not quite as bad as they've been painted. I own a lot of property in the area.'

'How much is a lot, Mr Drake?'

'A few hundred dwellings, a couple of pubs, two warehouses.'

'And how did Nelson's plans affect you? Would you have had to sell any of your properties under the compulsory purchase order? That might have cost you dear.'

'No, none of mine were affected. I'd offloaded a few when it seemed that Nelson's project was the one the government and the council were backing.'

'Do you contribute to the mayor's fund, Mr Drake?'

The businessman shrugged. 'Everyone does. You have to if you want to do anything new in this town.'

'I've been thinking,' Bodkin said, rubbing his chin. 'What happens to Kelly's factory plan?'

'It's dead in the water. His brother will take over the business now and he was always set against it.'

'For what reason?'

Drake shrugged again. 'You'll have to ask him, but I heard they had a big falling out over the plan. I am under the impression he wanted to build a new housing estate for the local workers, not just a few to replace the ones being demolished.'

'And Nelson wasn't keen on that idea?'

Drake shook his head. 'Rightly so in my opinion. It's a lot more expense. It would add thousands to the overall cost.'

'So, you'd be happy to ship workers in from Gillingham too, Mr Drake?'

'Some, the skilled ones, but I have plenty of tenants that might fancy the idea of working right next to where they live.'

'For the menial tasks?'

'A job is a job, training costs money.'

Bodkin shook his head. 'Does everything have to come back to the profit and loss column?'

'You're not a businessman, Inspector, or you wouldn't have to ask that question.'

'Horatio Kelly seems to think differently if what you say about it is true,' Bodkin replied.

'That company will go bust inside a year with him in charge. He's too weak, he doesn't have the mindset for business. You can't let the heart rule the head, it always ends in disaster.'

'Will you resubmit your bid now?'

'For sure, though Kelly might put in a revised bid with the new housing option added. There's another company too, from outside Spinton. They put in a well thought out bid.'

'Who was that, Mr Drake?'

'Erm... Sevenoaks Construction, I believe.'

Bodkin pursed his lips and looked hard at the businessman. 'Back to the gloves. Where are they, Mr Drake?'

Amy nudged Alice as Bodkin asked the question. 'He's so good, isn't he?' she whispered, excitedly.

Drake thought for a moment. 'I dropped them in the bin by the bus stop when I left last night. I'd parked my car outside my office and I had to pass the bus stop to get to it.'

Bodkin pursed his lips. 'That was very convenient, Mr Drake. We will check with the council. I know they empty the litter bins every day but the driver of the refuse truck might be able to tell us which part of the dump he dropped the load off at.'

Drake shrugged again. 'Good luck with that. I wouldn't fancy raking through everyone's rubbish.'

'It won't be me who lands the job,' Bodkin replied brightly. 'It's a menial task.'

Drake suddenly got to his feet. 'If that's it, Inspector? I have people to meet.'

Lorna followed suit and pushed her seat away from the table.

'That will be all for now, Mr Drake. But I will want to speak to you again. As they say in the western films. Don't leave town.'

As Drake turned to walk away from the table, Bodkin smiled at Lorna. 'We haven't had the chance for a proper chat yet, Miss Wetherby. Can we set a date? Would you like me to come to you or would you prefer to drop in at the station?'

'I'm in Maidstone at the company offices all week. They have to set me up with another account now that Nelson... well, you know.'

Bodkin nodded. 'When will you return? What if the next job is out of Spinton?'

'I have loose ends to tie up here, Inspector. The account is still open. We were dealing with the company, not just Nelson. I'll be back on Friday afternoon. I'd ... erm, I'd prefer to be questioned in my flat if you don't mind.'

'Friday evening it is,' Bodkin said, smiling. 'Now, where do you live? I assume you have a telephone?'

As Ferris began the final number of his set, Fats Waller's, It's A Sin To Tell A lie, Amy shuffled across and took the seat next to Bodkin.

'Did I hear right? He says he spilled wine on the gloves? It was hard to hear everything that was said from where I was sitting.'

Bodkin took her through everything that Drake had told him.

'Are you really going to search the rubbish dump?' Amy asked.

'No,' Bodkin replied. 'There's next to no chance of finding his gloves. As to whether I believe him or not... possibly. If they were covered in blood, he could easily have said they were in the bin at home, then bought a new pair in town and deliberately spilt some red wine on them. He could have bought some today after being questioned about them last night. Anyway, we can check about the wine spill. The caterers will know if they had a badly soiled table cloth after the event.'

Amy squeezed his arm and gave him a quick kiss on the cheek. 'I do love watching you work,' she said.

'You've been the one with all the surprises today, Amy,' Bodkin said bowing his head towards her. 'The feature in the Post was news to me. Well spotted by the way. Did you see how his face fell when you mentioned it. Almost as much as it had when I told him he was seen in town with Lorna today.' The policeman tipped his head to one side. 'Two bits of vital information in one day. Well done!'

'There are three bits, actually,' Amy said. I meant to tell you when you picked me up but when you didn't arrive it slipped my mind.'

'What's that? Something else in the paper?'

'No... our mysterious Mr H.K. I nipped up to our phone box earlier and looked through the telephone directory. There's a Mr Harold Kitson living at Skelton Grange, just over the crossroads from Horatio Kelly.'

Bodkin grinned. 'Sometimes I wish you were a man so you could work with me officially on the case,' he said.

'BODKIN!' Amy said, looking shocked.

The inspector laughed and took Amy's hand. 'Only on the odd occasion,' he said. 'I prefer you the way you are ninety-nine percent of the time, obviously. In fact, forget what I said. I wish they'd just let you join the force. We'd have a much better clear up rate.'

Amy smiled and kissed him on the cheek again. 'I wouldn't change a single hair on your head,' she said.

Bodkin smiled softly at her and put a soft hand on her cheek for a few seconds. 'How about one for the road. You've earned it.'

Five minutes later, Ferris came back to the table after leaving the stage to a rousing applause.

'I didn't get the encore, but then it's my first night. How do you think it went?'

'You were perfect,' Alice said. 'Have they offered you a regular spot?'

'Not exactly, though they have asked me to do another turn next month. They'll pay me a fiver if I do it. The manager said it will be a once-a-month slot. They have regular singers but they all take time off now and again. I'm now the official stand in.'

'WELL DONE, FERRIS!' Amy shouted and threw her arms around his neck. 'I'm afraid I'm a bit tiddly,' she added with a giggle.

'You'll always get at least one free drink if you come to see me on stage,' he replied. 'And I'll buy you all a drink out of my wages. I'll be able to afford it easily now. Just think, five pounds for an hour's singing.' The constable grinned at Bodkin. 'I saw you questioning that Drake, fellow. Do you think the drinks bill can go down on expenses? You were working after all.'

'There's more chance of nailing a blancmange to the ceiling, Ferris. I can hear the laughter now as the Chief Superintendent reads my expenses statement.' He got to his feet, then picked up his glass and raised it. 'I do prefer beer, but I could get used to drinking Manhattans.' He flicked his head towards the door. 'Come on, we'll just be in time for the last bus.'

As they walked out of the front door, Sandy Miles, the reporter stepped out of the shadows.

'Hello, Inspector. Do you have a comment for our readers about the article in tonight's paper?'

Bodkin's face hardened. 'Firstly, MISTER Miles, I'm off duty. Secondly, I haven't read the article, and thirdly, when I have something to say, you'll be in the queue to hear it along with every other reporter in the region.'

He stepped forward to push past the newsman, then stopped, turned back and whispered in Ferris's ear. 'Go back inside, Ferris. Warn Mr Drake that the press are waiting out here. Tell him to leave alone. We don't want Sandy Bloody Miles to find out that he and Lorna are an item yet. I want to know a lot more about their relationship before that happens.'

'Righto, boss,' Ferris replied, patting his pockets. 'I'll see you at the bus stop, sir. I've left my cigarettes on the table; I'll just nip back in to get them.'

Ferris caught up with the rest of the party at the bus stop a few minutes later. Amy had pulled on her jacket as the night air had turned chilly.

'There's no need to see us all the way home, Bodkin,' Amy said. 'You've had a really long day. Me and Alice will be fine. We used to do this every Saturday until you two latched onto us.'

'But I like seeing you home safely,' Ferris said. 'I enjoy the walk back from the farm, it gives me time to think about things.'

'Get an early night, Ferris,' Bodkin advised. 'You're on the front desk tomorrow, aren't you? I've got the day off; I'll see the girls home.'

'No disrespect meant, but if you're going, I'm going, sir,' Ferris replied. 'I haven't had much chance to talk to Alice tonight.'

Amy flashed Alice a quick glance. 'It's nice to be wanted, isn't it?'

'Here's the bus,' Alice replied. 'Come on then, Ferris, let's catch up on all that missed conversation.'

At Amy's gate, they said goodnight to Alice and she and Ferris walked up the lane towards the farm.

'I'll be fifteen... maybe twenty minutes,' Ferris called over his shoulder.

'There really was no need to see us home, Bodkin,' Amy said when they were alone.

'I like seeing you home. Not just because I think anything will happen to you on your own, but... well, to be honest, I just like being with you. I wish I could spend more time in your company. It's...oh, look seeing you is always the best part of my week.'

Amy stepped closer to Bodkin, wrapped her arms around him and laid her head on his broad chest.

'It's the best time for me too,' she said softly. She pulled back and looked up into his face. 'Especially when we're working on a case together.'

Bodkin rolled his eyes as Amy pulled him close again.

'I'm only joking, Bodkin. It's always lovely to see you, whatever the circumstances.'

'I'll nip across to the church and catch you when you come out in the morning if that's all right?'

'Of course it's all right, Bodkin,' Amy said, turning her face up towards his. 'You can come and sit next to my machine at work on Monday if you like.'

Bodkin smiled and lowered his head. They kissed.

Bodkin was true to his word and after the morning service, Amy walked out of the church with her parents to find him leaning against the left-hand side of the entrance. He swapped pleasantries with Mr and Mrs Rowlings then took Amy's arm and led her down the path towards the lychgate.

'I have some news I think you might like to hear,' he said as they walked past the Reverend Villiers gravestone.

'Really? Well, come on, out with it, man. Don't keep me in suspense.'

'I rang Chief Superintendent Grayson this morning. I'm trying to arrange an interview with Nelson Kelly's wife, Helen. It's a very delicate situation, her life must have been thrown upside down and I think we'll need to show a little bit more compassion than we usually do when we interview people. It won't be in the next few days; she's gone to her mother's house in Knightsbridge for a while. She'll be back at the weekend and I suggested that it would be a good idea if I had a woman with me when I conduct the interview. Grayson agreed that we have to be sympathetic to her position, so he suggested I take you with me.'

'ME!' Amy exclaimed. 'Why not that woman PC... Norris was it?'

'She's off work with stress. Friday night was a big shock to her. She'd never seen a dead body before, let alone one with a knife sticking out of its chest.'

'Poor girl,' Amy replied. 'It's not for everyone, this murder lark.'

'The only other alternative was Trixie,' Bodkin continued.

'Trixie!' Amy snorted. 'You might as well take the Post reporter with you.'

'That's what both Chief Super Grayson and I thought,' the inspector said with a laugh. 'I'll try to arrange the interview for Saturday, but make sure you're free on Friday night too, I want you with me when I question Lorna Wetherby. Keep your eye on her body language, let me know when you think she's lying, you're really good at that.'

'Does Mr Grayson know I'll be coming with you to that interview too?' Amy asked as Bodkin opened the gate for her to step through.

'No, but it's the same thing as the Saturday interview. If there's another woman in the room she may not feel so threatened. I want her to open up and there'll be more chance of that with you there.' Bodkin closed the wooden church gate behind him. 'Anyway, it's Grayson's idea to question female witnesses with a woman present. Modern policing, he calls it.'

They stopped on the pavement to wait for Amy's parents who had come out of the main gates and were walking down the hill towards them. Bodkin looked back at the lychgate they had just come through.

'Do you still get a bit nervous about using this entrance? It's where the vicar was found dead and close to where you were held hostage by his killer, after all.'

Amy shook her head. 'It was the most exciting day of my life, Bodkin. And I knew you'd come to rescue me anyway.'

'You couldn't have been sure of that, Amy.'

'I was,' Amy replied. 'As sure as night follows day.'

FIFTEEN

IN THE QUEUE TO CLOCK IN AT THE MILL ON MONDAY MORNING, BIG Nose Beryl was holding court.

'The police don't have a clue who killed him of course, but my cousin Edith told me that they are looking for his secretary, she's done a runner by all accounts. She was at the do right up to the moment he was killed.' Beryl tapped her nose with a long finger. 'Mark my words, she's for the drop when they find her.'

She was still handing out her 'inside information' as the workforce gathered in the changing room. Amy hung up her coat on her peg, then made a turban out of a headscarf and secured it with a couple of grips.

'Then there's his brother. He disappeared at the same time as the secretary, so that was a bit suspicious... then there's the girl on the catering staff who waited on him that night, rumour has it that she was having a fling with Nelson Kelly but he broke it off when she announced she was pregnant. She's eight months' gone now, and get this... her old man works for the same company and he was there on the night. He must have been more than a bit put out by that and he—'

'You really do spout nonsense, Beryl,' Amy said when she'd heard enough of her co-worker's ravings.

'What would you know about it?' Beryl asked.

Amy pursed her lips and held up her fingers.

'One,' she pushed a finger down. 'Mr Kelly's secretary wasn't at the do. Two,' she pushed down another finger. 'Mr Kelly's brother wasn't in attendance either.' She paused, then pushed down another finger. 'The catering staff aren't under suspicion and as far as I'm aware, there wasn't a married couple among them and none of the women were heavily pregnant.' Amy pushed down a fourth finger. 'Then of course there was the fact that I was there and witnessed the whole sequence of events. You're not just a little bit wrong this time, Beryl, you're one hundred percent wrong in everything you've said. If you did get it from this cousin of yours, she's as big a fantasist as you are.'

Carol Sims, Amy's best friend at work snorted with laughter along with many of the other women. Not many took whatever Beryl said, seriously.

'Oh, listen to Miss High and Mighty. She's mixing with the toffs now.' Beryl looked around for any signs of support. 'I don't believe you were there. Who would invite you to a posh bash like that?' She looked down her nose at Amy.

'I was in Chief Superintendent Grayson's party,' Amy replied, amiably. 'He was up for an award himself on the night and he wanted to thank me for the help I gave the police during the Reverend Villiers murder investigation.' She picked up her bag, fished around inside and pulled out a piece of coloured card. 'I've got my invitation here if you'd like to look at it.'

'You were with that fly by night copper of yours, I'll bet. He wangled you an invite.' Beryl looked suspiciously at the ticket. 'Anyway... how come you didn't mention it last week if you knew you were going.'

Amy decided not to let on that she had only been invited by

Bodkin on the Friday evening, when his superior officer pulled out.

'Because, Beryl, I don't like to boast. My private life is my own to comment on or share information about as I see fit. I wouldn't even have mentioned the fact that I'd been at the event to anyone but Carol and a couple of others if you hadn't come up with that ridiculous tissue of lies this morning.'

Amy pulled a small bag of mints from her coat and stuffed it into the pocket of her wraparound apron.

'Right, girls, let's get to it,' she said.

At twelve-thirty, Amy dropped the last finished dress of the morning into the bin at the side of her seat, stood up, stretched, then turned off her machine and made her way up the aisle to where Carol's machine was situated.

'I'm ready for a cuppa,' she said. 'And, I'm starving. As Bodkin is so fond of saying, "My stomach thinks my throat's been cut".'

Carol laughed as she examined her final garment of the morning.

'These dresses are easy, aren't they? I wish we could make them every day.'

'We get a good bonus on them too,' Amy agreed. 'But I think we're back on those pleated winter frocks next week. We'll have to go Hell for leather to make any extra on those blooming things, they're so fiddly.'

Carol dropped the garment in the finished bin and switched off her own machine. 'My turn for the teas,' she said as the friends walked side by side towards the canteen.

· · ·

'Have you got anything planned for the Whitsun Bank Holiday?' Carol asked as they ate their packed lunches at a table with five other women.

'Not really,' Amy replied. 'I'm doing a thing with the church in the afternoon. The poverty action group is going up to the Haxley estate to hand out a bit of food and a few essentials to some of the residents. I'm not usually involved in that, but Ada Strong has got to look after her mother following her operation, so I agreed to step in to make the numbers up. I might have two nights out over the weekend though as I won't have to get up for work on Monday morning. Do you fancy meeting up at the Old Bull on Sunday evening?'

'I'll see what my other half has planned,' Carol replied. 'He might have decided to take me out.' She laughed, loudly. 'I'm not holding my breath though, the last time he did that, the King was still a kid. Anyway, money is a bit tight at the moment.'

'He's happy at home, Carol. I think that's lovely,' Amy said. 'There aren't too many like him in this town. Take her old man for instance.' She nodded towards Beryl who was sitting with three of her cronies, heads together, flashing looks across to Amy's table.

'He's a brute,' Carol said. 'I honestly wouldn't wish him on anyone. Not even Beryl.'

'I know, but it's hard to feel any sympathy for her,' Amy said. 'I did notice she's not sporting a black eye this week so he must have behaved himself over the weekend.'

'Or it's his weekend in at the pit,' Carol said. 'They run a maintenance shift overnight and they're all on a roster.'

'That will be it then,' Amy said, finishing her sandwich and closing the lid of her tin box. 'Now then,' she shuffled her chair across the floor so she could be closer to Carol. 'Pin your ears back and I'll tell you the truth about what happened on Friday night.'

. . .

As the two friends were walking back to their machines to start the afternoon session, Amy was stopped by the foreman, Mr Bartholomew.

'Miss Handsley wants a word,' he said as he pointed up to the office on the Mezzanine floor.

'What have you done now?' Carol asked as Amy turned towards the stairs. 'If it's overtime. I'll take it if you don't want it. I could use the extra money.'

Georgina Handsley lifted a hand and waved her in as Amy approached the office door.

'Ah, our fashion guru. Come in, Miss Rowlings,' she said getting to her feet.

Georgina was a tweed-clad, dumpy woman of about sixty with thin, steel-grey hair tied back in a severe, old-fashioned bun which gave her the appearance of wearing a continuous look of surprise.

In the seat opposite was a heavily pregnant woman of about thirty-five years of age. She smiled at Amy as she entered the office.

'Miss Rowlings... Amy...' Georgina began. 'I have a proposition to put to you that I hope you will find interesting. It will mean time away from the Mill and I promise you, the work won't be anywhere near as heavy or tedious as you suffer every day at your machine.'

Amy tipped her head and smiled towards her employer.

'I'm already interested,' she said.

'Right, take a seat, please.' Georgina waved a hand towards a wooden chair that was positioned next to the door. 'We, Josie and I that is, have a bit of a problem. As you can see, she is almost due to have her baby and she's finding it more and more difficult to run her dress shop. I'm sure you know it... London Connection. It's just off the High Street.'

Amy nodded. It was the poshest dress shop in town. They carried all the major labels.

'Josie is my niece and also my partner in the business. She runs the ordering side of things while her sister temporarily manages the shop, deals with the customer complaints, etc... some of them need delicate handling, especially when you have to tell them that their body shape isn't what it was when they were twenty-one.' She paused for a moment as Amy nodded her understanding. 'The thing is, we've just lost the woman who does the dressing and measuring up for any alterations that might be required. She's off to London with her fiancé. She's been offered a job at Harrods, can you believe?'

'Blimey!' Amy exclaimed.

'This is where you come in,' Georgina continued. 'I can't spare you away from your machine for the whole week and I don't want you to lose anything by way of bonus payments, but I can spare you for a couple of days at a time. We can agree to some sort of average for the bonus you would have earned and the wages you'll get from your days working at the shop will be slightly higher than you earn here. So, here's the proposition. I'd like you to take on our ex-dresser's duties until we can find a suitable replacement. We've already placed an advertisement so it shouldn't take more than two or three weeks at most. I have been told that you have a keen eye for fashion and what might, or might not suit someone, I also know that you have the temperament needed to explain to our clients that they are not really overweight, it's just that sometimes the garments come in a little undersized.'

'So, I'll be advising clients what would look best on them and what wouldn't suit?' Amy asked.

'Correct,' said Josie.

'We have two more girls who help out with any alterations that might need doing. They're very good but still quite young. They work well under guidance though. You are there to advise them and check on the work. Most of the dresses are quite generously seamed so there is usually enough material to be let out. In more severe circumstances you'll need to talk the client out of buying the dress and assure her that one of the other, more generously proportioned garments is more her style.'

'That does sound interesting,' Amy said. 'How many days a week are we talking about?'

'We open half day on Wednesday and then, nine until five-thirty on Thursday, Friday and Saturday,' Josie said. 'Until I get back to work that is and we have the replacement dresser, then we'll be open for five and a half days as usual. Susan, my sister, has her own business, but she's been helping me out until after the baby arrives. She's lovely, but to be honest, Amy, she isn't that good at matching dresses to clients.'

Amy nodded.

'I'm happy to do it and I think I'd enjoy it. I do love picking out clothes myself and I also advise a couple of friends what they should buy, but I honestly don't like the sound of Saturday working. I have so much to do myself and I can't do any of it on Sundays, what with church and everything.'

'We do need someone with fashion experience in the shop on Saturdays. It's our busiest day,' Josie said, looking disappointed.

'I'm sorry,' Amy said, 'I'd like to help and I would have enjoyed it, but honestly, I really can't do Saturdays.'

It's the only chance I get to help Bodkin with the investigation, she thought.

'Could you recommend anyone who could do the job on a Saturday?' Georgina asked. 'Someone reliable.'

'Carol Sims used to work in a big dress shop in Maidstone before she got married and moved out this way. She's handy with a needle if needed too, she does alteration work from home to earn a bit extra.'

'Do you think she'd be interested?' asked Josie.

'I know she would. She was only talking about needing some overtime this lunch break.'

'Right, she sounds ideal,' Georgina said with a smile. 'Now, Amy. I'd like you to make your way to the London Connection for about nine o'clock on Wednesday morning so that Josie can show you the ropes. It's only a half day, but you'll be paid your full working hours. After that you'll work nine until five-thirty on Thursday and Friday for the next three weeks. Carol will work the same hours on the Saturday. Can you ask her to come up when you go back to your machine?'

Georgina got to her feet and clapped her hands together.

'Good, that's sorted then, don't worry about etiquette or protocol or anything like that. Susan knows how to handle the clients and she'll be doing most of the meeting and greeting. Once they have been suitably welcomed, you'll take over and show them what you think will suit. Then you can advise our two young seamstresses where any alterations need to be made.'

That's a bit of good news, getting away from the Mill for a couple of days a week, Amy thought as she walked down the stairs from the mezzanine. *Big Nose Beryl is going to have a fit.*

SIXTEEN

On Wednesday morning, Amy, wearing a black pencil skirt and a white blouse, arrived at London Connection twenty minutes early, and was let in by the cleaner who was just finishing up. She took off her coat and spent the next fifteen minutes studying the dressed, mannequins and the garments in the nicely lit niches that ran along one side of the shop. On the other side was a row of mirror fronted cabinets. Amy took a quick look inside one to find sets of shelves, covered with folded chemises and silk, knee length underskirts. The tops of the cabinets were piled high with hat boxes. On the floor was a short set of wheeled steps that presumably allowed the shop assistant to reach them.

Along the back wall was a wide, raised plinth on which stood three, immaculately dressed mannequins, all wearing hats. Half way down the shop floor was a low glass cabinet containing accessories priced at more than Amy would have paid for a dress where she shopped. On top of the cabinet were three metal stands showing off wide-brimmed hats. There were no sales rails like they had at Brigden's, but there were three long rails in the stockroom where different sized copies of the dresses on show in the shop were stored. Discreetly placed in the corner of the room was a narrow desk, on which sat a thick, black order book and a fancy-looking till. Alongside the order book was a typed, three-page stock inventory which gave detailed descriptions of the clothing available and the price of each item. Amy blew out her cheeks as she ran her eyes down the list. She'd have to save every penny she earned for four months or more to be able to buy the cheapest of the dresses.

Josie arrived bang on nine and, after a quick cup of tea, she showed Amy around again, pointing out where certain, unseen items were stored and going into a lot of detail about the sizing of the dresses.

'Each dress comes in three sizes. We find that's the right number to work with. There is a bit of give in each size, the only problems we tend to get is if a customer is particularly tall and slender, or short and… how shall we put it, more generously proportioned. We can get in touch with the London houses and have special versions of a dress made up, but it's costly and our profit margins shrink rapidly when we have to do that, so we discourage it in the main, and as was explained to you on Monday, we attempt to talk the client into trying on something a little more suitable.' She leaned in conspiratorially and whispered in Amy's ear. 'You will notice a range of dresses in the back of the shop that are, how shall we put it, generously enhanced?'

She spent the next two hours talking Amy through how the stock list worked.

'You won't need to familiarise yourself with the pricing, Amy. Susan is well able to do that. She'll run any shop bought items through the till too. If anyone has any questions regarding price or availability, just call Susan over.'

Susan had turned up about ten minutes after Josie. She was a pretty, petite young woman with mousey coloured hair cut in a page-boy style. Amy took to her immediately.

By the time twelve o'clock came around, Amy had only seen

four customers walk through the door and two of those had only come in to check on orders. The other two wanted to buy something from the accessory cabinet. Just after twelve, Amy got her first customer and spent the next forty minutes advising the lady over which dress would be most suitable to wear at a family wedding, after their discussion, she led her to the changing rooms where she tried on three of the four dresses that Amy had selected.

When the woman (who Amy now knew as Mrs Walker-Peters) had made her choice, Amy took precise measurements and jotted them down on a pad to hand over to Linda and Maggie, the two young women who worked in the tailoring shop on the first floor.

After double-checking her calculations, Amy led the woman back into the shop and handed her over to Susan while she went back into the changing room to pick up the selected dress and return the others to the rails.

At one o'clock, and relishing the thought of a free afternoon in the middle of the week, Amy walked out of London Connection, turned left onto the High Street and, as it was a sunny day, decided to walk down to the bus stop on Middle Street instead of having to stand in a queue and wait for the next bus from the stop over the road.

When she reached the bus stop, her eyes wandered down the hill to where the police station was situated. On a whim, she crossed the street and made her way to the newly built, red-brick, building. Pushing the front door open she stepped into a lobby where she found PC Ferris leaning on the front counter looking dreamily into space.

'Hello, Ferris,' Amy said, jolting the policeman back into the present.

'Hello, Amy. What are you doing here, shouldn't you be at work?'

'I've got the afternoon off.' Amy grinned at Ferris. 'Is His Nibs in?'

Ferris laughed. 'Inspector Nibs if you don't mind. Yes, he's here, shall I give him a shout?'

Ferris picked up the phone, dialled a number and spoke quietly into the mouthpiece. Two minutes later, Bodkin arrived behind the desk with a quizzical look on his face.

'Amy, what a pleasant surprise.' He looked suddenly worried. 'Is everything all right?'

'Everything is perfectly fine, thank you, Bodkin, I've got an unexpected afternoon off and I was wondering if you'd like to take me for lunch.'

Bodkin looked at his watch. 'I'm tied up for the next hour, I've got a meeting with the chief super, but I can make myself available after that. Where do you fancy going? The café on the High Street?'

'It's far too nice a day to be stuck indoors,' Amy said. 'I'll tell you what. I'll get the bus home and make us some sandwiches; we can eat them in the park. How does that sound?'

'Wonderful,' Bodkin replied with feeling. 'I'll drive round and pick you up after I've finished up here. I've been dying to get out in the sun all morning but I've been stuck inside writing reports.'

'Ooh, reports,' Amy said, winking at the inspector. 'You can report to me when you've done with Mr Grayson.'

When Amy walked into the house at one-twenty-five, she found her mother covering a plate of sandwiches with a tea towel.

'Ah, there you are love. Did you have a nice morning?'

'It was different, I was a bit nervous but then I've only had to deal with one customer. I don't think they get many people through the doors, but the ones they do get spend a lot of money.

You should see the prices of the dresses, Mum. Just one would keep us in food for a year.'

'Good heavens,' Mrs Rowlings replied as she shook the kettle. Taking it to the sink, she refilled it, then put it on the hob and lit the gas.

Amy took a brown paper bag from the cupboard and began to fill it with the sandwiches that her mother had left on the plate.

'Is there any ham left, Mum, and maybe a bit of cheese?'

'Are you feeling a bit peckish, dear?'

Amy laughed. 'No, Mum. I'm going for a picnic on the park with Bodkin, it's such a lovely day, it seems a shame to waste it.'

'You go up and get changed out of your shop clothes and I'll make another round up... did you say cheese and ham? Will he want any pickle with that do you think?'

When Amy came back down, she was wearing a floral print summer dress and a pair of open toed sandals. She carried a white knitted cardigan over her arm.

'I've packed the sandwiches into two separate bags, Amy. I cut Bodkin's bread a bit thicker than yours and I put an extra one in. I bet he went to work today without eating breakfast. Oh, and I've put a couple of slices of lemon cake in with them... and there's some of my homemade lemonade in the flask.'

'I'm going to have to watch out here, Mum. I think Bodkin might want to marry you.'

Mrs Rowlings blushed. 'What would he want with an old fuddy-duddy like me?' she said as she turned away and walked back into the kitchen. 'Joking aside. You ought to look after him, our Amy, he thinks the world of you. A blind man could see it. I think it's so romantic, the way he looks at you sometimes.'

'Bodkin. Romantic?... He...' Amy thought back to what the policeman had said to her at the gate on the previous Saturday... 'he can be... at times.'

Amy sat at the table and picked up the cup of tea that her

mother had poured for her. 'Ooh that's hit the spot, Mum. I've been looking forward to this since this morning's tea break. We only had one cup.'

'Did you want to keep this, or should I throw it away, love?'

Mrs Rowlings held up the brochure that Amy had brought back from Drake's office.

'No, give it here, Mum. It will give me something to read while I wait for Bodkin.'

Amy opened up the glossy brochure and read the introduction, then she turned over the page and read the list of companies that made up the conglomerate. When she noticed Sevenoaks Construction, she paused reading and stared at the large wooden crucifix on the far wall. *Where had she heard that name before?* Unable to remember, she turned the page again and read about some of the recently completed projects. On the final page was a listing of the company directors. As she ran her eyes down it, her mouth dropped open. Half way down the list of seven names was Harold Kitson.

SEVENTEEN

BODKIN PARKED HIS CAR ON A SIDE STREET IN PRETTY MUCH THE SAME spot he had found the previous Saturday. It was only a short walk to the alley that led to the park. As they came out from the gap between the last two bungalows, Russell Park opened up before them.

Pervis Drayman was sitting in the same seat he'd been in the last time they had seen him. He waved a brown beer bottle at them as they passed. Meg was chasing a stick, as usual.

'Where shall we sit?' Bodkin asked. The park was almost empty with only a young couple lying on a checked blanket. They seemed engrossed in each other.

'Let's go down to the Skelton end,' Amy said. 'The kids will be out of school in about an hour and the playground will be so noisy we won't be able to hear ourselves think.'

They walked through the park until it began to narrow, then Amy led him to the left and through a copse of trees. She stopped at the bank of a bubbling stream that ran the full length of the park, until it eventually emptied out into the river Medway. A mother duck swam along in the centre of the stream, followed by a bobbing line of six, brown and grey, ducklings.

Amy took a tablecloth from her basket, unfolded it and spread it out onto the ground, then she took out two plates and began to unpack the sandwiches that her mother had made for them.

'There's homemade lemonade in the flask,' she pointed out. 'Yours are the thick cut ones, Mum made them specially for you.'

'I think I'm a bit in love with your mum,' Bodkin said, taking a huge bite from his sandwich.

'I did warn her that you might be,' Amy said, smiling at the policeman. 'Dad had better up his game.'

Bodkin put his sandwich back on his plate, reached out and touched the back of Amy's hand. 'Thank you so much for this. It's a rare treat,' he said.

'Do you think I've brought you here to sit and sunbathe?' Amy said with a short laugh. 'I want to know what's new in the case and as I've finally got you to myself, you've got plenty of time to go through it all.' She paused then said. 'I've got some news for you when you're done.'

'What news?' Bodkin's ears pricked up.

Amy slapped his hand playfully. 'You first... now, come on, tuck in. Mum reckons you won't have had any breakfast so I can't take any of this lot back with me.'

Bodkin picked up his sandwich again and bit into it, thinking as he chewed.

'This mayor's fund is a bit of a puzzle, he said eventually. 'It appears that only businesses that have been awarded contracts with the council since the old mayor, Basil Thornalley took office, pay into it. There was something in place before he arrived, called the mayor's community fund which hands out small amounts to local charities and other good causes. As far as I know, that fund is still in existence. I've asked the chief super to get me permission to examine the books to see if any of the money donated by local businesses has been paid into it, but it's more complicated than usual because it's a local corporation managed fund. It seems we might be accused of interfering with democracy.' Bodkin finished his sandwich and reached for another. 'I smell corruption.'

'There's more than just a common or garden murder involved here then, Bodkin.' Amy took a bite of her own sandwich. 'Do you think the new mayor is in on it too?'

'Robert McKenzie stood on a sort of clean up the council ticket. Unlike the previous mayor he has assets of his own. He comes from money. Now, whether this means he's clean or not is a question we have yet to answer. He talked a good game in the meeting to select the next mayor, apparently, but some of those councillors aren't as shiny white as they appear. There may have been a few backhanders dished out.'

'It's terrible, Bodkin. We vote for these people thinking we can trust them and we can't, they all seem to be in it to serve themselves, not to serve the public.'

'Wealth and privilege, Amy, it always boils down to that. It's what I was saying the other day, they think they're entitled. The working man is between a rock and a hard place when it comes to who gets their vote because the candidates from all four parties come from the same gene pool. Even that guy standing for the communists went to public school.'

Amy finished her sandwich and poured them both a cup of lemonade. 'Women get to vote too,' she chided. 'Anything else to report?'

Bodkin thought for a moment. 'I've arranged an interview with Basil Thornalley, our esteemed former mayor, tomorrow morning.'

'Ooh, that's good, I'm working in town at the shop tomorrow and Friday. London Connection, do you know it?'

'I know of it,' Bodkin replied. 'I've never been inside.'

'Well, now's your chance, Bodkin,' Amy said. 'Come around at lunchtime. I'm free for an hour after one o'clock. If you fancy buying me anything while you're inside, there's a lovely cross-cut, bias dress going for thirty-five pounds.'

Bodkin almost choked on his sandwich. 'These are really good,' he said, quickly changing the subject. 'Is there any more?'

'No, that's your lot, but I've got a bit of cake in here if you're a good boy and finish off your report.'

Bodkin shook his head slowly. 'All right. We have a blood type from the handkerchief you found. We asked for it to be tested as a priority and for once the lab actually came up with the goods. It's type O positive and that's the most common blood group, so it's not much help to us really. However, Nelson was type O as well.'

'That's a shame. It would have been nice if he had belonged to a rare group.' Amy took a sip of her lemonade, then held her cup in both hands as she looked at the policeman. 'Now for my news. Are you ready for this? I've been bursting to tell you.'

Bodkin sat up straight and put his hand above his eyes to shade them from the sun. 'Go on then.'

'I was reading the brochure I picked up from Drake's the other day and guess who is listed as a director of one of the companies in the group?'

Bodkin shrugged and shook his head.

'Only Harold Kitson of Skelton Grange.'

Bodkin rubbed the dark five o'clock shadow that covered his chin. 'Now, that *is* interesting. We now have two names associated with a company bidding for the contract that Nelson won.'

'There was something else too. In the list of companies owned by the group, there was one called Sevenoaks Construction. It rang a bell but I can't remember why.'

'You heard it mentioned by Mr Drake the other night, Amy. He told me that Sevenoaks put in a rival bid for the contract that Drake Construction was chasing.'

'But why would two of his companies bid for the same contract? It doesn't make sense.'

'That's the question that's gone right to the top of my list for the next time I speak to him,' Bodkin said. 'Meanwhile I'd like to know more about our mystery man, Harold Kitson. He only lives a few hundred yards away from here, shall we drop in for a chat?'

CHAPTER

EIGHTEEN

S<small>KELTON</small> G<small>RANGE WAS A</small> V<small>ICTORIAN RESTORED</small>, <small>STONE-BUILT HOUSE THAT</small> had its origins back in the fifteenth century. It was an imposing structure with one large gable in the centre and two smaller ones that fronted a pair of dormer windows jutting out from the tiled roof.

At the front of the house was a large porch with a medieval style studded door.

On the well-kempt lawn, in front of the house, was a wrought iron table at which sat a double chinned, red-faced man wearing a white baseball cap with a black cat emblem, a purple velvet jacket and a pair of fawn, flannel trousers. On the table was a bottle of sherry, a single sherry glass, and the remains of a sandwich. At his feet, lay a fat, brown Labrador. As Amy and Bodkin approached, the man took a deep breath, pulled back his arm and threw a tennis ball with all his might.

'Go fetch, Cocoa, go fetch.'

The dog lifted its head, watched the ball land about five yards away, then yawned, closed its eyes and went back to sleep.

The act of throwing the ball seemed to have taken up most of the large man's energy. He wiped sweat from his brow with a soggy-looking handkerchief, then, as if he had just noticed their arrival, he took off the baseball cap, dabbed at this damp hair, then shielded his eyes with the brim as he looked towards them.

'Hello,' he said. 'Warm for the time of year, isn't it?'

'We're looking for Harold Kitson,' Bodkin said. 'Are you—'

'Good Lord no,' the man replied. 'I'm Clarence Hunt, I come every afternoon to exercise Mr Kitson's dog. He doesn't have time to walk it himself.'

Amy looked at the huge, flabby animal, then to the tennis ball lying a few yards away, then back to Clarence.

'He, erm... is it a he? Doesn't seem too keen on chasing the ball.'

'It's a she,' Clarence said, wiping his brow again. 'Her name's Cocoa. She's too old and lazy to chase things now. He picked up the bottle and drank from it. A bit like me, really.'

Bodkin nodded in agreement. If anything, the dog looked fitter than the man.

'Do you know where we can find Mr Kitson?' he asked.

'You just missed him. He was sitting out here having his lunch when I arrived.' Clarence nodded towards the partly eaten sandwich, then looked guiltily at the sherry bottle. 'He went inside to make a telephone call about half an hour ago, but never came back.'

'So, he's still in the house?'

'Well, he hasn't come past me so I assume so,' said Clarence. 'It's erm, probably better if you go round to the back door, the tradesman's entrance, so to speak... Not that he's stuck up or anything but that's where his study is situated. The bell on the front porch doesn't work.'

The rear of the building was nothing like as impressive as the front. At the back, the grass was uncut and grew in ugly clumps. At the bottom of a cobbled yard were two dilapidated barns, one of which was missing a roof. The other was so rickety-looking, it seemed like a strong gust of wind would blow it down.

The beautiful, lime mortared stone façade at the front of the house wasn't matched at the back. Here the stone looked weathered and had gaps where the mortar had fallen away. From above, they could hear a house sparrow singing as it perched on the edge of a large hole under the eaves where the stonework had crumbled.

Kitson was standing in the doorway with a cigarette between his nicotine-stained fingers. He was dressed in corduroy trousers, a blue and white striped shirt and a brown, linen waistcoat. His light, almost blond hair was parted on the left and flopped over his right eye. He seemed to be in deep thought as he stared down at the cobbled path and didn't notice their approach until they were almost next to him.

'Eurgh!' he spat as his head shot up. 'You scared me half to death. You really shouldn't creep up on people.'

Bodkin held up his hands, palms forward. 'I'm sorry about that. Are you Harold Kitson?'

The man gave Bodkin a quick glance, then looked Amy up and down for a lot longer than was necessary. She felt herself beginning to blush as his gaze came to rest on her chest and remained there.

'If you're from the council about my rates bill, I rang them this morning, the cheque is in the post.'

'I expect they'll be very happy to receive it, sir,' Bodkin replied. He pulled his warrant card from his pocket. 'I'm Inspector Bodkin from Spinton police and this,' he held his hand out towards Amy, 'is Miss Rowlings.'

'So, they're finally letting women into the CID, are they? Well, I hope they're all as pretty as you, my dear.' He gave Amy another long, lecherous, look.

Bodkin stiffened as he watched Kitson run his eyes over her.

'We have a few questions for you if you don't mind,' he said, with an edge to his voice.

'Of course,' Kitson replied, tearing his eyes away from Amy's chest. 'I'd invite you in but the place is a bit of a mess. My cleaner hasn't showed up for a week or more.' He pointed to a long bench seat at the side of the cobbled path, it had once been painted a dark green colour, but the top coat had flaked and faded so badly that you could see the original stained timber underneath.

His eyes never left Amy as she sat down and crossed her legs. Seeing Kitson was about to sit next to her, Bodkin pushed himself forward and plonked himself down leaving a space to his left for the businessman.

'Firstly, I'd like to ask a question about your business dealings,' Bodkin began.

Kitson narrowed his eyes as he tried to stare Bodkin out.

'Anything in particular?'

'Yes, I believe you own shares in the Drake Group.'

'What of it? It's hardly a matter for the police.'

'Quite correct,' Bodkin replied. 'Do you also own shares in Sevenoaks Construction?'

'No, I've never heard of it,' Kitson said.

'Really? I'm a little surprised by that answer because Sevenoaks Construction is part of the Drake group of companies and you are listed as one of its directors.'

'Ah, Sevenoaks, yes. I have investments all over the place, Inspector. I can't name them all off the top of my head.'

'I understand, sir.' Bodkin scratched the stubble on his chin. 'Do... did, you know, Nelson Kelly?'

'I've come across him a few times. Can't say I ever took to the man if I'm honest, I heard he's a bit of a charlatan, a manipulator.'

'That's interesting,' Bodkin replied. 'Who actually described him thus?'

'Oh, I can't remember now. Several people.'

'Francis Drake? Was he one of them?'

'He might have been, I honestly can't remember, I just know I was advised to be wary of doing business with him.'

'I see. What about his brother, Horatio? Are you on friendlier terms with him?'

'I can't say we're good friends. We're on nodding terms. He did give me a couple of investment tips at one time.'

'But isn't he a director of Kelly Construction? Surely if Nelson was a bit of a charlatan, you couldn't really trust his brother either?'

'Horatio is nothing like Nelson,' Kitson spurted.

'What do you mean, Mr Kitson? How are they different?'

'Well, Horatio doesn't treat you like you're an imbecile to start with. Nelson always looked at me like I was something he scraped off his shoe, he's been the same since we were at boardi...' He tailed off and screwed up his face as he realised his error.

'Boarding school? We'd have found out,' Bodkin said matter-of-factly.

'We were at Maidstone together until we were sixteen,' Kitson said.

'So, you know them both really well?' Bodkin replied.

'They weren't close friends, as I said. I never did get on with Nelson, he was a bully if you must know.'

'And Horatio?'

'I used to hang around with him now and then.'

'What about when you were back home... here?' Bodkin looked up to the crumbling façade.

'We spent a bit of time together in the holidays,' Kitson replied.

'What about more recently?'

'Not so much.'

Bodkin stroked his chin again. 'A few moments ago, you told me you hardly knew him, even though he lives less than a quarter of a mile away and there are fewer than a couple of dozen houses in the area. You must have been to the same parties. People with houses this size are always holding them.'

'All right! All right, I've met him socially, and Nelson, but I don't invest in their company. As I said, I was warned off.'

Bodkin looked thoughtful for a moment. 'If I were to ask Horatio about that, what would he say?'

'About what?'

'Oh, about your relationship, about whether you have ever invested, or indeed spoken to him about investing in Kelly Construction. They were the up-and-coming company in the region. Their order book was full and then they got this armaments factory contract, backed by the government. The price of their shares must have rocketed, meanwhile you were with Drake Construction and Sevenoaks, two companies that had missed out on that very lucrative contract. You must have thought about jumping ship when you heard the news from Drake.' Bodkin paused. 'Because I'm absolutely certain he would have known that his bid hadn't won, long before the public found out.'

'Horatio wasn't happy about the deal. Something about the housing situation.'

'So, did he advise you not to invest?'

Kitson sighed. 'He refused my offer, if you must know. I was going to sell off my Drake's holdings and invest in Kelly's but Horatio must have mentioned it to Nelson and he declined my offer.'

'But you could buy their shares on the stock market, anyone can.'

'No, it was a new company he was forming. Kelly Industrial. He was after cash investment before he floated on the stock market. It was all a bit complicated and I'm not sure it was entirely legal, especially seeing as the government was backing him. I suppose he wanted to show potential shareholders that the new company had a solid base.'

'So, Nelson Kelly personally declined your offer of investment. That must have been hard to take, Mr Kitson. Especially as you could see yourself making a big profit on the deal.'

'I didn't kill him if that's what you're thinking,' Kitson said, quickly.

'I'm just coming to that,' Bodkin replied.

He half turned and gave Amy a wink, then turned back to Kitson, who was squirming uncomfortably on the seat.

'Where were you last Friday evening, Mr Kitson?'

'I... I went to the Milton for a couple of drinks, it was quite early, probably about four o'clock, I'd just come from an appointment at my bank.'

'Which bank?' Bodkin asked.

'The Westminster.'

'What time did you leave the Milton?'

'I honestly can't remember, Inspector. It's all a bit hazy. I do seem to recall having a drink or two with Francis... Drake that is. He left about six-thirty, that's right, he was going to the presentation at the Town Hall.'

'Were you invited?'

Kitson nodded. 'Yes, but I couldn't bear the thought of seeing Nelson looking even smugger than usual, so I decided to give it a miss. I went on to a private club for a couple of hours.'

'This private club... what is it called?'

'Look, I really don't want to—'

'I don't really care whether you want to or not, Mr Kitson. You will tell me what your movements were on Friday night. You can tell me here, or you can tell me from the comfort of a cell at the station.'

'It was the Barwood.'

'The Barwood on East Street, above the book shop?'

Kitson nodded. 'You know it then?'

'One of the first cases I took on when I moved to the area involved members of that club,' Bodkin said. 'Something to do with larceny if I remember correctly.'

'I wouldn't know anything about that.'

'Back to Friday night. You were gambling?'

'I... Yes, I was playing blackjack.'

'For how long?'

'I honestly can't remember.'

'Come on, Mr Kitson, was it an hour, two... six?'

'I don't know... you see, the drinks are free at the blackjack table. I must have over indulged because my mind is an absolute blank after about seven o'clock. Mind you I'd had a fair few at the Milton before I even got there.'

'You can't remember leaving the club then? You can't remember how you got home?'

'No, I remember waking up with the hangover from Hell on Saturday morning. I was on the sofa, fully dressed.'

'Think hard, Mr Kitson. Can you remember getting into a taxi at around nine-fifteen on Friday evening?'

'No, honestly, I can't remember a thing.'

'On Saturday morning did you notice that your clothes were covered in blood?'

Kitson's head shot backwards.

'No... No! I would have remembered that, of course I would.'

'When you woke up, did you have a bloody nose, Mr Kitson?'

'No... as I said, I had the hangover from Hell but that's it.'

'So, you can't remember meeting Nelson Kelly at the fire escape of the Town Hall on Friday night and you can't remember sticking a kitchen knife into his chest?'

'WHAT? NO! Now look here...'

'Do you own any monogrammed handkerchiefs, Mr Kitson? They would have the initials H.K on one corner.'

'No, I don't own anything like that. I have monogrammed cufflinks. I got them for my twenty-first birthday but I don't own any initialled handkerchiefs.'

Bodkin got to his feet. 'Right, Mr Kitson, thank you for being so candid. I will want to speak to you again, quite soon I would imagine, so please don't leave the area.'

Amy got to her feet and followed Bodkin to the corner of the house. This time, Kitson's eyes were focussed firmly on the floor.

'Ooh, Bodkin, you gave him a right good grilling. Do you think he's our man?'

'He could be,' Bodkin said. 'He has no real alibi.'

Cocoa was still lying at the side of the table as the pair walked across the lawn towards the gates but Clarence Hunt had gone, along with the sherry bottle.

Amy was just about to comment on it when she noticed that Clarence had left the white handkerchief screwed up on the sandwich plate. Clearly visible in the bottom right-hand corner were the letters, H.K.

CHAPTER
NINETEEN

WHEN AMY AND BODKIN REACHED THE GATES OF SKELTON GRANGE, THEY saw Clarence shuffling down the road, heading towards the two Skelton farms.

'Mr Hunt!' Bodkin shouted as they hurried along the well-worn track behind him.

Hunt stopped and turned after hearing his name called and then waited until Amy and the policeman had caught up.

'I'd like to ask you a few questions,' Bodkin said.

'Not in the street if you don't mind,' Clarence replied. 'I only live a few yards away.'

He led them down a narrow, hedge-lined path, then across a nettle-strewn area of Couche grass until they came to a rickety, timber structure that looked like a converted stable block. It had seen better days, that was for sure.

'Don't let the exterior fool you, it's quite cosy inside. I rent it from Mr Kitson.' He unlocked the front door which opened with a creak that would have made it as a horror film sound effect, and ushered them inside.

The room was cluttered.

On either side of a timber-clad fireplace were two horsehair armchairs, the brown coverings almost bald in places. In the centre of the room was a solid-looking table, over which was stretched a dirty, cream-coloured tablecloth, not that much of it could be seen under the stack of unwashed crockery.

'My sink's blocked up,' he said by way of explanation. 'And the pipe underneath is leaking. I've had a word with Mr Kitson about it and he's promised to get a plumber in... that was about a month ago.' He took off his cap to reveal a scrawny mess of damp, greying brown hair, then he pulled off his purple velvet jacket and hung it on the back of a flaking door that led to somewhere or other. 'Thankfully the lavatory is working fine.' He continued quickly as Amy pulled a face. 'I mean to say, there's a sink in there, so I can wash the odd plate when I need one... and wash myself of course.'

Amy looked at the piles of newspapers that were stacked against the back wall, then across to the adjacent wall where an unmade wooden bed was situated.

On the wall opposite the fire was a badly-stained Belfast sink, next to it was an ancient gas cooker with two hobs and an oven door that looked like it was only held on with rust. On one of the armchairs was a fallen pile of what looked to Amy like children's paintings, but on closer inspection she could see the initials C.H. had been daubed across the bottom of each picture.

'You're a bit of an artist, then?' Amy said, twisting her neck to try to make out what subject Clarence had been attempting to capture. She guessed at the view from Skelton Grange but really couldn't be sure as everything was drawn at odd angles and the trees looked more like green topped lollipops than the oaks and elms they were meant to represent.

'Take one,' Clarence said generously.

Amy shook her head. 'No, it's all right. I've nowhere to hang it.'

Hunt pulled out a wobbly chair from beneath the table and

sat down heavily. Blowing out his red cheeks, he wiped his fore-head on his sleeve, then began to fan himself with a half-folded newspaper.

'You said you had some questions for me?'

He pointed to the chair opposite but Bodkin and Amy remained standing.

'The handkerchief you were using to mop your brow at the Grange earlier? Does it belong to you?'

'No, mine have a checked pattern. I get them from the market in Spinton when I need them.'

'So, how did you get hold of that one?'

'It was lying on the table when I arrived. It belongs to Mr Kitson... it had his initials on it at least.'

Bodkin pulled a brown paper bag from his pocket and pulled out the soggy hanky. 'Just to be clear, this was the handkerchief you saw on the table?'

Hunt craned his neck to see. 'It certainly looks like it.'

Bodkin stuffed the bag back into his pocket. 'Now, Mr Hunt. What else can you tell us about Harold Kitson? What's he been up to recently. Anything unusual?'

Clarence ran his hand over his chin. 'What's in it for me if I tell you?'

'A night in the cells if you don't,' Bodkin replied, staring hard at the overweight dog minder.

Clarence looked around the room, then back towards Bodkin in a manner that, without question, said that might be preferable to spending another one at home.

'Buy a painting,' he said.

'No!' Bodkin replied.

'Oh come on! It will be worth it, honestly.'

Bodkin sighed and grabbed the top sheet of paper from the listing pile. He'd seen better on the feature wall at the infant's school when he'd called around to investigate a break in. 'I'll have this one,' he said.

'Don't you want to browse through them?' he looked towards Amy. 'Are you sure you can't find room for one?'

Amy shook her head. 'My walls are full of film posters. Sorry.'

'How much for this one?' Bodkin fished a threepenny bit out of his pocket.

'A pound,' Hunt replied.

'You're having a laugh, aren't you?' Bodkin replied and held the painting over the pile, ready to drop it.

'Ten shillings then... five... all right, half a crown. It's got to be worth that to hear what I have to say.'

Bodkin fished into his pocket again and pulled out a two-shilling piece. 'Final offer,' he said.

Hunt gave him a sour look but took the money anyway.

'Right,' Bodkin said, glaring at Clarence. 'Out with it.'

Hunt wiped his sweating brow on his sleeve again and flipped the florin over and over between his fingers. 'You won't say where you got the information from? I don't want to lose my job.'

'Job? Sitting on your backside throwing a stick for a fat, old dog that doesn't want to fetch it?'

'I get five bob a week for doing that. Don't knock it,' Hunt replied, sulkily.

'Well done you for getting away with it,' Bodkin replied. 'Now... and I'm going to say this for the last time. What do you have to tell me?'

'He had a bonfire on Saturday afternoon,' Hunt said.

'And is that something unusual?'

'Of course it is. The gardeners usually do that... and he had his fire on the floor of the old barn... the one without a roof. The gardeners usually have them on the waste ground at the far side of the house.'

'What was he burning, do you know?'

'He said, old papers but I saw something that looked more like a piece of white material being chucked on.'

'He knows you saw him then?'

'Oh yes. I walked around the back at my usual time to get Cocoa. He'd just lit it. He did use some old papers and newspapers to light it but I'm absolutely sure that's not all he burned. He shooed me away and told me he'd bring Cocoa out to the front. He dropped something black... might have been a jacket or a pair of trousers. It's a waste really, he could have given them to charity.'

'What time of day was this, Mr Hunt?' Bodkin asked.

'It was just after one. I'll tell you something else too. He had a petrol can with him and I saw him empty it onto the flames. Silly bugger almost set fire to himself.'

Back out at the front of the house, Bodkin tore up the artwork and tossed the resulting litter into the air, leaving the thin strips to flutter into the long grass next to the hedge.

'It was worth two bob to be able to do that,' he said, wiping his hands down the seams of his trousers.

Amy smiled at him. 'I bet Alice's daughter Martha can do better and she's only been on solid food for a couple of weeks.' She waited as Bodkin held back a long, briar branch that ran across their path, then slipped past before he let it go again. 'That was interesting news about the bonfire though.'

'It was indeed,' Bodkin agreed. 'It will be a complete waste of time searching the place for that blood-soaked shirt now.'

'So, is he at the top of your suspect list, Bodkin?'

'Right up there... with Francis Drake,' Bodkin replied. 'I wonder if they were in it together? This might just be the piece of evidence that sinks him.'

CHAPTER

TWENTY

THE LEADEN SKY WAS LEAKING HEAVILY AS AMY GOT OFF THE BUS ON THE High Street on Thursday morning. Raising her umbrella, she ran across the road and hurried around the corner, trying to steer clear of the puddles, playing a sort of hop-scotch game as she tried to avoid getting wet feet. She was wearing a beige-coloured mac over a red blouse with the same, black, pencil skirt and black Oxford shoes she had worn the day before.

Tapping on the door, she looked through the glass impatiently, muttering, 'come on, Dora' to the cleaner who was using a vacuum at the far end of the shop.

When Dora finally spotted her and opened the door, Amy nodded her thanks, then turned back to the street and shook the rain from her umbrella onto the pavement.

'What a change from yesterday,' she said as she walked through to the staffroom where she took off her mac and hung it, along with the still-dripping umbrella, on a hook on the wall.

'Leave it opened up, love,' Dora said. 'It will dry quicker.'

'Isn't it bad luck to put an umbrella up inside?' Amy asked.

'Bugger,' Dora replied. 'I always do it at home, that must be why I got lumbered with my Cecil.'

Amy laughed and put the kettle on the hob.

'Fancy a cuppa before you go?'

Dora stuck her thumb up and began to pack the Hoover model 150 away in a cupboard.

'Did you have a nice afternoon off?' she asked as they sat down at the Formica table.

'I went for a picnic on Russell Park with a friend of mine. We had a lovely time,' Amy replied.

Susan arrived, bang on nine and Amy poured her a cup of tea while she took off her wet coat, opened up her umbrella and put it on the floor in the corner of the room.

'Amy thinks it's bad luck to put an umbrella up indoors,' Dora said.

Susan hurriedly lowered the umbrella and hung it on the hook next to Amy's.

'Don't want to tempt fate,' she said.

It was another quiet morning, the only customers being two elderly ladies who came in to try on a few hats and a frumpy, bad-tempered, middle-aged woman who came in to complain that the alterations that had been made to the dress she had ordered had resulted in her looking like a cottage loaf, or so her husband had remarked. Then, at a quarter to twelve, Amy saw a woman she half-recognised enter the shop. Susan scurried across the shop floor and the two women had a quick chat before the manageress called Amy over.

'Amy, this is Mrs McKenzie, the Lord Mayor's wife, she's attending the same wedding as Mrs Walker-Peters and she requires a new dress for the occasion, but she obviously doesn't want to wear the same one, or anything similar to the one Mrs Walker-Peters ordered yesterday. Could you show her a few possibilities, please?'

Amy held out her hand to Mrs McKenzie who took it and shook it gently.

'Have we met?' the mayor's wife asked as she stared hard at Amy. 'I never forget a face. It's just putting a name to it that's the problem.'

'I'm Amy Rowlings and I was at the awards presentation on Friday night. You must have seen me there. We didn't speak, but I did see you on stage with your husband when he made his speech.'

'What a dreadful thing to have happened to poor Mr Kelly,' she said. 'My husband knew him quite well. He was backing his bid for the new factory.... The land it was to be built on that is, not the factory itself.' She looked over her shoulder to where Susan was busying herself with the order book. 'Let's not be too formal, call me Shirley.'

Amy smiled. 'If you don't mind, I'd better stick to Mrs McKenzie, they don't like us to be overfamiliar with our customers.'

'Fair enough,' Shirley replied. 'I don't want you to get into any bother on my account. Now, what do you suggest I wear to this wedding?'

An hour later, and after trying on five dresses, Shirley decided to take Amy's advice and settled on a pale blue, body hugging, full length, sateen dress with a cowl neck and a hand-tied bow at the back.

'You have such a lovely figure,' Amy told her. 'And this shows it off to perfection.'

'As long as Mavis Walker-Peters is jealous,' Shirley said.

'I think the vast majority of the women at the wedding will be,' Amy said. 'I imagine you'll get plenty of offers to dance, too.'

'Good,' Shirley said with a nod of her head. 'It will do Robert good to realise what he's got.'

'Will Mrs Thornalley be at the wedding too... you know, the former mayor's wife?'

'God, I hope not,' Shirley said with distaste. 'I can't stand the woman.'

'Sorry,' Amy said. 'I didn't mean to...'

'Oh, that's all right,' Shirley said, touching Amy softly on the arm. 'Everyone knows we don't get on. The woman is almost as big a crook as her husband.'

'Crook? You mean a criminal crook?'

'What other sort is there?' Shirley asked. 'He's a fraudster, an embezzler and a thoroughly dishonest person. If he hadn't been mayor, and before that a prospective MP, he'd have been locked up by now, and quite rightly so.'

'Goodness,' Amy said, as she helped Shirley off with her dress. 'What has he done?'

'What hasn't he done,' Shirley said, she grunted as she pulled the dress over her head. 'He's been bankrupt twice, news of which only came to light after he became mayor. He was forced to step down as a parliamentary candidate in Essex because of that. His wife... Alma, is as bad. She'd take the coat off a beggar's back if she thought she could sell it on and make a profit.'

'So how on earth did he ever become mayor?' Amy asked, with a look of incredulity on her face.

'Back handers, promises of financial gain... the usual.'

'Via this mayor's fund?'

'Sort of. Robert is going to get someone to go over the books in the next couple of weeks. I doubt they'll find much though; he was too clever... still we can hope.'

'But how could he use money from the fund for his own personal use?' Amy asked.

'He didn't have to, dear. Many of the businessmen who wanted council contracts or to find ways around planning applications used to pay with cash or a cheque made out to him personally. He's almost broke, still paying off loans and debts from years ago. They must have used some of the money to pay for his kids to go to boarding school because they certainly can't afford to pay the fees on their earnings.'

'Doesn't he live in one of those big houses off the High Street?'

'He does, and it's mortgaged to the hilt. There's no value left in it.'

'Do you have any proof he took money for contracts?'

'Not directly, no. But it wouldn't take an accountant long to find proof if they had a look through his personal bank accounts. They'd find cheques paid in from a lot of the businesses around here, both big and small. Those men... and they would all be men, have been helping to keep him in a manner that he could never have afforded without their collusion.'

'Shirley,' Amy said quietly, looking towards the door of the fitting room in case Susan was about to enter. 'Would you mind giving this information to Inspector Bodkin. He's the policeman investigating Nelson's murder.'

Shirley shrugged. 'I'm not saying that he had anything at all to do with Nelson's murder, you understand? But he was backing a rival bid for the land.'

'Who was he backing, Francis Drake?'

'Surprisingly, no, dear, although the pair of them were as thick as thieves. No, for some reason he backed an out-of-town company... Seven something...'

'Sevenoaks Construction?' Amy blurted out.

'That's the one. Have you heard of them? I hadn't and nor had Robert.'

Amy gripped Shirley's wrist a little harder than she meant to.

'Please... Mrs McKenzie, tell Bodkin all about this. He's picking me up for lunch in a few minutes.'

TWENTY-ONE

As Mrs McKenzie fussed with her hair in the full-length mirror, Amy grabbed an armful of rejected dresses and opened the door of the changing room. At the other end of the shop, a dripping wet Bodkin had just entered. Susan was all over him like a rash.

'Hello, sir. We don't get many gentlemen in here, what can I help you with? Are you looking for a new dress as a surprise for you wife perhaps?'

Bodkin looked nonplussed. 'I'm, erm, I'm not married,' he said.

'Ah, then it's a surprise for your fiancée? A gift for your girl-friend maybe? How about a hat, or would she like something from our exclusive, accessories range?' She looked Bodkin up and down noting the rumpled look of his damp suit, thought about showing him something at the cheaper end of the market, but then, noticing the look of total embarrassment on his face, she suddenly thought she knew what he was looking for.

'Ah, the unmentionables? You men are always embarrassed by the subject. Heaven knows why.' She chuckled to herself as she hurried to the mirrored cabinets, opened one up and pulled out two pairs of silk Cami knickers. One pink, the other, powder blue.

She held them up in the air, one pair in each hand. 'Which one would the gentleman prefer?'

'I'd go with the blue if I were you, Bodkin,' Amy called as she came out of the changing rooms carrying a pile of discarded dresses. 'Pink really isn't your colour.'

They reached the Sunshine café on the High Street just as the rain began to get heavy again. Amy and Shirley shook off their umbrellas in the doorway as Bodkin held the door open for them. Once inside, Amy led Shirley over to a table by the steamed up front window, as far away from the other customers as they could get. They had just slipped out of their coats and taken their seats when Bodkin came back from the counter carrying a tray with a tea pot, milk jug, and three cups and saucers on it.

'The sandwiches are on their way, Amy. I got you ham.' He looked at Shirley as he sat down himself and passed her a cup and saucer. 'Are you sure you don't want anything?'

'Not for me thank you, Inspector. I'm having to watch what I eat. I want to make sure I still fit into that new dress on the day of the wedding.'

Amy poured the tea for all three and then sat back as Bodkin added sugar to his cup.

'Now then, Mrs McKenzie. Amy tells me you have some information regarding the former mayor.'

'Call me Shirley,' the woman said, laying her hand softly on Bodkin's sleeve.

'Shirley,' Bodkin echoed.

'Where do I start with something like this?' she said, and then spent the next twenty minutes talking non-stop about the Thornalley's without so much as pausing for a sip of tea. Amy ate her sandwiches in silence, checking her watch every few minutes. She still wasn't used to having a full hour's lunch break.

'They're not your favourite people on this planet, I can tell,' Bodkin smiled at her as he looked up from his notebook.

'A pair of crooks,' Shirley said. 'They ought to be behind bars.'

Bodkin caught the café owner's eye and ordered up another pot of tea.

'What about you, Shirley? How long have you and Mr McKenzie been in the area? I don't think our paths have ever crossed.'

'That's because we're not crooks,' Shirley said with a laugh.

Bodkin laughed along.

'We're from up north originally,' Shirley said after pouring tea from the fresh pot. She looked up and smiled to two old ladies as they came into the shop shaking the rain from their headscarves. 'Robert is one of the Humber McKenzies. The family tree dates back to Robert the Bruce's time. I was a Robinson-Smythe, my family are from the midlands, I met Robert at University and it was love at first sight. We moved here about two years ago. Robert has money, so he doesn't need to work, other than dabbling a bit in stocks, that sort of thing. He owns a couple of horses that he often goes to see race. One's running at Ascot this year.'

'And he's happy in a backwater like this?' Bodkin asked. 'Has he no ambitions other than to become mayor of Spinton?'

'Oh, he wants to become an MP eventually,' Shirley replied. 'He could get a safe seat somewhere if he wanted... eventually that is, it's who you know, not what you know when it comes to politics.' She took a sip of tea. 'Robert prefers to work his way up, gain experience along the way, take the knocks and learn from them. He's not one of these fly-by-night politicians. He wants to make a proper job of whatever he does.'

'Laudable sentiments, I'm sure,' Bodkin said, under his breath. 'Does, erm, Robert intend to carry on with the mayor's fund?' he asked.

'Oh yes, we've got big plans for it.'

'Do go on,' Bodkin replied.

'Well, to start with we want to do something with the children's home. It's rather Dickensian looking inside. We'd like to give it a bit of a refurbishment once there's enough money in the kitty. We'd like to give the kids a start after they leave there too, team up with local companies, maybe sort them out with an apprenticeship or at least a job. Girls used to leave children's homes and go straight into service at one time but that's not possible anymore, so we intend to set them up with courses... typing... waitressing... maybe machinist work at one of the clothing factories.'

'The sky's the limit, eh?' Bodkin muttered.

Amy shot him a look.

'We'd also like to set up a women's clinic. A free one... There are so many single mothers in this town. They need help and advice.'

'They'd be better off getting advice before they became pregnant,' Bodkin said before draining his cup.

'You're right of course,' Shirley said with a quick smile. 'But we have to start somewhere.'

'Indeed,' Bodkin replied. 'Will you be keeping the... what shall we call it... the donations system as it is or will you change the way the fund is financed?'

'Robert says, if it isn't broke, don't fix it.'

'The council could risk being taken to court if they leave such a corrupt system in place,' Bodkin replied, earnestly.

'Corrupt system? I'm not sure I understand.'

Bodkin's eyes widened.

'You've just explained how it all works, Mrs McKenzie. Businesses pay cash payments to the mayor and are awarded council contracts in return.'

'That's not the fund I was talking about. I think we're getting a little confused here. I was talking about the Mayor's Community Fund.'

'Does your husband intend to carry on accepting payments from businesses for contracts?' Bodkin asked.

Shirley suddenly checked her watch, then reached for her bag.

'You sound very suspicious of us, Inspector. If I had known I was going to be interrogated about my husband's affairs I probably wouldn't have joined you here. I was under the impression we were only going to discuss the Thornalley's.'

'I'm sorry you feel that way, Mrs McKenzie,' Bodkin said getting to his feet before Shirley. 'But this is a murder investigation. We have to look at everyone who had dealings with Nelson and you have admitted that your husband backed his bid. I will also have to look into whether they had any other interactions, financial or otherwise. I'm sorry, I know you don't like the intrusion but it has to be done.'

Shirley sighed. 'I understand, Inspector. Can I take it you'll be wanting to speak to Robert? I'll try to set up a time for the two of you to meet.' Her mood seemed to brighten. 'I'll tell you what. Come over to the house on Sunday afternoon. We're having a bit of a garden party. It's dress down, you won't need a black tie or anything like that. Bring Amy with you. I'd love to have a chat about which of the new lines of cosmetics I should be looking at.'

Amy stood and Shirley leaned across to give her a peck on the cheek.

'Goodbye, Inspector. I hope you find your man soon.' Shirley fastened her coat, picked up her bag and umbrella and walked slowly out of the café.

'BODKIN!' Amy snapped when Shirley had gone. 'You were very rude to her. She seems a very nice person who just wanted to help, and you treated her like a suspect.'

'What do I always say, Amy?' Bodkin replied. 'Everyone is a suspect until they aren't.'

'Well, I liked her,' Amy said.

'He's one of the Humber McKenzies,' Bodkin mimicked.

Amy shook her head. 'There's nothing wrong with being proud of your heritage, Bodkin. Look at my dad. He's only one sixteenth Scottish but he doesn't half play on it.'

'It's not her heritage, Amy, it's his,' Bodkin reminded her. 'And as for that Robinson-Smythe nonsense. Her father's name is Robinson, her mother's name was Smith and she's from a place called Ilkeston, it's an industrial town between Nottingham and Derby, I know because I've already had them checked out.'

'Oh... so there's no double-barrelled name then?' Amy asked, frowning.

'None. Her mum was a common or garden Smith. I doubt they met at university either. He went to Cambridge. That's a lot to aspire to for a young girl from an ironworks town.'

'She does seem nice though, she has some wonderful ideas about how to help the poorest in the area.'

'Miss goody-two-shoes if you ask me,' Bodkin replied. 'Maybe she's just a little too good to be true.' He looked across the table towards her. I'd put money on that corrupt system still being in place in five years' time.'

'But McKenzie is loaded, Bodkin. He doesn't need to embezzle money.'

'In my experience, Amy, people with money always want more money, especially if it doesn't cost them anything to get hold of it.'

He paused and picked up a teaspoon and turned it over in his hands. 'Anyway, everyone thought Thornalley was loaded but he didn't have a pot to... sorry, he's as poor as a church mouse. These people love to make us ordinary folk think they have it all but it's just an illusion with a lot of them. Many of them owe more money than we could expect to earn in a lifetime.'

'So, do you think McKenzie isn't as well to do as he claims?'

'He may well be Amy. I just can't see why a man who supposedly has everything, and can afford to live anywhere he chooses, would wash up in a dirty little backwater like this.'

'Well, I still liked her. I think you're a bit of a cynic when it comes to people with money and, or, status, Bodkin.' She checked her watch again. 'I'd better get back to work, they'll be opening again soon. 'What have you got on this afternoon?'

'I'm going to be standing in front of a desk while I get a ticking off from the chief constable,' Bodkin said. 'It didn't take our friend Mr Kitson long to put in a complaint.'

TWENTY-TWO

'I FORGOT TO ASK. HOW DID YOU GET ON WITH MR THORNALLEY THIS morning?' Amy asked as Bodkin took her arm and led her across the street.

'He was all sweetness and light, but he was very evasive. His wife was even worse. I didn't like her at all. She spoke for him whenever she could. I think she's the brains behind that partnership.'

'Shirley doesn't like her; with good reason it seems.'

'I wish I'd known what I've just learned before I questioned him,' Bodkin said, rubbing his chin as they stood outside the door of London Connection. 'I'd have asked him some very awkward questions.' He paused and looked into the distance. 'As for Mrs McKenzie? Well, there are a lot of reasons why she wants us to look at Thornalley. She might think it will take the focus off Robert.'

'You really didn't like her much did you, Bodkin,' Amy said with a laugh.

The inspector shrugged. 'It's not a matter of liking, it's a matter of getting to the truth.' He nodded to Susan who was walking up the pavement with the shop keys in her hand.

'Changed your mind about the underwear?' she asked, with a twinkle in her eye.

Bodkin blushed. 'I'd better get off, Amy. I've got a bit more to tell you about our former mayor but it will have to wait.'

'I can meet you tonight if you like,' Amy said. 'I don't have to get up early in the morning and the work here isn't exactly overtaxing, so I won't be tired.'

As Susan pushed open the shop door, Amy gave Bodkin a peck on the cheek.

'The Old Bull?' Bodkin asked as Amy pulled away. 'I'll pick you up at eight.'

'Good luck with the boss. I hope it isn't too awful,' Amy said over her shoulder as she followed Susan through the door.

The snug of the Old Bull wasn't busy. Thursday nights never were. The public bar on the opposite side of the counter was as busy as ever, the regulars came in no matter what night of the week it was. Some still had a little money in their pockets before pay day, but most bought drinks on tick. A credit system that the landlord kept updated on a blackboard that he kept behind the bar.

The snug was frequented mostly by women, or courting or married couples that didn't like the thick, smoky, and often rowdy atmosphere of the public bar.

The snug had a slate floor and an open fireplace that burned a welcoming fire from October through to April. The bench seats around the sides had once been pews that had been scavenged when St Michael's church had been given a facelift some thirty years before.

Bodkin caried the drinks over from the bar and placed them on a small, round table just in front of the window. Amy picked up her port and lemon and took a dainty sip.

'It's been so nice having the extra time with you this week,' she said, smiling.

'It's just a shame you can't work at the shop permanently,' Bodkin replied. 'Later starts, Wednesday afternoons off...'

'Ah but if I was permanent, I'd have to work every Saturday and I honestly don't want that. Besides which, if I'm honest, the job's a bit boring. It's okay when there's a customer in, but I do stand around twiddling my thumbs a fair bit and it makes the day drag. At the Mill I don't have time to get bored. It's like a race to the finish line from the minute I sit down at my machine.'

'It must make a nice change, all the same.'

'Oh, it's been lovely. Don't get me wrong, Bodkin, and Susan did ask me this afternoon if I'd consider taking the job on full time. The applicants they've had in so far aren't really what they hoped for.'

'What did you tell her?'

'I said I'd stay as long as it took to find the right person, but I'm hoping it won't be more than another week or two. Anyway, you would end up broke if you keep having to buy me lunch every day. And, I don't want to take the risk that you might get bored with seeing me so often.'

Bodkin reached across and put his hand on hers. 'I could never get bored with you. Not in a million years.'

'Right answer!' Amy said, her eyes bright. 'Now, tell me what you got out of Basil Thornalley... NO! first tell me what your boss had to say.'

'The chief constable is a man of few words Amy, and the ones he chooses to use at times like this are short and to the point. Basically, he told me that unless I intended to arrest Mr Kitson, I should back off a bit.'

'But... he's our... I mean, he's your prime suspect.'

'I wouldn't say prime exactly, but he's up there with one or two others,' Bodkin replied. 'The chief constable isn't keen on me questioning Horatio Kelly either, but in the end, he had to agree that there were some questions that required an answer. I've just got to go easy on him, he's lost a brother, after all.'

'But he might have been the one that killed his brother... or got someone else to do it for him.' Amy shook her head in disbelief. 'And what about Drake, has he been on the phone to the top brass as well?'

'Not that I'm aware of, but that could change when he finds out that we're digging into Thornalley's business dealings.'

'So, what are you going to do, Bodkin?'

'I'll do what I always do, Amy. Try to get to the bottom of it, whichever way I can. Anyway, I'll get a couple of week's grace. His High and Mightiness is off to London for a few days. There's a big, government led policing conference going on apparently. The other thing is, we're going to be shorthanded for the next few weeks. My sergeant broke his arm trying to apprehend a young thug last night and my chief Inspector is helping out the Gillingham police with a double murder. Oh, and our one and only policewoman has left. She didn't even hand in her notice. Last Friday night was too much for her. Grayson asked me to talk to you about the vacancy but I soon put him right on that score.'

'I won't be a tea lady for the police force. Uniform or not,' Amy said, firmly.

'That's pretty much what I said.' Bodkin lifted his glass and took another long pull from his pint. 'Grayson is worried. Apart from Ferris, we have two uniformed staff left, and one of those is coming up to retirement. So that leaves him and me as the only CID officers, and that's pretty much it for the foreseeable future.' He paused. 'I did tell him that you were coming with me to question Lorna Wetherby tomorrow as well as Mrs Kelly on Saturday. I didn't want the poor old so and so to get any more shocks via witness complaints.'

'So, you think he'll leave you to get on with it?'

'Oh, he'll be all right, providing I don't go right over the top and have them complaining en masse.'

Amy laughed. 'These posh boys are like a bunch of kids running to the teacher, aren't they?'

Bodkin snorted.

'Steady, Amy, you're beginning to sound like me.' He wiped his mouth with the back of his hand. 'They don't think they should be treated like everyone else. Intensive questioning should be held back for those that deserve it... the working-class criminals.'

Amy picked up her glass and lifted it in the air. 'Justice for all,' she said.

Bodkin lifted his own glass. 'Justice,' he said, then took a long swig.

'Back to Basil then. Did you learn anything at all?'

Bodkin put his pint carefully on the table and studied the ceiling for a moment as he thought.

'Neither Basil or his wife, Alma, are from Spinton, not even from Kent. We seem to import all our mayors. The one prior to him was a Welshman, I believe.'

'Owen Jones,' Amy said. 'A fire beathing Baptist. Dad had many a heated conversation with him while he was in office.'

'I heard a whisper that he was forced out in the end too,' Bodkin said.

'I think he might have been. He did leave suddenly, but I was only about fifteen, I can't remember much about it. I could ask Dad if you think it would help.'

'No, it's okay, Amy, I can't see the relevance to be honest.' Bodkin sipped his drink. 'The Thornalley's were from Luton origi-nally, but they sold up and moved to Essex. I don't know if it was under a bit of a cloud or not. I do know Basil had been bankrupted twice, but that was before they moved. Anyway, they stayed in Chelmsford for a few years, started up what seemed, on the surface at least, to be quite a successful business. Basil got in with the Liberal party and they selected him as their candidate at the election of 1931. Unfortunately for him, his past caught up with him and as an undischarged bankrupt, he wasn't allowed to stand for parliament and he was dropped by the party.

'He sold his business in 1933 and moved here for some reason that he didn't want to go into. Maybe he thought he could hide from his past in a small town like this. Anyway, as you are aware, he's been here ever since. He changed his allegiance to the Tory party, stood as a councillor and got in. Two years later he was voted in as mayor.'

'Did you ask him about the mayor's fund?'

'I did mention it but that's when Alma stepped in and threw a series of numbers at me so quickly that I couldn't keep up, but now that I've had the McKenzie woman's testimony I'll be going in firing with both barrels.'

'It's Shirley,' Amy said.

'Her,' Bodkin agreed.

'The thing was,' he continued, 'I was more interested in what he was up to on Friday night. He was out of the Assembly Room when Nelson was stabbed.'

Amy leaned forward eagerly. She had finished her drink but didn't want to interrupt Bodkin's narrative.

'Basil Thornalley, has a stomach ulcer it seems, so he has to refrain from drinking alcohol. Honestly to hear him go on about it I'm sure he expects to be canonised by the pope any day soon. He's such a brave soul. Anyway, on Friday he was thirsty and so he went to the kitchen to make himself a cup of herbal tea, something that helps ease his stomach pains. When he was mayor, they kept a stock of it in the cupboard because he used to drink gallons of the stuff. On Friday night, as he was pouring water into the pot, he heard Lorna scream and he rushed to the kitchen door and found her kneeling beside Nelson, covered in his blood.'

'So, he was a matter of yards away when the murder took place. Did he hear what the argument was about?'

'He says not. He didn't hear anyone shout "You've ruined me" as the cloakroom girl claims to have heard.'

'Even though he was slightly closer to the incident than she was?'

Bodkin nodded, got to his feet and picked up both their glasses.

'The thing is, Amy. He was only a few feet away from the corridor and the trolley where the kitchen knife was lying. He might have heard Nelson on the phone, picked up the knife and stabbed him when he was on his way back to the presentation. It would all have happened so quickly; he could have easily got back into the kitchen before Lorna came out of the cloakroom.'

CHAPTER
TWENTY-THREE

Friday was a busier day for Amy with three, society-wedding bound, customers in the morning and seven women in the afternoon, three of whom were making holiday plans and looking to see what they could add to their summer season wardrobe. Amy spent a lot of the time scurrying back and forth between cubicles as the women demanded to see a wide variety of dresses.

By the time five-thirty came around, Amy felt like she'd done a double shift at the Mill. Outside, the heavy rainclouds had moved on leaving behind lighter, broken clouds, the soft raindrops they produced (as Alice would have said) were as light as a maiden's kiss, on Amy's cheeks.

The air was warm, so, carrying her umbrella in one hand with her bag in the other and her coat draped over her arm, she walked across the road to the bus stop where there was already a line of people reading the evening newspaper, or chatting amongst each other.

Amy got off the bus at the Old Bull and took a slow walk home, enjoying the feel of the warm sun on her face. Mr Rowlings wasn't in from work, so Amy had an early tea before taking a strip wash in the bathroom. She took her bi-weekly baths on Tuesdays and Saturdays.

'Where is Bodkin taking you tonight?' her mother asked, as Amy emerged from the bathroom, brushing her flaxen hair. 'You're out together more and more. This will be the fifth time you've seen him since last Friday. Are things getting serious between you?'

Amy tried to avoid her mother's eye.

'Not so you'd notice, Mum. Last night was a one off really. We were just chatting about the murder case... in general terms, that is,' she added hastily. 'And we only met up on Wednesday because I got an afternoon off for the first time since... I can't remember the last one, actually.' She stopped brushing her hair and thought for a few moments. 'I'm, erm, seeing him again on Sunday as it happens, we've been invited to a garden party at the mayor's house.'

'Oh, I say, our Amy... First the awards night, now a garden party. You'll be telling me you're off to the palace next.'

Amy laughed. 'A Spinton garden party is a long way from the palace, Mum,' she said. 'I was only invited because I was with Bodkin when he was asked. He has an appointment with the mayor. He's got a few questions about Nelson Kelly's murder.'

'Please don't get too involved in it, Amy. We do worry about you sometimes.'

Amy gave her mother a soft hug. 'I know you do, Mum, but you shouldn't really. I've got Bodkin to protect me you know?'

'He's a lovely man,' Mrs Rowlings said, lifting a finger and wagging it at her daughter. 'You could do a lot worse. Maybe you should tie him down before someone else gets the chance.'

Amy's mouth dropped open. 'I'm not ready for a life of domesticity yet, Mum. I'm still young, I've got my whole life ahead of me. There will be plenty of time for weddings and families. I'm just not ready yet. Times are changing, a women's role is more than just washing nappies and cooking dinner.'

'I know how you feel about your independence, Amy, I'm just saying. Don't leave it too late. He's a good-looking man and someone might whisk him away, right in front of your eyes.'

'Too late? I'm only twenty-one, Mum. As for Bodkin, he's managed to get to be almost thirty without being tied down. I don't think he's exactly desperate for domesticity either. It's all work and sleep with him, although, I believe he might be beginning to think about the prospect.'

'There you go then, Amy.' Mrs Rowlings patted her daughter on the arm. 'Just make sure you're still at the front of the queue when he is ready to take the leap.'

Medway House was a recently-built, yellow-brick, residential building on the banks of the river. Standing twelve storeys high, the residents on the higher floors of the right-hand side of the structure had a wonderful view across the river to the rolling, green of the Kent countryside. Residents on the left-hand side, however, had definitely drawn the short straw, with their windows looking out over the dirty remains of Spinton's industrial past.

Lorna Wetherby was one of the unfortunate tenants. Her flat was on the tenth floor and looked out over the Victorian houses, long overdue for demolition, the cement works and the railway station. In the distance, Amy could just make out Long Lane with Alice's farm spread out like a patchwork quilt at the end of it.

'I brought Miss Rowlings along with me. My chief superintendent thought it might be a little more comfortable for you if there was another woman present,' Bodkin said.

Lorna nodded to Amy. 'That was very thoughtful of him.' She

turned away and headed for the open French windows at the far end of the kitchenette.

'It's not much of a view, is it?' she said, as she led them to a small balcony where a set of three deckchairs were laid out in a line, their colourful stripes reflecting back from the closed half of the timber-framed, French windows. In front of the chairs was a long, low, white-painted coffee table. On the table was a pitcher filled with slices of cucumber, lemon, and other exotic looking fruits.

'Pimm's?' she asked, lifting up the jug.

'Ooh, yes please,' Amy replied eagerly, 'I've heard about Pimm's but I've never had one.'

'This is their number one cup. It's based on gin. There's a number two and three cup as well, they're based on Whisky and Brandy I believe.' She poured a glass for Bodkin and handed it to him. 'I much prefer the gin base, it's so refreshing.'

Bodkin took a sip and nodded his head.

Amy took a tiny sip, followed by a longer one.

'That's lovely,' she said. 'Do they serve this at the Milton Cocktail Bar?'

'They do,' Lorna replied. 'You can get them made with ice in there, it's so good.' She looked sadly back into the flat. 'Unfortunately, I don't have a refrigerator, so I can't offer you any of that. I've had it standing in a sink full of cold water for an hour, and the air isn't so cloying up at this height so I hope it stays cool enough.'

Amy sipped again and closed her eyes, imagining the drink with small chunks of ice floating around in it. 'Next time we're in the Milton, I'm having these all night, with as much ice as they'll give me.'

Bodkin took a long pull on his drink, then licked his lips.

'We had better start saving up then,' he said.

They drank in silence for a few moments, then Bodkin put his glass on the low coffee table and leaned back in his deckchair.

Finding himself staring up at the sky, he heaved himself forwards, gripped both arms of the chair, then focussed his attentions on Lorna.

'Firstly, I'd like to know about your connection to Nelson Kelly. Was it purely employer, stroke employee, or did the relationship go a little deeper than that?'

Lorna played with a few strands of her dark, chestnut hair. Her green eyes looking out over the town. 'I like to think that we were friends too. We spent a fair bit of time together, especially when we were working on one of the projects he'd signed up to, but we weren't in each other's pockets if that's what you're thinking.'

'It didn't go deeper than business then? Only we have been told that you and Nelson were a lot closer than that.'

'Well, we weren't. Oh, I used to flirt with him a bit in public, he enjoyed that. That's probably where whoever it was that mentioned it to you got the idea from. Nelson used to think he was a magnet for women, he thought he was irresistible. He did try it on with me, but only once. He didn't take to being rejected very well.'

'So, you don't think he was faithful to his wife?'

'NELSON!' Lorna snorted. 'He wasn't capable of being faithful. His wife, Helen, was just a trophy. Someone to show off at the big events.'

'Did you get on with her? Did she suspect you and he were conducting an affair?'

Lorna thought about it. 'Possibly, but I don't think she'd have cared much one way or the other. She might have had high expectations of her husband when they first married, but those expectations would have been almost immediately shot down in flames. She knew what he was, Inspector. I think she was only there for the lifestyle in the end.'

'Can you think of any recent affairs? Someone who might get

angry after being dumped, or maybe a married woman whose husband found out about the affair?'

Lorna uncrossed, then crossed her legs again.

'None that I was aware of, but then it's Nelson we're talking about here. His little black book must be as thick as the bible.' She looked across at Amy. 'You'd have been high on his list of possibles if you mixed in the same circles. Possible, as in Nelson's view of the female population, Amy, not your actual availability.'

'This may sound a strange question, Miss Wetherby,' Bodkin said. 'You were obviously shocked when you found him last Friday, but since then, has it occurred to you that this is something that might have happened to him one day. Did he have any enemies, either political of business related?'

'Not in the political sense, no one you'd call an enemy at least.'

'He did have enemies in business then?' Bodkin asked.

'Rivals, strong rivals. Mind you, he had one of those inside his own company. His brother didn't approve of many of the things that Nelson did. He was particularly angry about the way he set up the bid for the factory land. It would have put a lot of families onto the streets, and he didn't intend to build any replacement houses at all. Horatio would almost certainly have backed the plan if he had.'

'But isn't he a director too? He must have had a big say in the way the plan was formulated.'

'Nelson is... was, a bully, Inspector. Horatio never could stand up to him. He'd argue his corner but when push came to shove, he'd just throw up his hands and give in. Helen used to side with Horatio a lot in those discussions, she's got something of a social conscience too. I believe she's a bit preachy, on social issues. I remember Nelson joking that if he'd have known he'd married a Socialist, he'd never have consummated the marriage.'

'He doesn't sound a very nice man at all,' Amy said as she finished her drink and looked hopefully towards the pitcher.

'He could be very charming too,' Lorna said, noticing Amy's hungry gaze and pouring out another round of Pimm's.

Amy smiled, gratefully. 'This is so good, thank you' she said.

Bodkin raised is newly refreshed glass. 'Can you take us through that night, Lorna? How was Nelson? Did he seem troubled by anything?'

'No, he was his usual self. He did aim a few sharp words towards the Post reporter but that was nothing out of the ordinary. I can't tell you how hard I tried to get the Post on our side. The editor was very obliging when we spoke on the telephone, but he always seemed to give that Miles character his head when it came to printing stories about Nelson. I don't know what he had against him, maybe it was just that he was so successful he thought he needed bringing down a peg or two, maybe it was his political persuasion. I really don't know.'

'I think he's just a louse, looking for an easy target, Miss Wetherby. He doesn't mind what or who he hurts when he pumps out the bile in his system. Once Nelson is forgotten about it will be someone else's turn.' Bodkin put his drink on the table. 'I haven't been here too long, but I know he's got it in for the police. He believes we should share information with him in the public interest and when we don't, he gives us a hard time over it, calling us incompetent or corrupt, or worse. He's right about the incompetence, in part at least. I'll own up to that on the force's behalf.'

Lorna laughed. 'I wouldn't like to do your job, Inspector. It must be an incredibly harrowing experience at times.' She turned her glistening, green eyes towards him. 'I think you're all so brave.'

Amy choked on her drink. 'Sorry... a lemon pip went down the wrong way,' she said, flashing Bodkin a quick, wide-eyed look.

Bodkin shrugged at Amy and gave her a puzzled frown.

'So, Nelson didn't appear to have anything on his mind then?

Other than making a good job of his acceptance speech... which he seemed to do well enough.'

'Nothing that he spoke to me about. He seemed his normal self. He had his eye on one of the catering girls, I saw him wink at her more than once, but apart from that, nothing out of the ordinary.'

'When you went to... erm, powder your nose, did you see Mr Drake in the cloakroom?'

'Yes, I did. He came out more or less at the same time as me, but he went back to the Assembly Room before I did.'

'Why didn't you speak... or even acknowledge each other, Miss Wetherby? You were close friends after all.'

'We had agreed beforehand not to speak to one another,' Lorna said. 'Nelson wasn't aware of our relationship, or at least I don't think he was, and Francis didn't want him to get suspicious. It wouldn't look good if he found out. He might think I was working under cover and passing information back to Francis.'

'But there was only a cloakroom attendant in there, she wouldn't have cared or even noticed if you'd have become involved in a passionate embrace, let alone saying a quick, "hello", she was too engrossed in her reading matter.'

'We stuck with the plan,' Lorna said. 'Anyway, I could have quite easily been given the sack if my company had found out that I was involved with a client's rival. We're supposed to be up front about that sort of thing.'

'And why weren't you up front about it?'

Lorna sighed and took a big gulp from her drink.

'I was given the contract before I met Francis. I wanted to get a good result for both me and the company. There was quite a large bonus coming my way. I didn't want to risk losing it.'

'Did you ever pass on any information about Nelson's bid to Drake?' Bodkin asked, leaning forward in his chair.

'No... well... yes... bits and pieces, but nothing he couldn't have found out from other sources... eventually.'

'Did he change his own bid accordingly?'

Lorna blew out her cheeks.

'I don't... Oh, all right, yes, he did, in the end there wasn't a lot of difference between his bid and Nelson's. Drake's offer was slightly higher, but only by a few hundred pounds. He didn't want to go overboard on the deal.'

'What about Sevenoaks Construction?'

'I don't know... Look Mr Bod... Inspector Bodkin. It was nothing to do with me. Francis did whatever he wanted; I couldn't influence anything.'

'Do you think the Sevenoaks bid was a bit of a stalking horse?'

Lorna looked puzzled. 'How do you mean?'

'Well, let's say for instance that Drake knows exactly how much Nelson has bid, because you told him. So, he puts in a big bid via his recently acquired company, Sevenoaks. A bid that is much higher than the Kelly bid, but it is doomed to failure because Nelson has the new mayor, the planning committee and the government on his side. But, when Nelson is killed, the Kelly bid is on the rocks because Horatio won't stand by it when he takes over the company. That leaves Sevenoaks in the prime position. Now, what if, for instance, Sevenoaks pulls out, citing financial difficulties or something. That would leave Drake with the only bid on the table. It would be game set and match.'

'Francis might be unscrupulous at times, Inspector, but he's not a murderer. He wouldn't kill someone just to get his own way. As far as I could tell, he had accepted that his bid had failed and he was ready to move onto the next project.'

'Hmm,' Bodkin stoked his chin. 'Did you get this apartment on a short-term lease, Miss Wetherby? Only a friend of mine was looking into taking one on and I'm sure he said that the minimum lease period was for a full twelve calendar months. What would happen to your tenancy agreement if your company called you back to Maidstone, or gave you an out of county client? Don't they have a lot of work in the London area?' Bodkin picked up his drink as Lorna turned her big, green eyes to him again. 'By the way, how did all the meetings go this week?'

'I have been told to tie up the loose ends on the Kelly contract. I'm going to be based in Ashford after that. Horatio is going to cancel. The whole project was built around Nelson as the company figurehead. Now that he's gone, Horatio isn't sure he needs much in the way of PR. That might change, but I'm not sure he'd want someone who worked so closely with his brother to run a new campaign.'

'How long will it take to... tidy up?' Bodkin asked.

'A couple of weeks, maybe three.'

'But the apartment has a twelve-month lease. How long have you lived here?' Bodkin waved an arm in the general direction of the flat.

'I've lived here for about three months.' Lorna stared hard at the drink in her hands. 'But I didn't take on the lease. The apartment belongs to Francis.'

'Thank you for confirming my suspicions, Miss Wetherby,' Bodkin said. 'Now take us back to the night of the murder again. You've just come out of the cloakroom, what did you see?'

'Nelson lying on the floor, he was staring up at me, he wasn't dead then.'

'Think hard now, Lorna,' Bodkin said. 'Was the door to the fire escape open or closed?'

Lorna closed her eyes as she concentrated. 'Open... I think... oh I really can't remember.'

'What about the door at the end of the corridor that runs along the side of the kitchen?'

'I honestly don't know... closed, I think, there were a lot of boxes and paper bags lying about in there.'

'Did you hear or see anyone else? The back of someone going into the Assembly Room for instance?'

'No, I was alone with Nelson... HANG ON! There must have been someone close by. I heard a noise from inside the kitchen... I'm sure I heard footsteps. Someone was in there, Inspector.'

'That was Basil Thornalley, the former mayor,' Amy said. 'He was making himself a cup of tea. He came to the kitchen door when he heard you scream.'

'Oh no he didn't,' Lorna said, flatly. 'There was no one in the doorway, I turned around when I heard the noise, there was no one there,' she paused.... 'Thinking about it... I'm sure I heard the click of heels as well as the softer shuffle of feet. There must have been more than one person moving around in there.'

TWENTY-FOUR

'Two people in the kitchen. Wow! That's a revelation.'

Amy walked alongside Bodkin as they left Medway House and made their way across the concourse to the car park.

Bodkin nodded. 'It's an interesting thought, isn't it?'

'Thought? But this changes everything, doesn't it, Bodkin? Drake may have come out of the cloakroom but instead of going back to the presentation he could have nipped into the kitchen to see Thornalley. They might have hatched a plot to kill Nelson... maybe the plot was already in place... maybe the phone call was part of it? Drake takes the opportunity to get Nelson out of his hair once and for all.'

'There are a few problems with that theory though, Amy,' Bodkin said as he unlocked the passenger side door for her and scurried around the front of the car.

'What problems?' Amy said when he was seated. 'The two of them could well have been in cahoots?'

'Oh, I think they could. It's just that the evidence doesn't point in that direction, not yet anyway.'

'How do you mean?' Amy asked as Bodkin turned onto the main road and headed back towards the town centre.

'Well, firstly there's the evidence of Debbie, the cloakroom girl. She said that she heard someone say, "You've ruined me". Now, Francis Drake, as far as we know at least, isn't on the brink of bankruptcy. I doubt Nelson winning that contract would have put him in penury. Thornalley, on the other hand, is a different kettle of fish. We know he's in debt up to his ears.'

Amy wasn't convinced. 'So, what if Drake eggs Basil on, and he does the deed, then they both hide in the kitchen. Basil could well have been the one that said, "you've ruined me".'

'What about the fire door? Someone opened it.'

Amy thought for a moment. 'Okay, what if Basil kills Nelson, and Drake nips up the passage and opens the fire door to throw us... you... the police, off the scent?'

'It's possible I suppose, but then we have very good testimony that a fair-haired man was standing at the emergency exit, talking to Nelson a few moments before he was killed. Terrence Derby gave a reasonable description and we know from the taxi driver that a man fitting that description and wearing a blood-stained shirt, got into his cab only a couple of minutes after the killing.'

'Kitson, yes, I know, but he was in with Drake too. Everything seems to be pointing in his direction.'

'We don't know that Drake was in the kitchen with Basil. We're just surmising, we might be trying to make things fit because we like the look of it that way.'

'True,' Amy said, placing her hands on her lap. 'But who else could it have been? Drake and Thornalley were both in the *area* at the time. I can't think of anyone else that was, apart from Lorna of course.'

'And she might be spinning us a yarn too. Did you see her eyes light up when you told her Basil was in the kitchen? She latched onto that straight away. It's funny how she didn't mention the two noises when we questioned her last week.'

'I saw her eyes light up when she was giving you the come on,' Amy said. 'Oh, I think you're so brave,' she mimicked.

'Was she really? Giving me the eye, I mean? I honestly didn't notice.'

'You never do, Bodkin. What is it those awful poets say... "her eyes were like limpid pools?" Well, hers were the size of two Lake Windermeres. I bet you didn't spot her crossing and uncrossing her legs either, and she never stopped fiddling with her hair.' Amy put her finger in the hair at the side of her head and began to twist it. 'I really don't know how you do your job, it must be so harrowing at times,' she simpered.

Bodkin shrugged. Amy let her hair fall back into place as she looked at the inspector.

'You'd be as good a detective as Sherlock Holmes if you ever learned to read women, Bodkin. Sadly, I don't think that will ever become part of your tool kit.' She patted him on the arm. 'Still, that's part of your charm I suppose.'

Amy bit her bottom lip as she thought about what Bodkin had said.

'As for spinning us a yarn about there being two people in the kitchen... you might be right. I mean, she could be dropping Francis right in it after that revelation, and I doubt she wants to do that. The other thing is, when we spoke to her last week, she was in shock, it was only a few minutes after she found the body, so her thoughts would have been all over the place.'

Bodkin changed down a gear to take an s-bend, then changed up again and rubbed his chin as he reached a section of straight road.

'Well, she'd certainly got over the shock by the next morning. You said she was laughing and joking with Francis as she got out of his car.'

'She definitely looked like she'd had a good night's sleep,' Amy replied.

Bodkin looked across. 'Or maybe, out of the goodness of his heart, Francis stayed over to comfort her in her hour of need.'

'You are a cynic, Bodkin. Just because they were seen together late the next morning, it doesn't mean they... spent the night together.'

'It's the copper in me,' Bodkin replied. 'You learn how to become a cynic the first week on the job.'

As Bodkin drove around the corner by the police station, Amy changed the subject. 'What are you wearing for the garden party on Sunday?'

The policeman glanced down at his suit. 'I was thinking of wearing this, actually.'

Amy's mouth gaped. 'You are joking. You've been in that thing all week?'

'All right, I'll wear my spare.'

'Is it even ironed?' Amy asked. 'Honestly, Bodkin you really should make more of an effort.'

Bodkin shrugged. 'I'll be working so I'll need to be dressed appropriately.'

'Will you be paid for going to the party?'

'Don't be silly, they baulk at paying us to work our scheduled hours as it is.'

'So, if you're not officially on duty, why wear a suit? Are you incapable of asking questions wearing a nice pair of trousers and a casual shirt? Shirley said dress down. That means wearing something comfortable.'

'I feel comfortable in my suit,' Bodkin said sulkily.

'Well, you're not wearing it on Sunday and that's that. Come on, your flat is only over the road, let's go and see what you've got hiding away in there.'

'I don't know... I...'

'Bodkin, do as you're told before you have to arrest me for

attempted blackmail, because if you don't agree to wear something other than your blooming suit, I'm not coming with you.'

'Amy...'

'Don't Amy me, Bodkin. Come on, let's see what you've got in your drawers.'

Trixie, the blonde bombshell who worked as a secretary at the police station, opened the door to her ground-floor flat as Bodkin held open the big, glass entrance door to allow Amy to enter the building. Trixie wasn't looking her glamorous best. Her hair needed setting and her face was devoid of make-up. She was wearing an off-white pinafore with gravy stains down the front. In her left hand was a soggy, limp, dish mop.

Amy smiled sweetly at her as she approached the stairs.

'Having a night in?' She pulled a sad face. 'Oh, I see, no date? That's such a shame.'

Bodkin put his hand in the middle of her back and gave her a gentle shove.

'Leave it, please, Amy,' he begged.

Trixie turned on her heel and with a flick of her head, she walked smartly into her flat and slammed the door behind her.

'Bags! Good heavens, Bodkin. Oxford bags? No one has worn anything like this for a dozen years or more.' Amy held the offending trousers up by the waistband. 'Those leg bottoms must be fifteen inches wide.'

'Sixteen,' Bodkin admitted. 'I got the widest ones I could get. They were all the rage back then.'

Amy tossed them onto the bed and turned back to the contents of the wardrobe. 'When was back then? How old were you?'

'About eighteen I think.'

Amy sighed, and pulled a tweed jacket from the short rail. 'This thing was out of fashion when fashion first became a thing. Honestly, Bodkin, I'm surprised you haven't got a frock coat and a stove-pipe hat in here.' She rummaged around until she found a white shirt. 'Hurrah! This one even has a fold down collar. We can make use of that.'

'It's the wrong size,' Bodkin moaned. 'It's got a size eighteen-inch collar label but I think it's more like a twenty. It buries me. The chest must be fifty inches. I'm only a forty-four.'

Amy shook her head as she stared at the remaining garments on the hanging rail. 'What's this?' she asked picking up a sleeve-less, diamond-patterned pullover.

'That's like new, I've never worn it.'

'I don't blame you,' Amy said, dropping it on the wardrobe floor. 'My Dad wouldn't be seen dead in that and he has very old-fashioned tastes.' Amy shuddered. 'You'd have been the star of the show at the British Open golf tournament if you'd worn that... In nineteen-twenty-two,' she added.

Bodkin stood in the centre of the room wearing a hang-dog, face.

'No wonder you only wear those two suits,' she said.

At the bottom of the wardrobe was a wide drawer. Amy pulled it open.

'Don't... that's my—'

'I've seen a pair of men's underpants before, Bodkin. My Dad wears them, I've ironed a few pairs in my time too.'

Bodkin pushed the drawer shut with his foot. 'Well, seeing as you don't like the look of any of my other clothes, it's going to have to be the suit on Sunday.'

'Oh no... It's a party, Bodkin. I'm going to be wearing a nice, summer dress. Everyone else will be wearing bright, colourful things. The men will be in short sleeves and slacks whether the weather is kind or not. I'm not having you turn up in something that looks like you borrowed it from a tramp.'

Bodkin looked down at his trousers. 'They're not that bad. I ironed them on Tues... or was it Monday?'

Amy smiled, sighed, then turned towards the door.

'I'm not going to Brigden's in the morning, Bodkin. We're going to Stan's Bargain Emporium to see what they have on their rails.'

'Second hand stuff... But...'

'The vast majority of my extensive wardrobe was bought from the second-hand rails, Bodkin. I don't think you can tell, can you? It's not like they're moth-eaten or whiffy. You're always complimenting me on how nice I look, and yet everything I wear, someone else has had on before me.'

'Oh, I know... but they're women's clothes. Women tend to look after their things better than men.'

Amy patted him on the arm. 'We aren't going to dress you in rags, Bodkin, never fear. Some of Stan's stuff is very good quality. Mum gets bits and bobs for Dad in there when he needs something.' She smiled at the policeman who was still looking unsure. 'And, even though the clothes are second hand or at best, factory seconds, they're still a good ten years newer than the stuff in your wardrobe.'

Bodkin ran a hand over his forehead. 'All right, you win, as usual. What time shall I pick you up in the morning?'

CHAPTER

TWENTY-FIVE

STAN'S BARGAIN EMPORIUM WAS A LARGE BUILDING SET OVER TWO floors. The clothing rails were on the ground floor at the back of the shop, away from the wide front window. Amy led Bodkin like a reluctant child across the floor until they came to the men's section.

'Right, Bodkin,' she said as she took a mint-green, short sleeved shirt with a pair of button-down, chest pockets, from the rail. 'Size forty-four chest. What do you think?'

'It's a bit... green,' he replied pulling a face.

Amy held it up in front of him. 'It looks nice. You can wear it tomorrow; you won't need a tie with it.' she said.

Turning back to the rail she held up three different white shirts until she found one that she liked.

'Spearpoint, eighteen-inch collar, forty-four-inch chest. Even you can't complain about this one, Bodkin.'

'No, I like it... spearpoint? What's all that about?'

'It's named after the shape of the long, pointed collar, Bodkin. Most people... our esteemed Prime Minister, Mr Chamberlain aside, stopped wearing winged collars a long time ago.'

'I know that,' Bodkin grumbled as he grudgingly took the

shirt from Amy. 'How much are we spending?' he asked, worriedly.

'The green shirt is two and six, the white one, three shillings. We've spent just over five bob so far... now.... Trousers... What size are you?'

'Thirty-two-inch waist,' Bodkin replied.

'What about inside leg?'

'Erm, thirty-six inches I think.'

'You think? Aren't you sure?'

'I am quite tall.'

Amy studied him closely. 'Yes, you are, but you're not six-foot ten are you, Bodkin? You look like you've got a long body to me. Your legs don't look particularly long.'

'The trousers of my spare suit were thirty-six inches in the leg, I remember buying it,' he replied.

Amy's shoulders sank. 'Yes, they were, and if you remember, Bodkin, I had to cut three inches off them so they didn't concertina around your ankles. You need a thirty-three at most... possibly a thirty-two.'

Amy ran her hand along the rail, pulling out a pair of trousers before checking the sizes and putting them back.

'Haven't they got anything in navy blue?' Bodkin asked after Amy had picked out two pairs of high waisted trousers, one grey and one brown.

'Your suits are navy; you need something else. Come on, Bodkin, help me out here.'

'I like navy, it suits me,' Bodkin muttered under his breath.

Ten minutes later, Amy was satisfied with her haul. Bodkin followed her to the changing room, both arms stuck out in front, carrying her selection.

'In you go, I'll wait out here,' Amy said, taking a seat just outside the door.

'Yes, Mum,' Bodkin replied, giving her a wink.

It took Bodkin twenty minutes to try everything on. Every few minutes he'd show his face at the glass door, check that no one was about, then he'd come out and stand in front of Amy while she ran her eye over him. By the time they headed towards the tills they had chosen three shirts, a thick striped navy jacket (just to please Bodkin) and the two pairs of trousers Amy had liked.

'That will be fourteen and six, all up,' the assistant said as she took the price tags from the garments at the till.

'Blimey, I didn't expect to spend...' Bodkin shot a glance at Amy. 'We got some bargains there,' he added, quickly.

'I'm donating five shillings,' Amy said, pulling two half crowns from her purse. 'I'm the one who insisted you get some new clobber after all.'

Bodkin shook his head. 'No, it's all right, Amy. You were right. I did need some new clothes. I'll come again in a few weeks and see what's in then.'

'Hey, we can do our Saturday bargain shopping together, Bodkin. That would be nice, wouldn't it?' Amy forced the two coins into Bodkin's hand. 'Please, Bodkin. My treat. I haven't spent anything at Brigden's today so it will only sit in my purse, tempting me all next week.' She looked at him pleadingly. 'Anyway, it's high time I bought you something, you're always spending money on me.'

'Oh, give them to me,' Amy said as they walked out of Stan's store with three, gaily coloured bags that Bodkin's new clothes were lying, neatly folded up in.

'They're just a bit... loud,' Bodkin said as he handed the large, yellow and pink bags to her.

'You're such a... MAN,' Amy said as she tucked her handbag into one of the offending carriers. 'My dad is just the same, that's why Mum does his clothes shopping for him.'

By the time they reached Bodkin's car, the sun had come out, its summer heat burning off the last of the grey clouds that had blighted the skies over the previous two days.

Bodkin checked his watch. 'We've got plenty of time before we go to meet Helen Kelly. I'll just drop these things off at mine, then we can think about an early lunch.'

'Take them to mine, Bodkin. I'll run an iron over everything and check the seams properly this afternoon. You can either take them back home tonight on the way out, or get changed there tomorrow.'

'I can manage an iron, Amy, I don't want to put you to any trouble.'

'It will be less trouble if I do it properly this afternoon instead of having to perform an emergency ironing session tomorrow lunchtime,' Amy replied. She smiled at the policeman. 'I'm not belittling you, Bodkin, honestly, it's just that I'm a lot better at it than you are.' She put her hand on the car door latch as they pulled up outside the cottage. 'When it comes to catching crooks, you're the bees' knees, but when it comes to swinging an iron, you're a very poor second.'

Bodkin followed Amy across the pavement and through the little white paling gate. When they reached the front door, she stopped, put down the shopping and fished the front door key from her bag.

'You don't think I'm a bit of a bully, do you, Bodkin?' she asked, looking at him seriously. 'I know I boss you around sometimes and I can understand if you don't like it. It's not that I mean anyth—'

Bodkin put his finger softly on her lips and kissed her on the forehead.

'I love you bossing me about,' he said. 'I wouldn't have it any other way.'

CHAPTER
TWENTY-SIX

Hillcrest was a large, Edwardian house that had been built at the turn of the century at the same time that the library and Town Hall had been constructed. It was well named as it was the last house on the left-hand side of the hill just before the High Street met Main Street.

The house itself was set back about thirty feet from the road with a wide, twin pillared entrance leading to a square-shaped, loosely-gravelled, parking area.

Bodkin pulled up alongside a smart-looking, Riley Kestrel saloon and whistled as he climbed out of his own Morris, police car.

'It's a work of art, isn't it?' he said to Amy as he stood admiring the coachwork.

'It's a car, Bodkin,' Amy replied. 'They get you from A to B in comfort and they're a bit quicker than the bus. One car is pretty much the same as another to me.'

'You wouldn't think like that if you were a driver,' Bodkin said, still staring at the sleek, red car.

Amy slowly shook her head and walked into the porch where she pressed a white-buttoned doorbell. The door was opened almost immediately by a woman with medium brown hair cut in the page boy style with a parting on the right. She looked to be in her early thirties. She was wearing a knee-length, white dress with a rose print. She smiled at Amy as she stood in the doorway.

'We have an appointment with Helen Kelly,' Amy said.

'I'm Helen Kelly,' the woman said, smiling towards Amy. 'Are you Miss Rowlings? Chief Superintendent Grayson said you'd be coming. It really is very kind of you to sit in. I've never been questioned by the police before. I thought that it might be quite intimidating so I'm grateful for some female support.'

Amy pointed into the parking bay where Bodkin was still admiring the Riley. 'He'll be along in a minute; he's got a thing about cars.'

Helen nodded. 'It's a man thing. Nelson used to change his to a new model every few months. I'd just about get used to driving it and he'd come home with something completely different.'

'Bodkin,' Amy called.

The inspector looked up from his reverie. 'Sorry,' he said, quickly. 'I was just admiring your car.'

'Take a seat, I'll just organise a pot of tea,' Helen said as she led them into a large room with a square of flower-patterned carpet, on which sat two facing, cream coloured, leather sofas. The walls were covered in a leaf-patterned wallpaper. In the bay window was a dark oak dining table with six, upholstered, soft-seated chairs, positioned around it. Between the two sofas was an oak coffee table.

Amy sat down on the right-hand sofa as Bodkin examined the row of photographs on the mantlepiece.

'She's not dressed like the grieving widow, is she?' he said, turning around and taking a seat on the sofa opposite Amy.

'I have to admit, I expected a more sombre looking woman,'

Amy said. She looked up quickly as Helen came back in with a tea tray.

'Clara has the afternoon off,' she said as she placed the tray on the table. 'Help yourself to biscuits.'

'Clara?' Bodkin asked.

'Oh, sorry, she's our... my housemaid. She's a lovely young girl, a bit scatter-brained, but she's a real treasure. Nelson thought very highly of her.'

Amy shot a quick glance at Bodkin. Helen's eyes had narrowed slightly when she mentioned her husband.

'We're so sorry for your loss, Mrs Kelly,' Bodkin said, accepting a cup of tea from Helen. 'It must have come as a terrible shock.'

Helen's face fell, she turned away and dabbed at her eyes with a lace trimmed handkerchief.

'Are you any closer to finding out who did such a terrible thing?' she asked with a slight croak in her voice.

'Enquiries are ongoing, Mrs Kelly,' Bodkin said. 'But I'm afraid we're not in the position to charge anyone yet.'

He took a sip of tea, pulled a face, then put the cup back on its saucer.

'Earl Grey,' Helen said. 'I'm sorry, would you have preferred breakfast tea?'

'No, it's fine, thank you, Mrs Kelly. I'm used to something a little more... robust, that's all.'

Amy looked to the ceiling, then turned her attention back to Helen.

'When did you last see your husband, Mrs Kelly?'

'I assume you mean alive? Well, that would have been on Friday afternoon. He was working on his acceptance speech in his study. He came out at around six, and went down to the cellar to get a fresh bottle of rum. I didn't see him after that as I went up to my bedroom to read.'

'Your bedroom?'

'Yes, Nelson and I had separate rooms.'

Bodkin smiled, softly. 'I'm sorry if some of the questions seem a little intrusive, but we really do have to find out all we can about Nelson, and unfortunately that means I have to ask a few delicate questions.'

'I understand,' Helen replied. 'I suppose you have to rule me out too.'

'Was it a happy marriage? How close was your relationship?'

'Happy... What is a happy marriage? I think women want more out of it these days. I don't know of anyone who is still madly in love with their husband, not anyone who has been married for any length of time at least.' She picked up her tea, sniffed the fragrance, then took a delicate sip. 'We rattled along together, Inspector. There was no animosity.'

'Here's one of the questions I warned you about,' Bodkin said, holding Helen's eye. 'We have had reports that Nelson was something of a ladies' man. Is that an accurate assessment?'

'With knobs on,' Helen replied firmly. 'Ladies' man is a very inoffensive term, isn't it? What you really mean to ask is, was my husband a philanderer, a serial adulterer? And the answer is yes. He had dozens of affairs,' she looked sideways at Amy. 'He'd have loved you.'

'So, you've always known about his... dalliances?' Bodkin asked.

'The first one... the first one I knew about at least, was about three months after we were married. I was told later that the relationship had been going on while we were engaged. That tells you all you need to know about Nelson.'

'Did you argue about it? Were you angry?'

'At the start, yes. I was furious. We had a few hum dinging rows about it, but after a while I realised that I was wasting my time. He was never going to change.'

'Did you ever considered asking for a divorce, Mrs Kelly?'

'Call me Helen, please,' she said as she got to her feet and walked over to a dark-wood sideboard where she took a cigarette from a cedar box and lit it with a Ronson table lighter. She took a long draw, then tilted her head back and blew smoke towards the ceiling. 'Regarding divorce... no, not yet, it probably would have happened at some stage though.' She walked back to Bodkin's sofa and placed a soft hand on his shoulder. 'When the time was right... Are you married, Inspector?' she asked, looking into his upturned face.

'No, I'm not.'

'Then you can't really know what it's like.' She took her hand off his shoulder and sat down in the seat next to Amy again. Slowly crossing her legs, she blew a long stream of smoke across the table towards the policeman. 'Anyway,' she waved her hands expansively, 'why would I want to give all this up?'

'There would be some sort of settlement, surely?'

Helen sniffed. 'Yes, but I like it here. Everything you see in this house is only here because I wanted it to be here. I chose the carpets, the wallpaper, the shell-shaped bath... everything.'

'But didn't you feel insulted by his actions? He's known for what he is all around town, it must have been difficult for you to be the subject of so much gossip.'

'Why do you think I don't accompany him on his official jaunts?' She flicked ash into a clam-shaped ash tray. 'I've got my own circle of friends now and I hang around with them. They know exactly how I feel about Nelson. They think he's pathetic. Especially when they found out he'd been having an affair with Clara.'

'Clara? Your housemaid?' Amy's mouth dropped open.

'She's the only Clara I know,' Helen replied. 'Look, she's pretty, she's very young and she's female, why wouldn't he?'

'How old is Clara, Mrs... Helen?' Bodkin asked.

'Eighteen, nineteen maybe.'

'And you weren't angry? Why didn't you sack her?' Amy asked.

'Because, as I said, she is a very good worker, then of course it meant that while he was accommodating her, he left me alone at night. He does... sorry did, have a very strong sex drive. Oh, he didn't get up to anything like that when I was at home, he didn't even use his own bed. They used to go to her room at the top of the house when I was out.'

'Did you ever talk to her about it?'

'Good God no. That would have been both embarrassing and demeaning.'

'But she knew that you knew?'

Helen shrugged. 'I honestly have no idea.' She leaned forward to stub out her cigarette, then sat back and crossed her legs again.

Bodkin blew out his cheeks, began to speak, then stopped himself. He shot a glance at Amy, screwed up his face, then went ahead anyway.

'What about you, Helen? Are all your friends female or...'

She laughed out loud. 'Out with it man! Are you asking if I have had affairs too?'

Bodkin nodded slowly. 'Yes, I suppose I am.'

'Then I'll answer. Yes, but not until last year.'

'Why leave it so long?' Bodkin held up a hand. 'I'm sorry, that was...'

'Because I didn't meet the right man.' She looked at Amy and tilted her head. 'You know what I mean, don't you, my dear? We aren't like men; we don't just jump into bed with the first one that comes along. There has to be more to it than that, doesn't there?'

'I erm, I wouldn't know,' Amy replied quietly. 'It sounds about right though.'

'You mean you and him... You've never...?' She pushed out an arm and patted Amy's hand. 'I'm so sorry, I just assumed that you were an item.'

'We're good friends,' Amy said, blushing scarlet.

'I'm sorry, Amy,' Helen said again. 'I thought it was so obvious. I'm usually right about things like that. I have an instinct. I knew when I was meeting one of Nelson's conquests the moment I was introduced.'

'How did you get on with Nelson's brother?' Bodkin said, changing the subject.

'Horatio? All right, I suppose. He's a gentle sort, completely the opposite of Nelson.'

'Is Horatio married?'

'Not now, no. He was until five years or so back. She ran away with the circus?'

'She did what?'

Helen laughed. 'That's not entirely true. She ran away with the man whose family own a travelling circus. One of the big ones. They have interests in the larger fun fairs around the country too. He wasn't involved in any of that. He was the black sheep of the family. He and Nelson got on like a house on fire. In fact, it was through Nelson that Tabatha met him in the first place.'

'We've had it from a reliable source that you backed Horatio in arguments with Nelson over several business contracts.'

'By reliable source, you mean Lorna Wetherby.'

'I can't comment on who told us,' Bodkin replied.

'I can't think who else would have known. You haven't spoken to Horatio yet, so it wouldn't have been him.'

'Was Lorna having an affair with Nelson?'

Helen shrugged. 'I assume so, she's pretty enough.'

'Back to the contracts. How many times did you support Horatio in an argument with Nelson?'

'Once or twice. The factory was the big one.'

'Did you have a say in board meetings?'

Helen laughed again. 'No, Inspector, my name was only on the directors list for expediency. I didn't have a vote. When I backed Horatio, it was at a family gathering, I think it must have been Christmas, we were all in here and we'd all had more than enough to drink. Horatio let fly at Nelson for not replacing the housing he proposed to knock down in order for the new factory to be built. It wasn't official then of course, but Nelson said it was all cut and dried. I backed Horatio up. Have you seen the state of those houses, Inspector? How they can expect anyone to live in them... children especially. They all need to be demolished, but those poor people should be given alternative housing. The problem is, there isn't any and there are none in the planning stage either.'

'But Horatio backed the plan in the end, even though he wanted houses to be built for the workers?'

'Not just the potential workers, those being displaced to make room for the factory too. I was behind him one hundred percent, but Nelson had managed to get a sneaky look at his competitor's bid... don't ask me how... probably via Thornalley... and he told Horatio that if Kelly Construction didn't win the bid, then Drake Construction would, and as he wasn't offering to build any houses either, he said we'd just be handing the factory to him on a plate and the residents of the area would be no better off.'

'And Horatio backed down at that stage.'

'There wasn't much point in arguing after that revelation.' She stood up and went to get another cigarette. After lighting it she walked back to her seat, sat down and blew out a plume of blue-grey smoke. 'Nelson was a bully, Inspector. Not just in business. He always expected to get his own way. He did when he was a child and he has done ever since. His father doted on him when he was alive, he never had five minutes for poor Horatio. He was ever the disappointment.'

Bodkin straightened, then leaned towards Mrs Kelly. 'Helen,

can you think of anyone, anyone at all, who held a grudge against your husband? For business or personal reasons?'

'Most of the people he knew despised him. Oh, there were always those hangers on, people hoping to get a bit of business, or a hot tip about some woman or other put their way, but he didn't have many true friends, Inspector.' She blew out smoke then extinguished her cigarette. 'He had lots of enemies, I suppose. Irate husbands who had been cuckolded. Small businessmen he had helped into bankruptcy and taken over their holdings. There are probably a lot of women who held grudges over the way they were treated too. I don't envy you if you have to work your way through that lot. You'd be at it until Christmas.'

'Would Francis Drake be on that list? What about Harold Kitson?'

Helen shrugged. 'You'd have to ask them, Inspector. They didn't get on, that's for sure, but that's the way it is when two businessmen are up against each other.'

'Have you met Mr Kitson?'

Helen nodded slowly. 'Yes, a few times. He came around here once asking to speak to Nelson. They had a bit of a ding-dong in his study. That would have been a few months ago. I haven't seen him since.'

'What did you make of him. Did you like him?'

'He was a bit of a sleaze if you ask me, Inspector. No, I didn't like him much. I met him at a couple of parties. He used to undress you with his eyes. Every time you looked around he'd be staring at you with a leer on his face.'

Amy nodded. 'He did that to me too.'

Helen patted her hand again. 'I'd get used to that sort of thing happening if I were you, my dear. You are a very attractive young lady. Nelson's ghost will be...' She held up her hands towards Amy. 'I'm sorry, I was just speaking out of experience.'

'I've only got a couple more questions, then we'll leave you in peace,' Bodkin said. The room had become very warm. He ran a finger inside his collar to loosen it. 'Who is mentioned in the will? Are you the main beneficiary?'

'I'm not a hundred percent sure, but I think I get the house and most of his personal wealth. Horatio will definitely get the business. I think he'll be successful too. He won't make as many enemies as Nelson, that's for sure.'

Bodkin got to his feet. 'Thank you for being so candid, Mrs Kelly.'

Amy got up, smiled at Helen, then followed Bodkin to the door.

'One last thing,' Bodkin asked as he put his hand on the door handle. 'When was the last time you spoke to Nelson?'

'In person you mean?'

'Is there any other way?'

'Well, I spoke to him on the phone on the night he was killed.'

Bodkin let go of the handle and turned back to face the widow.

'Were you the person that made the call to the Town Hall, Mrs Kelly?'

'Yes. Is there something wrong?'

'How did you know you could get through to him, which number to ring?'

'I got it from the telephone directory.'

Bodkin scratched the hair behind his ear. 'Could you tell me the purpose of the call, Mrs Kelly? What was so important that you felt the need to call him in the middle of a civic presentation?'

Helen flushed a little. Her eyes flicked away from Bodkin's for a second.

'I wanted to check if he had his front door key. I had decided to go and stay with my sister for the night, she lives at Burham, near Gillingham. Clara had asked for the night off, so there would have been no one here to let him in.'

'Was it a sudden decision or had you planned to visit your sister?' Bodkin asked.

'It was an instant decision, Inspector. She rang at about nine o'clock on Friday evening. She was upset... that foul creature of a husband had been at her again. He should be strung up for the way he treats her. He's a bigger bully than Nelson. He's handy with his fists too, at least Nelson never sunk that low.'

'I'm sorry to hear that, Helen,' Bodkin said, sympathetically. 'Why didn't you go in the end? I was under the impression that the police contacted you here on the night of the murder.'

Helen put her hand to her throat. 'Oh, she rang me back about half an hour later. She said he'd apologised and promised never to do it again.'

'Good luck with that,' Amy said, under her breath.

'Could you give me your sister's contact details please, Mrs Kelly? I'd like a quick word with her to confirm your story.'

'I'm afraid she'll be out of the country by now, Inspector. Barty, that's the louse she's married to, took her to the South of France on Monday, his way of saying sorry I suppose.'

'How very convenient,' Bodkin said as he opened the car door for Amy. 'I didn't buy that business about her sister at all.'

'Nor did I,' Amy replied. 'Why would she offer to go down there to comfort her sister? Surely her sister would have come to her if her husband had turned volent again. Helen would almost certainly have made things worse for her, turning up out of the blue. He would have taken it out on her the moment they were alone again. You see it all the time in this town.'

'It's not always possible to get out of the house, Amy, but I do agree. If she did make that phone call, then her husband can't have been within earshot, so he'd either gone out after assaulting her, or, it didn't happen.'

'She's definitely hiding something, Bodkin,' Amy said as the policeman started up the car. 'She's the second woman in the space of twenty-four hours trying to use their feminine wiles to put you off your stride.'

'How? What did I miss this time?'

'Oh, she is out of the same acting stable as Lorna. Slowly crossing her legs, blowing smoke at you, fiddling with her hair, holding your eye for much longer than necessary. Then of course there was the way she put her hand on your shoulder. Such a familiar thing to do, yet you've only just met her.' Amy leaned back in her seat and sighed.

'I don't know what it is that you've got, Bodkin but if you ever find out, you should have it bottled. You'd make a fortune.'

Bodkin let go of the steering wheel and held his hands up.

'Is there a course you can take on understanding women? I think I need to go on it if there is.'

'Stick with me, Bodkin, I'll teach you all you need to know.'

Bodkin ran a hand over his forehead, then put it back on the wheel to turn onto the Gillingham Road.

'I did notice one thing, other than her attempts to seduce you that is.' Amy said.

'Did I miss something else too?'

'It was when she said, you hadn't spoken to Horatio yet... How did she know?'

CHAPTER
TWENTY-SEVEN

On Saturday afternoon, Amy checked the stitching on Bodkin's new clothes, then, satisfied with the seams, she ran an iron over the two shirts and pressed both pairs of trousers before draping them over wooden hangers and hooking the clothes on the handles of her wardrobe and bedroom doors. As she was folding up the carrier bags, she heard something chink. When she looked into the bag, she found the two half crowns she had handed to Bodkin in the store.

At four o'clock, she took a bath using her favourite rose baths salts that Alice bought for Christmas and birthday presents every year. Amy never grew tired of receiving the gifts.

After a half-hour soak, she pulled on her floral dressing gown, wrapped a towel around her hair and went up to her room to play music until her mother called her down for tea.

'What are you going to see tonight?' Mr Rowlings asked between mouthfuls of his potted beef sandwich.

'We're seeing A Star Is Born, with Janet Gaynor.'

'That ought to be good then,' Mr Rowlings said. 'I remember her in the early films she made. I think she got an Academy Award for one of them.'

'The first ever Academy Award for best actress,' Amy said.

'She knows her stuff when it comes to films does our Amy,' Mrs Rowlings said, proudly.

James Rowlings smiled fondly at his daughter.

'She ought to, she's never got her head out of her Photoplay magazines and she must have seen just about every film that's ever been made.'

'I like to totally immerse myself into a film... or a book for that matter. They allow you to escape the daily drudgery of life.'

'What are you reading at the moment?' Mr Rowlings asked.

'A Poirot book, Dumb Witness. I don't think it's Agatha's best, but then her worst is better than someone else's best.'

'I need a new book,' Mr Rowlings said. 'Did you say you were working in town this week, Amy?'

'Thursday and Friday, Dad. Do you want me to nip to the library in my lunch break? I'll have finished Dumb Witness by then.'

Mr Rowlings patted the copy of Graham Green's Brighton Rock that sat on the small table at the side of his chair.

'I'll finish this today. I fancy something a bit lighter next time. P.G. Wodehouse has a new one out, The Code of the Woosters, or something like that. Could you see if they have it in? If not just grab me one of his older books. He's always worth a second read.'

'I love Jeeves and Wooster, they're so funny,' Amy replied. 'The one thing I dislike is that all his younger, female characters seem to be fluffballs, but then again, Bertie himself wasn't actually the full shilling, was he? Old Aunt Agatha kept him on his toes.'

Alice turned up at a quarter to six with her face only partly made-up.

'You said I could borrow that lovely lipstick and nail varnish,' she reminded Amy.

'They're on my dressing table,' Amy said. 'Up you go.'

Just as Alice reached the top of the stairs, Bodkin knocked on the door.

'I've driven over in the car,' he said. 'I got a bit behind again.'

'That's not like you, Bodkin,' Amy said, rolling her eyes. She gave him a peck on the cheek and led him into the living room.

'Look what the cat dragged in,' she said.

Mr Rowlings looked up from his book and nodded to the policeman. 'Have you caught him yet, Laddie?'

Bodkin shook his head and bit the inside of his cheek in an attempt to stop himself laughing. Mr Rowlings was only one sixteenth part Scottish, and usually spoke with a broad, Kentish accent but for some reason, whenever Bodkin turned up, he slipped into a Scottish brogue. After the first few minutes he'd forget and he would resume the conversation in his usual manner.

'Not yet, sadly,' Bodkin said with a slow shake of his head.

'Cup of tea?' Mrs Rowlings shook an empty tea pot at him.

Bodkin checked his watch.

'I'd love one, Mrs R. We've got plenty of time tonight; I'm in the car, we won't have to run for the bus.'

'Is it easy? Driving, I mean,' Amy asked. 'Do you think you could teach me, Bodkin? My Uncle Maurice promised that he would, but he's hardly ever around these days. He's always just setting off for somewhere or *is* somewhere, and I've never had the chance to get behind the wheel.'

'I'd love to,' Bodkin replied, 'but sadly, the police force owns the car and if the top brass ever found out I'd be for the high jump.'

'Don't worry about it then, Bodkin, I don't want to get you into any more trouble than I already have.'

'I'll teach you,' Alice said as she walked into the living room waving her wet fingernails in the air. 'What do you think, Amy?' Alice pouted showing off the freshly applied lipstick.

'It really suits you,' Amy replied. 'It goes so well with your auburn hair. You look fabulous.'

'I'm really pleased with the effect too. What do you think, Bodkin?'

'I'm sorry?' Bodkin looked from Alice to Amy, then back. 'What am I looking at?'

'Oh, you're hopeless,' Amy said, as she pulled out a chair at the table and sat down.

'What?' Bodkin was still puzzled.

'Never mind those two, they're just teasing you,' Mrs Rowlings said, handing Bodkin a cup and saucer. 'Sit yourself down, I've made you a potted meat sandwich, I bet you didn't have any dinner.'

Amy smiled as she poured herself a cup of tea. 'Bodkin gets his tea poured and served on a silver salver,' she said, winking at Alice. She patted the chair next to her, inviting her best friend to sit. 'Did I hear you correctly just then. You said you'd teach me to drive?'

'If you like, but I've only got the old truck to teach you in.' She shook her head as Amy pointed to the teapot. 'Better not, I had two cups before I came out. I'll spend more time in the lavvy than in my seat tonight if I have any more.'

'Your old truck,' Amy mused. 'Of course!' She patted Alice's thigh. 'Thank you, my darling.'

'You'll have muscles like Popeye after driving that,' Bodkin said. Alice's rusty, open-backed lorry was over twelve years old and its best days were well behind it.

'But the good news is, if you can drive that, you can drive anything,' Alice said.

They sat in silence for a few moments, then Bodkin suddenly leapt to his feet.

'Am I wearing the new stuff tonight, or am I all right in the suit?' he asked.

'You won't need the tie and jacket, Bodkin. It will get a bit stuffy inside the Roxy.'

'Okay, but I'm all right for tonight, I don't need to get changed?'

Amy got to her feet and hurried up the stairs, she came down a minute or so later with Bodkin's new clothes draped over her arms.

'Thanks, Amy,' Bodkin said with a grin. 'I came in the car, so I'll drop them on the back seat.'

'You're not leaving these on the back seat overnight, Bodkin, they'll be as wrinkled as your suit by tomorrow morning. Take them in and hang them up in your wardrobe after you park the car up.'

'I didn't mean overnight,' Bodkin protested.

'Are you two going somewhere special tomorrow?' Alice asked.

Amy grinned at her. 'We have an invitation to the mayor's garden party tomorrow afternoon.'

'Goodness!' Alice exclaimed. 'You are moving in different circles now, aren't you? Don't forget your old friends when you're swanning about in Buck House.'

Amy patted Alice on the arm. 'If I ever get to Buckingham Palace, you can be sure that you'll be standing right alongside as we queue to meet the King. I'd wrangle you an invite for the bash tomorrow but I'm only there myself because Bodkin wants to grill the mayor.'

'Make sure the roast pig is off the spit first,' Alice replied. 'As for the palace. I'll pass, thanks. I'd rather we went to the Kent County Show to take a look around the pens.'

• • •

The Rectory was an imposing, early eighteenth century building which was positioned in three acres of land just off North Street at the top end of Spinton. It had, as its name suggests, once been owned by the church, but they divested themselves of the property in the late eighteen hundreds when worshiper numbers began to decline. The current vicar lived in a smaller property next to the church. The front door of the house was open as Amy and Bodkin arrived and after standing around for a few minutes and after trying the doorbell twice without success, Bodkin wiped his feet on the huge coconut mat and stepped into the hall with Amy following closely behind.

'Shouldn't we go around the back, Bodkin?' she asked.

'I have no idea,' Bodkin said, giving the waist of his grey, twill trousers a tug. 'These things feel like they're falling down,' he hissed.

'Shh, stop moaning, Bodkin, you look nice. That short-sleeved shirt really suits you.' She touched his bicep. 'I didn't realise you had muscles.'

They found themselves in a wide hallway which was lined with likenesses of some of the former church notaries. There were four huge, solid oak doors leading off, two to each side. On the right as they entered, was a dark-wood staircase leading upwards.

They followed the hall until they came to a huge, square sitting room, with a pair of large, French windows built into the far wall. Amy could hear the sounds of voices filtering into the room.

'This way,' she said as she took Bodkin's arm, and together, they stepped into the well-kempt garden. There were about two-dozen people present, the men dressed casually in slacks and shirts with just one or two elderly men wearing yachting style, double breasted, blazers. The women wore summer frocks and wide-brimmed sunhats.

Amy looked around the garden where the guests were standing in small groups. Set out alongside the back wall of the house was an open fronted marquee with rows of trestle tables inside, containing plates of thinly cut, triangle sandwiches, sausage rolls, Vol-au-vents and dishes of sherry trifle.

'Alice would have been disappointed, there's no pig on a spit,' Amy said as she dragged Bodkin away from the trestles. 'There'll be plenty of time for food later,' she whispered, leading the policeman across the lawn towards the smiling figure of Shirley McKenzie, who was standing with a small group of middle-aged women.

'Amy, Mr Bodkin,' she cooed. 'I'm so pleased you could make it.' She took a step back and studied Amy. 'I love that dress, where on earth did you get it?' She leaned forwards and took a closer look at the red, halter neck, polka dot summer dress that Amy had picked out from her wardrobe. 'Stunning,' she said. 'Did you buy it in London?'

'Brigden's, in town,' Amy said. 'I buy all my clothes from there.'

'I've never been in,' Shirley said, 'but I'll make sure I do in future if they're selling things of that quality.'

Amy held her hand to her mouth to muffle the sound of her voice. 'It's all second-hand stuff,' she muttered.

'Well, you wouldn't know it,' Shirley said with a genuine smile. She turned to Bodkin. 'You look much more relaxed out of that suit, Inspector.'

Bodkin's eyes had wandered back to the marquee. Amy nudged him in the ribs.

'Bodkin,' she hissed.

'Yes, it is,' he replied, snapping his head around to face Shirley. 'A lovely day for it.'

'You'll have to excuse him,' Amy said as Shirley took her arm and led her across the lawn towards a group of men who were sipping glasses of gin and tonic while they discussed the latest cricket matches.

'Can I get you a drink, dear?' she asked as a white-coated waiter appeared carrying a tray full of empty glasses.

'Erm, would you have any Pimm's number one?' she asked.

'I know we do; I gave the caterers my own recipe this morning. Would you like ice with it?'

'Ooh, yes please,' Amy said. She looked up at Bodkin. 'What are you having?'

'Pimm's for me too, please,' he said as the waiter nodded towards him. 'With extra fruit and cucumber, I'm hungry.'

When their drinks had been served, Shirley took hold of her husband's arm and led him away from the leather on willow fanatics.

'This is Amy Rowlings, Robert and this is Inspector Bodkin. Would you like to talk to him now to get it over with, or leave it until later?'

'There's no time like the present,' Robert said, amiably. He shook Bodkin's hand then bowed his head slightly towards Amy. He pointed down the garden to a small orchard. 'Shall we talk over there? We shouldn't be overheard.'

Amy gave Bodkin a quizzical look as if to ask whether she should accompany them, but when Bodkin flicked his head towards the apple trees, Amy took a sip from her clinking icy Pimm's and fell into step.

McKenzie was a well-built man with wide shoulders and a shortish neck. His brown hair was parted on the left, short on the sides, long on top and combed back from his brow. He had an oval face, a well-proportioned, nose and, for a man, generous lips. His eyes were piercing blue. He was dressed in a pair of tan slacks and wore a sky-blue, short sleeved shirt in a similar style to the one that Bodkin was wearing.

'How may I help you, Inspector?' McKenzie said when they reached the first line of fruit trees. He paused when he noticed that Amy had followed them and gave her a strange look.

'Miss Rowlings is helping us on this case,' Bodkin explained. 'Chief Superintendent Grayson will confirm it if you'd like to call him to check.' Bodkin crossed his fingers behind his back and prayed that the mayor wouldn't bother.

'Are you hoping to join the police at some stage... erm, Amy, is it?'

'They don't allow women into their little club,' Amy said. She took another sip of her drink. 'Which is ridiculous because–'

'Amy has very strong feelings on the matter, Mr McKenzie.' Bodkin's interruption stopped Amy mid-rant. 'She's working with us on an ad hoc basis; she runs a private detective agency called ARIA.'

'Kent police accredited,' Amy said, fishing around in her bag for one of her pink cards.

'How unusual,' Robert said. 'I wish you luck with your enterprise, my dear.' He smiled, then looked towards Bodkin. 'We might have another Nancy Drew on our hands.'

'Ah, you read Carolyne Keene?' Amy said. 'I'm not sure if you know but she's not a real author, it's just a pen name. The books are ghost-written. Can you imagine that? Going to all the trouble of writing a detective story, then not being able to put your name to it.'

'My wife likes them whoever writes the things, she also like Dorothy L. Sayers. She's always got her nose in a book.'

'I'm a Poirot fanatic myself,' Amy replied. 'I love everything Agatha does. I wonder if Shirley has read her Miss Marple story, The Murder at the Vicarage. That was really good. I was hoping she'd write more with that character because you don't see too many female detectives, but she seems to be happy writing Poirot at the moment.'

Robert pursed his lips. 'I wish I had time to read, I miss it.' He turned to Bodkin. 'Right, let's get started, what do you want to know?'

'Firstly, I'd like to know a little bit about your background,' Bodkin said. 'Just to put things into context.'

'All right, where do I start? I come from the East Riding, Inspector, my family have been there for generations.'

'The Humber McKenzies,' Bodkin replied.

'You've been talking to my wife,' Robert said with a grin. 'She was the first person I ever heard say that. She used to use the phrase when we became an item at Cambridge. She did it to annoy the posher element amongst the students. They could never find the name in Debrett's, but it didn't stop her doing it. She'd hear one of them say, 'oh, I'm one of the Epsom Fothering-hays,' as if it meant anything to anyone outside of their area, and she'd come out with that. She still enjoys bigging me up.'

Bodkin grinned back at the mayor. 'You met at Cambridge? Shirley must have had a hard time getting in there, coming from where she does.'

'They couldn't turn her down really. She was too good not to be at university. Her results put mine to shame. She got a first you know? In History.'

'Good for her!' Amy said, much louder than she intended.

'She's a very intelligent woman,' Robert said to Amy. 'She keeps me on my toes.'

'I know a woman like that,' Bodkin said, flashing a wink at Amy.

'Has your family always had money, Mr McKenzie?' Bodkin asked. 'I'm sorry about the line of questioning but Nelson's death could be tied to this factory contract. We have to know the background of all those involved.'

'I have nothing to hide,' Robert said. 'Just a minute, let's all get a top up before we go on. What are we having? More of Shirley's Pimm's?'

The mayor stepped out from the shade of the orchard and waved to one of the waiters to get his attention. Holding up his fruit filled glass, he pointed to it then held up three fingers.

'Where were we,' he said when the waiter had delivered their drinks. 'Ah yes, money. I was born into it but my father wasn't. Some old ancestor of ours had gambled away the bulk of the family fortune in the eighteenth century. My father set up his own business importing silk, cotton and quite a few other things that were hard to get hold of over here. It wasn't that difficult a task, we had the empire behind us of course. He did spend rather a lot of time abroad, he set up companies in America, Canada and Brazil as well as the three companies he had over here. Sadly, he died of a fever in Africa in the mid nineteen-twenties and my uncle took over the firm. He must have got wind of the forthcoming crash in nineteen twenty-nine because he sold the lot before it all happened. He made a huge profit. He died about five years ago, and everything was left to me. I was well provided for. I'll never have to actually work for a living if I don't choose to. I've got a couple of race horses that I like to see run, and I play the stock market now that it's returned to normal.'

'Do you have any children, Mr McKenzie?' Bodkin asked.

'Sadly not, we haven't been blessed yet, but there's still plenty of time for that. We live in hope'

'Your wife tells us you're interested in using the mayor's community fund for charity purposes.'

'I'd like to. The children's home isn't fit for purpose in this day and age. I am a patron of two children's charities, Mr Bodkin, so I do have some idea of what will be needed. My wife is interested in women's issues and I'd like to help her out with that if I can.'

'And Mr Thornalley's so called Mayor's Fund?'

'We're trying to work out exactly what that was all about,' McKenzie replied. I've got a firm of accountants going through the records, such as they are. It's a difficult one because the money given for access to contracts was never paid into a fund account. The payments went directly to the former mayor. He was corrupt and I'm going to prove it.' He took a sip of his drink. 'I can see what's going through your mind, Inspector, but honestly, take a look around you. I own every last blade of grass here. There is no mortgage on the property, I have no loans under my name and my shares portfolio is worth a couple of hundred-thousand pounds. I can make more money just sitting around eating my breakfast than most men earn in a decade. I have absolutely no need to continue with Thornalley's so called, mayor's fund. You can check everything I've just told you. I'll tell my accountants to let you see the books if you like.'

'There's no need for that, Mr McKenzie,' Bodkin said, scratching the newly formed stubble on his chin. Thank you for being so candid. I did have reservations about you, I will admit, but you have put my mind at rest.' He took a mouthful of fruit into his mouth and chewed on it. 'Is there anything you can tell me about the night of the murder. You were with the former mayor and his group of friends I believe.'

'Yes and no. We don't get on, Mr Bodkin. He knows that I know what he was up to, he even had the gall to offer to explain how his scam worked, if I allowed him to be a part of it after he left office, but I was having none of it. New brooms sweep clean and all that.' Robert paused for thought. 'On Friday night he was rather on edge. He was all right until he had a conversation with Francis Drake, then his entire demeanour changed. It was, of course, common knowledge that Drake's business had lost out to Kelly's over the factory construction deal. I wondered if Drake was demanding back some, or all of the money he'd paid Basil to help smooth the wheels for his bid, but I can't be sure about that.'

'Drake was in good humour himself?'

'He was on top form. I got the impression he had enjoyed having Thornalley on toast. That or he was expecting some good news. He was full of himself. He didn't even have a go at me for backing Nelson's bid and scuppering his own.'

'Was there much difference between the two bids?'

'In the end, no, though Drake's was a revised bid that suddenly came very close to what Nelson was offering. I think he got hold of some inside information, possibly from Thornalley, but it could have come from Lorna Wetherby.'

'How did Nelson get the government onside. Does he have friends in high places?'

'Some, but I have more, Inspector. I helped out in that respect. As I saw it, anything that Thornalley backed can't have been a good thing for this town. He is a crook, there's no two ways about that. So, after speaking to Nelson, and after getting his assurances about his next public project, I was more than happy to throw the council's resources behind him. I had the backing of enough councillors, by that time there were only one or two still talking to Thornalley, let alone wanting to put money and votes into something they knew might be illegal.'

'Back to last Friday. Thornalley disappeared from the Assembly Room, did you see him either leave or return?'

'I saw him leave and head down towards the kitchen. He's addicted to that herbal tea he used to keep in there. It does his ulcer some good, I believe.'

Bodkin nodded. 'So, I heard... And Mrs Thornalley?'

'I'm not sure about her, but Drake followed him out, and that PR woman, Wetherby?, she left a couple of minutes before him. She went out almost straight after Nelson. I remember because I was talking to her when the girl from the cloakroom came in to say he had a telephone call.'

'You didn't see anyone else leave the room?'

'No, but then I was tied up with that local reporter... Miles, is it? He's a nasty piece of work. He was trying to talk me into making disparaging remarks about Basil. I wasn't about to do that. Not until I had all the facts at my disposal.'

Amy, who had already finished her second Pimm's and was beginning to feel a little more self-assured, held up her hand as if asking permission to speak.

'Yes, Amy?' Robert said.

'You mentioned Nelson's next public project just then. What did he have planned?'

'Oh, it was all very hush-hush. Not even his brother knew about the plan.' He thought for a moment. 'Ah well, it can't hurt him now, can it? Nelson and I came to an understanding. Once again, I agreed to call in a few favours from government and use the council's financial clout to back the scheme. It was going to be a difficult thing to pull off, but we both thought that with the right backing, it could be achieved.' He paused again as if still usure he should talk about it. 'What we had planned was to knock down every single house on that Victorian estate. I would issue a compulsory purchase order, offering no more than thirty pounds per dwelling, then we'd get the demolition teams in.' He looked from Amy to Bodkin. 'After that, we intended to build hundreds of brand-new houses with all modern facilities. It would be a mix of privately owned and council owned properties. The tenants would have paid no more in rent than they are paying now and they would have had security of tenure for the rest of their lives. Nelson took a bit of persuading, but he could see there were big profits to be made. It was win-win for the council, as we would end up with a lot of modern houses and at the same time, we'd be ridding ourselves of the slum that should have been demolished years ago.'

'Blimey!' Amy said, a little more loudly than she meant. 'It's a good job Drake didn't know anything about that. He owns hundreds of those houses. There's no way he would have been compensated for what he'd lose on the rents.'

Bodkin rubbed his chin again. 'Then again, perhaps he did get wind of it.'

'If he did, he didn't get it from me,' Robert replied.

'Thank you, Mr McKenzie,' Bodkin said. 'You've been very helpful. I think I need to spend a bit more time with our ex-mayor and his wife.'

'You'll get your chance a little sooner than you thought, Inspector. I told you my wife was a clever little so and so. She invited them yesterday afternoon and they agreed to come.' He looked across the lawn from the orchard towards the marquee. 'And you're in luck. They've just arrived.'

TWENTY-EIGHT

AMY AND BODKIN FOLLOWED ROBERT BACK ACROSS THE LAWN UNTIL HE came to a group of people standing with their backs to him.

'Basil... Alma,' he said, enthusiastically, 'thanks so much for coming.'

The couple turned around with smiles on their faces.

'It's a pleasure, Robert,' Alma said, as though she felt they were the stars of the show. 'We always like to show our support, especially as this is your first garden party as mayor.'

Basil Thornalley didn't seem to be the slightest bit interested in what his wife was saying, his eyes were firmly focussed on Bodkin.

'Hello again,' Bodkin said, grinning widely. 'Long time no see.'

'What are you doing here?' Alma asked, noticing Bodkin for the first time. She looked Amy up and down with distaste. 'And who is this? I don't think we've met.'

'I'm Amy Rowlings of ARIA Investigations,' she said, handing the former mayor's wife one of her pink cards. Amy held out her hand, but instead of shaking it, Alma handed the card back.

Amy dropped it in her bag, then caught the eye of one of the waiters and ordered up another Pimm's.

'Drink, Bodkin?' she pointed a finger towards the waiter. The policeman shook his head and turned back to Thornalley.

'Can we have another chat?' Bodkin asked, 'only certain things have come to light since we spoke last.'

'We're here for the party, man,' Alma hissed. 'Can't we do this at another time, we have reputations to keep up you know?'

'We can chat here or down at the station, it's entirely up to you,' Bodkin replied. 'I think your... reputation, such as it is, would suffer less damage if we spoke openly.'

Basil gave in. 'All right, but not here, it's too public.'

'Let's go to the orchard,' Bodkin suggested. 'It's nice and quiet in there.'

Basil Thornalley was a squat man who wore a permanent frown. His hair was lank and thin, much longer on the right, the extra length enabling him to comb it over a large bald area of pink scalp. He was a tubby man, his blue striped shirt stretched so tightly across his stomach that Amy felt the buttons could give way at any time. He had a round face with narrow eyes, that looked out suspiciously beneath a thick monobrow. When they came to a halt in the orchard, Amy noticed he was sweating profusely.

His wife was a female mirror image of him, the only real differences being that she wasn't balding, she had plucked her eyebrows and she wore a blue striped dress instead of a shirt.

'What on earth do you want to know now?' Basil snapped before taking a big slug from the glass of whisky he was carrying.

'There are quite a few questions, actually,' Bodkin replied. 'Firstly, I'd like to know more about your dealings with Francis Drake and Sevenoaks Construction.'

'There's nothing more to tell,' sniffed Basil. 'I, as mayor, backed their plan to buy demolition land and build a factory on it.'

'I'm already aware of that,' Bodkin said, testily. 'Did you ask him to contribute to your so called, mayor's fund before you decided to back his bid?'

'He was a generous donor. I didn't need to ask. My backing was nothing to do with how much he paid into the fund anyway. I backed him because it was the right bid.'

'Did Nelson 'donate' to the mayor's fund too?'

'Yes, but that doesn't guarantee anything.'

'Who gave you the most money?'

'I don't think I have to answer that, I–'

Bodkin took a step towards the former mayor and leaned in so that their heads were only a few inches apart. 'I think you do, in fact I'm sure of it.'

Basil took a step back. 'This is intimidation,' he said.

Bodkin straightened up and smiled thinly at Thornalley.

'I'm not sure if you're aware of this, Mr former mayor, but the council's accounts are being scrutinised by a team of accountants brought in by Mr McKenzie. They couldn't find a single reference to this, mayor's fund, although that's hardly surprising because it doesn't exist.' The inspector narrowed his eyes as he looked at the heavily sweating man. 'So, this begs the question, where did Drake's money go? You've just admitted that he handed money over.' Bodkin turned to Amy who was watching events with interest. 'Do you see the problem I have here? I can't see where the money went?'

Amy put her hand to her chin as she thought. 'Perhaps it's a magic money pot,' she said.

'Was it a magic money pot, Mr Thornalley? Or did Drake pay you in cash. Money you put into your personal bank account, possibly to pay for your children's school fees?'

'It's nothing to do with me,' Alma burst out. 'Basil saw to the workings of the fund.'

'Really?' Bodkin said, with a puzzled look on his face. 'Yet the other day, you were the one who answered every single question I asked.. You even said, "I'll deal with this" to him at one point.'

Alma's mouth opened and closed like a goldfish.

'There was nothing underhand going on,' Basil blurted. 'Nothing illegal.'

'Oh, I think there was plenty of skulduggery going on, Mr Thornalley,' Bodkin growled. 'You see, I have a nose for criminal behaviour and I can smell a great stinking pile of rottenness.' He flashed a look at Alma. 'I can smell fraud... with more than just a hint of embezzlement, in fact, my nose is so sensitive it's picking up the aroma of corruption too.' He looked back to Basil. 'That's a long time in jail, Basil and that's before we come onto the question of murder.'

'Murder! I didn't murder anyone, what the hell are you talking about?'

'You had the perfect opportunity, Basil,' Bodkin said. 'You were in the kitchen, just a few feet away from the knife that somehow ended up in Mr Kelly's chest. You had motive... He ruined the deal you had set up with Drake... I've heard Drake had a quiet word with you on the night of the murder. Did he ask for his money back? How much did he bribe you with by the way? Was it all cash or did he offer you a few shares or some another form of payback once the factory had been built?'

'It was a private conversation, it had nothing to do with—'

'Have it your way, Mr Thornalley, but I'm going to see Francis again tomorrow, and I'm going to ask him all about your involvement. The problem for you is, he could quite easily say that you asked him for a cash donation. I'm pretty sure he'll have a receipt lying around somewhere, businessmen tend to cover their backs like that. After I've spoken to him about what he was actually promised, I'll nip around to your bank and I'll ask to see the records of your accounts.' He leered at Basil. 'I can do that you know.'

Basil began to shake.

'Where did the money go, Basil?' Bodkin asked.

'Into a new personal bank account we set up. There were two signatories. Me and Alma.'

'So, both of you could withdraw cash to, how shall we put it, hand out to a worthwhile cause. Like your children's exclusive boarding school?'

'We did pay some of it into the community fund, the youth club got money, as did the scouts and guides, then there was the old folks Christmas concert, that cost money to set up.'

'How much money have you taken from local businesses since you became mayor?'

'I honestly don't know... quite a lot.'

'How much was in the legitimate community fund when you left office?'

'Around four hundred and thirty pounds.'

'Four hundred and thirty pounds! That's quite a lot of money, Mr Thornalley. How come you didn't use it for worthwhile causes? What use was it sitting in a bank account when there's so much poverty and need in the community?'

'We wanted to make a big splash, something that would put Spinton on the map.'

'What would that have been?'

'We hadn't made up our minds, but something the town would be proud of. A swimming pool or something.'

'So, you were saving up for a swimming pool. Would this have been in the town or your back garden? Did you intend to take money out of that account when you needed it too? Bodkin glowered at Basil, then turned his attention to Alma who was staring, wide-eyed at her drink as though it might be about to explode. 'As

I said, I will go to the bank and look into any accounts you might own. I will be able to see any transactions you've made between banks in case you have been squirrelling the money away out of town. Now, answer truthfully or I'll arrest you this minute. Did you use the money from your bogus mayor's fund for your own benefit?'

Basil hung his head, then nodded. 'It was just the school fees to start with. We were having a bit of a cash flow problem, so Alma had the idea about asking businesses to hand over money to be sure of getting council contracts. We had planned to pay some of it into the community fund, but the school put the fees up the following year. Then there was the mortgage. We got behind on it, so we needed a bit more.'

Alma suddenly screwed up her face. 'It's all your fault, you and your big ideas. Always robbing Peter to pay Paul. All you did was get us deeper into the mire.'

'What about you?' Basil spat. 'It was you who demanded we live the lifestyle we did. You were the one who wanted the best dresses, you couldn't bear to wear anything in public twice, you wanted the biggest parties. You had to have the smartest car, the latest gadgets. You had the bloody garden landscaped eighteen months after it had been done, just because Mrs Walker-Peters had hers designed by that up-and-coming landscape architect. You wasted thousands just to convince people we were up there with the town's elite, so don't point the finger at me.'

Amy made an O shape with her mouth as she and Bodkin exchanged glances.

'The financial investigation is on-going, Mr Thornalley,' Bodkin said when the pair had finished arguing. 'I'm sure you'll have a good explanation for everything. It does puzzle me why four hundred and thirty pounds is still sitting idle in the community account, just waiting for the new mayor to do something with it.'

'There was only about thirty pounds in there. It wasn't a well-supported fund. I paid the four hundred in when I lost my position,' Basil said. 'I was hoping for another term. I would have paid more money into the community fund over time, please, believe me.'

'And where would the money have come from; your shady little deal with Drake?'

'He said we'd all make a lot of money out of the factory build.'

'I bet,' Bodkin said, sourly. 'All those lovely, government grants. You in charge of doling it out... but Nelson put the mockers on that. He had McKenzie and his friends in government behind him, didn't he? And he had a second public amenities project in the pipeline to boot. Did you know about that, Basil?'

'Second project? No, I only ever knew about the proposed factory.'

'And boy were you planning to milk that for every penny you could get out of it.'

'No one would ever have known. I only needed one more term in office.'

Bodkin pursed his lips and shook his head slowly. 'Spinton doesn't know how lucky it is,' he said. He clapped his hands. 'Now then, back to the night of the murder. You went to make a cup of herbal tea. Did you notice anything unusual; hear anything suspicious, maybe?'

'Not until the girl screamed. Then I went to the door to see what the fuss was about and I saw... well, you know what I saw.'

'You didn't hear anyone arguing beforehand? You didn't hear something like, "you've ruined me" shouted out?'

Basil shook his head, still looking at the floor. 'No, I didn't hear anything like that.'

'I find that strange, Basil, because the incident happened right outside the kitchen door, which incidentally, was open, so, if the girl in the cloakroom heard angry words shouted out from where she was, surely you must have heard it too.'

'I'm a bit hard of hearing as it happens,' Basil said. 'You can check with my doctor.'

'Oh, I will, be sure of it,' Bodkin replied. 'Now, you told me last week that you rushed to the door when you heard the scream. Are you sticking with that story?'

'Yes, I am. It's the truth,' Basil said, meekly.

'Was there anyone else in the kitchen with you at the time of the murder, Mr Thornalley?'

Basil looked uncomfortable. 'No,' he said softly.

'Are you absolutely sure? Was Mr Drake in there with you for instance?'

Basil shook his head. 'No, there was no one.'

'You do realise that lying to a police officer while he is in the process of conducting a murder investigation won't go down well with the courts, Mr Thornalley. If you repeat what you've just told me before a judge you could well be charged with perjury.'

'Drake wasn't there,' Basil repeated.

'So, who was in there with you? We know there was someone, because Lorna Wetherby heard two sets of footsteps scurrying away from the door... And there's another thing, Lorna also states that when she looked behind her, there was no one standing in the doorway, so her evidence contradicts yours. Who is telling the truth, Basil?'

Thornalley shot a quick look at Alma from under his lids.

'All right,' she said. 'I was there, I was in the kitchen with Basil.'

'At last, we're getting somewhere,' Bodkin said, staring hard at Alma. 'Why didn't you tell the truth in the first place if you had nothing to hide?'

'We just didn't want to get involved,' Alma said. 'Surely you understand that? We had enough problems on our plate without becoming suspects in a murder investigation.'

'What were you doing there, Mrs Thornalley? Isn't Basil capable of making a cup of tea?'

'I had overheard something that newspaper chap said. He was talking to McKenzie, asking him some very in-depth questions about Basil's time in office, so I thought I'd better warn him, give him a few minutes to think up something to throw him off the scent.'

'I see, and did he think of something plausible?'

'He didn't have time to, it was only a few minutes later that we heard the woman scream.'

'So, you both went to the kitchen door?'

'Not to it, no, near enough to be able to see out, but then we crept back to where we were.'

'On your way to the kitchen, did you see anyone in the corridor?'

'Only Nelson on the telephone.'

'Could you hear what he was saying?'

'Not a lot of it, but he was very angry about something. He raised his voice... said something like, "you had better be... you better had" something like that.'

'But you still say that you didn't hear an argument outside the kitchen door only a minute or so later?'

'No, but I was busy telling Basil about the reporter. Our minds would have been elsewhere.'

'Can you remember seeing the emergency exit door when you came to the kitchen door to see what had happened? Do you know if it was open or closed?'

'I really don't know; I was too shocked by what had happened to take in anything else.'

'When did you come out of hiding?'

'When the crowd gathered around the body, we sneaked out and stood at the back.'

'Were you wearing gloves on the night, Basil?'

'Yes, we both were as it happens, why do you ask?'

'It's a question we're asking everyone. Do you have them at home?'

'Yes of... damn, no. I took them off to make the tea, I didn't want to risk spilling anything on them. My hands shake a bit when the old ulcer plays up. I put them in the pocket of my jacket.'

'Well, I assume your jacket is at home?'

'Sadly not. I took it to the dry cleaners on Main Street along with my dress shirt on the Saturday. I dropped off Alma's dress too.'

'Why did the dress need cleaning, Mrs Thornalley?'

'Some oaf at the buffet, bumped into me carrying a greasy plate of food. I cleaned it up the best I could, but there was still a slight stain. I hope it will come out all right, they use some really harsh chemicals when they clean the clothes.'

'So, you haven't picked them up yet?'

'No, I keep meaning to but there's always something else to do,' Basil said.

'Well, don't worry about finding the time,' Bodkin said. 'I'll pick them up for you tomorrow. The gloves will still have been in the pocket, I assume.'

Basil ran the back of his hand across his freely perspiring forehead. 'We should have come clean at the start; I know that now. It's just that...'

'Is there anything else we should know,' Bodkin said, as he narrowed his eyes at Basil.

The couple looked at each other again, then Basil nodded.

'Tell him,' he said quietly.

Alma clasped her glass to her chest with both hands. 'It was when I first got into the kitchen. I was giving Basil a hard time, trying to get him to come up with something. Anyway, I just happened to look away from him for a moment and I saw someone standing in the doorway, watching us.' She grimaced, then turned to Basil. 'He's not going to help us like he promised, is he?'

Basil shook his head. 'No, he won't lift a finger, tell him.'

'It was, Francis, Inspector. Francis Drake.'

CHAPTER
TWENTY-NINE

'Ooh, I love it when you turn the thumbscrews, Bodkin,' Amy said as the couple followed the Thornalleys across the lawn. 'You'd have made a wonderful inquisitor at the Tower of London in Tudor times.'

'People like those two really get to me,' Bodkin said, still with a hint of anger in his voice. 'Besides which, I'm hungry and I'm never in the best of moods when I'm hungry.'

The policeman stopped dead halfway across the lawn. 'What is it with this town and charity funds? It isn't two months since we arrested Councillor Constance De Vere for embezzling thousands from her own charity and attempting to do the same with the church's children's fund.' He shook his head and looked at the gathering of the town's elite as they stood around in small, chattering groups some twenty feet away. 'Are they all bent?'

Amy patted his arm. 'Not all of them, Bodkin. Some of them are honest.'

Bodkin rolled his head slowly from side to side. 'I suppose I'd trust Robert with my rates charges.'

'Are you going to arrest the Thornalleys for embezzlement?' Amy asked, before Bodkin could begin another rant.

'Eventually, when I have all the evidence. My main concern at the moment is Nelson's murder.' He gave Amy a grim smile. 'It's typical that we're so shorthanded when a case as tricky as this one comes up. If we had a full complement of officers, I'd have two of them crawling all over Drake and Thornalley's financial records.'

'Drake's been dragged into the frame again, hasn't he?' Amy said, thoughtfully.

'He's never been out of it, Amy,' Bodkin replied. 'He's front and centre as things stand. He's still not the only candidate though.' He nodded towards the side gate where the Thornalleys were making a quick exit. 'They're not out of the frame themselves yet.'

'And we have two men who came in white gloves and left without them,' Amy muttered.

'Whoever killed Nelson was probably wearing them... unless the killer picked the knife up with a monogrammed handkerchief or something. Kitson isn't out of this yet.'

'Do you believe them when they say they didn't hear the argument?'

'Not entirely,' Bodkin replied. 'But listening to Alma having a go at Basil just now, it is plausible.'

'And, what was that about the accountants not finding any reference to Basil's mayor's fund? Have they really finished going through the council's accounts?'

'No, they've got a long way to go yet. That was just an educated guess. I thought I'd throw it in just to see if it unnerved him or not. It seems I hit the jackpot.'

'Clever man,' Amy said, taking his arm. 'Now, let's go and find you some food before you bite someone's head off.'

. . .

'So, how did the party go? Come on fill us in, did you pick up any juicy gossip?'

Alice put Martha into her high chair and fastened down the little table at the front.

'Well,' Amy said, sitting down at Alice's big, old, oak table and shaking her head at the plate of sliced fruit cake that Alice was waving in front of her. 'At least two of the pillars of Spinton society, shop at Brigden's I can tell you that... the dresses they were wearing were on the second-hand sales rails near where I buy mine, not on the 'just in' rails. I saw both of those dresses a couple of weeks ago, but they weren't in my size, or colours. Actually, they weren't their colours either, primrose yellow doesn't work for everyone. Especially not when worn with a maroon shawl.'

'Who was it?' Miriam asked.

'The alderman's wife, Sarah Thomas was one of them. I don't really know the other one very well although her picture has been in the papers attending one do or another. I'd have put money on her shopping at London Connection. Maybe Bodkin is right and these people aren't as well off as they try to make out they are.'

Miriam looked up from her knitting pattern.

'What was it my old dad used to say when he was alive...? All fur coat and no drawers, something like that.'

'Miriam!' Amy said, laughing along with Alice.

'Did Bodkin get to grill the McKenzies? Is he still suspicious of them?' Alice asked.

'No, he knows they're decent people. I really like them, Shirley especially. She kept feeding me glasses of iced Pimm's. I was quite tiddly by the time we left. Oh, Alice, you've got to try one when we go to the Milton again. They're gorgeous, especially on a hot day.'

'Pimm's? Never heard of it,' Alice said.

'It's actually Pimm's number one,' Amy said. 'It comes in a

bowl with cucumber, lemons, strawberries, anything that's available by the looks of it. It's like a dessert in a glass.'

Miriam, Alice's long-time friend and housekeeper, looked up from her knitting again. 'My sister used to make them when she worked at Claridge's in London. She said they were very popular.'

'You know what?' Amy said. 'We three ought to have a night out. Hit the cocktail bars. Miriam can ask her sister which drinks we ought to try out.'

'We'd need to save up for quite a while if the Milton's prices are anything to go by,' Miriam replied. She was quiet for a moment, then she said. 'My John bought me a cocktail when we had that weekend together on the coast. I had a Singapore Sling; it's made with gin, cherry brandy and some other stuff. I was sick as a dog after drinking it.' Miriam was seeing a local builder who wasn't quite as keen on the idea of marriage as she was.

'We could go to the Café Blanc,' Alice said. 'It's posh, but not anywhere near as pricey as the Milton. Godfrey took me, it's where I had my first Martini.' Godfrey was a lawyer and Alice's married lover.

'Martina,' Amy corrected her. 'Don't try to be all knowledgeable now, Missy. They're always going to be Martinas. We decided that a long time ago.'

'You decided,' Alice said with a short laugh. 'You'd get away with ordering one, even at a posh bar. You have an air of innocence about you. I wanted the earth to swallow me up when I did it.'

'Café Blanc it is then,' Amy stuck up her thumb. 'Now we just need some rich men to escort us.'

On Monday morning, Amy had an hour's lie in and arrived at the breakfast table just as Mrs Rowlings was clearing the plates that she and Amy's dad had used for their breakfast.

'What do you fancy, Amy. A fry up? You'll need something substantial inside you today if you're going to be walking around the Haxley estate.'

'Eggs and bacon would be nice, if there's enough left,' Amy replied, reaching for the teapot.

'Leave that, it's stewed, I'll make a fresh one, dear.'

'It's very kind of you to help out with the poverty group on your day off, Amy. I hope it won't be too upsetting for you when you see the conditions some of those poor people have to live in,' James Rowlings said as he picked up his morning paper. He held up the front page. 'I see the Post's chief reporter is having a go at the police again.'

Amy read the block headline. 'Murder Squad Reduced to Skeleton Crew!' She shook her head and looked puzzled. 'Where does he get his information from? He has to have a contact inside the police force.'

'So, it's true then is it?'

Amy nodded and smiled up at her mother as she placed the teapot and a toast rack on the table.

'There are only two CID officers at the station at the moment and one of them is Mr Grayson, the chief superintendent. Nice as he is, he doesn't pitch in when it comes to the investigation. Mind you, he must be feeling the pressure too. I mean, who's looking after the common or garden burglaries, assaults and shoplifting offences? Someone has to do it?'

'So, poor Bodkin is on his own for this investigation,' Amy's mother said as she carried in a plate of eggs and bacon.

'Not really, Mum,' Amy replied as she cut a small piece from one of the rashers of bacon and broke the egg yolk with it. 'I'm helping too.'

. . .

Amy met the church team on the outer edge of the Haxley estate, the network of narrow streets built by the Victorians to house the influx of workers that arrived in the early eighteen-fifties to take up jobs at the newly built iron works, and the small, but plentiful, individually-owned coal mines that were dotted about around the area. There were four hundred, two-up two-down terraced houses in all and the vast majority were in a poor state of repair. Rats and mice were a common problem. They scurried around in plain sight, even in the daytime. The council was forced into action when the rat problem spread to the nicer parts of the town. A hundred or so houses in the worst affected part of the estate were demolished and the rat catchers laid down poison bait on the waste ground, or sat on piles of broken bricks, shooting at them with air rifles.

The worst part of the estate was in the Ebenezer, Trafalgar and Albert Street areas. Those particular streets had been built over the top of some recently vacated, mine workings and the houses had suffered the effects of subsidence, many of the structures left with twisted roof beams, cracks in the brickwork and rising damp. All of the houses were still occupied, but only Ebenezer Street, which was closest to the area of wasteland where the new factory was to be built, had been earmarked for demolition. With the death of Nelson, that issue seemed to have been taken off the agenda and the residents of the crumbling, rat infested line of terraced houses, heaved a collective sigh of relief.

'We're just concentrating on Ebenezer today,' Benjamin Carmichael, the group's leader said as he opened the back door of his nineteen-thirty model, blue-painted, Morris Light Van.

The five volunteers stepped forward one at a time and loaded the baskets they had brought with them with loaves of bread, packets of tea, sugar, biscuits, and a few tins of canned food.

'There's no milk as it's bank holiday. The bread was baked on Saturday but it's still edible. If anyone requires baby formula or a few nappies, then you'll have to come back to the van for them. Only give out a couple of nappies at a time. We're really running short. They're in the front seat if anyone needs them. There are also a few packs of Harrington's mutton-cloth rolls. If anyone asks why you're giving them soft, disposable, car polishing cloths, explain that they are to be used to line the nappies with. There are also a few knitted baby clothes, sized from new born to eighteen months for the more desperate mothers.' Benjamin took a deep breath. 'Unfortunately, and this is going to disappoint many of the residents, there are no cigarettes this week. I know this will cause a bit of angst but I haven't been able to get hold of any this time around.'

When everyone had loaded up their wicker baskets, Benjamin gathered them all together, then blessed the food before saying a short prayer, asking God to protect the poor and needy.

'Jean,' he said, when he had finished the prayer. 'Can you start at the top end, ignore numbers twenty-one, eighteen and seventeen. The man living at twenty-one doesn't need charity, he owns the entire row of houses, and you'll only get abuse from the men in the other two. They'll still be suffering from the after effects of last night's drink. June and Margaret, start at fifteen and work towards me. I'll be working up from number ten. Marylin, start at number five, Amy, as it's your first time with us, I'm starting you at number two, so you'll only have three houses to cover.' Benjamin held up a key, then looked around suspiciously in case he was being watched.

'I'm putting the back door key under rear-left tyre. Please make sure you aren't being spied upon when you retrieve it to refill your baskets. I'd leave the door open but to be honest, and I hate to tar every resident with the same brush, if I did, the van would be emptied withing five minutes if it hadn't been driven away, that is.'

Amy watched as Benjamin carefully slid the key under the

back tyre, then he knelt and said a short prayer, asking God to keep it safe from prying eyes.

Unlike the other streets in the area, there was only one row of tightly packed houses on Ebenezer Street. On the other side of the road was a high wall, behind which the railway track ran.

Amy made for the bottom of the street, smiling at a queue of children as they lined up for their turn at Hop Scotch. Just beyond them, three girls were engaged in a skipping game. 'Charlie Chaplin went to France to teach the ladies how to dance,' the two non-skippers chanted while a young girl of about ten, did her best to stop the whirling length of clothesline getting tangled up with her dirty-looking boots.

Between every set of four houses ran a narrow alley which allowed residents and visitors access to the rear of the properties. Amy walked along the alleyway, four houses up from the final dwelling on the street and found herself on a narrow strip of cobblestones that marked the boundary between the back of Ebenezer and the rear of the Trafalgar Street properties.

She pushed at a roughly made, wooden gate at what looked to be the second house along. It opened into a cobbled courtyard that hosted a shared outdoor lavatory. On the right-hand side of the grimy courtyard, standing balanced on one leg, with her hands stretched above her head, attempting to hang a wet shirt on the clothes line, was a stick-thin girl of about seven or eight years of age. Her long legs appeared swollen, her short, dark hair looked dry and brittle. The skin on her forearms was red and blotchy and she had an angry-looking rash on her right thigh. The dress she was wearing, whilst clean, was several sizes too small and had obviously been mended several times. She looked across at Amy as she heard the gate creak. When she smiled, Amy could see that her gums were a deep red colour and she had several missing teeth.

'Hello,' Amy said. 'Let me help you with that.' She put her basket down, took a wooden clothes peg from the faded bag that was hooked over the line, and pinned one side of the shirt's bottom hem to the line, then, taking the peg from the girl's hand she repeated the process on the opposite side. 'There,' she said. 'That ought to dry quickly today.'

The girl nodded and looked hungrily at the basket.

'Is there anything to eat in there?' she asked.

Amy picked it up, broke off a piece of bread and passed it to the young girl.

'I'm Amy,' she said. 'What's your name?'

'I'm Beth,' the youngster replied.

'I bet it's nice having a day off school,' Amy said.

The girl shrugged. 'I don't go very often; I have to help Mum with the washing.'

'Is mum inside?' Amy asked as the girl stuffed all of the bread in her mouth, wincing as she began to chew furiously at it.

She pointed along the courtyard to the open back door of number one.

'Can you get her for me?' Amy said as she walked slowly across the cobbles. She had just reached the rear end of the house when the door of number two opened and a woman wearing a faded and heavily repaired, check-patterned, pinafore, stepped out into the yard. Amy put her at about forty, but her whitening hair made her look much older.

'Don't get too close to that one,' she said pointing at the young girl's back as she skipped up the steps to her back door. 'They reckon she's got the scurvy,' she hissed. 'Among other things,' she added, eyeing up Amy's basket. 'Is that for me?' she asked.

'I'm not sure,' Amy said. 'I'm supposed to start at number two but it looks like that little girl could do with some feeding up.'

'They're not allowed church handouts,' the woman replied. 'They're heathens... according to Ada, anyway.'

Amy wondered what the family had done to warrant her church depriving a child of charity. It must have been something serious.

She was just about to ask the question when a thin, but pretty woman of about thirty came to the door of number one. Her dark hair was plastered to her head with sweat, she wore a grey, knee length dress under a soggy, but clean-looking pinafore. She raised a blotchy red arm and pointed a long, thin finger at her neighbour.

'Don't you go telling your lies, Freda Simkin. If the lady wants to know why we're not on the church's needy list, I'll explain myself. At least she'll get the truth that way.'

Amy smiled at Freda, 'I'll be with you in a few minutes. There's lots more food on the van, you'll get your share of it.'

'Just watch her,' Freda said, giving the young mother a dirty look. 'She'll have everything out of that basket before you could blink an eyelid.'

Freda walked quickly back into her kitchen and slammed the flaking, green-painted door behind her.

'Blimey!' Amy said as she turned back to the young woman. 'She's got it in for you, hasn't she?'

'It's charity day,' she replied. 'Her Colin's off work today for the bank holiday, she'll have run out of tea and he'll be giving her grief about it. She's not usually that nasty, especially when she wants me to iron one of his shirts in a hurry so he can go to the pub looking half-decent.'

'I'm Amy Rowlings,' Amy said. 'Can I come in? This is my first day on the job, I'd like to know why my church says a hungry child should be refused food.'

'I'm Karen Hamilton and I'm not going to pray, before you start with the God bothering,' the woman said giving Amy a stern look.

'I wouldn't ask you to,' Amy said. 'If you put the kettle on, we can have a chat.'

'There's little point,' the woman said. 'There's no tea in this house either.'

Amy fished about under the muslin cloth that covered her basket and pulled out a packet of Brook Bond Dividend tea and held it up. 'There is now,' she said.

CHAPTER

THIRTY

AMY FOLLOWED KAREN UP THE THREE BACK STEPS AND INTO A DINGY room, lit by an electric light bulb that hung on a dangerous-looking single wire from the ceiling. The room was stiflingly hot. On the back wall was a deep white sink that was filled with murky water. At the side of it was a gas copper boiler which pumped copious amounts of steam into the already clammy atmosphere.

At the side of the copper was a long, two-inch thick, wooden trestle on which sat a knotted, white sheet. Next to that, and opposite the door, was a battered, cast-iron mangle, its wooden rollers set to the narrowest of gaps. On the floor below, was a galvanised metal bucket that was half full of water.

The walls were once painted some dark shade of green but most of the paint had flaked away leaving black patches of mould covering much of the back wall. Water dripped from the ceiling onto the clay-tiles that had been laid on top of a compacted earthen floor. Amy waved her hand in front of her face; she was finding it difficult to breath in the moisture-laden air.

Karen pushed open a thick, timber door and stepped into the living area. The walls in this room weren't quite as mould-ridden as the scullery but there were still large patches of damp on every wall in the room, including the one that contained the built in, cast-iron, open range. On the right-hand side of the range was a black painted oven, a fire was burning in the grate, despite the heat of the day. On top of the oven was a large metal pot. Inside was the remains of a thin stew. There was a solid, well-scrubbed, oak table sitting on the clay tiled floor in the centre of the room with two, rickety-looking chairs pushed underneath. In the centre of the table was a hexagonal shaped plate on which sat a very stale-looking heel of bread. Cut into the grimy, far side wall was a door which presumably led upstairs. Large lumps of plaster had fallen away from the wall, leaving the bare bricks underneath, on show.

Karen picked up the scorched-black, bone handled kettle from the table and carried it through to the scullery to fill it at the sink. When she returned, she set it on the iron grill that sat just above the fire.

Amy passed the quarter-pound packet of loose tea to Karen and she tipped three spoonsful of the black leaves into a cream teapot that had the picture of a coaching inn on the side, the lid had been painted to look like a roof.

'That really is lovely,' Amy said, admiring the artwork.

'It's the only decent thing in the house,' Karen said. 'It belonged to my mother-in-law. It was left to my husband when she died.'

'Is your husband at work?' Amy asked.

'He's no longer with us,' Karen said. She quickly changed the subject. 'You're going to be in trouble when they find out you gave us the tea,' she said. 'Especially as I haven't prayed for it.'

'As I said, I'm not going to ask you to pray, and...' Amy emptied the contents of the basket onto the table. 'You won't have to pray for that little lot either. I'm sorry there's no milk but it had gone off in the heat over the weekend.'

'We're used to having it without milk, aren't we. Beth?' Karen said, looking at her daughter.

'I like it better with it,' Beth replied.

'You're going to get sugar in it today too,' Amy said, pointing to the large blue and white printed bag. 'There's two pounds of it in there.'

Karen walked to a tallboy on the wall opposite the fireplace and brought out three dainty, china cups and saucers, bearing a pattern that matched the teapot.

'We only use these when we have guests,' she said, proudly. 'So, they don't get used much.'

'Is there anywhere I can get some milk,' Amy said suddenly. 'I do prefer my tea with a dash of it.'

'Gideon's shop is just around the corner on Trafalgar,' Karen said. 'But don't tell him you want it for me or he'll probably send you away with a flea in your ear.'

'Why?' Amy looked puzzled.

'Because I owe him money. I'm behind on my slate and he won't let me have anything until I've paid most of it off.'

'How much do you owe... if you don't mind me asking?'

'Fifteen and six,' Karen said. 'I really didn't intend to let it get to that state of affairs but I had a bad spell in the winter and couldn't get the washing dry, so I got behind with the washing, and my slate.'

'Is that what you do, then,' Amy said. 'Other people's laundry?'

'There's no shame in it,' Karen said.

'Oh, I'm sorry, I didn't mean to offend you. Of course, there's no shame in it. It must be really hard work though.'

'I do fourteen hours a day in the summer, seven days a week. We have to hang the washing all around the house to get it to dry when the weather is bad. Beth should be at school but I've had to keep her away on Mondays and Tuesdays to help me get the sheets through the mangle, I can't manage them on my own. I can just about get away with it for the rest of the week as I do clothes on Wednesdays and Thursdays, ironing in the evenings and all of Friday if I get a lot in.' She pointed to the corner of the room where six hessian sacks were piled up. 'That's the rest of the week's work, but there'll be extra thrown in too.'

'I don't know how you do it,' Amy said.

'Nor do I at times, but I have to. The rent on this dump is ten shillings a week and the most I've ever earned is seventeen and six. I always make sure I pay the rent; we go without a lot to make sure I do. I'm not like some of them around here, who will pay the rent man or the tallyman 'in kind'. I'd rather we starve.'

Amy shuddered. 'Do these men accept... that sort of payment in lieu of the rent?'

'Goodness me no, but they'll let you off with a week's payment now and then, you still have to pay it back though. Some women owe two or three pounds in back rent. The tallyman has them over a barrel, so to speak.'

Amy shook her head. 'Do the landlords know this is going on? I assume the rent man works for a landlord?'

'Mine doesn't, not now at least. The houses on this street were bought out a few months ago and the new landlord collects himself.' She paused. 'He's a decent man, at least he's never asked me for favours, unlike the rent collector we had before the sale. He was disgusting.'

'Will the shop be open on a bank holiday?' Amy asked, suddenly remembering she had offered to get milk.

'Gideon never closes. He even opens on Christmas Day,' Karen replied.

'Okay, Beth, would you like to come with me,' Amy said as she picked up her empty basket. 'You can show me the way.'

Beth nodded, but looked at her mother, suddenly unsure of herself.

'Go with Amy,' Karen said. 'But wait outside the shop, don't let Gideon see you or he might be a bit off with her and we won't get the milk then.'

Gideon's One Stop Shop was only a three-minute walk away. To get to it, Beth led Amy across the cobbled space at the back of her house and along a narrow alley that brought them out directly opposite the shop on Trafalgar Street.

Outside, on the pavement lay a vast assortment of goods, everything from crates of green beans to small sacks of coal. In a crate just by the door were two, string mesh bags with six oranges in each one.

'You'd better wait out here, stand in the doorway where I can keep my eye on you,' Amy said to Beth before pushing at the half glass door of the shop.

The shopkeeper was a small-framed man of no more than five-feet-six in height. He had narrow shoulders, a stubby nose and dark brown, receding hair. He wore a spotless, white apron over dark shirt and brown trousers.

'Good afternoon,' he said, looking around Amy to the door where Beth's face was pressed up against the glass.

'Could I have a pint of sterilised milk, a tin of evaporated, and a pound of butter, please?'

Gideon took a long-necked bottle from the shelf behind him, then reached up and picked up a can of Libby's evaporated milk, after handing them to Amy he knelt on the floor and took a pack of Isaly's butter from a shelf under the counter.

'Anything else?'

'Yes, what veg do you have?'

'We have some spring greens, beans, some early season carrots, new potatoes.'

'I'll have a couple of pounds of spuds, and a pound each of the rest please,' Amy replied. 'Oh, and how much are the oranges? I wasn't expecting to see those.'

'They're a shilling a bag, which is why they're still sitting out there,' Gideon said. 'I made a big mistake when I bought them. I should have known that my customers wouldn't buy oranges. Most of them think fruit is bad for the kids, even the ones that can afford it.'

'I'll have a bag... oh, and half a dozen apples.'

'Hello, young Beth,' Gideon said as he opened the door. 'Why don't you come and wait inside?'

'Mum said I can't come in without her,' Beth replied.

'Well, you had better do as your mum tells you,' the shop-keeper said as he began to stuff handfuls of veg into a cardboard box.

'Is she with you?' he said, after weighing the veg on his white scales.

'Yes, she showed me the way to your shop.'

'Is this lot for Karen?' Gideon asked, as he tipped the contents of the box into Amy's basket.

'Yes,' Amy admitted. 'She's got nothing but a bowl or two of thin stew to last her the week. I thought I'd help her out. I'm with the church poverty group. We're in the area today.'

'It's very kind of you, Miss,' Gideon said. 'I've done all I can to help her but there are limits as to how much of a slate I can allow her to run up. It's not fair on the other customers. I've let her have an extra five bob on top of what I normally allow.'

'She wants to pay it off, but it's so hard for her. I honestly don't know how they get by. She's got her hands in the sink for fourteen hours a day. Beth never gets any treats and she needs medicine for that rash of hers.'

'There are plenty around here in the same boat,' Gideon said. 'I wish I could help, but...' he shrugged his shoulders. 'She's suffered a lot in the last few years, what with her younger child and her husband going the way they did.'

'What happened?' Amy asked.

'It's up to her whether she wants to talk about that,' Gideon said. Stuffing his hand into a heavy glass jar, he pulled out a sugar-coated pineapple cube and popped it into his mouth.

'I'll have two quarters of those as well,' Amy said. 'One bag for Beth and one for my dad.'

Gideon weighed out the sweets, then dropped an extra one into each bag as Amy looked around the shop. On the counter was a silver ham slicer with the remnants of the ham sitting at the back of the machine.

'I don't suppose you've got a ham bone I could have?'

Gideon looked at the machine, then cut off the last few slices before picking up the ham bone. He wrapped it in newspaper then passed it over the counter to Amy.

'That will help thicken the stew,' he said.

'How much does that come to?'

'Three shillings and sevenpence,' Gideon said. 'The ham bone is on me.'

Amy pulled the two half-crowns that Bodkin had sneakily slipped into the Brigden's bag and passed them to Gideon.

'Tell Karen I hope she has better luck soon,' he said as he handed over the change. He thought for a moment. 'Look, I'll tell you what. If Karen will do my washing every week, I'll freeze her old slate and she can pay it off that way. At two bob a week she'll have it cleared inside a couple of months. That way, I can set her up with a new slate and she'll be able to afford to get a few items in every week with the money she makes without getting too deep in debt.'

Amy held out her hand, Gideon took it gently and shook it.

'Thanks so much, I'm sure that will help her a lot,' she replied with a soft smile. She turned away and began to make her way to the door.

'Oh, wait a minute,' Gideon said as he turned back to the shelves. Lifting up a tall glass jar he pulled out a striped lollipop.

'For Beth,' he said, with a wink.

'That's from Gideon,' Amy said as she passed the lollipop to Beth. 'Don't eat it just yet though I want you to have something else first. She untied the string at the top of the bag of oranges and pulled one out. 'Have this first,' she said, handing the orange to Beth.

Beth looked at it, wondering what it was. She lifted it to her mouth and tried to bite it.

'Whoa,' Amy said, holding the girl's wrist. 'Haven't you ever had an orange before?'

Beth shook her head.

'You have to peel the skin off,' Amy said. 'Pass it here and I'll show you how.'

Amy took the orange, dug her nails into the fruit, then began to pull the peel away. When she had completed the task, she pulled one of the segments away and held it out to Beth.

'It breaks into little pieces,' she said. 'Open wide.'

Beth opened up and Amy popped the orange segment into the child's mouth. The girl bit into it, then opened her eyes wide.

'It's sweet,' she said.

'It's good for you too.' She pointed to the string bag. 'There's another five in there, that's one a day for the rest of the week.'

Karen was just pouring boiling water into the teapot when Amy and Beth returned. The youngster proudly holding her oval-shaped lollipop.

'I've had an orange thingy,' she said to Karen as she skipped into the living room.

Amy put the basket on the counter, took out the bottle of sterilised milk and passed it to Karen.

'I got you a few bits, I hope you don't mind,' Amy said, nodding to the basket.

'I won't say I'm not grateful. Thank you so much,' Karen said, holding up the ham bone. She took a long sniff at it. 'That's going straight into the pot,' she said.

As Beth skipped around the room, taking occasional licks at her lollipop, Amy and Karen sat down at the table and sipped at their tea.

'Gideon sent you a message,' Amy said, then explained what the shopkeeper had proposed.

'He's a good man,' the young mother said, 'I hate it when I can't pay him anything off my slate. I know it's a bigger one than I should have had.'

'This is a great way to get out of debt,' Amy said. 'Do you think you can manage the extra work?'

'I'll make sure his is a priority,' Karen said. 'I'll nip in to say thank you tomorrow.'

'He was telling me that you've had a hard time of it,' Amy said. 'He wouldn't say what happened, just that he felt so sorry for you.'

Karen's eyes misted over.

'When I said my husband... Jimmy, was no longer around. I meant he's dead.'

'Oh my goodness,' Amy said. 'He must have been very young.'

'It was four years ago; he was only twenty-eight.'

Amy kept quiet, waiting for Karen to continue her story.

'A big hole appeared in the roof after a snow storm,' Karen said. 'Jimmy told the landlord about it but he wouldn't do anything. We could see the stars from our bedroom at night, so

Jimmy climbed up on the roof to have a go at fixing it, but the wind got up and he fell off. He landed on the cobbles in the yard.' Tears began to run down her cheeks. Amy hurried around the table to comfort her.

Karen sniffed and wiped her eyes with the back of her hand.

'I can't say we were comfortably off, but Jimmy was working and we were just about managing. I did a bit of laundry for some extra cash, but Jimmy didn't like that. He didn't feel like he was the man of the house if I had to work.' Karen picked up her cup and stared into it as though she was studying the tea leaves. 'A fortnight later, my baby, Anna, caught scarlet fever and died within a week. Honestly Amy, if it hadn't been for the fact that I still needed to care for Beth, I'd have done everything I could to join them, in heaven or wherever it is you go.'

Amy squeezed Karen's hand and wiped away a tear from her own eyes, thinking how easy her own life had been in comparison.

'So, that's why we find ourselves in these dire circumstances,' Karen said. 'And I honestly can't see a way out. Beth should be in school five days a week but I can't do without her when the bedding comes in on a Monday morning. It takes two days to clear that. I can't pull heavy sheets through the mangle on my own. Beth will sometimes miss Wednesdays too if I get extra work in.'

'What have the school said?' Amy asked.

'Mrs Silverstein is a very understanding woman, thank goodness. She gives Beth stuff to bring home and work on over the weekend. I'm not quite as pushed then, so I can spare an hour to help her with it.'

'Can't the welfare people do anything? There is a child suffering after all.'

'I'm going nowhere near them, and I really hope they don't come anywhere near me.' She poured tea into her cup, then refilled Amy's before adding a spoon of sugar and a dash of milk. 'Ooh,' she said, smacking her lips. 'I can't tell you how good it is to have milk in my tea, it's been weeks.'

Amy smiled. 'Why don't you want the welfare people to become involved, Karen? I'm sure they could help you.'

'Last summer,' Karen began, 'Jane Barker, who lived at number seven, became a single mother after her husband ran off with... well, it doesn't matter who he ran off with... anyway, she was left in the same predicament as me, only she had two young girls to look after. She managed to get a job in the pit canteen but it was only ten hours a week, and it didn't pay nearly enough... so she went on the game. Not in a serious way, just a couple of nights a week, Friday and Saturday, she used to hang out with the girls who stand outside the station. That helped a bit and she was managing to get by, but then some nosey so and so... I have a good idea who it was, reported her to the welfare. When they came around and saw the conditions the family were living under, they took the kids away. Jane was devasted. She couldn't afford a fancy lawyer, but she went to the court to plead her case. The magistrate turned her appeal down flat and the kids were sent to a home down in Maidstone. Jane took it badly and began to drink heavily, then one night, she scaled the wall at the other side of the street and chucked herself under the London express.' She banged the table in anger. 'I know it's wrong to take your own life, it's a cardinal sin and all that, but, honestly, if the welfare people ever take Beth away from me, I'll do the same.'

'Oh my goodness, the poor woman,' Amy said as tears filled her eyes again. 'Honestly, Karen, most people in this town, even the less well-off ones, have no idea how the families on this estate live.'

'The businessmen certainly don't, they just look to make money out of our suffering.'

They were silent for a few minutes, then Amy went back to her seat on the opposite side of the table.

'I still don't understand why the church won't help.'

'It's my own fault. That Ada Strong came around with the food basket a few months ago. I was in a bit of a state as Beth had fallen ill and I couldn't afford the five shillings to get the doctor. Anyway, Ada, as usual, wouldn't take the food out of the basket until I had joined her in a prayer. I was in no mood to thank God for anything so she had a right go at me, calling me a heathen who didn't deserve the effort she put in. She said the authorities should bring the workhouse back. Well, that was it, I laid into her. I asked her what sort of God would leave a young family to starve for half the week, what sort of God takes a young husband away from his family in such a terrible way. What sort of God would allow such a sweet little baby to die in my arms because, yet again, I didn't have the money for the doctor.' Karen thumped the table again and glared across at Amy. 'What sort of loving God allows all that to happen?'

Amy clasped her hands together. 'I don't have the answer,' she said softly. 'I wish I could tell you why. I doubt even the vicar could, he'd just go on about God moving in mysterious ways.' She paused and reached across to take Karen's hand. 'I'll bring Benjamin in to have a word with you. I'm sure the decision to bar you from the food parcels will be overturned when he hears what you've been through.'

'I'm still not going to pray for it,' Karen replied with a cheeky grin.

The two young women sat silently for a few more minutes, then Amy said. 'Beth needs to see a doctor. The lady next door said she has scurvy and other contagious things; how does she know about that?'

'I stupidly told her,' Karen said. 'I took Beth to the Free Hospital a few weeks ago. They checked her out, told me she had... oh I can't even pronounce the disease, it's the thing that causes the rash she has, but she also has scurvy to go with it. The doctor said give her vitamin C, you get that by eating lots of citrus fruit, but I can't afford to buy it, and Gideon didn't sell it anyway. He said the wholesaler charged too much and he didn't think his customers could ever afford to pay the prices he'd have to ask.'

'I have a feeling he got the oranges in for Beth,' Amy said. 'He won't admit it of course, but he knew when he bought them that his customers would just leave them to rot.'

'I wouldn't put it past him,' Karen said with weak smile. She got up from the table and went to the drawer of the tallboy. When she came back, she had a white sheet of paper in her hand with some illegible scrawl written on it.

'They gave her a prescription at the Free. I've been trying to save up to get it filled ever since, but there are four different medications and she'll have to take them all for at least a month. The lady pharmacist in town said it would cost six shillings if she had every item listed on the script.' Karen hung her head and the tears flowed again. 'I've only managed to save half of it so far. We have to pay the rent and eat out of what I earn.'

Amy picked up the prescription and tried to read it but couldn't make head nor tail of what had been written. Suddenly, she had a thought.

'Karen, can I take this with me for a day or so. There are one or two people I know who might be able to help.'

'Not the welfare,' Karen said, sharply.

'No... not the welfare. The thing is, the church used to have a charity fund for people like you and Beth. It was closed down when one of the councillors tried to embezzle money from it. I'll ask the vicar if he's started it up again. A young, troubled girl I know called Violet, had her treatment paid for by the fund... sadly she's been moved away now. And, the new mayor, Mr McKenzie and his wife want to set up something to help women and children living in poverty. I think this,' she held up the prescription, 'could be just the thing to get them started.'

'Don't lose it, please, Amy. I'll have the money myself in a few weeks.'

Just then, there was a knock on the open living room door and Benjamin stuck his head into the room.

'Amy, we were getting worried about you. Is everything all right?'

'Karen,' Amy said, getting to her feet. 'This is Benjamin, he runs the food aid program.' She turned to her charity team mate. 'Benjamin, this is Karen and this,' she pointed across the room to where Beth was licking the last sticky bits from the lolly stick, 'is Beth. I think you should hear what they have to tell you.'

THIRTY-ONE

'I HEAR SOMEONE HAS BEEN HOBNOBBING WITH THE TOFFEE NOSES AT A garden party this weekend,' Big Nose Beryl said in her annoyingly high-pitched attempt at a posh voice.

Amy ignored her and continued to make a turban out of a clean headscarf.

'She thinks she's all hoity toity now she's working in that posh shop. Too good for the likes of us.'

'I've always been too good for the likes of you, Beryl,' Amy said to much laughter.

Beryl scowled. 'You're only a Mill girl, the same as me,' she snapped. 'I've had my moments with the upper crust you know. You're nothing special.'

'I bet the crust was stale too,' Carol called out getting even more laughs.

Beryl plonked herself down on her part of the bench, took off her shoes and pulled on a pair of worn, pink slippers. 'All right, just tell us, why were you there?'

'I was there because I was invited by the mayor's wife, Shirley McKenzie, if you must know, Beryl. She came into the shop on Thursday and we got chatting.'

'Oh, we got chatting,' Beryl mimicked. 'What did you two have to chat about? The width of a seam in a Handsley's nightie.'

This time it was Beryl's turn to get a laugh.

'We chatted about fashion if you want to know, then we went for a cup of tea at the Sunshine café. We got along so well that she invited me to her garden party. She's really nice, very friendly, I like her a lot. She said she'd like to meet me and Alice at the Milton the next time we go in. Ferris has a regular singing spot, starting next month.'

'You're so full of yourself aren't you. Who cares who you're going to be supping posh wine with next month?'

'You for a start, Beryl, you'll be the first to ask about it. And it won't be posh wine we'll be drinking anyway, it will be Pimm's number one... with ice.'

After lunch, Amy was once again summoned to the office where she was asked to work on Wednesday morning at London Connection.

'Two of the ladies you assisted are coming in for their final fitting, Miss Rowlings, and they have asked for you to be there when they try their dresses on for what will hopefully be the final time before they pay and have the items delivered.' Georgina Handsley pursed her lips. 'You are very highly thought of, it seems, Amy. I believe you turned down the offer to work at the shop full time.'

'I did, Miss Handsley. I was flattered to be asked but I value my Saturdays off too much. The free Wednesday afternoons would be lovely of course, but I have my little rituals on Saturday and I wouldn't be able to carry them out on any other day of the week.'

'I can't say I'm too displeased, Amy,' Georgina said, patting her on the arm. 'We really would miss your experience on the shop floor.'

'So, you have another Wednesday afternoon off, you lucky thing,' Mrs Rowlings said when Amy broke the news after work. 'Mind you, no one can say you don't deserve it, you work hard enough.'

Amy gave her mother a hug and went through to the bathroom to wash her hands and face before tea.

'Oh, Alice left a message when she dropped off the fresh eggs. Bodkin rang. He said something about speaking to Helen Kelly again and asked if you could spare an hour tonight.'

Amy walked back into the kitchen, wiping her hands on a towel.

'Did he say what time?'

'Alice said, around seven. Bodkin will pick you up.'

Amy almost hugged herself. 'Ooh this is exciting news. I wonder what Bodkin has discovered.'

Bodkin arrived at seven on the dot. Amy hurried to the front door when she heard him knock.

'What's all this about, Bodkin?' she asked. 'Have you found some new evidence? We only spoke to Helen on Saturday.'

'Evidence? No, but I have been thinking about something that was puzzling me, and I want to have a chat to Helen's housemaid, Clara, so I thought I'd kill two birds with one stone. You are invited because she's bereaved still and I wouldn't want to go against Grayson's orders. He was the one who said you should be there when I question her, after all.'

Amy grabbed her jacket from the peg, shouted, 'see you later' to her parents, then hurried out of the front door, slamming it shut behind her.

Bodkin held the passenger side door open for her before walking steadily around the front of the car to the driver's side.

'You're such a gentleman, Bodkin,' Amy said as he clambered into the old Morris.

'There are still a few of us around,' he said with a grin.

Amy half turned in her seat and rubbed her hands together. 'So, what's the thing that's been puzzling you, Bodkin? I'm amazed it's just one thing if I'm honest. This case seems full of riddles. I've been thinking it all through too, but it has more holes than a Swiss cheese.'

'The woman in the coat,' Bodkin replied.

'Woman in the coat?' Amy frowned at the policeman.

'The woman in the fur coat, the one who old Pervis mentioned. The lady who hurries across the park alone, at night.'

'Ah, *that* woman, what about her?'

'I had a walk down the side of the library and up that path at the back of the big houses today. Have you ever been up there?'

'No, not all the way up, it used to be too overgrown when me and Alice explored it. Too many stinging nettles.'

'It's been cleaned up since then, thankfully, but if you were to take a walk up there now, do you know where you'd end up?'

Amy shrugged.

'The path ends at an impenetrable hawthorn hedge, but the last back gate you see before you reach that hedge, belongs to Hillcrest. The home of Mrs Helen Kelly.'

THIRTY-TWO

'Just think, I could be doing that soon,' Amy said, watching Bodkin's movements with interest as he started the car, slipped it into gear, then pulled slowly away from the kerb.

Bodkin flashed her a quick glance before looking ahead again as he approached the junction with the Gillingham Road.

'You might find Alice's truck a little heavier to steer than a little car like this,' Bodkin replied, straightening up after taking the corner.

'Alice manages,' Amy said, 'though I might leave it until the Mill closes for Factory Fortnight in the last week of July. I could be driving on my own by the time I go back to work in August.'

'I've always found it strange that factories do that, but they all seem to, especially in the clothing industry.'

'It gives them chance to do a deep clean and get all the maintenance done,' Amy replied. 'Mum said they used to do it when she worked at the Benson's factory, and that was before I was born.'

Bodkin turned right onto Middle Street, then changed gear as he pulled out to pass a stationary car, parked just outside the police station.

'Don't forget to put some of Alice's overalls on if you're going to jump into that old truck. The front seats are covered in years' worth of animal droppings.'

'I'll put a towel down,' Amy said. 'I wouldn't be seen dead in overalls.'

At Hillcrest, Bodkin parked the car and turned towards Amy as he shut off the engine. 'Amy... this evening, if Mrs Kelly starts... I mean, if Mrs Kelly...'

'If she starts flirting with you again?' Amy suggested.

'Yeah, could you let me know somehow? Tip me the wink, wave your hand, just let me know when she's doing it.'

Amy shook her head. 'I'll try, Bodkin but I doubt you'll see it, even then.'

Amy sighed as the policeman once again stopped on the driveway to admire the Kelly's car. 'Ask Helen if she'll sell it to you, Bodkin,' she said as she walked up to the front porch on her own.

'I couldn't afford this on a chief constable's pay,' Bodkin said, sadly. 'It doesn't hurt to dream though.'

Amy looked heavenwards and then pushed the white bell push. The door was opened by a young girl wearing a knee length black dress and a white apron. Her dark blonde hair was tied back and she wore a black headband that held a starched, pleated, piece of linen in place above her forehead.

'Oh,' she said, 'Mrs Kelly was expecting the police.'

'He's still admiring the car,' Amy replied. 'I accompany him when he speaks to Mrs Kelly. I'm Amy, Amy Rowlings.'

'You work with our Jenny at the Mill, don't you? I've heard her talk about you.'

'Nothing too bad, I hope,' Amy said as Bodkin managed to tear himself away from the car and came to join her in the porch.

'She says you're going out with a copper. Is this him?'

'I'm Inspector Bodkin,' the policeman introduced himself, jumping into the conversation before Amy could respond. 'You must be Clara.'

'Yes, sir,' the maid responded with a slight bend of her knees. 'Mrs Kelly is in the lounge.'

Clara stepped back to allow Bodkin and Amy to enter, then she stuck her head out of the open front door and looked down the drive before closing it and leading them to the front room.

'Mr... I mean, Inspector Bodkin... Oh, and Amy Rowlings,' she added quickly.

Helen Kelly crushed out a cigarette then slowly got to her feet. She turned to them with a forced smile on her face. She was wearing a sable, mid-calf dress with a deep V neck and three-quarter sleeves, the waist was tight, and sported three padded buttons that held the neckline together.

'What a pleasure it is to see you both again,' she said, her smile broadening but not touching her eyes. 'And so soon too.' She dismissed the maid with a gesture of her hand. 'You can go now, Clara.'

'It's Clara we've come to see as a matter of fact,' Bodkin said, 'but I do have a couple of questions for you too.' The inspector flashed a quick smile. 'We'll begin with Clara if that's all right?' Helen began to sit, but Bodkin stopped her by lifting his hand, palm facing towards her. 'We'd like to speak to Clara alone if you don't mind, Mrs Kelly. I'll send her out when we're done. It shouldn't take too long.'

Helen Kelly straightened up and after giving Clara a hard stare, walked out of the room.

After being invited to sit, Clara sat with her hands clasped together on her lap and looked between the two visitors.

'I didn't do anything to Nel... I mean, Mr Kelly,' she said, uncertainly.

'No one is accusing you of anything,' Amy said with a smile, determined to try to put Clara at her ease.

Bodkin scratched behind his ear, then smiled himself. 'How long have you worked here, Clara?'

'It will be two years in August,' she replied.

'Do you like working here?'

'Yes, sir. It's better than working in a factory,' she flashed a glance at Amy, 'Sorry, but I did a bit of factory work when I left school and didn't like it. The hours are longer on this job, but the work is easy enough.' She leaned forwards conspiratorially. 'I sometimes think I'm only here for show. She gets a team of cleaners in twice a week to give the place a proper going over. I just tidy up after the Kellys. I lay the fires and wash their sheets, smalls and the odd tablecloth, but they send most of the stuff to the laundry in town.' Clara paused. 'I prepare breakfast, usually boiled eggs and toast, kippers on Sundays, that sort of thing. Old Mrs Crispin from East Street comes in to cook for them in the evenings or if they're entertaining. She used to work in the kitchens at the Milton.' She looked from Bodkin to Amy again to see if they were impressed by the news, then continued with her answer. 'Not that Mr Kelly was home for dinner very often. He used to eat out a lot.'

'What about Mrs Kelly, did she eat at home?'

'More often than Nel... Mr Kelly, but not every night by any means. She goes out two or three evenings a week and gets back late, I think she belonged to a bridge club or something, oh, and she went to the theatre in Gillingham a lot. Mr Kelly would sometimes stay in on those nights.' Clara blushed and bit her lip as if she had said something she didn't mean to say.

'How old are you, Clara?' Bodkin asked.

'Eighteen, I'm nineteen in September.'

'How long have you and Mr Kelly been... how shall I put it... physically close?'

Clara dropped her head.

'I don't know what you—'

'We know all about it, Clara,' Amy said softly, reaching out and touching her gently on the arm.

'It's not all over the town, is it?' Clara's head snapped up, she looked at Amy with a horrified look on her face. 'Big Nose Beryl doesn't know does she? My dad will kill me if he finds out.'

'Beryl doesn't know, and doesn't need to know,' Amy said, patting Clara's arm again. 'She definitely won't hear it from me.'

'When did it start, Clara?' Bodkin asked. 'Don't go into explicit detail, just give us the basics.'

'It started last New Year,' the housemaid replied. 'Mrs Kelly was out for the night, she said she was going to see her sister in Burham but Nelson didn't believe her. He was staying in because he had a big business meeting with some investors the next day, and he wanted to prepare for it. Anyway, it got to nine-thirty and so I knocked on his study door to ask if he needed anything before I went up to my room. He invited me in and gave me a glass of wine. He told me how much he and his wife appreciated my hard work and asked me if I liked working here. He was really kind to me. He gave me one of his posh cigarettes, then another, then we had more wine and before I knew it, I'd been in there for over an hour. I was quite tiddly if I'm honest.' Clara blushed as she thought back to that night. 'Anyway, he said I'd better get off to bed and that he'd lock up. He gave me the remains of the wine to take up with me, and I went to my room. I'd just got undressed and into my nightie when I heard a knock on the door, then it opened and his face appeared.'

Clara stopped speaking and looked towards the door. 'What if Mrs Kelly...'

'Don't worry about that, Clara,' Bodkin said waving his hand dismissively. 'Just get on with your story.'

'There's not much more to tell you about that night. He came in and well... I think you can guess the rest.'

'And after that night. How often did Mr Kelly come to your room?'

'Once a week, sometimes twice. Whenever we were on our own, I suppose.'

'Did he make promises to you, Clara?'

'He did say he loved me. He gave me a few presents and some extra cash so I could buy make up, new stockings, and... well, little things like that.'

'Do you know how old Mr Kelly is... was...?' Bodkin asked.

Clara shrugged. 'Thirty-five... forty? Why does that matter? He said he loved me and that one day we would be together.' She looked up to Bodkin, then winked at Amy. 'Age is just a number if you're in love, isn't it?'

Amy looked down at her hands as Bodkin cleared his throat. 'I think he took advantage of your inexperience, Clara,' he said.

'He was nice to me. He said we could go to London for a while when his divorce came through.'

'Divorce? He told you that? He was probably lying to you, Clara.'

'He said that he'd get around to it after the factory had been built. He was too busy to deal with lawyers over private stuff at the moment.'

Bodkin put a hand to his chin and shook his head, slowly. 'If you only knew how many married men made that promise to their lovers, Clara. He took advantage of you, that's all there is to it.'

'He didn't, he loved me,' Clara said, defiantly.

'Let's just leave that for a moment, shall we?' Bodkin said. 'Did you ever meet Mrs Kelly's sister?'

'The one from Burham? No. She never came here.'

'Are you sure she actually exists?'

Clara shrugged again. 'I don't know to be honest, she stayed there often enough... or at least she said she did.' Clara's mouth suddenly opened wide. 'Do you think she was having an affair and used her sister as an excuse?' She put her hands to her mouth. 'Oh my goodness! Nelson was telling me the truth then. He said she was seeing someone.'

'Where did you go on the night that Mr Kelly died, Clara?'

'My sister has just had a baby. We got the train down to Gillingham to see her.'

'We?'

'Mum, Dad, my stupid brother... We stayed overnight. Half of us slept at her place, half at her mother-in-law's house. We came home the next day. I got back here about lunch time. That's when I heard the terrible news.'

'How was Mrs Kelly taking it? Losing Nelson, I mean.'

'She cried a fair bit. Especially when I entered the room. The other Mr Kelly came around in the early afternoon. They sat in here with the door shut, I think they were comforting each other. I went upstairs and unpacked her cases. She didn't call for me the rest of the day.'

'You unpacked her cases?'

Clara nodded. 'They were still at the top of the stairs where she'd left them the night before. She said she had packed them to go to her sister's but then she had been visited by the police so she never went.'

'What time did Horatio Kelly go home?'

'I heard his car drive away about two-thirty ish.'

'Now, back to Mrs Kelly. When she went out in the evenings, did she ever leave by the back door, or did she take the car?'

'I don't know about going out the back, my room is at the front of the house, but I know she didn't use the car at night, she didn't like driving this one. I saw her get into a taxi once or twice though, it didn't pull right into the drive, it stopped and waited by the gates. It was always the same taxi firm.'

'Really?' Bodkin asked. 'Which one?'

'Adams,' Clara said. 'It wasn't black.'

'Thank you, Clara,' Bodkin said, getting to his feet. 'Can you ask Mrs Kelly to come in now. You have been very helpful.'

'You don't believe he loved me, do you?' the housemaid said. She pushed her fingers inside the collar of her dress and pulled out a silver locket on a thin chain. Flicking it open she showed first Amy, then Bodkin the likeness of a young-looking Nelson.

'See! He did love me,' she said triumphantly. Her jaw dropped as she looked over her shoulder to see Helen Kelly standing in the open doorway.

'So that's where it went,' Helen said, as she stared at her housemaid who was still showing off the necklace.

'It's mine,' Clara said, firmly. 'Nelson gave it to me.'

'He gave it to me first,' Helen replied. 'The night we became engaged. It was typical of him. Here's something to remind you of me when I'm not around. He never did ask for a locket with my picture in it.'

'It's mine... he gave it to me... I didn't steal it, honestly,' Clara looked at Bodkin, her eyes watering.

'It was in the bottom of my jewellery box the last time I saw it,' Helen replied. 'That was years ago though. I haven't worn it since I found out about his first affair.'

Clara wrapped her fingers around the locket, protectively.

'Oh, keep it,' Helen said. 'You've earned it, I suppose.'

As Clara hurried from the room still clutching the locket, Helen walked across to the cigarette box, selected one and lit it. 'You said you had a few more questions for me?'

Bodkin closed the lounge door and held out his hand towards the sofa.

'Sit down, please, Mrs Kelly. I won't keep you long.'

Helen smoothed down her dress, then sat down. She crossed her legs slowly and blew smoke across the table towards Bodkin. Amy stared hard at the policeman, willing him to turn his face towards her, but his eyes never left Helen.

She moved her position so that she was looking directly at the policeman.

'You look tired, Mr Bodkin,' she said, pulling a sad face. 'I hope this case isn't taxing you too much.' She took another draw from her cigarette, then began to wind her hair around the index finger of her free hand, her eyes looked down towards her chest, suddenly shy.

Amy, who had been making repeated hand signals towards Bodkin slapped the table with her right hand. Bodkin almost leapt out of his seat as he spun around to look at her.

'A fly,' Amy said. 'It was annoying me.'

Bodkin tipped his head and gave Amy a quizzical look. She bit her lip and said nothing.

'Your sister,' Bodkin began. 'Where did you say she lived?'

'Burham,' Helen said. 'I can give you her address, but as I told you, she isn't there at present.'

'If you could give it to me before I leave, I'd appreciate it,' Bodkin replied. 'Now, this is where it gets a little bit personal, Mrs Kelly.'

'Call me Helen, please,' she said as she recrossed her legs then leaned forwards towards the inspector.

'Clara told us that she had to unpack your suitcases when she got home the day after Nelson died, is that correct?'

'Yes, I didn't unpack. I pay her for that sort of thing.'

'How long did you intend to stay at your sister's house?'

'Overnight, possibly the Saturday too. I don't like to stay too long when they're having problems. They've usually kissed and made up within a day or two.'

'But you packed two suitcases. You wouldn't need that many clothes for an overnight stay, would you?'

'It might have been two nights.'

'That's still a lot of luggage. Were you intending to go out while you were down at Burham? I thought you were just going to offer a bit of comfort.'

'I like to be prepared for all eventualities.'

'Mrs Kelly, the last time we spoke you admitted to having an affair. Who was the man you were involved with?'

Helen stubbed out her cigarette, walked across the room and lit another one.

'A gentleman wouldn't ask that question. I'm disappointed in you, Inspector.'

'I'm a policeman, Mrs Kelly. I'm paid to ask questions like this. Now, are you going to force me to take an educated guess?'

'Guess away,' she said, as she tipped back her head and blew smoke at the ceiling.

'Horatio Kelly?'

'Horatio? Oh my God. You have got a vivid imagination, Inspector,' she said, still with her back to Bodkin.

'Do you own a fur coat,' Mrs Kelly?'

'What a strange question.'

'Could you just answer, please?'

'I do, as a matter of fact, why do you want to know?'

'Do you like to walk in the park in the evenings, Mrs Kelly?'

'The park? Occasionally, not for a while though.'

'So, you didn't go for a walk on the night of Nelson's death?'

'No, I told you, I was here, packing. It took a while, there were two cases, remember?'

Helen stubbed out her cigarette after taking a long draw from it. She leaned back on the sofa and brushed imaginary ash from her dress. Bodkin rubbed the stubble on his chin between the thumb and index finger of his left hand.

'Horatio came to see you the afternoon after Nelson's death. Why did he want to see you so urgently, Mrs Kelly?'

Helen looked towards the window at the sound of a car pulling up outside.

'Ask him yourself, Inspector. He's just arrived.'

CHAPTER
THIRTY-THREE

Horatio Kelly was a fair-haired, handsome man of around thirty-five years of age with a square jaw, a straight nose and a pair of piercing blue eyes. Standing a little over six feet, he wore cream flannel trousers and a sleeveless pullover over a white shirt, looking every inch the amateur cricketer. He held out his long-fingered hand as he was introduced to Bodkin by Helen.

'Sit down, Horatio,' Helen said, placing a soft hand on his shoulder and pecking him on the cheek. 'I'll organise some tea... or would anyone prefer coffee?'

'Tea for me, please,' Amy said. 'I'll be awake all night if I have coffee.'

Bodkin nodded his agreement and Helen left the room to find Clara.

'You're a hard man to pin down, Mr Kelly,' Bodkin said as Nelson's younger brother sat down on the sofa next to the policeman.

'I've had a lot to do, Inspector, what with business uncertainty, the funeral and what have you.'

'I can imagine it's been difficult, but to cancel three appointments is going a bit far.'

'As I told the chief constable, I'm a very busy man and I am grieving, don't forget.'

'My condolences on your loss,' Bodkin replied.

Horatio turned sideways on to give Bodkin a narrow-eyed look. 'Thank you, I appreciate your comment,' he said, looking as though he didn't believe the policeman was being sincere for a moment. 'And how are you, Miss... Rowlings isn't it? I've heard a lot about you just recently.'

'Nothing too bad, I hope,' Amy said with a smile, wondering why it was that everyone was suddenly talking about her. It was the second time she'd heard it inside half an hour.

'You work at Georgina Handsley's factory, I believe.' He turned to face Bodkin again. 'Strange that someone with no connection to the police should be so involved in a murder inquiry.'

'Oh, she has a connection to the police, Mr Kelly. Miss Rowling's runs an investigations agency called ARIA, and she is registered with the Kent police force... that's the whole of Kent, not just Spinton. And, as it happens, Amy and I have a very similar outlook on our respective jobs. Neither of us likes to leave any loose ends.'

Kelly looked back to Amy as Bodkin went on.

'Such was my superior officer's concern for the wellbeing of Mrs Kelly, and because Miss Rowlings has helped us solve two murders recently and because we have no female officers in Spinton, he thought it prudent to have a woman attending the questioning, especially when the lady being interviewed has been so recently bereaved.'

The policeman gave Horatio a hard stare. 'So, Mr Kelly, you are quite welcome to demand that Miss Rowlings vacates the room while I question you, but she will be joining me should I wish to speak to Nelson's widow again. You can telephone the chief constable now if you wish. We'll wait here while you make the call.'

Kelly thought about it for a moment as Bodkin winked at Amy. 'It's no skin off my nose, Inspector,' he said. 'I've got nothing to hide, I'm just concerned that some business details might slip out in conversation afterwards.'

'I can assure you Mr Kelly, that Miss Rowlings is the master... or should I say mistress of the buttoned lip,' Bodkin said. 'I assure you that nothing you say here will be spoken about outside of this room to anyone other than me. Besides, Amy might be one of the most intelligent women I've ever met, but she has no interest nor has she ever had any dealings with business. She won't be rushing out of this meeting to splash her life savings on a rival's share issue.'

Nelson pursed his lips. 'I suppose I was coming across as being a little reticent,' he said.

'No, you're coming across as being a little arrogant, Mr Kelly, especially where Miss Rowlings is concerned.'

'Then I apologise,' Kelly said. 'Miss Rowlings, I have been very rude. Please accept my heart-felt apologies. I'm under quite a lot of stress at the moment. I can assure you; I am much more of a gentleman than I appear.'

Amy smiled and leaned towards him. 'I understand completely, Mr Kelly. I'm quite happy to leave the room while you answer Bod... Inspector Bodkin's questions, but should you allow me to stay, I will promise you that anything you say here, not just the business-related remarks, will be treated with the strictest confidence.'

Nelson nodded and gave Amy a warm smile.

'Right then, let's get down to brass tacks,' Bodkin said. 'Did you love your brother, Mr Kelly.'

'Love him? Of course I loved him. We were flesh and blood.'

'Did you like him though?'

Horatio thought about it. 'Sometimes, sometimes not. It depended what mood he was in.'

'He's been described as being a philanderer, a narcissist and a bully, do you recognise any of those descriptions?'

'The first two are bang on, everyone who knew him would agree to that, but bully?'

'He used to bully people; we have it in evidence statements.'

'He could be forceful, yes. Some people might call it bullying, I suppose.'

'Did he bully you, Mr Kelly?'

'No... look, I don't know where this is leading but...'

'It's hopefully leading us to the murderer, Mr Kelly.'

'You don't think I had anything to do with his death? That's preposterous.'

'I'm not saying you did, sir. But I hope you understand, I do have to ask these questions.'

Just then Helen tapped on the door and pushed it open.

'Could you give us another ten minutes, please, Mrs Kelly?' Bodkin asked with a smile.

Ignoring Bodkin, Helen put the tea tray on the table and returned to the door. As she pulled it to, she gave Kelly a soft smile.

'I'll be just outside if you need me for anything,' she said.

Bodkin poured tea for all three, then handed the drinks around.

'Where were we?' he said, when they were settled again. 'Ah yes, bullying. We have it on good authority that Nelson has been a bully since childhood. Leopards don't tend to change their spots, do they, Mr Kelly?'

'Ah, all becomes clear. You've been talking to Harold Kitson, haven't you? Nelson and Harold never saw eye to eye.'

'So I gather. His childhood was blighted by it.'

'I suppose Nelson could be harder on some people than others.'

'He was your father's favourite son too, that can't have been very nice for you, Mr Kelly.'

Horatio took a sip of his tea, then he sighed before answering.

'It wasn't nice, Inspector. Nothing I did was ever good enough. I got better marks than Nelson in most exams, but I never once got a "well done" from my father. I won the lead role in King Lear one year but that was overshadowed by Nelson scoring a ton in the inter school cricket tournament. I got used to it in the end, but I can't say I ever fully accepted it. Mother wasn't quite as bad, but he was still her blue-eyed boy, everyone knew it.'

Horatio paused for a moment, then went on. 'He even got the best name. I mean, Nelson... it sounds so commanding, doesn't it? Dad was a naval officer in his youth, so he gave us both a bit of his hero. I got Horatio, unfortunately. Can you imagine what it was like at school with a name like that? I used to get called Horrorshow.'

He paused again.

'Horatio was Hamlet's only friend in the play, that's one more friend than I had... Harold apart, and he wasn't much of a friend, he used to just hang around me because he thought it might give him some protection from Nelson. It never did of course.' He took another sip of tea. 'It got better at university. Nelson didn't go, my father wanted him to learn the ins and outs of the family business as soon as possible. I made a few friends at Oxford, my future wife being one of them. The name calling finally stopped, no one called me Horatio there. I was always, Harry, Ray, sometimes Terrence, which might seem little better than Horatio, but at least it was different.'

'Your marriage didn't last?'

'No. I assume you've already heard the sordid details so I won't add to it. She left me, that's all that needs to be said.'

Bodkin nodded. 'I'm sorry about that.'

'Oh, I'm not. Not anymore that is. I was devastated at the

time, but now I think I got off lucky. It cost me a bit of course. I didn't want a messy divorce, so I admitted to adultery and paid her what she wanted. It meant me re-mortgaging the house and I had to ask Nelson to agree to let me have a director's loan on the company to pay her off, but it was money well spent.'

'Did he agree to the loan or did he want something from you in return?'

Horatio shot Amy a glance, then clasped his hands together. 'I had to give him the controlling interest. He wanted ten percent of my equity. We had owned fifty percent each. After that, what he said pretty much went. He organised the share flotation and to be honest the company did really well out of it, but he was still the majority shareholder.'

'You argued about the factory deal, didn't you?'

'Yes. Nelson has always thought I'm too soft to be in business as I have a strong social conscience. I used to work with the poor when I was at university. There was a church group that ran soup kitchens and the like, this was during the mid-twenties, before the stock market crash and the Depression, but there was still a hell of a lot of poverty about… people couldn't feed their children. Nelson always argued that if they can't afford to feed them, they shouldn't have them, but that's such a simplistic and cruel thing to say. He didn't understand, and he didn't want to understand. He only ever thought about profit. That was drilled into him by my father.'

'So, you argued about the lack of housing in the big plan? Were the arguments heated?'

'Yes. I used to give as good as I got in the main, but I couldn't persuade him to build even enough houses to replace the twenty or so that were to be demolished. Those poor people would have had nowhere to go. They'd have been out on the streets, there is no spare housing capacity in the town.'

'Mrs Kelly backed you in those arguments I've heard,' Bodkin said.

Kelly nodded. 'Yes, she was very supportive.'

'Do you like her, Mr Kelly?'

'Of course I like her. She's a wonderful woman, she deserved so much better than Nelson.'

'Back to the arguments. How heated, was heated? Did you ever blow a gasket, come to blows?'

'I'd have lost straight away if it had. Nelson was a boxing champion at school. I played chess and croquet.'

'Were you angry that he'd got his way yet again? He didn't have a heart, did he? He had a swinging brick.'

Horatio shrugged. 'Nelson was Nelson. You couldn't win.'

'And you resented that.'

'In part. I wanted to do something for those poor people, have you seen the state of those houses? You wouldn't let farm animals live in them. Helen agreed with me.'

'So do I,' Amy said quietly. 'I've seen them, the conditions are truly dreadful. One young father died trying to fix a hole in the roof in the middle of winter. The owners should have faced criminal charges.'

'You've been to Ebenezer Street?' Kelly said, looking at Amy in a new light. 'I bet you have nightmares about it.'

'I'm just frustrated that no one will help them,' Amy replied. 'They don't ask for much.'

'Frustrated... Yes, I was frustrated, I also felt totally powerless. Here was I, part owner of the company that was going to knock their houses down, and I couldn't do anything to help them. I felt impotent, totally, utterly impotent.'

'Why did Nelson even bother to argue the case, Mr Kelly? He wielded all the power. He didn't need your agreement.'

'He was trying to raise money for the project. He needed me to back him if potential investors asked questions. It was as simple as that.'

'So, you gave in without a real fight. He might have changed his mind if you could have persuaded an investor or two to get behind a bid that included a few houses. Harold Kitson for instance?'

'Ah, poor Harold. No, he wouldn't have backed me up at all. He was in a bit of a financial hole, much worse than I was. He was looking to make a quick buck. As soon as he knew that we had won the bid, he wanted to take his money out of Drake's companies and put it into ours. Word got out about the winner a good while before it was announced.'

'But Nelson turned him down flat? Why did he do that if he wanted money from people with the same instincts as him?'

Horatio shrugged again. 'I'd say you'd have to ask Nelson, Inspector, but of course, you can't.' Kelly thought for a moment or two. 'He was absolutely insistent that Kitson wouldn't be allowed to invest. It wasn't like him at all. Nelson would snatch someone's hand off for a fiver.'

'How did he buy you off then? You've just said he needed you onside for the other investors.'

'He offered to pay off my director's loan and promised me enough money to pretty much pay off my mortgage. It was a very good offer. I felt I was betraying my principles but I couldn't really turn it down, I was struggling. Sooner or later, I'd have had to sell off some or all of my company shares and that would have horrified my mother. She always thought her sons should both be involved in the firm. I had already let her down by getting divorced. She saw that as a family disgrace. Nelson played up to that. I know his own marriage wasn't worth the paper it was written on, but he wouldn't have divorced Helen, not while mother was alive. He was the apple of her eye and he didn't want her to be disappointed in him too.'

'So, you were pretty much debt free by this point, Mr Kelly? That must have dampened your social justice ardour somewhat.'

'No, it didn't, I felt guilty... anyway it never happened. Once the bid was won, Nelson went back on the deal. I had nothing in writing, I just took him at his word.'

'You must have hated him. First the housing, then cheating you out of what you were promised...' Bodkin rubbed his chin. 'You got it all in the end though. You had the last laugh.'

'I don't see anything funny about it. Anyway, I don't get Nelson's half of the business, that was *his* last laugh. I was supposed to get it. Mother always said that if anything should happen to either one of us, the other should fully own the company... or the majority holding after the share release at least.' Horatio wiped his hand over his brow. 'But he didn't even stick to that. Helen is to get his money and his shares. That's why I'm here today. I came to tell her that she's now the majority shareholder in Kelly Construction.'

'That must be hard to take, Mr Kelly. It's lucky that you and Helen have such a good relationship.'

'I hope it stays that way because I've got other news for her. Drake has offered to buy me out. He doesn't know that Helen is the largest shareholder, yet, he's assuming I own the lot.'

'Are you going to sell?'

'I don't know. I want to see what Helen thinks first. If she sells, I will, I don't want to be subservient to someone like Drake.'

'I can well understand that,' Bodkin replied.

The room fell silent for a time, then the policeman spoke again. 'Are you in love with Helen?'

Horatio immediately blushed.

'Come on, Mr Kelly, she's a very good-looking woman. Who wouldn't find her attractive?'

Amy shot Bodkin a look from under her eyelids.

'Of course I find her attractive, as you said yourself, who wouldn't?'

'Were you having an affair with your sister-in-law, Mr Kelly?' Bodkin asked, turning a stern eye on him. 'Did she used to come and see you down at Oaklands when Nelson was out on the town?'

'That's preposterous!' Horatio spluttered.

'We know she was having an affair, Mr Kelly. She's been seen hurrying across the park. That path runs straight past your house, doesn't it? Has she been nipping in through the back door so none of your neighbour's notice her? What if I told you she'd been seen, Mr Kelly. A married woman, hiding her face under the collar of her fur coat, sneaking towards your house.'

Kelly turned purple. 'I'm not going to discuss this. My private life is none of your business.'

'When it comes to murder, everything is my business,' Bodkin snorted. 'Where were you on the night that your brother was killed, Mr Kelly?'

'I was at home.'

'Alone?'

'Yes, as it happens.' Horatio glared at Bodkin. 'Look here, if you're going to treat me as a suspect, then I'm not going to say any more without my solicitor being present.' He turned towards Amy. 'And if I find you've repeated a word of the allegations about my personal life, I'll have you up in court for defamation. Do you understand?'

THIRTY-FOUR

BODKIN'S NEXT QUESTION WAS CUT OFF WHEN HELEN PUSHED OPEN THE door and walked back into the room. She looked belligerently at Bodkin.

'Oops,' Amy whispered to herself. 'Someone has blotted his copybook.'

'I'd like you to ask these people to leave, Helen,' Kelly said, glowering at Bodkin. 'I know he is trying to uncover my brother's murderer, but there are some questions, deeply personal questions that a gentleman doesn't answer.'

Bodkin spread his arms wide. 'Many murders happen because of deeply personal feelings, Mr Kelly. I will get an answer to my last set of questions, either from you, or from someone else. I have part of the answer already, as I told you. It won't take me long to dig up the rest.'

Horatio's face fell. Helen hurried to his side and put a soft hand on his cheek feeling a tear run down her fingers.

'I think he's right. We have important things to discuss.' She clapped her hands together. 'Clara will see you out,' she said.

'I will need to speak to both of you again,' Bodkin replied as he allowed Amy to leave the room first. 'So, you had better get your stories straight.'

Horatio pushed his lips together tightly as Helen walked towards the back of the room to get a cigarette from the box.

'Oh, one last thing,' Bodkin said, turning back. 'Were either of you aware that Nelson had put forward a second proposal for a large demolition and construction project, which was to be discussed once the original plans had been passed by the planning committee?'

As Helen and Horatio exchanged puzzled glances, Bodkin could see that they weren't.

Helen followed Bodkin to the lounge door and blew a long plume of blue-grey smoke into the hallway as the policeman and Amy followed Clara to the front door.

'What did he have in mind, can you tell us?' she asked.

'I'll see, it depends what you two can come up with as a trade-off. Fair exchange and all that.'

'You were pushing your luck again, Bodkin,' Amy said as she climbed into the inspector's black Morris. 'Mentioning the chief constable, I mean... oh and then making out that Helen had actually been seen going into this house via the side gate.'

'I thought it was worth the risk,' Bodkin replied, as he slammed the door and put both his hands on the steering wheel. 'I'm getting so frustrated with these two. They're both hiding something, I know it.'

'The affair probably,' Amy agreed.

Bodkin started the car and made a half turn reversing manoeuvre. 'Possibly much more than that,' he said as he pulled out onto the road.

They drove in silence for a minute or two, then, as they passed the library, Bodkin looked sideways at Amy.

'So, how do you think I handled her tonight? Was she attempting to seduce me again?'

'She dropped you like a hot brick the moment Horatio arrived,' Amy said, trying to keep herself from smiling.

'Oh, I did spot that there seemed to be something between them.'

'I've just been thinking about her and I don't think she knows she's doing it,' Amy replied thoughtfully. 'She seems to be like it with every man she sees.'

'Well, that's my bubble well and truly burst,' Bodkin said, smiling as he turned his face back to the road.

When Amy got home, she made a pot of tea for the family and carried it through to the lounge. Mrs Rowlings was sitting on the sofa flicking through her copy of Woman's Own. Her father put down his evening paper as she passed him a cup and saucer.

'That reporter has been at it again. He's all over the front page with his assertions.'

Amy picked up the paper and skim read the front page.

Thieves Thrive As Tecs Take Time Out!

Sandy Miles. Exclusive.

'The man's an idiot,' she said eventually, throwing the paper down in disgust. 'Bodkin is the only working detective they have at the moment. The poor man got dragged away from a murder investigation today, just to review some case files on a spate of burglaries. I know burglary is seen as a serious crime, especially if you're the one who's had your possessions stolen, but honestly, how can this... person, have a go at Bodkin just because he feels that murder is the more serious offence.'

'Has Bodkin gone home now, Amy?' her mother asked with a concerned look on her face.

'No, he's gone back to the station. He's got to do some more work on the thefts.'

'Poor man. No wonder he always looks so tired and dishevelled.'

'Bodkin always looks dishevelled, Mum, it's part of his charm,' Amy said with a grin.

'I worry about that young man,' Mrs Rowlings said. 'He works far too hard for his own good.'

'It comes with the territory,' Mr Rowlings said, grinning at Amy. 'That's why I won't have a telephone fitted. I'd be at the factory's beck and call.'

Amy looked to the heavens and shook her head.

'I get the message,' she said, before adding. 'Oh, I know what I meant to ask you, Dad. Is the church poor fund up and running again? The one that Mrs De Vere tried to steal from? Only I met a woman yesterday and she can't afford the prescription for her daughter. I thought they might be able to help her.'

'I don't think so... in fact I know it isn't, Amy. The bishop hasn't decided what's happening with that yet. It all got a bit messy, didn't it?' He paused, then pursed his lips. 'I can ask the vicar if you like?'

Amy thought back to the case she'd helped Bodkin solve only a few weeks before. 'It got *very* messy but don't bother asking him, Dad, it's okay, I've got someone else I can talk to about it.'

When Amy got to her room, she pulled out her jotter pad and picked up her pen, then after collecting her thoughts, she began to write down the names of the suspects, next to them she wrote down the motive they might have for wanting Nelson dead. She had almost finished her list when her mother tapped on the door to say that it was after ten and that she and Mr Rowlings were going to bed.

Amy took one last look at her work in progress, then flipped the jotter shut and got undressed ready for bed. Before she switched out her beside lamp, she picked up her pen and jotter again, and quickly read through her notes, adding a final thought regarding other possible suspects before turning out the light.

Poirot's motive list

Revenge, Gain, Jealousy, Fear.

Clues...

Relationships.

Opportunity.

Drake and Lorna. Evasive. Gloves stained on the night and which now cannot be produced for evidence. Definitely Gain for Drake, possibly Revenge or Jealousy for Lorna. You've ruined me argument? Kelly's second public housing plan would have seen Drake having to sell off all his property and he would lose out on thousands in rent over the next few years. Firstly, did he know about the second plan and secondly, would it ruin him? How strong are his company assets beyond the housing portfolio? Appeared to have a plan in place if Nelson somehow had to pull out of the running for the factory build. Lorna was first on the scene and therefore the last to see Nelson alive. She was covered in his blood. She did appear to be in distress, but she could be a really good actress. Drake and Lorna both had the opportunity.

Horatio and Helen. Evasive. Gain for both, they could have planned this together to take control of the company. I don't think jealousy is a motive, but revenge might come into it. Opportunity? Both were absent from the event, but the phone call could be relevant. I don't believe it was about her sister for a moment. Could it have been a ruse to get Nelson to open the Fire Exit door? Horatio and Kitson would look similar from the back, especially in the semi darkness. Neither has a complete alibi for the night in question and both are not telling all they know. Horatio very secretive about the relationship. The lady in the fur coat? Looks likely. The Ruin Me argument... works for Horatio in some contexts... Helen's reputation could be at risk.

Harold Kitson. Revenge for the bullying. Fear of becoming bankrupt? Evasive. Bloody shirt, getting out of the taxi well away from home. Was it a call of nature, or didn't he want to let the driver know where he lived? Burned his clothes, tried to buy into Kelly's company and was refused. WHY? Opportunity. Might have been spotted at the emergency exit so if he did get Nelson to open the door on some pretext, he wasn't too far away from the knife. The, you've ruined me argument is strong.

Shirley and Robert McKenzie. Gain is the only motive I can think of but they really don't need the money. Would have to have paid someone to murder Nelson as both were in the Assembly Room at the time of the murder. Opportunity? No. Ruined me? Hardly likely.

Basil and Alma Thornalley. Do they know more than they are admitting to? They could be listed under both Gain and Revenge. Desperate for money and could have lost everything after being forced out of the mayoralty. Opportunity. Both of them were as close as you could get to the scene. Possible scenario, Basil shouts "You've ruined me", Alma uses the knife...

Who opened that emergency door?

Other Suspects? Sandy Miles. Catering staff. Cleaners... no evidence.

The next morning, Amy arrived at the shop at eight forty-five to find Susan already in her place by the till.

'Good morning,' she said with a wave. 'I'm just getting the receipts ready for Mrs Walker-Peters and Mrs McKenzie. Both of the dresses are ready to go.' She looked at her appointment book. 'You've got Mrs W.P at ten-thirty and Mrs Mac at twelve, so you have plenty of time to get the final fittings done.'

She looked back to her notes as Amy walked towards the staff room.

'Oh, did Georgina tell you. We'd like you to box up the dresses and deliver them to the customers this afternoon.'

'No, she didn't say, but that's fine. Erm, how do I get to the customers? I can't really carry two boxed up dresses on the bus.'

Susan laughed. 'No, you can't. I've booked a taxi for you at three o'clock. You should have plenty of time to pack the dresses before then. I've already got the boxes out and there is a mountain of tissue paper in both of them so you won't have a problem there. We're closing at the usual time as it's Wednesday, so I'm trusting you to lock up. I'll leave the spare keys on the desk when I go at one o'clock.'

Mrs Walker-Peters was picky. Very picky. Amy was sure she was going to pull a magnifying glass from her bag at any moment to examine the stitching around the area of alteration. Then she was 'almost certain' that the dress she was looking at wasn't exactly the same colour as the one she had tried on. Amy could tell she was just being a pain for the sake of it so she decided to revert to flattery.

'This is the only one we have, Mrs Walker-Peters. It's an exclusive. It's too expensive to have more than one of these in stock. Luckily it was perfect for you in every way. The colour completely compliments your skin tone and hair colour and it couldn't be a better fit really. The seamstresses only had to take it in an inch.'

'In... they had to take it in? I thought it felt a bit tight.'

'That was the seam, Mrs Walker-Peters. It's adjustable, they fold them over slightly so it can be taken in, or let out. It's always a little bunched up when it arrives, that's why it probably felt tight to you.' Amy flashed a smile at the woman. 'It was definitely taken in half an inch on each side, I've seen the report.'

Mrs Walker-Peters preened as she examined herself less critically in the mirror. 'Well then. In that case, I'm happy with it. She turned her back so that Amy could undo the fastenings. 'I knew something was different.'

Shirley McKenzie arrived just as the older, Mrs Walker-Peters was leaving. They exchanged pleasantries at the door, then just before she left, she leaned towards Shirley and said in a loud stage whisper. 'I got an exclusive... see you at the wedding.'

Amy led Shirley though to the fitting rooms and took her new dress from the rail. After pulling it on and trying it with several different pairs of shoes, she declared herself satisfied.

'I wasn't sure which size heels to wear with it,' she said. 'But now I think I'm going to risk it and go with the black, three-inch slingbacks.'

'Good choice,' Amy said, 'you have the ankles for them.'

'Your flattery is accepted and appreciated,' Shirley said with a smile. 'I'd die to know how thick you had to lay it on with Mrs Walker-Peters. I bet you had to use a trowel.'

'I wasn't...'

Shirley patted her arm. 'I was only joking, Amy, but we all like a bit of a compliment, don't we? I wish more men understood that.'

Amy helped her off with the dress and laid it down on the pile of tissue paper in the long, cardboard box that Susan had left out for her.

'I believe it is being delivered after three, is that right?' Shirley said.

'Yes, I'm bringing it over myself, by taxi.'

'You're delivering it? That is nice. We can have a cup of tea and a chat.'

Amy took a quick look towards the door in case Susan was earwigging, then leaned in towards the mayor's wife.

'I was hoping to catch a word with you, Shirley. There's something I'd like to ask you about.'

Shirley pulled up her skirt, fastened most of the buttons then spun it around so it was in the right position.

'Could you just fasten the hook and eye, dear? It's always a fiddle.'

Amy did as she was asked and then helped Shirley on with her jacket. When she was fully dressed, Shirley checked herself in the mirror, patted her hair into place, then turned back to Amy.

'What was it you wanted to discuss?'

Amy pulled Beth's prescription from her pocket.

'This prescription is from a lady who lives on Ebenezer Street, the house is an absolute hovel but she looks after her daughter the best she can. She takes in washing and works on it for fourteen hours a day. Her daughter, Beth, has to miss school to help out.' She paused to collect her thoughts, then went on. 'Anyway, Beth's got scurvy from not eating properly, she also got something else that her mother couldn't pronounce, she's got a skin rash too, a bad one. She's only seven, Shirley, and her mum can't afford the prescription. She's been saving up for it but has only managed to raise three shillings and the prescription costs six with all the items that are on it. She's a lovely little girl and her mum is desperate to get her well again. She lost a baby to Scarlet Fever and her husband fell off the roof and died when he tried to fix it.'

'Oh my goodness! The poor woman,' Shirley replied with a look of horror on her face. 'We don't know how lucky we are, do we?'

'So, do you think that this might be a case you can help with?' Amy said. 'Can you use the community fund? You said you wanted to help children.'

'I'm pretty sure the fund can help, Amy. It's about time it did something useful.'

Amy threw her arms around Shirley's back and hugged her tight.

'Thank you so much, I can't tell you how much this will mean to Karen.'

'What time do you close for lunch?' Shirley asked.

'One, then I've got an hour off before I box up the dresses and do the delivery run.'

'Hmm,' Shirley said, thoughtfully. 'The chemist closes for lunch at the same time. I'll tell you what. Give me the prescription and I'll nip over now and have a word with Agatha. She owns the pharmacy now, you know? Imagine that, a female pharmacist, isn't it wonderful?' Her eyes lit up. 'Women are on the march, Amy.' Shirley picked up her bag and slipped the prescription inside. 'Agatha will get the stuff made up and she can send the bill to me. I'll explain about the circumstances and that any future prescriptions for Beth will be paid for out of the community fund. I can't see there being any problem at all.' She grinned as Amy pulled away from her. 'Meet me in the Sunshine café at one-thirty, and I'll hand over the goodies.'

As promised, Shirley met Amy in the café and handed over a brown paper bag with the medicine inside.

'Agatha said there's a linctus, some cream and something called ascorbic acid. I've been told to make sure that this doesn't cause her mother any alarm. It's perfectly safe and will clear up the scurvy in no time. She might need more of the other medicine next month, but she says, if Karen is still worried about Beth after using this lot, she's not to go all the way to the Free Hospital, just drop in at the pharmacy and she'll have a look at her. No cost.'

Amy took the bag, leaned across the table and gave Shirley another hug.

On the way back to the shop, Amy walked through the market

place where the bustling Wednesday market was in progress. She nodded to one or two of the sellers as she walked between the fruit and veg stalls. As she passed Glenys Waldon's wool stall she spotted a new trader who had a mixture of bric-a-brac and second-hand, children's toys on his stall. In a tall pile at the back, was a collection of jigsaw puzzles. Amy selected a one-hundred-piece puzzle with a picture of Buckingham Palace on the front and a two-hundred-and-fifty-piece puzzle of Windsor castle. Having paid sixpence for the pair, she walked back to the shop feeling as excited as if she had bought the puzzles for herself.

At three o'clock, Amy picked up the keys from the table and walked to the shop front to open the door for Rory, the Adams taxi driver.

'Hello again, Amy, this is getting to be a regular thing, isn't it? The fates seem to be pushing us together.'

'Ah, but beware, Rory, the fates can be fickle,' Amy said as she put the second box onto the back seat of the taxi.

'Tell me about it,' Rory said, sadly. 'Oh, while you're here. Can you take a message for Mr Bodkin, you see I've just seen that man... the one in the bloody shirt. He was going into the bank as I was dropping a fare off.'

'We think we know who it was, Rory, but thanks for the information. I wonder if he's still in there?'

'I haven't seen him come out yet,' Rory said. 'Hey, I'll tell you what. Let's do a bit of detective work. I'll park up outside the bank, then tip you the wink when he comes out.'

Amy thought about it. 'All right, let's have a look, but only for five minutes, we have to deliver the dresses, don't forget.'

In actual fact, it took less than three minutes for Harold Kitson to make an appearance. He strolled out of the bank with a worried look on his face, and walked into the road without looking for traffic. Amy, who was sitting in the front passenger seat, lifted up the brown medicine bag to cover her face as Kitson crossed the street in front of the taxi.

'That's him,' Rory said. 'No doubt about it. I can see him almost falling out of my cab when I close my eyes.'

Amy watched Kitson walk past the Post Office on the opposite side of the road before she risked putting the brown bag back on her lap again.

'I'll report to Bodkin later today, Rory. Thanks for the information. You're a very useful man to have on our side.' Amy stared out of the windscreen as she had a sudden thought. 'Rory. Have you ever picked a woman up from Hillcrest? It's the last house at the top of the High Street.'

'Yes, I think her name's Helen something. She's a very attractive woman, long legs... very...'

Rory tailed off as Amy gave him a look.

'How many times did you pick her up and where did you drop her off?' she asked.

'I must have picked her up half a dozen times in the last few weeks, but Denny Lang, another driver, had a regular fare with her on Saturday nights. He used to wind me up, telling me she'd been flirting with him. He knows I fancy her.'

'Yes, yes, that's all very interesting but where did you drop her off?'

'Skelton,' Rory replied. 'It was never at an actual address, just at the crossroads.'

THIRTY-FIVE

Mʀs Wᴀʟᴋᴇʀ-Pᴇᴛᴇʀs ᴡᴀs sᴛɪʟʟ ʙᴀsᴋɪɴɢ ɪɴ ᴛʜᴇ ɢʟᴏᴡ ᴏꜰ Aᴍʏ's flattering comments when she dropped her dress off at Longstairs, an aptly named, large house on the outskirts of Spinton. Amy counted twenty-four steps leading up to the front door. So delighted was the recipient of the dress that she gave Amy a half crown tip.

'Will you still be there when I come to look at the autumn fashions?' she said as she handed the money to Amy. 'I was told you were only temporary.'

'I help out when they need me,' Amy replied, 'so I might be there. Thank you for choosing London Collection.'

Shirley McKenzie was in the back garden, sipping an iced drink when Amy arrived, so when no one answered the front door, she carried the box around to the side gate and shouted over it.

'I'm so sorry, Amy. I thought you'd be a little bit later than this, it's only just ten past three.'

'Mrs Walker-Peters didn't bother to inspect the dress again when I dropped it off. Susan thought that she might,' Amy said with a grin.

Shirley opened the gate and Amy carried the box through to the garden and into the lounge via the open French windows.

'Just put it on the sofa, please, Amy, I'll unpack it and take it upstairs later.' She picked up her purse from the table and fished around in her loose change. Finding a crown, she pulled it out and offered it to Amy. 'There you are, my dear. Thank you for your expertise.'

'Five shillings? I can't accept that, Mrs McKenzie, not after all you've done today.'

Shirley pushed the heavy coin into Amy's hand and folded her fingers over it.

'You deserve it for being so kind to people who need help,' she said with a smile. 'Please don't say anyone would do the same, because we both know that the vast majority of people wouldn't.' She patted Amy's hand, then closed her purse with a click. 'You're the Good Samaritan that didn't pass by on the other side of the road, Amy.' She put the purse back on the table. 'Now, can I get you a cold drink?'

'No, thank you, Mrs McKenzie. I'm going over to Ebenezer Street to drop Beth's prescription off while I've got the free taxi service.' She held the silver coin in the air as she turned towards the door. 'Thanks for this. I know exactly what I'm going to spend it on.'

Amy got back into the taxi and asked Rory to drop her off outside Gideon's shop on Trafalgar Street, and with the two puzzle boxes stuffed under one arm and the prescription bag in her hand, she pushed down the handle on the half glass door and gently eased it open.

'Do you want me to wait for you?' Rory asked through his wound down car window. 'You're booked for another hour yet if you need me.'

'No, I'll be fine now, thanks, Rory. Well done again for spotting our man, and for the tip off about Helen.'

'Hello again,' Gideon said, smiling towards her as she stepped into the shop. 'You look like you've been busy.'

'This is all for Beth,' Amy said, happily. 'I've just popped in to see if you still have the other bag of oranges and I'd like a quart of milk please, the fresh, pasteurised stuff.'

'I do still have those oranges as it happens,' Gideon said. 'I thought I was going to have to eat them myself before they went off.' He walked over to the shop front and picked up a mesh bag from a crate that was sitting in the window. 'You can have them for what they cost me, so that will be a shilling altogether, ninepence for the oranges and threepence for the milk. I'll give you a box to carry everything in.'

Amy put the puzzles and medicine on the counter, pulled out her purse from her pocket and handed the silver crown to the shopkeeper.

'Could you put what's left from this onto Karen's new slate, Gideon. It will help stop her getting behind again if the weather turns and she can't get the washing dry. Don't tell her though. I don't want her to think I'm treating her as a charity case.'

Gideon nodded his head slowly.

'It's our secret, Amy.'

Amy carried the carboard box through the alley and slid sideways through Karen's gate. The back door was open as Amy approached, but before she could knock, she was confronted by Freda, Karen's next-door neighbour. She hung her nose over the box that Amy was carrying.

'Are you handing out a second lot of rations,' she asked, poking her finger at the milk. 'I could use some of that? I've got none for Colin's tea.'

'This is nothing to do with the church,' Amy said as she heard Karen's footsteps on the step behind her. She turned away and smiled at the young mother as she stepped back to allow her to enter the scullery. Noticing the fresh milk in Amy's box, she looked across at her neighbour. 'I've got half a bottle of sterilised if you want it, Freda? Wait there a minute, I'll get it for you.'

When Amy placed the cardboard box on the table in the back room and handed her the brown pharmacy bag, Karen burst into a flood of tears.

'Beth's having a lie down upstairs,' she said between snuffles. 'They sent her home from school today because they're worried about that rash of hers being contagious.'

'Oh no,' Amy said, as she wrapped her arm around Karen's shoulders. 'Still, look on the bright side, there's something in the bag for the rash and there's some medicine for her scurvy, she'll be good as new in a week or so.' Amy took her arm from around Karen and held up the oranges. 'These are for both of you to share this time. They'll do you good too.'

As she was talking, the side door opened and Beth walked into the room rubbing her eyes.

'AMY!' she cried as she rushed across the room and flung herself into her arms. After a full minute's hug, she turned around to see what was in the box that Amy had brought with her.

'Amy brought your medicine round, so you'll be back at school in no time,' Karen said croakily as she wiped her eyes on her sleeve. 'And look, we have proper, fresh milk.' She opened the bottle, filled one of the china cups with it and passed it to Beth.

As Beth drank, Karen opened the brown bag and took out the contents. 'We'll start you on this little lot as soon as you've finished your milk,' she said.

Amy went on to explain about the community fund and how Shirley had gone out of her way to help.

'So, you see, not all politicians are in it just for themselves.

Any medicine Beth needs now will be paid for by the fund. Not just for these ailments but anything she needs in the future.' Amy reached out and stroked Beth's hair. 'I think the fund could help you with medicine too should you need it, Karen. I'll have a word with Shirley about it.'

Karen sighed softly. 'Please don't think I'm ungrateful, Amy, I honestly can't thank you enough for all you've done for us, and I can't put into words the joy and relief I feel at this moment. I just wish there had been a little help when my baby needed it.'

When Beth had been given her medicine and the cream had been applied to her skin, Amy took out the two puzzles and handed them to the young girl.

'Are those for me?' she squealed excitedly.

'Who else would I buy them for?' Amy said. 'Come on, let's clear the table and we'll have a go at making Buckingham Palace.'

At five o'clock, Amy said goodbye and promised to come back soon to see how Beth was doing with her medicine.

'Don't you go buying things for us, Amy,' Karen said as she gave her a hug on the top step. 'You've done more than enough and it's not like you're rolling in money yourself. We'll be fine now that I can work the old slate off.'

Amy tilted her head as she looked at Karen. 'I'm not being a nosy, do-gooder, honestly. The thing is, seeing how you and Beth have been forced to live has made me realise just how fortunate I am to live the life I do. We don't have a lot of money at home, but we do live relatively comfortably.'

'Never feel guilty, Amy,' Karen replied. 'You work hard for the bit you have. Don't apologise, you've earned it.'

. . .

As Amy walked along Ebeneezer Street on her way back to town, she spotted a man climb out of a green van and run across the street, trying to avoid the worst of the deep pot holes that had been left, unrepaired by the council for years. She squinted into the sun as she watched the man fish a key from his pocket and open the front door of number twenty-one.

'Terrence Derby,' Amy whispered to herself. 'He must be Karen's new landlord.'

Amy hurried along the street until she came to the last red-brick terraced house. On the road outside was a pile of rotten-looking timber mixed in with broken floor tiles and rusty lengths of iron pipe. Across the road was his small, green van with the words, Derby Cleaning Services, hand painted in white along the side.

Remembering that most people on the street didn't really like answering the front door to visitors, Amy walked back along the road until she found the alley that led to the rear of the properties. Derby shared a gate with number twenty, and as Amy stepped through it, she found herself in a shared yard that was identical to Karen's. She walked quickly to the back steps and after climbing the first one, she rapped on the newly painted, red door.

The greying, Terrence Derby was wearing the same faded blue jacket and baggy grey trousers he had worn when she had first met him at the Town Hall. His dreadfully scarred hands were in full view as he opened the door wider to look quizzically at her.

'If you're from the council, I'm moving the rubbish at the weekend,' he said.

'I'm not from the council, Mr Derby. I'm Amy Rowlings, we met at the Town Hall a couple of weeks ago. The night that—'

'I remember you now,' Derby said. He looked at her suspiciously. 'You were with the policeman.'

'That's right,' Amy said, 'but I haven't come to see you

regarding the murder. I think Inspector Bodkin has all the evidence he needs from you on that matter.'

'Oh that's all right then.' Derby rubbed the back of one hand with the palm of the other and winced. 'Sorry, I need to put cream on them, they're starting to dry out.'

'Please, don't let me stop you. I just wondered if I could have a quick word on behalf of one of your tenants?'

Derby stepped back into the scullery. 'Please, come in, Miss Rowlings.' He showed her into his back room which had been recently replastered. It was a complete contrast to Karen's back room. The fireplace had been taken out, rebuilt and now sported marble tiles with a dark oak surround and a matching mantle-piece. The earthen tiled floor had been covered in pale grey linoleum. There was an old table, similar to Karen's in the centre of the floor and there was a tall, mahogany Welsh dresser on the back wall, the top two shelves holding stacks of patterned plates, teacups and saucers. In the corner of the room was a small, low table with a black telephone perched on top.

'You're on the phone I see,' Amy said nodding towards the handset.

'It was only put in the other day; I've only used it once. It is a bit of a luxury but I am a businessman now so I can afford it.'

'You should get some business cards done,' Amy said. 'I can give you the name of a good printer.'

As she waited to be invited to sit, Derby looked around the room with a smile on his face.

'It's still a work in progress,' he said, 'but the gas cooker is in place in the scullery and I'm almost ready to paint the walls in here. The plaster needs another week or so to fully dry out.

'It's lovely,' Amy said as he held out a hand, inviting her to sit at the table.

'Can I make you some tea?' he asked.

The last thing Amy really needed was tea as she'd spent the

last hour and a half drinking cup after cup at Karen's, but she smiled politely and nodded her head.

'That would be lovely, thank you.'

Derby went out to the scullery and Amy heard the running of a tap, then the metal clunk as he put the kettle on the stove. When he returned, he was rubbing some greasy looking ointment into his damaged hands.

'Ah, that's better,' he said. 'It cools them down pretty quickly; they chafe a bit if I let them dry out too much.'

Amy looked at the tight, shrivelled, red skin, now glistening with the white coloured cream he had applied, and shuddered inwardly.

'I'm sorry you have to see this, Miss, I usually wear my gloves if I have company, I know it's not a pretty sight.'

'I'm sorry you have to go through such pain and discomfort,' Amy said. 'I can't imagine what it must have been like for you when your ship was attacked.'

Derby flinched at the memory, then he turned away, picked up a clean looking cloth and wiped off the worst of the sticky gunk from his hands. When he was finished, he tossed the cloth into a basket on the floor next to the dresser, then took two cups and saucers from the top shelf and placed them gently on the table. The crockery had a blue, periwinkle pattern on them.

'My mother left me these,' he said.

'They're lovely,' Amy said, thinking about the hand painted set that Karen owned.

Derby picked up a matching tea pot from the centre of the table and took it out to the scullery. When he returned, he put it carefully down on the square wicker mat, then went back out to get milk from the cold shelf in the pantry.

'So, you've come to ask something on behalf of one of my tenants? They can ask me themselves you know? I don't bite.'

'Karen has nothing but good things to say about you, Mr

Derby,' Amy said. 'You're so much better than the last landlord she had. The rent collector was... well, he was vulgar and opportunistic, at best.'

Derby shook his head as he poured the tea. After splashing milk into both cups, he offered Amy the sugar bowl.

'I don't hold with such things, Miss Rowlings, and please, call me Terrence.'

'In that case, I'm Amy,' she replied sipping at her tea and wondering where the nearest lavatory was outside of the Haxley estate. She assumed it would be at the railway station, she wasn't about to ask Terrence if she could use his.

'Which of my tenants are you representing, Mi... I mean, Amy?'

'Karen Hamilton, she lives right at the far end of the terrace, at number one,' Amy replied. 'She has a young daughter, Beth, who gets very ill due to the damp conditions. She looked around the room. They would love to live in a place like this.'

Terrence grimaced. 'All the steam she creates doesn't help with the damp,' he replied.

'She has to do the washing to survive,' Amy argued. 'Anyway, that would only really affect the scullery and every scullery on the street will have damp walls, everyone does their washing in there, that's what it's for. Her living room has dreadful damp, there is vermin running around and she's plagued with silverfish around the range. The roof still has a bit of a leak from the damage that ended up causing the death of her husband...' She paused for a moment, 'and she gets worms and slugs coming up from under the floor. Could you do anything to help her, Mr Derby? I don't suppose there's another house on the row coming up soon is there? One in a better condition than the one she's in?'

Terrence lifted his scarred hand to his chin. 'I'm sorry, Amy, no one has given notice to quit and everyone is pretty much up to date with their rent so I can't just evict a family, it wouldn't be fair. Anyway, all the houses are in pretty much the same condition and I can't do anything about them until I've got some spare cash. I promise you though, once I have, I'll make a start on the renovations.'

'Will they look like this when they're done?' Amy asked. 'That would be fabulous.'

'I won't be able to make them all as good as this one, Amy, this is my own house and it will be renovated to a better standard than the others. The vermin thing is an estate issue, not just this street, but I will have a go at the council about it.' Derby took a deep swallow from his tea cup. 'In the meantime, I'm spending most of my spare income doing this place up.'

'Can you give her an idea of how long it might be and what sort of improvements you've got planned for the properties?' Amy asked.

Derby frowned. 'I made a business plan when I took out the bank loan to buy these houses and I have to stick to it or the bank may call in my loan early. As for improvements. You can tell her I'll try to do something about sealing the floors, I'll definitely do something about the damp. We can install what they call, air bricks, near to the base of the walls, that will stop more damp coming up, once that's done, we can dig out the floor, lay some more bricks, then lay tiles or even concrete on top of them. Once the air bricks are in, the old lime-plaster can come off the walls and we'll redo them with modern gypsum. It's quite an expensive job though and it will take me years to get them all updated.'

'I don't mean to pry, Terrence, but how many years will it be before you can make a start? And can you *please* make number one your first project?'

'Seeing as how you've been so pleasant; I'll seriously consider it. Most people only want to shout at me when they complain about the state of the houses, but I've only owned them for a few months. As I said, I have to pay the bank off first. I borrowed fifteen hundred pounds to buy this entire street and as you can easily work out, at ten shillings a throw, I make ten pounds a week from the twenty properties, if I use all the rental income to pay off the loan and the interest, it will take me three and a half years.'

'That's a long time for her to wait, Mr Derby, I understand you have to give your own finances priority, but Beth is a sick child and she really does need to live her life in better conditions than she's in at the moment, and they can't just up sticks and move, there's nowhere for them to go.'

Derby picked up the teapot and left the room again. When he returned some five minutes later, he was carrying a fresh brew.

'There,' he said, placing the teapot on the table again. 'Let's have another cuppa and I'll tell you the whole story, maybe by the time I've finished you'll have a better idea of my circumstances.'

'I'd love to hear it, but could you hold the tea for two minutes, Mr Derby,' Amy said, getting to her feet... 'I am feeling rather... uncomfortable. Do you mind if I pay a visit to your lavatory?'

THIRTY-SIX

After visiting Derby's outdoor lavatory, which, thankfully, was spotlessly clean, Amy rinsed her hands under a standpipe in the yard, then, feeling much more comfortable, she re-joined Terrence in the house.

'I became a businessman just under a year ago,' Terrence said. 'Before then I made my living the best way I could with hands like these. I did a bit of ledger work at Mortenson's bank and in my spare time I worked on tax returns for one or two local, small businesses, but that didn't bring much in. People were reluctant to use my services because I didn't have my own set of offices and I used to turn up to the customers' premises on a bike after the business had closed for the day. I was living at home with my mother at the time.' He looked down at his hands again. 'It's hard to find a wife when you have hands like these.'

Amy leaned across and patted him on the forearm. 'I'm sure there's a good woman out there somewhere who would appreciate what you can offer,' she said, sympathetically.

'She's hiding herself well if there is,' Terrence said, sadly. 'It's not just the hands, unfortunately, Amy, I've got scarring over a lot of my body.'

'There's always someone. Don't give up hope,' she replied.

Derby looked long and hard into his tea cup, then he sighed and continued his story.

'Mum died last year and I was left the house in her will. It was bigger, and in a lot better state of repair than these are, to be honest. It was dry inside, but it needed some work. To cut a long story short, I was offered four hundred pounds for it and I bit the man's hand off. Mum had left me just over a hundred pounds in her will, but I didn't want to spend it all doing the house up. I needed that money to live on. I was earning a pittance at the bank; I reckon I could have earned more as a labourer or a miner, but my hands wouldn't allow me to work in those industries. Then the two small businesses I was doing the books for, both suddenly ceased trading. One was taken over by a bigger company and the other owner decided to retire. Anyway, I was left with a bit of money in the bank but I was living in lodgings. Then I met Mr Allenby who ran a small business repairing water and gas pipes for the council. They used to employ their own plumbers but the mayor had been running a cost cutting program and Mr Allenby had convinced him that his firm could do the work a lot cheaper than his own workforce could.

'Allenby was my way into the cleaning contract. I had been thinking of setting up my own business for a while, but wasn't sure what services I'd actually be able to offer. Allenby told me that the cleaning contract for the town's principal buildings was up for renewal and the current contractor was about to be deprived of it because he refused to pay the mayor's new, inflated contract price. He wanted three hundred pounds for a five-year contract that paid fifteen pounds a week to clean the three buildings, the Register Office, the Town Hall and the library. Previously it had been a hundred pounds. I had a little over five hundred pounds burning a hole in my pocket and I thought, what could be easier than cleaning? It was the same thing I did at home every week.'

Derby fished about in his coat pocket, pulled out a packet of cigarettes and offered one to Amy.

'I don't smoke, but thank you,' she said.

Terrence walked to the sash window and lifted the bottom half, then he sat on the window sill and lit his cigarette, blowing smoke out into the yard, thinking as he puffed away.

'The fates seem to have been with you when you met Mr Allenby,' Amy said.

Derby took one last draw on his cigarette, flicked the stub into the yard, then after fanning the air around Amy with his hands, he closed the window and walked back to his seat.

'The beauty of the cleaning contract was that it was all evening work, and that meant I could keep my job at the bank during the day. I had no one to come home to at night, so I didn't mind the extra hours. I bought a few second-hand vacuum cleaners and a load of brushes, buckets, mops etc and put an advertisement in the Post asking for experienced cleaning staff. As luck would have it, I ended up with three of the cleaners the deposed company had employed, and they knew the buildings well, so I could really have just left them to get on with it. In the end, I decided to muck in myself as that would save me money on employing a fourth cleaner.'

'So, that all worked out well for you?' Amy said. 'But how did you end up with the houses?'

'Ah, now that was Mr Drake's idea. I met him when I was working at the Town Hall one night and we got talking. He was thinking about hiring a new cleaning company to look after his offices, they're in town, next to the Westminster bank. He said if I could undercut the firm that was cleaning for him at the moment, he'd be happy to let me take it on. Then Mr Thornalley took me to one side and booked us to clean his house, it's a big one too. After that, Mr Kelly... Nelson that is... the man who sadly died, offered to let me take on cleaning his house, the big one on the High Street, Hillcrest. Things were going so well that I had to increase my workforce by adding four daytime cleaners.'

'Things were taking off for you then,' Amy said, smiling at Terrence.

'In spades,' Derby said. 'Before I knew it, I had a whole new side of the business. Because my girls did such a good job, and we were cheap, the word got round amongst the neighbours. I was still working at the bank so I couldn't muck in during the day, but the girls were so efficient they didn't need me anyway, and because we could run the team, one short, I was making even more money.'

Derby suddenly burst into a coughing fit. 'Sorry,' he spluttered, 'my lungs were damaged in the ship fire.'

'Smoking won't help them, surely,' Amy replied.

'It's an old habit, and it's a comfort to me. We all need something to settle the spirit, don't we?'

When Terrence had finished coughing, he wiped his mouth on the handkerchief he pulled from his pocket, then he went on.

'A couple of weeks after starting to clean for Mr Drake, we got chatting again, and he asked me if I'd ever thought of investing in property. I told him that I didn't have the funds available or I'd seriously think about it. I said that in a year or so I'd be looking to buy a house for myself. He laughed at that, and said that he meant, serious investment. He then told me that he was looking to offload a whole street of houses. Twenty-one in total and if I was interested, I could have them at a knock down price. I told him I'd think about it, but he said he needed the answer within a day or two and that he was doing me a big favour as he had people queuing up to buy them.

'When I asked how much he wanted, I was shocked. I could get the whole lot for fifteen hundred pounds. That was only about seventy-one pounds, ten shillings each, and as I had just sold one house for four hundred, albeit in a different area, I thought it was a bargain price. I went to have a look at them in my lunch break the next day. This house was empty and I was a bit surprised at the state they were in, but I was so excited by the prospect of owning my own property portfolio that I shut out all the negative thoughts that were building up inside my head and went to see my boss, the manager at Mortenson's bank. He put me onto another man, a Mr Holloway, who dealt with the property market. He was a friend of Mr Drake's and a big investor in his businesses, so he knew all about the houses that were being offered. He told me that with a little bit of investment to refurbish the buildings, they could be worth double the asking price inside five years, and if the houses were renovated to at least a minimal degree, then the rents could easily be increased.'

Derby rubbed the palms of his hands together.

'I thought about it for all of two minutes before I agreed, and within a few days I had signed the documents that made me a property owner. I moved into this house straight away, so that saved me the money I'd been spending on my lodgings. I started work on the refurbishment the following Saturday and I've been working on it ever since.' He looked around the room with look of pride on his face. 'I've done all right with it, haven't I? Mr Allenby helped out with the plumbing and there's a couple of builder's labourers that live on the estate. I just had to give them a bit of beer money to do the donkey work.'

'You've done really well for yourself,' Amy said, clasping her hands together. 'But weren't you worried when Nelson Kelly announced the plan for the new factory and the mayor set the price for the compulsory purchase order? It was a lot lower than the price you paid for the houses.'

'I was very concerned; in fact, I went to see Mr Drake about it, but he said I wasn't to worry and that he had plans in place himself for the factory build. He showed me a plan of the derelict land with the factory drawn at a different angle to Nelson Kelly's design. He said he'd got the mayor behind his project and that Kelly's scheme was just a pipe dream that would never see the light of day.'

Derby paused, then went to the window and opened it again before lighting another cigarette. He coughed after one draw, then recovered and continued his story.

'As the time got closer to the announcement of the winning tender, I began to get worried again. I hadn't heard anything from Mr Drake for a couple of weeks, then I learned that Mr Thornalley had been ousted and that Councillor McKenzie was taking over. Then worse news came. He was backing Nelson Kelly's bid. I went around to see Mr Drake in his office, but once again he put my mind at rest. He told me that he was investing in Nelson's company himself, and that would give him a say as to which floorplan the contractors would use to build the place. He said that he could easily persuade Mr Kelly to adopt his plan as it was a fair bit cheaper than his own design, mainly because there would be no demolition costs. So, I went home feeling a lot more relaxed about things and just got on with my work. Then came that terrible evening at the Town Hall. I'll never forget looking over Inspector Bodkin's shoulder and seeing Mr Kelly lying there. I still wake up in the night thinking about it.'

'Have you spoken to Mr Drake since Nelson's death, Terrence?' Amy asked.

'Yes, he asked to see me in his office a few days after Mr Kelly died. He offered to buy the houses back from me at a small profit, but I declined and said that I intended to stick to my business plan. He just smiled at me and said I was a fool to look a gift horse in the mouth and that I would come to regret it. Then he told me to get out. The next day I found out I'd lost the contract for cleaning his offices.'

'That's a vindictive thing to do,' Amy said. 'The more I hear about him, the more I dislike him.'

Derby nodded. 'That wasn't the end of it. A few days later I was called into the manager's office at the bank and was told that my services were no longer required.'

'Oh no! how awful,' Amy replied.

'The manager said he was going to check the details of my loan, but I wasn't worried about that. I'd had it looked at by a lawyer before I signed it, so they can't change the terms of the contract even if they wanted to. As long as I keep up the monthly repayments, they can't do a thing about it.'

'Drake didn't try to make your household customers drop you too, did he?'

'It wouldn't work if he had tried. We are cheaper than anyone else in the area. It really doesn't matter how much money these people have; they still like to save a few shillings here and there.'

'So, you still clean the Kelly house, Hillcrest.'

'The girls do. I've only bumped into Mrs Kelly once since it all happened. She was walking towards the Skelton crossroads as I drove past. I'd been down there to quote for a cleaning job at one of the big houses. I pulled up and wound my window down, but I just didn't know what to say to her.'

Amy's ears pricked up. 'Was she walking towards the crossroads from the direction of Russel Park?'

'No, from the Skelton side, I passed her just before she reached the crossroads. There was a taxi parked up at the junction.'

CHAPTER
THIRTY-SEVEN

AFTER LEAVING EBENEZER STREET, AMY DECIDED TO ENJOY THE EVENING air, so she took a slow walk past the Dragon pub and the railway station, and came out on the Main Street via the alleyway at the side of Brigden's. From there, she turned the corner to the High Street and walked past the three bus stops opposite the Town Hall, then she strolled down the hill to where the road merged with Middle Street.

The police station was a new building that stood at the junction with the main Gillingham Road. Amy pushed the dark-blue door open and stepped into the foyer where she found PC Ferris standing behind the dark-wood counter.

'Hi, Amy,' he said, brightly, 'to what do we owe the pleasure?'

'Is His Majesty at home?' she asked, flicking her head towards the door that led to the interior.

'He's been promoted, has he? He was only His Nibs the last time you came.'

Amy shrugged. 'He can't be a king, can he? Kings have lots of minions working for them, Bodkin has to do most of the work himself.'

Ferris leaned forwards and beckoned Amy towards him

conspiratorially. 'I hear from the palace that reinforcements might be on their way. Lord Laws, aka Chief Inspector Laws, formerly of this parish, is about to return for a few days with a couple of constables in tow.'

'I have mixed feelings about this news,' Amy said with a grimace. 'Laws doesn't like me getting involved with Bodkin's cases. Is he going to be looking into the Nelson Kelly murder, or is he just coming back to help out with the spate of burglaries and robberies?'

'I have no Idea, Amy,' he shrugged, 'he doesn't like me either if it helps.'

Amy patted his hand. 'Never mind, eh? We'll survive.'

'We always do,' Ferris gave Amy a wink. 'Inspector Bodkin has been in the records office all afternoon, going over old burglary cases. I bet he's ready for a cup of tea, I'll give him a shout.' The constable picked up the phone and dialled a single number.

'Is Mr Grayson in?' Amy asked as Ferris waited for Bodkin to pick up.

'No, he's down at Maidstone trying to drum up a few more recruits. He'll be back tomorrow. Did you want him for something? I can make an appointment.'

'No, it's all right, I was just wondering how much help Bodkin is getting today.'

'Not a lot, Amy. I offered to help but Grayson insisted I stay on the desk in case we have any more complaints of theft. We've had a dozen or more burglaries in the last fortnight. We don't get many more than that in a year, usually.' He put the phone back on its cradle. 'Nope, he isn't answering.' He looked over his shoulder towards the corridor that led to the police station's offices. 'I'd go and look but I've been told not to leave the front counter.' He thought for a moment, then left the desk and walked around to the side door to let Amy into the station, proper.

'There's only me and Bodkin here, so no one is going to spot you and ask questions. Trixie has already gone home so she won't be able to make any trouble for you. He pointed along the passage. Straight to the bottom, then turn left, go to the end, then down a set of stairs, the record office is right next door to the evidence room. You can't miss it, there's a big sign on the door, saying, Evidence.'

'What are we going to see on Saturday night?' he called after her as she set off.

'Oh, it's a re-release of a George Formby comedy, Keep Fit. I love George, he's so funny.'

Ferris suddenly pulled a buck-toothed, grin and began to sing in a mock Lancashire accent. 'When I'm cleanin' winders.'

'Stick to Bing Crosby songs, Ferris,' Amy said, chuckling to herself as she walked along the corridor.

She found Bodkin leaning against the wall in the passageway outside the evidence room. He was reading a report held inside an open buff folder. He looked up through baggy eyes as he noticed her approaching.

'Hello,' he said. 'Do you come here often?'

'Only when Chief Inspector Laws isn't around,' Amy replied. 'I honestly can't believe that you and Ferris are the only two people in the building.'

Bodkin waved the buff folder in the air. 'Back Door Billy and Jemmy Jemson wait for no man,' he said.

'Who on earth is Back Door Billy?'

'He's a burglar who usually—'

'Breaks in through the back door?' Amy suggested.

'Correct, give the lady a cigar. Meanwhile, Jemmy Jemson...'

'Breaks into houses using a Crowbar... sorry, Jemmy.'

'You're too good at this,' Bodkin said, opening the door to the records office.

'The nicknames aren't very imaginative, are they?'

'No,' Bodkin agreed, 'but then the press made up the names, not me. Blame the likes of Sandy Miles.'

'Speaking of him, did you see last night's edition of the post? He's found out that you and Ferris are pretty much the last men standing. He's practically inviting the criminal element in the town to get about their nefarious activities with little chance of being caught.'

'I saw it. He's not very happy with me, is he?'

'I think you have an informer, Bodkin. In fact, I'm sure of it.'

'Oh, I know, and the list of suspects isn't a long one, is it?'

'It's Trixie,' Amy said. 'I'd bet my wages on it.'

'Just because she gets right up your nose, it doesn't mean she's the culprit, Amy. Anyway, I've decided to get to the bottom of it once and for all. I've set a little trap.'

Amy rubbed her hands together excitedly. 'Ooh, do tell. I won't spill the beans, honestly.'

'Just keep your eyes on the Post for the next few days. If you see a police-based story about a fruit and veg warehouse robbery, it's Albert Foss, the constable who's about to retire... my money's on him by the way. I think he's taking back handers from Miles to help boost his retirement pension.' Bodkin paused as he smiled at Amy. 'On the other hand, if you see a piece telling the world that our three police cars are so old that they aren't fit to drive, then it's Trixie. I told each of them a different story when I was chatting to them in the canteen.'

'Ferris is ruled out, obviously.'

Bodkin nodded. 'Ferris hates the press even more than I do; he only ever reads the entertainment pages.'

'Speaking of Ferris, he's upstairs on the desk doing terrible impressions of George Formby,' Amy said.

'God help us on Saturday,' Bodkin replied with a grimace.

The policeman dropped the buff file on the desk, then, after closing and locking the records office door, he led Amy back up the stairs to the ground floor.

'Why did you lock the door, Bodkin? It's a police station,' Amy said with a puzzled look on her face. 'It's not like anyone is going to steal things from here.'

'I'm not trusting anyone with anything until the person responsible for leaking information has been caught,' Bodkin said. 'Though I'd love to catch Sandy blooming Miles in possession of some of our criminal record files. I'd have him up before the beak before he could type one of his ridiculous headlines.'

Bodkin opened the door to his office and stood back while Amy entered. Picking up the kettle he shook it, then plugged it into the wall socket next to his filing cabinet.

'Tea?' he asked.

'Not for me, honestly Bodkin, I've drunk enough of it today to empty the hold of a tea clipper.'

Amy sat in the chair at the front of Bodkin's desk, crossed her legs, then went into detail about her conversation with Derby. Bodkin took notes as she was speaking.

'Oh, and there's a bit more pertinent news. Rory the taxi man has been ferrying me around all afternoon and he can definitely identify Kitson as the man with the bloody shirt.'

'That's good, it will be important if he ever gets taken to court,' Bodkin replied.

'He also told me that he regularly picked up Helen Kelly from Hillcrest and dropped her at the Skelton Junction.'

Bodkin rubbed his hands together. 'So, some nights she took taxis, other nights she walked through the park to see her lover. I wonder what she'll have to say about this. I think I'll give Horatio a ring now and ask him for a comment. That ought to take that holier than thou look off his face.'

'Don't call him. She wasn't seeing Kelly,' Amy said quickly. 'She was seeing Kitson.'

'Kitson!'

Amy nodded. 'Terrence Derby spotted her walking along the road that Kitson lives on. There was a taxi waiting at the crossroads.'

Bodkin put the handset back on its cradle and rubbed at his stubbly jaw as he thought.

'Well, that is a surprise. I hadn't considered those two being an item. He just doesn't seem her type, I mean, she's an extremely attractive woman, she can do much better than him.'

Amy narrowed her eyes at the policeman. 'All right, Bodkin, don't go overboard.' She leaned back in her chair and studied her nails. 'Anyway, you're in a queue behind two lecherous taxi drivers.'

'I only have eyes for you, Amy,' Bodkin said with a look of mock-shock on his face.

'I should think so too,' Amy replied giving him the stern eye. 'Right,' she said, clapping her hands, 'what else is new?'

'Nothing really,' Bodkin replied. He picked up a buff folder from his desk. 'The head of the catering staff called back in response to my query about wine-stained tablecloths. He said there were always about four or five after any event and that night was no exception. He couldn't pinpoint any particular tables that the stained cloths were taken from either.'

'So, that means we can't rule out Drake's rather thin story about his missing gloves then.'

'No, that's a line of investigation that is closed to us now. We have no way of finding out whether he was lying or not.' He put the folder back on the table, then opened it up and rummaged through the paperwork until he found what he wanted. 'I'll read these two statements to you, Amy. I'd like your opinion. If it was left to me, I'd let you go through the whole evidence folder, but I don't want you to be compromised if Laws ever asks you if you've handled police files.'

Amy nodded. 'I understand.'

'Okay,' Bodkin picked up the first sheet. 'This is Raymond Giles's statement. He's the team leader of the caterers.'

We got to the Town Hall early on the evening of the presentation. There were six of us altogether. Me and five girls who had travelled in the back of the van to make sure the food wasn't tipped out all over the floor. We parked up at the top of the alleyway that runs between the Town Hall and the Library but we had to wait for fifteen minutes for the Council's staff to leave before we were allowed to get our stuff inside. We were waved in by a black-haired man, wearing a blue suit, standing near the stairway to the upper rooms. We carried all the boxes through to the kitchen, then I left the girls to unpack it while I went to move the van a little further up the street. I didn't want a fine for leaving it parked on the pavement all evening.

Anyway, when I got back, I looked for the man we had seen in the entrance lobby on our way in, but there was no sign of him. I assumed he had gone home. Now, I know this might seem unimportant but he didn't close the front doors. They were open right from the time we turned up to when the guests started to arrive at seven-thirty. We were all busy in the kitchen or setting up the trestle tables in the Assembly Room, anyone could have come in and hid themselves away until the presentation started.

Amy sat in silence while Bodkin read, then she thought out aloud.

'No one else has ever mentioned this man. He sounds like a council official, but why would he leave the front doors open all that time when he wasn't there to guard them?'

'We know who the man is and he's been questioned. He is a councillor called David Broughton. He was waiting for his girl-friend to come down from the offices above, she works in the typing pool. I only mention this because in his evidence; Mr Giles mentions that the front doors were open all evening and as he says, anyone could have just walked in and hid themselves, maybe in one of the rooms upstairs, then joined the presentation party when it was in full swing.' The policeman rubbed his chin again and dropped the sheet of paper back in the file.

Amy pushed a few strands of hair away from her face and then pursed her lips. 'It doesn't help us a lot really, though I suppose it's possible that Horatio or Kitson sneaked in while no one was about.'

'I don't really buy it but it is a loose end,' Bodkin replied as he picked up the second sheet. 'Now this *is* interesting, this tells us exactly how the murder weapon got to be where it was.' He picked up the sheet and began to read.

'This is the evidence of one of the catering staff, a Miss Zena O'Keefe. She is the youngest of the crew.'

When we arrived in the kitchens, Mr Giles told us to start unpacking the food and get rid of the boxes. There were some bins outside the back door apparently but the door was locked so we had to just pile the boxes up in the corridor. I had just finished unpacking the beef roast when Mr Giles came back and told Marlene, Hilda and Rosie to start setting up the buffet trestles. They were also told to get the tablecloths onto the guests' tables. I was left in the kitchen with the food but I wasn't sure what he wanted me to do so I went to look for him. He wasn't in the best of moods; I can tell you. Anyway, he took hold of my arm and almost dragged me back to the kitchen, then pointing to the roast beef and the big ham, he told me to get carving.

The knife we used to use was lying on a trolley with a couple of serving plates, so I picked it up along with the carving fork, boiled a kettle and washed them in hot water before I got to work on the ham and beef joints. When I finished, I put the full serving plates back on the trolley. I was going to wash up the carving knife and fork again, like I'm supposed to, but I heard Mr Giles's voice shouting for me. "Where is that damned girl with the cold cuts?" I panicked a bit and dropped the carving set on the trolley next to the plates, then I pushed the trolley out of the kitchen and up to the Assembly Room. Mr Giles took the serving plates and began to distribute the meat across a few of the trestles, then he handed the empty plates back and told me to park the trolley up in the kitchen.

However, when I got to the kitchen door, the other girls were rushing in and out carrying the rest of the buffet. Suddenly I felt Mr Giles's hot breath on the back of my neck. "Don't stand around like a blooming statue, girl, get those dessert bowls out."

So, I parked the trolley up by the kitchen doors and did as I was asked. I didn't get back to the kitchen again after that. I was told to help serve the guests drinks when they arrived, so the trolley stayed where I'd left it. I do feel bad about it, because if I'd done my job properly and washed the carving set, they'd have been sitting on the drainer in the kitchen out of sight of any murderer.

'The poor girl, blaming herself,' Amy snapped. 'If it was anyone's fault it was that man Giles for being on her back all evening.'

Bodkin nodded agreement. 'She's right though. If the knife had been left where it should have been, our murderer would never have been given the opportunity to kill Nelson. We're not looking at a premeditated murder here. No one went to the event intent on killing Mr Kelly. It was a spur of the moment attack.'

Bodkin yawned and rubbed his eyes. 'I think I could sleep on a clothesline,' he said.

'Knock off early, Bodkin,' Amy said. 'You'll be no use to anyone if you're too tired to think straight.'

'I'll give it another hour or so,' Bodkin replied. 'But I will take a bit of a break while I give you a lift home.'

'I think we should get our heads together soon,' Bodkin said as he pulled up outside Amy's cottage. 'How about I come over tomorrow night, then we can compare notes?'

'That sounds good to me, Bodkin, and it will get you out of the station for the evening.'

Bodkin smiled as Amy climbed out of the car. 'See you tomorrow. I'm off to see if I can catch up with Back Door Billy.'

Mrs Rowlings was waiting by the door as Amy waved Bodkin off at the gate.

'Amy, where on earth have you been? I thought you did another half day. I've been expecting you home since half past one.'

'It's a long story, Mum,' Amy replied. 'I'll tell you over dinner.'

'Your dad has already had his. He fancied egg and chips; I've got plenty cut up ready if you'd like the same. The chip pan's still quite hot, they won't take long.'

Amy walked into the living room and gave her father a kiss on the cheek. 'How was your day?'

Mr Rowlings put down his paper. 'Not as interesting as yours it seems. What were you doing up by the station tonight? I saw you walk by when I was on the bus.'

'I was across at the Haxley estate again, Dad. Shirley McKenzie paid for Beth's prescription and I went over to deliver it.'

'Ah, the Good Samaritan,' Mr Rowlings said, fondly. 'You're always going out of your way for people less fortunate. I'm proud of you, my dear.'

Amy gave her father a hug and walked across the room to sit at the table. Lying on top of a place mat was an envelope with her name written on it. She recognised the handwriting immediately as belonging to Alice. She picked it up and tore it open eagerly. Alice usually just left a verbal message so she was intrigued to find out what was inside.

Amy, I took a telephone call for you from a gentleman who would like you to follow his wife to see what she gets up to. He left a phone number. He got mine from one of your pink cards.

Love Alice.

PS. I told him you'd ring him back this afternoon.

'Hold the chips!' Amy shouted as she got to her feet and headed for the door. 'I'm nipping down to see Alice.'

Mrs Rowlings followed her with a bowl of cut chipped potatoes in her hand. 'She said a man wants your gum shoes.'

THIRTY-EIGHT

'Ooh, look it's the young Jane Marple,' Alice said as Amy stepped in through the kitchen door. 'The kettle's on.'

'Not for me, thanks,' Amy said, rubbing her stomach. 'I'm a bit acidy.'

'How are things at the shop?' Miriam asked as she bounced baby Martha on her knee.

'It's been good, thanks, Miriam, I get a bit bored, but today has been interesting.'

Amy sat down at the well-scrubbed, ancient oak table and picked up the piece of paper that Alice slid across to her.

'That's the message I got. I wrote it all down so I didn't forget anything.'

'Mum thinks someone wants to eat my chewy slippers,' Amy said with a grin.

'She wha... ah, I did say that a man was asking for a Gumshoe. Sorry, I didn't mean to confuse her.'

'I did explain what a Gumshoe was once, but I think she's forgotten. She's like it with a lot of American terms. The last film she went to see was a Jimmy Cagney movie and all the way home she was asking me why he called his girlfriend a 'broad' when she was as skinny as a rake.'

Alice laughed. 'I didn't want to leave a verbal message because I know your mum and dad aren't too keen on the sleuthing.'

'To say the least,' Amy replied. 'They're all right if they know I'm with Bodkin though.' Amy paused for a moment. 'Mum's still saying I should pin him down while I have the chance. She's convinced someone else will come along and sweep him off his feet before I get to see him again.'

'Bodkin? Swept off his feet? It would take a far bigger brush than I've ever clapped eyes on,' Alice replied.

'She worries about him. She thinks he needs mothering.'

Alice nodded slowly. 'She's right about that at least. I noticed he was looking a bit peaky last week.'

'He looks even peakier now,' Amy said. 'The poor man hardly sleeps.'

'I'm not surprised, if what you read in the papers is true,' Miriam said, before blowing a raspberry on Martha's tummy. 'The Post reckons there are only two policemen looking after the whole town. They're forecasting a festival of crime. Has Bodkin worked out who is passing the stories on yet?'

'Keep your eye on the headlines for the next couple of days, Miriam, but don't believe all you read,' Amy said. 'Bodkin has a clever plan to try to wheedle out the informant.'

With Alice sitting on a chair a couple of feet away, Amy picked up the phone and dialled the local number that her best friend had written down.

'The Timms residence, Kristina speaking.'

Amy froze for a second and put her hand over the mouthpiece.

'I recognise that voice,' she whispered to Alice.

'I was hoping to speak to Mr Timms,' Amy said with a slight change of accent.

'Edgar... it's your floozy,' Amy heard Kristina shout.

A few moments later a man's voice came on the line.

'Trixie, what on earth are you thinking of, calling me at home?'

Amy put her hand to her mouth to cover a giggle.

'It's erm... it's not Trixie, Mr Timms, it's Amy Rowlings from the ARIA agency. You left a message.'

Timms wasn't impressed.

'You were supposed to call back earlier than this,' he hissed. 'My wife is back now; she's probably listening to us as we speak.'

'I'm sorry about that, Mr Timms, I'm involved in a rather important case at the moment and I'm afraid I'm a little caught up in it.'

'Are you saying you don't want to take on my investigation? I assumed when I pulled that little pink card from my wife's handbag, that you were a professional service with more than one agent.'

Amy cupped her hand over the mouthpiece again.

'I know who it is,' she hissed towards Alice. 'I met them at the Town Hall.'

'I'm afraid I am the only agent available at the moment, Mr Timms and as I said, I'm awfully busy, but I'll get back in touch as soon as I have a bit of free time.'

'Don't bother yourself,' Timms snapped. The line went dead.

'Well, well, well, the not so happily married Timms family. She's out running wild, while he's seeing that bimbo, Trixie, who lives in the flat below Bodkin.' She put her hand on her hip and began to swing it slowly whilst doing a very good impression of Mae West. 'I generally avoid temptation... unless I can't resist it,' she drawled.

'You can't be sure it's her,' Alice said. 'Although how many Trixies can there be in a small town like this?'

'It's her. I'd stake my record collection on it,' Amy replied.

'But why didn't you take the job? I bet there was good money to be had.'

'I agree with Dad about adultery,' Amy said. 'It's best not to get involved in someone else's sinful pursuits.'

'But you're investigating an adulterous relationship in the murder inquiry, aren't you?'

'That's different,' Amy replied. 'That's Bodkin's case.'

Alice got to her feet and walked to the lounge door; Amy was about to follow when she suddenly had a thought. Picking up the local telephone directory, she skipped the advertisements and flipped through the pages until she got to the people whose surname began with the letter T.

'Talbot, Tansley,' Tebbit... Timms, Mr. E. The Limes. 124 High Street, Spinton. Wait a minute. I'm sure Polly Starbuck lives at 118a and she's in the flat above the grocers. That must mean that the Timms live on the other side of the alley that runs past the library.'

'So, why is that important?' Alice asked.

'Because, my darling, there's a gate at the back of her house that leads directly onto the park.'

With Alice still looking confused, Amy slammed down the phone book and quickly picked up the handset again.

'Operator, can you put me through to Spinton police station. I'd like to speak to Inspector Bodkin.'

CHAPTER
THIRTY-NINE

Amy had a busy time of it at London Connection on Thursday morning with two of the shop's larger- framed customers insisting on trying on dresses that they wouldn't have squeezed into after a year of dieting.

At lunchtime, Amy picked up her bag and walked the short distance to the library to exchange her book and try to get the new Jeeves and Wooster for her father. She was delighted to find a copy of P.G. Wodehouse's latest comedy, knowing full well that she would read it herself as soon as her dad had finished it. Her own choice was a murder mystery by Georgette Heyer, Death In The Stocks, which she had been looking for on the shelves for a few weeks.

As she came out of the library, she turned left to walk past the alleyway that divided the council building from the Timms' household. On instinct, she turned into the alley and walked slowly towards the park, stopping now and then to look into the Timms' garden through a knot hole in the fencing, but as there was a rather thick hedge growing on the other side, her view was limited. At the end of the alley, Amy turned right and walked to the back gate of the property. After looking over her shoulder to make sure she wasn't being observed, Amy flicked the latch of the gate and pulled it open. She found herself looking onto a beautifully kept garden with a wide, lush, green lawn bordered by flower beds and shrubs. On the right-hand side of the garden was a double swing chair. Sitting on the chair was Kristina Timms, she put her book down at her side as she noticed Amy standing at the open gate.

'Well, are you going to stand there and gawp all day, or are you coming in?' she said.

Amy stepped onto the lawn and closed the gate quietly behind her. She held out her hands in a gesture of apology as she walked towards the slim, dark-haired woman.

'I'm sorry, I...'

'You were looking for Edgar?'

'No... yes... not really.'

Kristina got to her feet. She was wearing a green, knee-length tea dress with puff sleeves and white sandals. She pursed her lips as Amy approached.

'Yes, no, not really? What a strange reply to a simple question.'

Amy bit her lip.

'I wasn't looking for him, but had he been here I'd have asked for a word,' she said.

'Was it you on the telephone last night? I thought it might have been his fancy piece. She's very young, or so I hear.' She turned back to the swing seat. 'Come on then, sit down and tell me why you're sneaking in through my back gate.'

'Firstly, can I say that I have no intentions of investigating you,' Amy began.

'Well, that's good to know. Is that why he rang you? I wondered why your card was lying at the side of the phone when I answered it last night. The silly old fool forgot to put it back in my bag.' She paused as Amy sat down. 'I was thinking of calling you myself as it happens.' She picked up her glass of lemonade and took a sip. 'Our marriage is over. It would take something the size of a double sheet to patch it up this time.'

'I can't really discuss what he said to me,' Amy replied. 'Not that there is much to say anyway. He didn't like my response.'

'He wants a quick divorce, dear,' Kristina said, 'and he wants to blame my adultery for the collapse of the marriage, even though the affair he's embarked on at the moment is just one of many he's had over the years.'

'I turned him down,' Amy said. 'Partly because I don't want to get involved in messy divorce cases but mostly because... well, I think I know the woman he's seeing. We don't get on and she might get the idea that I was just being vindictive if I stuck my nose into her affairs.'

'But it would be me you wouldn't have been investigating, wouldn't it?'

'True, but after he mentioned a certain young woman... he thought it was her on the phone at first... I sort of know I'd have had to look into his behaviour too. Oh, I'd be hopeless at divorce cases, I'd feel sorry for one side or the other, especially if one of them was being dumped for someone younger.'

'I wouldn't have been dumped, Amy... it is Amy, isn't it?'

Amy nodded.

'This time, I'm every bit as much at fault as he is. Although at least the person I'm seeing is more or less my own age. Edgar is still chasing his long-lost youth. He just doesn't realise how ridiculous he'll look with a young blonde, twenty-year-old on his arm. He's fifty-four you know?'

'She's older than that,' Amy said with distaste. 'She's a floozy who thinks she's Mae West.'

Kristina patted Amy's hand. 'I hear more than a little bit of bitterness in that statement. I won't ask what the reason is, though I can imagine.'

'She lives in the flat below a friend of mine,' Amy replied. 'She's forever flirting with him.'

'Ah, she fancies your boyfriend, does she? Well, he's probably more her age at least.' She patted Amy's hand again. 'Don't worry, dear, if he's half the man you deserve, he'll ignore her.' She looked at Amy appraisingly. 'He'd be mad to drop you anyway. He'll never find a more attractive young woman.'

Amy blushed and looked at her knees.

'So,' Kristina said, after a few moments silence. 'Why did you break into my garden today?'

'It's to do with the investigation I'm helping Inspector Bodkin with,' Amy replied. 'Could I ask... Do you own a fur coat?'

After leaving the shop at five-thirty, Amy took a leisurely stroll down Middle Street to the police station. Ferris was once again on duty on the desk.

'Have you been there since yesterday evening?' Amy asked.

'It feels like it,' Ferris replied, 'but, as it happens, no. I'm on the evening shift, Albert Foss has been manning the fort all day and the chief super has found a couple of volunteers to look after the desk for the next week or so. One's a female constable from Gillingham, the other is coming up from Sittingbourne for the week. He sounds a nice sort of bloke. He rang me today to sort out which shifts we're going to be working.'

'That's good news. Is someone covering Saturday evening? We can't have you missing George Formby, can we?'

'Young, Linda Blissett will be filling in, at least I assume she's young. All the female constables I've seen have been under twenty-five.'

'Your luck might be in then, Ferris,' Amy said with a wink. 'It's just a shame she won't get to hear you sing at the Bell.'

'Oh... I haven't told you, have I? I've lost my spot at the Bell.

They found out about my monthly booking at the Milton and they don't want to share singers with them.'

'But they weren't paying you, were they?'

'No, but the manager was about to make me an offer. Nothing like the fiver an hour I'd get at the Milton though. He was talking more like five shillings for the two, hour-long slots.'

'Stick with the Milton then, Ferris,' Amy replied. 'You're far more likely to be spotted by a talent scout in there.'

She nodded towards the corridor behind him. 'Is Bodkin at home or is he out hunting Back Door Billy?'

'He went home about twenty minutes ago. He said he wanted to put something on his eye.'

'His eye? What's wrong with his eye, did he bump into something?'

'Yep, he bumped into Back Door Billy,' Ferris said.

Amy left the police station and walked the short distance to Bluecoat House, the two-storey block of flats where Bodkin lived. After pressing the bell on the front door five times without getting a response, she walked a few paces back and looked up at his window. The curtains were open, as was the small, top window.

She was just about to leave to walk to the bus stop when Trixie opened the window to her front room and stuck her head out.

'He's not in, he left with a dark-haired woman about an hour ago... they were arm in arm... and laughing about something.'

'Nice try,' Amy said. 'But I already know he was at the station only twenty minutes ago.'

'Ah, I meant fifteen minutes, I lost track of time,' Trixie replied before pouting and pulling a sad face.

'She was very young, and very pretty.'

'He likes them young,' Amy said with a smile. 'Like someone

else I know, but he's much, much older than Bodkin.' Amy frowned as she pretended that she was thinking hard. 'What's his name now... Edward... No, Edgar, that's it, Edgar.'

Trixie's mouth dropped open.

'You should keep your nose out of other people's business,' she spat as she pulled her head back and slammed the window shut.

Amy backed away smiling to herself. After taking one last look up at Bodkin's window, she turned away from the building. As she did, she spotted a Black Morris car, parked up at the right-hand side of the block of flats. She dipped her head to look inside as she walked towards it and saw the policeman sprawled out in the driver's seat, his head hanging over the back of it. His eyes were closed. She could hear his snores, even with the car windows shut tight.

Amy walked around the front of the car and tapped lightly on the driver's window. When that didn't rouse him, she tapped a bit harder, when that failed, she pulled open the door, placed a hand on his shoulder and gently shook him.

'Eh...What?' Bodkin's head snapped forwards. He looked totally disorientated for a moment, then his one good eye focussed on Amy, the other was half-closed and ringed by a purple and black bruise.

'Wake up, Rip Van Winkle,' Amy said with a smile. She leaned closer to get a better look at his swollen eye. 'Back Door Billy has a decent right hook by the looks of it.'

'He took me unawares,' Bodkin complained. 'Anyway, you should see him, he's got two shiners.'

Amy shook her head sadly. 'Throwing punches is never the answer, Bodkin. What happened, wouldn't he come quietly?'

'He wouldn't even come noisily,' Bodkin said as he began to yawn. 'Not at first, anyway.'

The policeman yawned again, then raised his fingers to touch his swollen eye. 'How long have I been asleep?' he asked.

'No more than fifteen minutes, I'm sorry to say,' Amy replied. 'I dropped into the station and Ferris told me you'd gone home.' Amy flicked her head towards the flat. 'Then, the bimbo of the year, nineteen thirty-nine, told me you'd left on the arm of an attractive young woman.' She stretched her neck to look into the back of the car. 'But... the lady vanishes.'

'That's a good title for a film,' Bodkin said as he rolled his shoulders to ease the cramp.

Amy walked around to the passenger side and climbed into the front seat. 'Home, Jeeves,' she said, as she placed her hessian bag on her knee.

'I have a few things to sort out at work, Back Door Billy is in one of the cells.'

'He'll still be there in the morning, Bodkin,' Amy replied. 'Is there anyone to check on him overnight?'

'Albert Foss is coming back in. He was on the desk all day but he wants some more overtime.'

'Well then,' Amy said. 'Unless Albert wants to give Miles a new headline about a notorious criminal with two black eyes escaping from the cells at Spinton nick, he'll probably still be in his when you get to work tomorrow.' She patted Bodkin's arm. 'Come on, let's get some food inside you. Mum said she was going to make a shepherd's pie for dinner when she found out you were coming round tonight. She does like to spoil you.'

Bodkin yawned again, then started up the car. 'Shepherd's pie is my favourite meal,' he said.

'I know,' Amy replied, 'so does Mum, that's why she's made it.'

As they drove along, Amy shot Bodkin a glance, the policeman looked back at her through his one good eye.

'What?'

'I was about to mention that I did a bit of sleuthing in my lunch break and I have definitely uncovered the identity of the lady in the fur coat. It was Kristina Timms. She's been seeing Horatio for a few months now.'

'So, she's his alibi for the night that Nelson was killed. We know she was over there that night because the old man and his dog spotted her walking back crying. I wonder what that was all about?'

'She didn't say why she was crying but she hasn't given him an alibi. He wasn't there when she turned up.'

CHAPTER FORTY

'There you are, Bodkin, tuck in,' Elizabeth Rowlings said as she placed a plate of shepherd's pie on the table in front of him.

'Wow!' Amy exclaimed as she stared at the plate, piled high with mince and mash. 'You've given him enough to feed a flock of shepherds.'

'He needs feeding up,' Mrs Rowlings replied. 'He's nothing but skin and bone, the poor man.' She walked back to the kitchen to get her own plate. 'I don't have any steak to put on that eye, but I've got half a pound of mince left over.'

Amy and Bodkin exchanged glances. Mr Rowlings didn't appear to have noticed and continued eating in silence.

After an apple pie and evaporated milk dessert, Bodkin offered to do the washing up, but Mrs Rowlings wouldn't hear of it.

'Sit yourself down on the sofa, or would you like to lie down for a nap? Amy can sit at the table with me.'

'I'm fine thanks, Mrs R,' Bodkin said. 'My eye will be fine too. It's not the first one I've had in my career.'

'There's an interesting story on the front page of the evening Post,' James Rowlings said, looking up over his paper. 'It seems that someone has run off with a lorry load of fresh fruit and veg while our police force wasn't looking.'

'Got him!' Amy exclaimed. 'Albert's in for the high jump now, isn't he? Do you think they'll sack him? He'll lose his pension surely, the silly man.'

Rowlings looked quizzically across the room as Amy began to explain Bodkin's cunningly laid trap.

'How long has he been a constable?' he asked. 'He was on the beat around here when I was a kid.'

'Well, he's sixty-five. He did make sergeant once, but he was demoted again when he was caught with a box containing two hundred packs of cigarettes that had been stolen from a delivery van. He didn't steal them himself; it was his payoff for keeping quiet.' Bodkin shook his head. 'I think Grayson was going to ask him to stay on for a few months to man the front desk.'

'Are you going to report him tomorrow?' Amy asked.

'No, I'll just have a quiet word. I don't want to ruin his retirement. He's been in the force since he was fourteen. I will have a word with Miles though, let him know that I'm aware that he's been bribing a police officer.'

Amy leaned over and squeezed Bodkin's arm. 'You're such a nice man,' she said.

Bodkin shook his head. 'I'm not being kind really, but I do feel sorry for him. He'll get a pittance as a pension and his pay as a constable wouldn't have been enough for him to have put any money aside.' The policeman touched his eye tenderly. 'I would bet that old Albert has sported enough of these over the years. He's earned his pension. I'm not going to be the one that deprives him of it.'

At seven o'clock, Amy got to her feet and stretched her arms above her head. 'Right, Bodkin, let's get started. Have you got your notes? Mine are upstairs.' She looked at her father who had just picked up his new book. 'Is it all right if I take Bodkin up to my room, Dad? We can't really discuss the case down here with you and Mum listening in.'

'You are not taking a man up to your bedroom, Amy,' Rowlings said as he put his book back on the table. 'I know I can trust you both, but it is rather unseemly.' He got to his feet and patted his stomach. 'I think I'd like to wash that excellent dinner down with a glass or two of whisky.' He made a 'get up' motion towards his wife. 'Come on, Elizabeth, grab your coat. We'll have a walk up to the Old Bull. We haven't been in there for months.'

Bodkin walked out to the car to pick up his personal case notes while Mr and Mrs Rowlings walked arm in arm up the road towards the pub. When he returned to the lounge Amy was waiting for him, clutching the jotter containing her own thoughts.

She opened her notebook and spread it out on the table to show Bodkin the two pages of neatly written observations.

'Right, this is what I've got, though it needs to be updated with the latest news about Helen and Kristina.'

Bodkin opened his buff file and tipped out twenty pieces of crumpled, hastily scribbled notes. Amy shook her head as she looked at the crumpled scraps of paper sheets and torn out pages from his notebook that littered the table.

'I sometimes wonder how you ever managed to crack a case if this is how disorganised you are, Bodkin.'

The inspector tapped his head, then winced as he felt a stab of pain in his wounded eye.

'I keep it all up here,' he said. 'I have lots of little rooms inside my head where I store everything pertinent to the case.'

'I bet those rooms are in a right state too,' Amy said, as she tried to arrange Bodkin's notes into some kind of order.

An hour later, the pair had updated and co-ordinated their notes, adding the latest information that Amy had collected over the last couple of days. Bodkin, who had been listening intently as

Amy gave him the finer details of her meeting with Kristina, leaned back in his chair and rubbed at his stubble covered chin with his right hand.

'So, I think we've got everything we know about all the main protagonists written down now, Amy, the only problem is, we've still got the same number of suspects and none have cast iron alibis.'

Amy grinned at the policeman. 'I love it when you say "we".'

She turned to a new sheet in her jotter and wrote the names of the suspects in large letters.

BASIL THORNALLEY

Bodkin rubbed his chin again.

'He's in the frame. He was in the vicinity. He has a weak alibi. In my top three.'

Amy put a tick next to Thornalley's name, then pointed to the next name on her list.

ALMA THORNALLEY

'Whilst female murderers are very rare, women can, and do, kill if they feel threatened. She's not out of the running.'

'Lorna?' Amy put a tick next to Alma's name then pointed to the next name on the list.

LORNA WETHERBY

'She could have done it,' Bodkin said, thoughtfully, 'She was covered in his blood when we found her and she was the last person to see him alive after all. She's not one of the main contenders for me, but that could change of course.'

FRANCIS DRAKE

'He's still my number one suspect,' Bodkin said. 'Whether he did the deed himself or orchestrated it. He was at the kitchen door, when Nelson was on the phone.'

Amy put two ticks alongside Drake's name, then asked what Bodkin's thoughts were about the next name on the list.

HAROLD KITSON

'Kitson is very high on my list, number two, jointly with Basil Thornalley. We know he was outside the Town Hall at the right time. He's a contender.'

Amy put a tick next to Kitson, then pointed to Helen Kelly's name.

HELEN KELLY

'She wasn't at the event, we know that, but that telephone call is still bugging me. Now we find she's secretly been seeing Kitson. She can't be the killer but she could have been part of a plot. Put her in alongside, Lorna.'

HORATIO KELLY

'No alibi for the night. He said he was at home, but we now know that he wasn't. Nelson let him down and he must have been angry about that. Definite contender.'

TERRENCE DERBY

'He could have had a motive, but not the opportunity. And his mind was put at rest by Drake on more than one occasion, so he didn't think that his money was really at risk. Add the fact that Drake was planning to buy the properties back. He wasn't in the vicinity at the time of the murder anyway.'

CATERING STAFF

'Raymond Giles isn't the best example of a team leader, but I honestly can't see what he would have had against Nelson, the same goes for Zena and the other female staff members... It's not beyond the realms of possibility that one of them had been having an affair with Nelson. We have to bear them in mind because of their proximity to the murder weapon I suppose, and Zena's prints were on the knife.'

SANDY MILES

'Was he trying to create the ultimate headline? I'd need to read through the witness statements again to completely rule him out. Kristina Timms said she'd been talking to him just before the murder but witnesses can become confused. I'd like to know the exact time she was in conversation with him. It could have been a few minutes before the balloon went up, or just before Lorna found the body, so he may have had time to leave the room, unnoticed for a couple of minutes.'

'Everyone is a suspect until they aren't?' Amy said.

'Correct,' Bodkin said, sticking up his thumb.

The inspector collected all his notes and stuffed them haphazardly back into the buff folder.

'Bodkin!' Amy tutted at the policeman. 'I've just sorted all those notes out for you, now they're in a mess again.'

Bodkin tapped his forehead.

'It's all up here. Now, shall we go up to the Old Bull and buy your mum and dad a drink?'

Amy nodded. 'A port and lemon would go down nicely after all that brain bashing.'

They found Mr and Mrs Rowlings sitting by the unlit fire at the far side of the sparsely-populated, snug. Amy sat down with them as Bodkin went to the bar to order drinks. He had just returned to the table, when PC Ferris burst through the door.

'Thank God I've found you. I've been looking everywhere. I rang Alice, I've been to Amy's house and your flat, this was my last hope.'

Bodkin put the tray of drinks on the table and turned to face the constable.

'What on earth has happened, Ferris?'

'It's Back Door Billy. He's dead.'

CHAPTER FORTY-ONE

Friday morning was busy in the shop. Amy had two customers waiting to see her by eleven o'clock and she had to skip her morning break to deal with them. By lunchtime she was parched, and as soon as she left work at lunchtime she hurried across the street, making for the Sunshine café for a pot of tea and a sandwich.

She was just about to open the door to the café when she heard a familiar voice.

'Amy! Oh, thank goodness. I have some news and if I don't tell somebody soon, I'm afraid I might burst.'

Amy turned around to find herself face to face with Shirley McKenzie.

'Hello, Shirley. You do look rather excited I have to say.'

Shirley performed a mini tap dance. Then she glanced over her shoulder before looking Amy in the face, her eyes bright.

'I've just come from seeing the doctor... I'M PREGNANT!' she squealed, throwing her arms around Amy's neck.

'CONGRATULATIONS!' Amy squealed back. 'That is exciting news. I bet Robert is just as excited as you are.'

'He doesn't know yet. He's in a meeting until three so I

won't be able to telephone him. Oh, Amy, I can't tell you how long I've waited for this, we both have, Robert is going to be over the moon with the news.' She let go of Amy and wiped the tears of joy from her eyes. 'I'm sorry for burdening you with this but I had to tell someone or I'd have just stood in the middle of the marketplace and shouted it out for the whole world to hear.'

'Let my buy you a cup of tea and a slice of cake to celebrate,' Amy said. 'I'd take you for a proper drink but I've got to go back to work this afternoon.'

Amy led Shirley to her favourite seat by the window and placed her bag on the floor at the side of her. Shirley was still grinning like the Cheshire Cat as Amy took both of her hands across the table.

'You'll be a wonderful mother,' she said.

'Do you have any plans... dreams... of motherhood... when you're married of course?'

'I haven't really thought about it,' Amy said. 'But I have saved my old rag doll and my favourite story books, so there must be something going on in the back of my mind. It won't be for years yet though. I'm only twenty-one, there's lots of time.'

Shirley patted Amy's hand, then sat back as the tea tray was placed on the table by the waitress.

'You'll have beautiful children, Amy, you are gorgeous and Inspector Bodkin is a very handsome man.'

Amy blushed and concentrated on pouring the tea. 'Have you got any names in mind, for the baby, I mean?'

'If it's a girl, I'm determined it's going to be Sarah, after my late mother. If it's a boy, Robert's always insisted that he will be called Rufus after his grandfather, but I'm having none of that.' She leaned across the table. 'He'll be called Arthur if I get my way. I've always loved the tales of King Arthur and his knights.'

'I like Arthur, stick to your guns,' Amy replied.

Shirley took a sip of tea and grinned again. 'We've waited so long for this.'

'Can't you get a message to him in the meeting?' Amy asked.

'No, he's in London,' she leaned across the table again and whispered. 'He's trying to get backing for the housing estate plan. We want to go ahead with demolishing the slums and building some housing the town can be proud of.'

'So, you're going ahead with Nelson's second project then?'

'We're going with both his projects. We just don't know who will build them yet.'

'So, Drake could still be in with a shout for both projects?'

'I suppose so, we have to do things by the book, but the bid that's best for the town will win, not necessarily the highest.'

'I really hope it's not Drake.'

'We want a local company if we can manage to get one. We don't know what's happening to the Kelly organisation now. We're assuming that Nelson's brother will take over.'

'I'll let you in on a secret,' Amy said, 'but please, don't let on you know anything, you can tell Robert of course but don't let it go any further than that.'

'What is it? I'm intrigued now,' Shirley said.

'Helen Kelly has been left all of Nelson's company shares, she's the main shareholder now.'

'WOW! That is a surprise. Mind you, I've heard through the grapevine that she and Horatio were of the same mind when it came to the factory project. Both wanted to replace the houses that would have been demolished. What they didn't know of course, was that Nelson intended to go even further than they did.'

'So, what happens now?' Amy asked.

'We're setting up a meeting of all the interested parties next Sunday evening. There will be another item on the agenda too, the cessation of Basil's notorious, mayor's fund.'

'Hmm,' Amy mused. 'So, you'll have Drake and both the Kellys in the same room; that should be interesting.'

'We'll be having the meeting at The Rectory; it will be a bit less formal that way.'

'Who else will be there?' Amy asked.

Shirley thought for a moment, then ticked off names on her fingers.

'Francis Drake. Horatio Kelly. Helen Kelly... I'll have to make sure she gets an invitation now. There will be a representative from Sevenoaks Construction as they put a bid in last time the project was tendered. Oh, that will be Harold Kitson. I'm sure I saw his name mentioned somewhere.'

'Wow!' Amy exclaimed. 'You only need to invite the Thornalleys and you'll have all of our murder suspects under one roof.'

After work, Amy took a walk down to the police station on Middle Street and once again she found Ferris behind the front desk.

'I thought you'd got reinforcements, Ferris,' she said. 'Have they changed their minds about that?'

'No, it's all good. Linda Blissett is on the desk at seven. She's over at the police accommodation, unpacking her case.'

'Is Bodkin free?'

'When is he ever free these days, Amy? There's been a queue of people waiting to see him all afternoon. Grayson's only just gone. He came back this morning to oversee the Back Door Billy investigation.'

'So, where's Bodkin now?'

'He's been going over Albert's Back Door Billy statement with him before he faces the grilling from the investigation team they're sending up from Maidstone tomorrow. He should be done with that soon because Albert went home a while back. Mrs Kelly is sitting in his office, waiting; she came in asking to see him about fifteen minutes ago.'

'Helen Kelly? I wonder what she wants?' Amy said, more to herself than to Ferris.

'No idea,' Ferris replied. 'No one tells me anything.'

Just then, Amy spotted Bodkin walk into the corridor behind Ferris.

'Bodkin,' she shouted, then waved as the inspector turned around.

'Just the person I need,' Bodkin said. 'Ferris, open the door for her. I think Mrs Kelly might feel more comfortable with another woman present. I have a feeling she's about to tell us something she couldn't bring herself to reveal the other day.'

FORTY-TWO

HELEN KELLY WAS SITTING ON THE SEAT IN FRONT OF BODKIN'S DESK when Amy walked into the office. Spotting Bodkin, Helen stood up and greeted him with a curt nod.

'Please, don't get up, Mrs Kelly,' Bodkin said as he entered the room. Dragging out a chair, he positioned it against the wall opposite to where Helen was sitting, then he motioned for Amy to sit before walking to his own chair behind the desk.

'What can I do for you, Mrs Kelly?' he asked.

'I have been made aware of a visit Miss Rowlings made to a friend of Horatio's yesterday, and I've come to get something off my chest before anyone jumps to the wrong conclusion regarding his movements on the night that Nelson was killed.'

'I'm happy to listen, Mrs Kelly, but I think it would be better coming from him,' Bodkin replied.

'Oh, he won't tell you anything about it, he's far too much of a gentleman. He believes affairs of the heart should be treated as personal and private.' She paused for a moment. 'He's also feeling rather embarrassed and more than a little bit guilty about the way he treated Kristina.'

Bodkin ran his tongue over his teeth as he studied Helen. 'Go on,' he said.

'Horatio and I have become very close over the last three months... oh nothing happened between us, but we had both been treated despicably by Nelson and we found ourselves consoling each other, mostly over the telephone. Horatio had been seeing Kristina for a while, but typically, he felt guilty about it because she was a married woman and she had told him that she was going to leave Edgar. I had been seeing Harold Kitson, but it was nothing serious, at least not on my part. He seemed to be convinced that we might one day become an item, but he was wrong. It was a dalliance, something I did to annoy Nelson as much as anything else. I knew it would, they had been bitter enemies since school.'

Helen crossed her long legs and smoothed down her skirt before winding the hair at her temple around her finger.

'I would have ditched Harold for Horatio at the drop of a hat, but he wouldn't dream of cuckolding his brother. We did talk about a life together at some point in the future, but Horatio wanted to get his finances sorted out first. Again, typical of him. He couldn't bear the thought of being a kept man.

'Anyway, Horatio told me that he intended to end it with Kristina. She was coming on too strong and what started out as just an occasional visit from her was now happening three or four times a week. Horatio was sure they'd be found out before long.' She took a silver cigarette case and a Ronson lighter from her bag. 'Do you mind if I smoke?' she asked.

Bodkin pointed to an empty ash tray on her side of the desk, and she lit a cigarette and blew a plume of smoke into the air.

'We had a long telephone conversation on the Friday lunchtime. Nelson was actually in the house at the time but I didn't care anymore. I'd had enough of him. Horatio told me that Kristina had rung and was determined to come around that night, but he didn't want to see her, so I suggested he pretended not to be at home when she called. I knew once he'd ended it with Kristina that I'd want to take her place, even if it was just platonic for a while. I decided there and then that my time with Harold was over. I telephoned him, but he wasn't at home, at least he wasn't answering the phone. So, I left it for an hour or so, then rang again. This time I got him and I'll be honest, he wasn't in the best of moods when he slammed the phone down on me. I've never had such foul and abusive language directed at me before. Even Nelson didn't stoop to that sort of thing.'

Helen paused and took another long draw of her cigarette. Amy wafted her hand in front of her face as the smoke was blown directly at her.

'He accused me of leading him on at first, which was true, I suppose, but then he revealed the real reason he was so keen to keep the relationship going. He saw me as a cash cow. He knew I'd be well looked after if Nelson and I divorced and he had no money of his own. The house was mortgaged to the hilt and what assets he had were tied up with Drake, the losing bidder for the factory contract. He was a desperate man, caught in a financial trap and he thought I was going to be his way out.'

Helen stubbed out her cigarette, then crossed her legs again and brushed ash from her skirt.

'He'd already had a few drinks; I could tell by the way he was slurring his words. Anyway, as I said, he slammed the phone down on me and that was the last time we spoke. I rang Horatio back and told him I'd ended it with Kitson. He began to cry.'

She paused for a moment as she looked at Amy.

'My heart was his from that moment. He blurted out that he loved me. No one had ever told me that before, not even Harold when he was doing his best to win me over, and certainly not Nelson. He has only ever loved himself.'

'This is all very interesting, Mrs Kelly, but where is the relevance to the night in question?' Bodkin asked.

'I was coming to that.' Helen pulled out her cigarette case again, then tutted and dropped it back into her handbag.

'After Nelson left, I sat and thought long and hard about things. I had a couple of drinks and just stared at the wall for an hour or so, trying to work out what Nelson's reaction would be when he found out about us. He wouldn't take it lying down that was for certain. It appeared that I was going to be on my own for the evening. Clara had gone to a family thing down in Gillingham. I tried reading but couldn't concentrate, so I put the radio on. It was then that I decided that I was going to leave Nelson. I almost ran upstairs to pack a couple of cases. I could stay at my sister's house in Burham. I'm sorry but I told you a little white lie the other day, Inspector. They had already gone abroad and wouldn't be back for almost a month. So, I packed the cases and dragged them to the top of the stairs. A few minutes later the doorbell went and I found Horatio standing in the porch. He'd had a few drinks and just blurted out that he couldn't live without me. We went into the lounge and I poured us another drink and we just sat holding hands and talking quietly. That was when I told him I was leaving Nelson and where I would be for the next few weeks. He asked me if I was sure this is what I wanted to do, so to prove it, I got the number of the Assembly Room from the telephone directory made the call.'

Helen reached for her cigarettes again, lit one, then mouthed, 'sorry' towards Amy.

'Well, I don't think you need to have much of an imagination to guess what happened next.' She looked directly into Bodkin's eyes, then down at her knees. 'I told Nelson that I was leaving him, and Horatio and I ended up in bed.'

'What was Nelson's reaction when he answered the phone? Did you tell him you were leaving with his brother?'

'No, just that I was leaving him. Had I mentioned Horatio he would more than likely have left the presentation and come home to confront me. As it was, he wouldn't have deemed it that important. I've threatened to do it often enough.'

'So, was he angry?'

'Peeved, I'd call it. Annoyed, but not particularly angry.'

'But you didn't leave him, did you, Mrs Kelly?'

'I fully intended to, believe me. We were going to use Horatio's car as it was parked outside. We needed to sober up a little before either of us would have been fit to drive. He couldn't just leave his car there, Nelson would have spotted it as soon as he got home… we were going to go together, but we stupidly fell asleep and I only woke up when the police knocked at the door. I went down in my dressing gown to let them in. They didn't realise that Horatio was upstairs in my bed all the time they were there.'

'Did he stay with you for the whole night?' Bodkin asked, 'only that wou—'

'No, as soon as the police had gone, he got dressed, had a strong cup of coffee, then left to drive home. There was no way we could run away after that news. What would the police have thought?'

'We'd have thought the pair of you were in it up to your necks,' Bodkin replied.

Helen's eyes looked down at her chest as Bodkin stared hard at her.

'It would have saved us a lot of time and effort if you had mentioned this at the start, Mrs Kelly,' he said. 'Horatio will have to corroborate your story whether he deems it ungentlemanly or not.'

'He won't, Inspector. Honestly, you don't know him.'

'He will,' Bodkin replied, 'or I'll arrest him for withholding vital information and wasting police time.'

. . .

'Well, what did you make of that story, Bodkin?' Amy asked when Helen Kelly had left.

'I'm not sure I buy it,' Bodkin replied. 'They could be trying to create a smoke screen. It's all very convenient isn't it? I honestly can't see why they hid this from us.'

Amy bit her bottom lip as she thought. 'Kristina Timms was crying for a reason that night. It might have been because she had arranged to meet her lover and he wasn't home.'

Bodkin pulled a face. 'Possibly... and I suppose we now have an answer as to why Kitson got so drunk that he didn't know what he was doing that evening.' Bodkin rubbed his chin. 'Hmm, he would have been very angry, maybe it was him at the emergency exit, arguing with Nelson after all.' He got to his feet. 'I think I'm going to have a word with the manager of the Barwood club. The place was shut the last time I called round.'

Amy nodded. 'That will be another loose end tied up. We don't like loose ends do we, Bodkin?'

'We don't,' Bodkin agreed.

Amy walked with Bodkin along the corridor towards the front desk.

'What's happening with the Back Door Billy thing? Did he have a heart attack in his cell or something?'

Bodkin shook his head. 'Albert gave him a whack on the bonce with his truncheon when he attempted to escape.'

'Oh my goodness!'

'Billy had been whinging on about getting a cup of tea and Albert got sick of hearing it, so he went and made him one. When he got back, he made Billy stand at the back of the cell while he opened the door to put the mug on the floor, but Albert's a bit slow, and Billy rushed him.' Bodkin pointed to his own eye. 'You think this one is bad; you should see what Albert's look like.' Bodkin shook his head. 'Anyway, Billy made a dash for the back door but Albert caught up with him before he could get it open.

Billy tried to hit him again, so Albert whacked him with his truncheon. He went out like a light and never recovered.'

'So Back Door Billy lived up to his name right to the end then,' Amy said.

'Good one. I hadn't thought of that,' Bodkin said.

'It's sad that he died though.'

'It's always sad when someone dies, even a low life like Billy, but when I look back at the things he's done... he once held a knife to a heavily pregnant woman's throat until her husband handed over her jewellery box.'

Amy shook her head. 'My sympathy only extends so far. Is Albert in trouble now?'

'He's a bit of a hero to be honest. Grayson is going to offer him the desk job after all. We just have to go through the formalities of an investigation from the Maidstone team tomorrow, but it will be fine. I'm involved because with Grayson being away, I was technically in charge of the place.' The inspector grimaced. 'Our old friend, Chief Inspector Laws is back tomorrow. He's bringing a couple of constables with him. He's already read the case notes for the murder so he'll have his own take on that.'

'You've been running the entire station yourself for ages now. It isn't fair to drag you into it.' Her shoulders dropped. 'Laws, eh? I'd better stay clear of this place while he's here. He really doesn't like me getting involved in cases, does he?'

Bodkin grinned. 'We won't tell him then.'

Amy smiled back. 'I still don't think it's fair that they drag you into something you weren't even there to witness.'

'Heavy is the head that wears the crown,' Bodkin replied.

'If you're quoting Henry the Fourth, it's uneasy is the head that wears the crown,' Amy said.

'I wasn't,' Bodkin said. 'It's just something my dad used to say.'

. . .

On Saturday morning, Amy caught the nine o'clock bus and got off at the junction of the High Street and Main Street, then walked around the corner to her favourite shop, Brigden's Nearly New Store.

One or two items caught her eye but she finally settled on a dark blue, flared skirt from the second's rail that was priced at six shillings and sixpence. After examining it carefully, she found that there were a couple of rows of untidy stitching on the waist band, so after draping the skirt over her arm she marched up to the till, where the manageress, Eileen, was writing out price tickets.

'It's got a faulty seam and I'm going to have to unpick it and—'

'Five shillings,' Eileen said without looking up.

Smiling to herself, Amy walked out of Brigden's swinging the colourful bag in her right hand. After paying her weekly visit to the Post Office to pay five shillings into her savings account, she walked along the pavement to the Sunshine café to enjoy her regular, Saturday cup of espresso.

After the café, she made her way to the busy market to pick up some fresh veg for her mother. As she was passing the toy stall, she spotted Karen, bartering with the stall owner.

'I can't afford five shillings, anyway, it's not worth that much,' she said to the obviously exasperated man.

'It's worth it to me, I paid four and six for it,' he replied.

'Well, you were robbed,' Karen said, turning around with a look of frustration on her face.

'What's the matter?' Amy asked.

'Oh, I'm after a doll for Beth's birthday. I can't afford a new one obviously, so I thought I'd try to get a nice, clean second hand one, but he's asking far too much for it.'

Amy took Karen's arm and began to lead her back the way she had just come.

'Let's try Stan's Emporium,' she said. 'He's always got something in.'

Amy led Karen through the wide front door of Stan's Bargain Emporium before turning left and taking the wide staircase that led to the second floor. They found the toy section on the left-hand side and walked between the boxes of cowboy hats, boxed game sets and spinning tops until they came to a shelf full of dolls. Some were missing an eye, others an arm or leg. There was a sign pinned to the shelf inviting customers to pull a limb off another doll to complete the one they wanted to buy. Karen walked along eyeing the toys with a sad look on her face.

'None of these are good enough for a birthday present,' she said. 'Beth won't mind it not being new but it will have to be intact, with both legs the same length at least.'

Amy pointed to a doll that was still in a box, albeit looking rather tatty and crushed.

'What about this one?' she said, 'it says she's lost her voice. She's supposed to say, Mama.'

Karen picked it up and examined it.

'She's lovely and Beth won't mind the fact that she can't talk anymore, but she's five shillings, the same price as the one on the market.'

'How much do you have?' Amy asked.

'I've got the three shillings I was saving for the prescription plus the sixpence I've managed to put by this week.' Karen said. 'I should really save it in case we ever need the doctor, but after the mayor's wife said we could see the pharmacist instead, I thought I'd risk it. She got very little last Christmas, just a couple of packs of card games and a packet of sweets.'

'I could give you the rest,' Amy offered.

'No, I'm not taking any more of your money, Amy, anyway, it's my present, not a joint one.' She sighed. 'What else have they got?'

'Hang on,' Amy said, looking into the broken packaging. 'There are a few doll's dresses in here too.'

'It doesn't make the doll any cheaper, Amy.'

'No, but... okay, here's my idea. Your share of the toy will be three and sixpence, I'll put up the other one and six for the doll's clothes, then I can give them to Beth for her birthday. It will save me looking for something else.'

Karen thought about it.

'That would work,' she said, happily.

Amy picked up the box, put the doll carefully back inside, then handed it to Karen with a shilling piece and a sixpence from her purse. Karen paid at the till and the assistant stuffed the doll box into a gaily coloured carrier bag with the Stan's Bargain Emporium logo, emblazoned on the side.

After chatting for a while outside, Amy and Karen went their separate ways, Karen walking towards the station with a definite spring in her step, and Amy walking towards the bus stop with the doll's clothes lying alongside her new skirt in the Brigden's bag.

After unpicking the faulty seam and restitching it, Amy pressed her new skirt and hung it on a hanger in the bathroom to steam any reluctant creases out of it while she had her Saturday afternoon bath, then she sat in her dressing gown talking to her parents as she rubbed at her hair with a towel.

'Do you know, I'm tempted to come with you tonight,' Mr Rowlings said after Amy had told him that there was a George Formby picture on at the Roxy.

'Hee hee, turned out nice again, 'ant it?' he said as he

performed the worst George Formby impression that she had ever heard.

Amy and her mum sighed in unison.

'That was terrible, Dad. Why is it that whenever anyone hears the name, George Formby, they feel compelled to do an impression of him?'

Mr Rowlings shrugged. 'I don't know but everyone does it,' he said.

'Men do it,' Amy replied. 'I've never heard a woman try it.'

'Women are far too sensible to attempt it,' Mr Rowlings replied. 'Quite right too in my opinion, it would really mess up their lipstick, trying to get the buck toothed look right.'

'Bodkin says he'll meet us at the Roxy again,' Alice said as she patted her loose curls into place while looking into Amy's bedroom mirror. 'Chief Inspector Laws arrived a day early and he's had to update him on both the murder case and the death of Back Door Billy, whoever he is.'

Bodkin and Ferris were waiting for them as they got off the bus just below the Roxy on Middle Street. Bodkin was wearing the trousers and shirt he had bought from Stan's.

'You look very relaxed without a suit and tie,' Alice said as she approached the two policemen.

'Have you seen my George Formby,' Ferris said after Alice had greeted him.

'Don't, please, Ferris,' Amy begged.

'All right, what about this?' Ferris crouched down and walked back and forth along the pavement, performing an impression of Groucho Marx. 'I just shot an elephant in my pyjamas, how it got into my pyjamas I don't know.'

Amy slapped her hand to her forehead. Bodkin stood shaking his head. Only Alice laughed.

'I was thinking of putting that into my act? What do you think?' Ferris asked.

'Stick to singing, Ferris,' Bodkin replied. 'You're not too bad at that.'

As they walked up the steps to the cinema, Bodkin took hold of Amy's arm.

'I've just been to the Barwood Club to have a word with the manager. He remembers Kitson from the night Kelly was killed. He told the bouncers to throw him out for being drunk, but more importantly for accusing a fellow card player of cheating. Amazingly, the bouncer in question was called Sam Strong and he told me that Kitson had become quite violent as he was shown the front door and swung a fist at him. Needless to say, Sam gave him something back for his troubles. In his case, a bloody nose and a thick ear. He said that Kitson's shirt was a bit of a mess as he shut the door on him.'

'So, is he out of the frame now?' Amy asked as they walked along the aisle between the rows of seats.

'Not entirely, he could still have turned up at the fire door, but it's looking unlikely. The blood he had on his shirt was almost certainly his own.'

'So that's two suspects off the list in the space of two days,' Amy said.

'Pretty much, providing what Helen Kelly told us is the truth.'

'I think I believe her,' Amy said. 'Men might boast about their conquests but women tend to keep quiet about theirs. I doubt she'd have confessed to sleeping with Horatio if it wasn't true.'

'Two down, three to go,' Bodkin said as they took their seats. 'The only real evidence we have is the overheard conversation and the mysterious man at the fire door.' He sighed as he leaned back in his seat to watch the movie trailer on the screen. 'It's not a lot, is it?'

Back on Middle Street, after the film, Bodkin took Amy's arm and led her down to the bus stop.

'Old Bull or the Bell?' he asked.

'I vote the Old Bull,' Ferris said. 'I'm not too bothered about going into the Bell now they don't want me to sing anymore.'

'The Bull it is then,' Alice said, as she looked carefully at Amy. 'Are you sickening for something? You've been very quiet. You didn't even laugh at the film and it was hilarious.'

Amy looked up suddenly. 'Oh, I'm all right, Alice, thank you. I was trying to work something out while the film was on and I think I've managed to do it.'

She put a hand on Bodkin's arm and turned to face him.

'Bodkin, I think I've worked out who murdered Nelson Kelly.'

FORTY-THREE

'WHAT TIME IS IT, BODKIN, DO YOU THINK THAT SHIRLEY MCKENZIE will be at home?'

'It's nine-fifteen, she might be, why?'

'As I mentioned, they're having a meeting tomorrow night. They're going to discuss the new planning applications for the factory and housing projects too. The majority of our original suspects will be attending. I'd like to ask if Shirley will add one or two more to her guest list. Plus us, of course.'

Bodkin nodded slowly. 'Do you really think you've got this cracked?'

'I might need one last bit of evidence, or a stroke of good fortune, but yes, I'm pretty sure I know who did it, I'll explain on the way.'

Amy said goodbye to Alice and Ferris as Bodkin ran back up the hill to stop one of Adam's taxis as it made its way slowly up the street; Rory, the driver, craning his neck looking for a fare as he passed the people on the pavement outside the cinema.

'The Old Rectory, and make it snappy, Rory.'

'Am I on the clock for this or...'

'It depends how much the fare is. I want you to wait for us at the Rectory. I don't know how long we'll be there. If it's a while, I'll write you a chitty and you can get it from petty cash at the police station again.' He turned towards Amy who had just climbed into the back seat, and put his finger to his lips.

'Explain when we're alone,' he said.

Shirley was both surprised and delighted to see Amy as she opened the door to the couple.

'I really need to ask you a favour,' Amy blurted out. 'It's rather a big one.'

Shirley led Amy and Bodkin along the corridor, past the lines of pictures of old clergymen and into the lounge where Robert was sitting in an armchair in front of a beautifully decorated, folding Japanese screen. He got to his feet as they entered the room.

'Congratulations on your happy news,' Amy said, leaning forwards to plant a light kiss on the mayor's cheek.

Bodkin held out his hand and shook Robert's warmly. 'You said you hadn't given up hope,' he said to the beaming Robert.

Shirley invited them to sit and offered them a glass of sherry which both Amy and Bodkin refused.

'If you could let me have a sheet of paper and a pen, instead,' Amy said.

Shirley looked puzzled but opened the draw of an old, highly polished desk and took out a sheet of top quality, headed notepaper and a silver pen.

Amy sat down at the desk and immediately began to write a list.

'Could you do your best to ensure that all of these people attend the meeting tomorrow night,' she said. 'They are all on the telephone network.' She paused before speaking again. 'I know it's a lot to ask, but could you tell them that they'll hear something to their immediate advantage regarding the new plans for the Haxley area.'

Shirley studied the list carefully.

'I can be very persuasive when I need to be. I'll do my utmost to get them to attend, but I'm still confused as to what's this is all about?'

'Oh, that's easy to explain. We're hoping to unmask a murderer,' Amy replied.

FORTY-FOUR

AMY HAD A STRANGE DREAM THAT NIGHT, FINDING HERSELF IN THE middle of one of Hercule Poirot's murderer revelations. It had been some time since she had read Peril at End House, but the novel had obviously stayed in her memory and she saw herself clearly standing alongside the great man as he exposed the Crofts as forgers by getting Nick Buckley to play the part of her own ghost at the fake séance.

When she woke, early the next morning, she was sure that she had solved the murder mystery, but she knew she needed one last piece of solid evidence for her to be able to prove it beyond a reasonable doubt. She had been left with an outline of an idea that the great Belgian detective had urged her to consider. She lay in bed for a good half an hour, staring at the ceiling whilst trying to figure how to make her own, ghostly witness ruse, work.

At church, Amy struggled to concentrate on the service as the vicar read out the words that her father had written for him. She was still thinking about her plan for the evening when she was approached on the slate and gravel path outside the church by Bodkin. He was wearing his usual, scruffy blue suit with a stained black tie.

'Penny for them,' he said, making Amy jump.

'You can have them for nothing, Bodkin,' she replied with a quick smile. She looked him up and down. 'It's Sunday, I thought you were Mr Casual at the weekends now?'

'I've got to go in to see Laws again. He's got a bee in his bonnet about the Kelly murder. He seems to think it's a cut and dried case with only one suspect worth pursuing.'

'Oh dear,' Amy said. 'I hope his wife hasn't been giving him any grief this morning over breakfast. He's bad enough when he's in a good mood.'

'I've been going over your solution since last night,' Bodkin replied, seriously, 'and I honestly think that you've got it spot on. Well done, once again, I'd only got it down to the last three with an outside possibility.'

'You'd have got there soon, Bodkin, just don't divulge any of this to Laws, I'd hate him to claim credit for solving the murder after all our hard work.'

'Mum's the word,' the inspector said before putting his finger to his lips.

'Poirot gave me an idea for how to get the final strand of evidence last night.'

'Did he indeed,' Bodkin replied. 'I wish he'd come and have a chat to me sometimes.'

Amy gave Bodkin a quick peck on the lips as the two parted at the lychgate entrance to the church, then she stood, deep in thought as she waited for her parents, imagining one or two of the many scenarios that might take place at the mayor's meeting.

At seven o'clock, Amy and Bodkin arrived at the Old Rectory, Bodkin wearing his suit and Amy wearing her new navy skirt with a white, button up shirt and brown, heeled sandals. Shirley met them at the door and showed them into the lounge where Robert was standing with his back to the fireplace.

'Is everything ready?' Bodkin asked. 'Did everyone agree to attend?'

Robert nodded. 'Shirley can be very persuasive. They were all delighted to have been invited.'

Amy walked to the back of the room and ran her hands over the lacquered surface of the folded Japanese screen.

'This is perfect for what I have in mind. Are we holding the meeting in here?'

'No, it would be rather cramped,' Shirley replied. 'I thought we'd hold it in the old Parish Meeting Room.'

Could you carry this through for me, please?' Amy asked.

Robert and Shirley exchanged glances.

'Of course,' Shirley said. 'Where would you like us to place it?'

Amy followed Shirley to a large room at the front of the house while Robert and Bodkin carried the antique screen between them.

The meeting room was oblong in shape with two doors coming off it on the right-hand side. At the far end of the room was a foot-high dais with an oak lectern in the centre. The wooden seats that would have sat in rows along the length of the room had been removed and replaced with a dozen comfortable-looking chairs with red-velvet padded seats and backs. The seats were laid out in pairs with small, round tables in between. On a long table on the wall between the two doors a temporary bar had been set up with bottles of whisky, gin, brandy and vermouth, along with small bottles of tonic water, a soda syphon and an ice bucket.

'Could you put the screen in front of the door at the bottom end, please, Mr McKenzie?' Amy said as she looked around the room. 'This is perfect,' she said smiling at Shirley.

'But what do you need the screen for, Amy?' Shirley asked as Robert opened out the folded screen.

'It's to hide my ghost,' Amy replied.

Amy and Bodkin returned to the lounge with the McKenzies and the four sat for half an hour sipping sherry and chatting about the new mayor's future plans. At seven-thirty on the dot, the doorbell rang to announce the arrival of the first of the guests. Amy stood behind the open lounge door and listened as Shirley McKenzie welcomed Francis Drake and Lorna Wetherby.

'Come in,' she said, 'and welcome to the Rectory, it's so lovely to see you, thank you for coming tonight.'

'I was intrigued, and I have to say I'm delighted to see that you are getting on with reorganising the factory project so soon after Nelson's untimely death. We'll be ready to go with our bid as soon as we hear the details.' Drake extended a hand, inviting Lorna to go in first.

Amy craned her neck to listen as Shirley showed the couple into the meeting room. 'What can I get you to drink?' the mayor's wife asked as Robert left the lounge to formally greet his guests.

Five minutes later, Harold Kitson arrived and was shown into the meeting room. He was closely followed by the Thornalleys, who greeted Shirley effusively, thanking her over and over again for inviting them to such an important meeting.

A few minutes later, Helen and Horatio Kelly arrived together. Shirley was just about to close the door behind them when Terrence Derby arrived, out of breath after running from the street where the taxi had dropped him off.

'Sorry I'm a little bit late,' he panted, 'but the taxi went to the wrong address to pick me up.'

Shirley put him at his ease with a bright smile and led him through into the meeting room where the other guests were assembled in two distinct groups. The Kellys standing a good few feet away from what had quickly become a gathering of Drake supporters.

Amy stepped back from the lounge door as Shirley hurried back in.

'They're all here,' she said, excitedly. 'Robert is going to do a bit of a welcome speech, then they'll start to discuss the new projects. Is that when you want to join us?'

'Yes, give them a few minutes to get settled,' Amy said. 'I think fifteen minutes ought to do it.'

Shirley was just about to go back to the meeting when the doorbell rang again. Amy and Bodkin exchanged puzzled glances.

'I thought all the guests were here?' she said as she walked back to her position behind the open door. A few seconds later Amy heard the voice of Chief Inspector Laws as he demanded to be allowed in.

'We're here to make an arrest,' he boomed. 'Please step aside, Madam.'

Bodkin groaned when he heard the all too familiar voice. Getting quickly to his feet, he hurried along the corridor.

'I'll see to this,' he whispered in Shirley's ear as he reached the front door.

'Good evening, sir, this is a surprise. What are you doing here?'

'Bodkin! Good grief, man. Move aside, I've come to arrest the murderer you couldn't manage to catch yourself.'

Bodkin cleared his throat. 'Could you come with me before you do that, sir. I'd like to explain something to you.'

As Shirley pulled the door shut behind them, Bodkin led Laws and two burly constables along the corridor to where Amy was waiting in the lounge.

'Miss Rowlings,' Laws said, shaking his head. 'I'd like to say it's a pleasure to meet you again, but as I suspect you're involving yourself in police business, I'm afraid I'll have to refrain.'

'Hello,' Amy said with a slight wave of her hand.

'Right, let's get down to brass tacks. What are you and Miss Rowlings doing here?' Laws asked.

'We were invited,' Bodkin replied. 'We are friends of the mayor and his wife.'

'Oh...' Laws was obviously impressed. 'I wasn't aware you moved in these circles, Bodkin. You'll have to introduce me properly after I make my arrest.' He looked around the room with pursed lips. 'Mrs Laws would love to attend one of the mayor's parties herself.'

'I'll certainly do that, sir,' Bodkin replied, giving Amy a quick eye roll. 'Who have you come to arrest?'

'Kitson of course. Who else?'

'Kitson,' Bodkin echoed.

'Bodkin, I've only had the case files and your notes since yesterday but it only took a half an hour of reading to work out who murdered Nelson Kelly. It's as plain as a pikestaff man. I really can't see why you've been blundering about causing havoc among the well to do of the town, when the solution was at your fingertips pretty much from the start. Kitson killed Kelly, took a taxi home, then burned his clothes the next day. Why would anyone who had nothing to hide, do that? He even left a clue on the roadside, the handkerchief he'd used to pick up the knife to make sure he didn't leave any prints on the weapon.' He shook his head with a sad expression on his face. 'Honestly, Bodkin, I expected better, you're an experienced officer, you should have been able to work it out for yourself. Sometimes, the obvious answer is the correct one.'

As Bodkin was about to reply, he held up a podgy pink hand.

'Don't try to make excuses, man. Constable Roecastle, Constable Parks, find Kitson and arrest him.'

'Just a moment, sir, please.' Bodkin closed the lounge door and held out a hand inviting Laws to sit.

'How did you know he was here?'

'We followed him. I decided to pull him in this evening and we drove down to his house at Skelton. Unfortunately, he was pulling out of this drive as we approached, we flashed our head-lamps at him but he either didn't notice or ignored us, so we turned around and followed him back to town to see where he was going.'

'Why didn't you follow him into the house when he arrived?'

'It was obvious that there was going to be a bit of a party. I wanted to see who else was invited.'

'The guest list includes the entire list of suspects, sir. Every person who had a reason for wanting Nelson dead. The mayor kindly helped us get them all in one place.'

'Wasting more time, Bodkin? I've told you who did it, why don't you just arrest the man here and now?'

Just then Shirley tapped on the door and entered the lounge.

'Amy... Inspector Bodkin, we're just about ready for you,' she said.

FORTY-FIVE

'WHAT ON EARTH IS GOING ON, BODKIN?' LAWS SPLUTTERED.

'Would you like to sit in, sir? Everything will be explained.'

Laws was about to protest again, but Shirley took him by the arm.

'Could I get you a drink, Chief Inspector Laws? Robert and I have heard so much about you. You'll have to come to dinner one night... maybe to one of our little garden parties.'

'That sounds very nice,' Laws said, 'Mrs Laws would love to come. She is a very good friend of the chief constable's wife you know.'

Shirley kept hold of his arm and began to lead him down the corridor. Half way along, she looked back over her shoulder and winked at Amy.

'Inspector Bodkin and Amy have organised a little gathering. I'm sure you'll find it interesting, Chief Inspector.' She put her hand on the handle of the door. 'There's a particularly good double malt waiting for you inside.'

'You two, wait out here,' Laws rasped at the two constables who were about to follow him into the meeting room.

'Guard that door, please,' Bodkin said, pointing down the

corridor. 'We don't want anyone to leave before I say they can.' Bodkin watched one of the constables walk back along the hall and position himself outside the far door, then turned to the other policeman. 'You, come inside. Let's give them a show of force.'

'Robert... everyone, this is Chief Inspector Laws... I think you all know Inspector Bodkin and Miss Rowlings.'

Robert shook Laws' hand and beamed a smile towards him. 'Whisky?' he asked.

'Thank you, I was just saying to your good lady that my wife would love to meet you. She's a friend of—'

'What the hell are you doing here, Bodkin? This is a private meeting,' Drake exploded. He pointed to the officer guarding the door. 'What's going on here?'

'All will be revealed,' Bodkin said smoothly as Laws sipped at his whisky before sitting down in the seat opposite Harold Kitson.

The inspector walked over to stand in front of the dais where he motioned for Amy to come forward.

'Firstly, I'd like to thank you all for attending this evening,' he said, as he looked around the room at the confused faces of the guests. 'I'd also like to extend my thanks to Mr and Mrs McKenzie for allowing Amy and me to be present at such a prestigious gathering.' He paused, then went on. 'Quite soon there will be a new contest to gain control of the waste land over at the Haxley estate. I'm sure you will all be busy over the next week or so preparing your bids. I wish you luck in your endeavours.... HOWEVER!' Bodkin raised his voice as Drake got to his feet to interrupt. 'I am more concerned with the consequences of what happened after the contract had been awarded the first time around. A respected businessman lost his life and his death was directly related to the fact that he was the victor in that contest.'

The inspector stared hard at Drake, who, after holding

Bodkin's eye for a few seconds, downed his whisky, then walked across to the drinks table to get another.

Bodkin waited for him to return to his seat before he continued.

'Right, now that we're all comfortable again, I'd like to ask Miss Rowlings here to sum up our investigation. I'm sure you'll all find what she has to say of the utmost interest.' Bodkin leaned towards the dumbfounded Amy. 'It's your Poirot moment,' he whispered.

'Are you sure?' she hissed.

Bodkin didn't reply. Taking two steps back, he held out his hand towards the space he had just left. 'Miss Rowlings,' he said.

Amy flashed a nervous glance at Bodkin, then brushed a few stray hairs from her face.

'Nelson Kelly was murdered. He died by way of a single stab wound to his heart. A shocking event in itself, but what is even more shocking, is that he was killed by someone he knew. Someone he had a short but explosive argument with in the corridor, just a few yards away from where he had just received the Businessman of the Year award.'

'Tell us something we don't know,' Drake muttered.

'More importantly, what are you doing up there? You're not even involved with the police,' Laws added.

Amy pulled a pink card from the pocket of her skirt and held it up so that Laws could see it.

'I'm Amy Rowlings, the lead investigator of ARIA investigations.' She pointed out the small print line at the bottom of the card. 'Kent police accredited.' Amy looked directly at Laws before tucking the card back into her pocket. 'Chief Superintendent Grayson asked me to accompany Inspector Bodkin to interview Mrs Kelly because he thought she might feel more comfortable if another woman was present. The same went for Lorna Wetherby. After that, I had to stick around because the police were so undermanned and there was no one else they could call upon to help with the investigation. Inspector Bodkin was being dragged from pillar to post, working all the hours God sent, not only on the murder, but on every other crime that occurred in Spinton, including burglaries, theft and assault. This case needed more than one pair of eyes and I was happy that I was able to help him.'

Amy walked to the drinks table and poured herself a glass of water and added two large chunks of ice. After taking a sip and pulling her thoughts together, she continued.

'This was an investigation that yielded very few clues at the start. It was quickly established that the murder weapon had been left on an unattended trolley at the side of the kitchen door. There were only one set of prints on the knife handle, those of the young woman who used it to carve the slices of meat that were eventually laid out on the buffet tables. The only other person to touch the knife was the murderer, but that person left no prints behind, meaning that they were almost certainly wearing gloves when the attack took place.'

'Or they picked up the knife with a monogrammed handkerchief and left the victim's blood all over it,' Laws called out.

Amy ignored the heckling.

'The gloves are a very important clue,' she continued. 'Gloves that were worn, then discarded, gloves that were taken off and sent to be chemically cleaned, gloves that were worn, but then, probably changed at some point during the evening.' Amy paused and took another sip of water. 'Another thing we had to take into account was the argument between Nelson and a person that hasn't yet been identified. The row was a short one, but was overheard by a young woman in the cloakroom. The door was open and she was only a few yards away from the incident. Sadly, there was no direct line of sight, so the lady in question couldn't identify the person involved. Then there was the emergency exit door. It had been closed all evening, as it normally was, but when Lorna

Wetherby found Nelson dying on the floor, the fire door was swinging open.'

Amy shot Bodkin a quick glance. He smiled back at her reassuringly.

'That left a couple of questions that required an answer. Had the door been opened by Nelson himself during, or following, the phone conversation? If he hadn't received the call that night, he would almost certainly still be alive today. The second question that arose was, who was the caller? Had the call been deliberately timed so that the killer was in place, outside the emergency exit, when Nelson picked up the receiver? We had first hand evidence that around that time, a well-dressed man with fair hair was seen in conversation with Nelson at the fire door.'

Amy shrugged and lifted her hands, palms out.

'And that was everything we had at the time. There wasn't a lot to go on at all.' She picked up her glass and took another sip of iced water. 'Then, the investigation started in earnest and we began the questioning. We didn't get a lot from the attending guests, but one or two important facts were discovered.'

Amy turned towards Lorna Wetherby.

'Lorna was covered in Nelson's blood when we found her and she was the last person to see him alive. Lorna was there on the night in her PR capacity. We soon picked up strong rumours that she and Nelson had been engaged in an affair. Nelson's wife suspected it, as did the Post's scandal monger reporter, Sandy Miles. I have to say here that Lorna forcefully denies having a relationship with Nelson, but she has admitted passing on sensitive business information to the man she definitely is in a relationship with, Francis Drake. We know that Lorna was out of the Assembly Room at the time of Nelson's death, but there are a couple of things that don't fit with the idea that she was the killer. Firstly, the open fire escape door had to be a factor, and as Lorna had just come out of the cloakroom when she says she found

Nelson on the floor, then she probably didn't have time to open it herself, and what would have been the point, anyway? Secondly, unless she's a freak of nature, she couldn't impersonate a male voice well enough to fool someone who was sitting only a few yards away. While it might be a possibility that both she, and a man were with Nelson at the time of his death, it is only a remote possibility. The girl who was working on the desk in the cloakroom, Debbie Vallance, overhead the argument and she said she only heard two male voices.

'That leads us to Francis Drake,' Amy said as the businessman's head snapped up. 'He was in the cloakroom at the same time as Lorna. He insists they didn't acknowledge each other even though they were in a relationship. That's something I find very odd.'

'I've explained that,' Drake stormed.

Amy narrowed her eyes as she thought.

'Hmm... it wasn't a very convincing explanation as I remember. You didn't want to let on that you knew each other in case it got back to Nelson and he became suspicious of what information she might be passing on? I'm not buying that. Anyway, back to business. As I said, Mr Drake was in the vicinity at the time of Nelson's death. He was seen at the kitchen door by the Thornalleys not long before Lorna found the body. Drake and Kelly were bitter business rivals. Both had submitted bids for the factory build, Drake had even put an extra bid in from a recently bought company, Sevenoaks Construction. He was using it as a way of outflanking the Kelly organisation.' She looked across at Drake who was glaring back at her. 'It all looks a bit suspicious now. This is how I think it was meant to work. Nelson puts in his bid. Lorna Wetherby gifts the Kelly bid information to Drake, who then offers a slightly higher amount. Sevenoaks then put a much higher bid in, one that was pretty much guaranteed to win under the Thornalley bidding system, but then, the mayor is ousted and a new, honest mayor takes his place. After studying the bids and after receiving backing from the government for the scheme, Nelson's offer is accepted. Now, the question is, why did Mr Drake leave the big Sevenoaks bid in place, when his man on the inside, Mr Thornalley, had been removed, and there wasn't much chance of it being successful under the new regime?

'There are two reasons that I can see. One. There was a chance, albeit a very small one, of it being accepted. Two. With Sevenoaks in the running, it would make the process look as if there was more competition that there actually was. If Mr Kelly had been forced to pull out for any reason... and his death was obviously a good one, then Sevenoaks would be ordered to pull their bid, leaving Drake Construction as the only offer on the table. That's one perfectly sound reason for Mr Drake to want to see the back of Nelson Kelly. What with the way the world is at the moment, an armaments factory being built with guaranteed government orders, it would be worth millions over the next few years.'

'It's business,' Drake suddenly shouted. 'That's all it is, things like that happen all the time, it doesn't mean I'd murder someone to get hold of a contract.'

Amy shrugged.

'Maybe it is, just business, Mr Drake, but as I said, it doesn't smell right to those of us who aren't involved in such practices.' Amy was silent as she gathered her thoughts, then she went on. 'Mr Drake might insist that what I'm about to say next is just something you might expect an astute businessman to do, but personally, I'd call it deviousness. Part of Nelson's plan was to demolish the row of houses that makes up Ebenezer Street, with no new houses built to replace them. The houses were to be bought out under a compulsory purchase order with a price on each dwelling set at thirty pounds. When Mr Drake got wind of this, he immediately sold the whole street off to Mr Derby, a man new to business, who wasn't aware of the order the council were about to enact. Mr Drake sold the houses to Mr Derby for seventy-five pounds each. To convince the new buyer that he was getting a bargain, Drake instructed one of his larger investors, a man who was employed as a property advisor in the same bank that Mr Derby worked at, to convince him to take out what would, for him, be a huge loan, to enable him to buy the properties.'

This time it was Drake's turn to shrug. 'Business is business,' he said.

Amy pushed away a few loose strands of hair.

'Indeed, Mr Drake, but then, straight after Nelson's death, you made an offer to buy back the properties and when Mr Derby refused, you instructed the bank manager to sack him. Not only that, you try to get them to withdraw the loan agreement that he had signed. Unfortunately for you, they weren't able to do that, though they did attempt it.'

'That's a lie,' Drake said. 'Why would I go to all that trouble over a few houses?'

'Because you like to be in control, Mr Drake,' Amy replied. 'It's as simple as that.'

Terrence Derby suddenly got to his feet. 'It's not a lie, Mr Drake. I have the letter from the bank.'

Drake ignored him and turned his ire on Amy again.

'Is that it? Is that your case against me? It's not much is it?'

'There's also the fact that you are trying to buy out the Kelly business, so you will be absolutely certain of getting the factory contract. You made Horatio Kelly an offer within a few days of Nelson's death, but that's not all,' Amy said. 'Let's get back to the first clue I mentioned. The gloves.' Amy sucked on her lip as she thought. 'The presentation was a black-tie event and even the men were expected to wear white gloves. Mr Drake wore his, we know that because there was a photograph in the evening paper and he can clearly be seen wearing them as he enters the Town

Hall. Jump forward a couple of hours to the time immediately after the murder, and his gloves have magically disappeared.'

'I explained that. I spilled wine on them, they were ruined. I put them in my pocket and tossed them into the bin when I got home.'

'That was convenient,' Amy said. 'The thing I'd like to ask now is, what else did Lorna tell you about Nelson's plans. Did she tell you for instance, that he was embarking on a second venture, and that an agreement with the mayor had already been made. He was planning to knock down the entire, Haxley estate and replace the lot with brand new, modern housing, some to be sold privately, some to be owned by the council. Once again, there would be a compulsory purchase order in place with the owners being compensated at thirty pounds per dwelling. You own hundreds of those houses, Mr Drake, it would have lost a lot of money in rents over the next few years. That plan had to be stopped at all costs.'

Drake looked at Lorna, then back to Amy.

'It's the first I've heard of it,' he said.

'Really?' Amy shook her head. 'I doubt that very much.' She took another sip of her iced water.

'Now, we come to the Thornalleys.'

Basil drained his glass of whisky and clutched it to his chest. Alma put her hands together as if in prayer.

'I'm lumping both of you together because everything you've done has been done in unison, the pair of you are joined at the hip.' Amy held Alma's glare until the former mayor's wife looked away. 'To say they have a chequered past would be an insult to a chess board. I'm not going to go into their dodgy dealings before they came to Spinton because it would take me half the night, and it has no real relevance to the case. However, the grasping criminality they have engaged in since they arrived in our town, certainly has.'

Amy shook her head slowly.

'Where on earth do I start? Okay, this will do. The Thornalleys dreamed up something they called, the mayor's fund, ostensibly to raise money for good causes. Their children's private school would be the main good cause, by way of its fees. After a while, they realised that they could lay off loyal council employees and charge local businesses a tariff to win the contract for their services over the next few years. The Thornalleys played this game for all it was worth and quite soon they were living the kind of lifestyle they had previously only ever dreamed of. They engaged a local plumbing business to take over any repairs that needed doing in the town. They charged Mr Derby three times the amount they had previously charged to obtain the cleaning contract, but that was chicken feed compared to the money they took from both the Kelly and Drake organisations for any construction work that came up. The sad thing was, the fools didn't bother to put as much as a penny away for a rainy day, and as soon as Robert McKenzie came onto the scene and forced a vote in the council chamber, they were in a big mess. They had tried, unsuccessfully, to get Nelson Kelly on their side for the factory deal, so they had put all their eggs in one basket by taking up with Drake. When Mr McKenzie used his London contacts to get backing for the Kelly bid, the Thornalleys were staring ruin in the face. There was no way on earth that Alma, in particular, was going to accept that.'

Amy broke off for a few moments to refill her glass.

'On the night of the murder, Alma was seen in earnest conversation with Mr Drake, after that, she became aware of the Post reporter sniffing around, asking questions, so she hurried out to the kitchen to find Basil who was making himself a cup of herbal tea. Now, according to them, they were so engrossed in trying to think up some story that would put the press off their scent, that they failed utterly to hear the argument that was taking place only a few feet away from them. They do claim to have seen Mr Drake standing at the door to the kitchen just before Lorna found the body, but to be honest, not even the person who they were relying on to get them out of the hole they'd dug for themselves could trust them not to try to drop him in it for the murder. Basil and Alma had the opportunity to kill Nelson and they had an excellent reason for wanting him out of the way.'

Amy took another sip of water, then licked her dry lips.

'Then, of course, we once again come back to the matter of the gloves. Basil claims that he took them off and stuffed them into his pocket in case he happened to spill tea on them. That sounds an even flimsier excuse than Mr Drake's. Unfortunately, Mr Thornalley put his suit into the dry cleaners for a chemical wash the following day, with the gloves still in the pocket.'

Amy looked directly at the Alma and Basil as she went on.

'The Thornalleys had motive, they faced total ruin and social contempt. They had the opportunity, and they told us a tissue of lies before we got at least some semblance of truth out of them. I'm sure we still haven't heard the whole truth, but that might come out further down the line. When they are investigated for embezzlement.'

With the former mayor and his wife looking anywhere but at Chief Inspector Laws, Amy concentrated on the next suspects.

'Now, we come to Horatio and Helen Kelly.'

'Please, Miss Rowlings, could you keep certain names out of this?' Horatio asked.

'I'll keep one name out of it as she's done nothing at all to deserve a mention,' Amy agreed. She smiled at Helen Kelly as she shifted about in her seat.

'Can I just ask, why am I even here?' Derby said, jumping to his feet. 'I've done nothing.'

Bodkin took a step forward and made sit down motions towards the property owner.

'You're here because the houses you bought from Mr Drake, the ones he did all he could to take back from you, are an integral part of this investigation, Mr Derby. Now, please sit down.'

The inspector turned back to Amy. 'Please, go on.'

'Horatio Kelly seldom agreed with his brother when it came to the company's business dealings. He was totally against the demolition plan for Ebenezer Street and wanted the company to be much more socially responsible. Horatio was in some financial difficulty. His house had a large mortgage on it after the divorce settlement, and he has an outstanding director's loan with the company. Nelson had promised to help him out with both issues if he backed down over the factory plan. Horatio did, but with much regret. There has always been a lot of bitterness between the two brothers. Nelson was the blue-eyed boy in the family. His father groomed him to take over the business when the time came. Horatio resented Nelson's wayward lifestyle. He hated the way he treated Helen. He felt impotent and unimportant, more of a hanger on than a proper partner in the family business. It all came to a head when Nelson, after promising to wipe out Horatio's loans, reneged on the deal when he knew he'd secured his brother's reluctant backing for the factory plan. Horatio had no alibi for the night in question until very recently, but I'll come to that in a moment. Mr Kelly, as you can see, is a tall, well-dressed, fair-haired man. He pretty much fits the description of the eye witness, Mr Derby, who spotted a fair-haired man arguing with Nelson at the fire door. So, you see, Mr Kelly has a strong motive for killing his brother.'

Amy cleared her throat and took a sip of water as Horatio protested his innocence.

'Helen Kelly has admitted to making the telephone call that led indirectly to her husband's death. The question we had to ask was whether the call was used to set Nelson up. Would someone be waiting on the other side of the fire exit door at a prearranged time? Did Nelson then, for some reason, open the door to speak to whoever was there? Was he told to go to the door by his wife, or did the waiting man hammer on the emergency exit to get Nelson's attention?

'Mrs Kelly lied to us initially when she explained what the telephone call was all about, citing an emergency visit to her sister's house and asking whether Nelson had his key with him. Later we learned that she had actually phoned her husband to tell him she was leaving him, and she wouldn't be at home when he got back. Nelson, as you can imagine was a little irked by this news. However, it couldn't have come as a huge surprise as their marriage had been on the rocks for years and he had been involved in numerous affairs. Nelson had even been bedding the maid right under Helen's nose, so, just like Nelson's brother, she had a reason to be resentful. Add to that her burgeoning relationship with Horatio, she even backed him in an argument with Nelson over the housing issue, and you can see that there was a major problem between them. Helen, for reasons known only to herself, became involved in a relationship with Harold Kitson.'

Amy paused to look across at him. 'Kitson thought the relationship was deeper than it was, but more about that later. Helen Kelly, dumped Mr Kitson unceremoniously when she realised he was only interested in the money she would get from her husband after their divorce. She had also just been made aware of Horatio's true feelings for her. She now claims that on the night of Nelson's murder, she and his brother were together at Hillcrest, where she has lived for the last decade with Nelson. According to Mrs Kelly, she had packed her cases and was ready to leave with Horatio, but then the police had arrived to inform her of Nelson's death, and their flight was no longer possible, as it would have looked incredibly suspicious.'

Amy was silent for a moment, then she went on.

'So, as you can clearly see, although neither of the two were actually at the event, they did have motive. The pair could well have decided that they would like to run the company in a more socially responsible way. Horatio would be debt free and after a few months of official mourning the pair could set up together and live happily ever after on Nelson's money.'

'That's a ridiculous assertion,' Helen spat. 'I didn't even know I was getting his shares until the other day.'

'Even then, Horatio would have received them and you would have got the house, plus his money,' Amy said. 'So, the assertion is not a ridiculous one. People have been killed for much less.'

Helen threw herself back in her seat as Amy went on.

'Now we come to Harold Kitson.'

Harold straightened up in his chair as Amy addressed him.

'Mr Kitson isn't the most likeable of men. He's an arrogant lech who thinks, just like Nelson did, that every woman he takes a shine to, could be his. Sadly, for him, this is just a figment of his over sexualised imagination. Mr Kitson is heavily in debt; like Horatio, his house is mortgaged to the hilt, he has no money to speak of, his only real asset being the shares he holds in the Drake group of companies. Shares he was desperate to sell, to enable him to switch loyalties and buy into the Kelly organisation when he found out, before it was announced officially, that Nelson had been successful in his bid, and that he was also planning to wipe out most of the assets the Drake company owned. So, he went to see Nelson in his study to beg him to be allowed to invest in the new project. Nelson, being Nelson, would probably have accepted his money, even though he detested the man and had done since childhood, but something stopped him. I think Nelson knew all about Kitson and Helen's affair. Whatever the reason, he threw Kitson out on his ear, leaving him desperate to find the finance he needed to fend off his creditors. The only hope he had now was to either prise Helen away from Nelson and live off the money she would get from a divorce, or hope against hope, that somehow,

Drake's company managed to get hold of that big factory contract. He would have become a very rich man over the years had they done so.'

Amy licked her lips to moisten them, then went on.

'Unfortunately for Harold, Helen had seen right through him and had telephoned on the day of Nelson's murder to tell him it was all over. He was devastated by the news and he knew he was now in a big hole. As I said, the only hope he had was for the Drake businesses to come good, but unless Nelson was out of the way, that wouldn't happen any time soon. So, Harold goes out to drown his sorrows. He meets up with Drake in the Milton, goodness knows what sort of a conversation they had, but, whatever transpired, Harold ended up drinking far too much. From there he went to the Barwood Club where he lost heavily at the card tables. Later we know he got into a taxi with his shirt covered in blood. He got out of the taxi before he got anywhere near where he lives and dropped a bloody handkerchief on the grass verge. The next day he was seen burning the clothes he'd been wearing the night before. So, the question is, was Mr Kitson the fair-haired man seen arguing at the fire door by our eyewitness? He did get into a taxi right outside the Town Hall after all. The trolley bearing the murder weapon was only a few feet away from the emergency exit. It wouldn't have taken more than a few seconds to have picked it up and stuck it in Nelson's chest. Mr Kitson had motive, that was for certain. Nelson's demise benefitted him as much as it did Drake.'

'What more evidence do you need, Bodkin?' Laws got to his feet. 'Arrest him, man. I told you it was blatantly obvious.'

'If you'll just bear with us for a few more minutes, sir,' Bodkin replied. He turned back to Amy. 'Is it time to bring her in?'

CHAPTER
FORTY-SIX

AMY NODDED.

'Yes please, Inspector. I think we're ready for her now.'

Bodkin picked up a chair from the side of the drinks table and carried it behind the Japanese screen. There was a scraping sound and then Amy heard the door open and the sound of a muffled voice. A few moments later the policeman came in and positioned himself by the screen, then there was the sound of a chair scraping again before the door closed and Bodkin reappeared. He gave Amy a quick, thumbs up, then turned his attention to whoever was now behind the screen.

'Are you ready? Okay we'll get started,' he said with a friendly smile.

Amy took a sip of water and ran her tongue over her lips before brushing away a few stray hairs that fell onto her face.

'Behind this beautiful, antique screen, is the young lady who was on duty in the Town Hall cloakroom on the night of Nelson Kelly's murder. She is very young, and understandably reluctant to stand in front of you as she helps us identify a murderer. She only heard voices that night, so there is no need for her to see the faces of the people we ask to speak.'

Amy walked across the floor until she was standing about four yards away from the screen.

'Okay, I'd like you to imagine that the screen is the entrance to the cloakroom. I'm standing more or less the same distance away as Nelson was when the argument broke out.' She looked across towards Bodkin. 'Could you and I swap places please. I'd like you to play the part of Nelson Kelly.'

The policeman stuck up a thumb and the pair swapped positions. As Amy reached the screen, she tilted her head to look behind it.

'Don't be nervous, it's all right. Just nod when you hear the person you heard that night. Shake your head if you don't recognise the voice.' Amy turned back to Bodkin and stuck up her own thumb. 'Righto, Inspector Bodkin, we're ready.'

Bodkin took in the confused-looking faces as they looked towards Amy, then at each other.

'Shall we start with Mr Thornalley?' Bodkin said.

Basil choked on his whisky.

'ME?' he spluttered, 'why me? I wasn't even in the corridor at the time of the murder.'

Bodkin ignored his protest and motioned to him to come forward.

'If you wouldn't mind, Mr Thornalley.'

'But I...'

'Oh, just get on with it, Basil,' Alma spat.

Basil got to his feet and edged around the empty chair in front of him before walking in his shambling gait towards the policeman. Bodkin patted him on the arm and handed him a piece of paper.

'Just read those words out loud when I give you the signal, Mr Thornalley.'

Bodkin cleared his throat and looked sternly at the former mayor.

'It's just business, it's nothing personal,' he said, before pointing towards Basil.

'You've ruined me!' Thornalley said, nervously.

Bodkin looked towards the screen as Amy mouthed, 'louder.'

'Let's try again, a little louder this time,' Bodkin ordered.

'You've ruined me!' Basil said, raising his voice.

Amy looked behind the screen, then shook her head.

'Next one up please.'

Bodkin turned to the rest of the guests.

'You're next up... Mr Drake.'

'What! This is preposterous.' He slammed his glass onto the small round table in front of him. 'I will not take part in this charade.'

'Oh, I think you will, Mr Drake,' Bodkin replied. 'It's either that or at least one night in the cells for obstructing a murder inquiry. You can call your lawyer if you like, but that does seem a little bit over the top when all we're asking you to do is say a few words.'

Drake screwed up his face and snarled at Bodkin as he stormed towards him.

'You haven't heard the last of this.'

'I look forward to reading your written complaint,' Bodkin replied, smoothly. 'Are you ready? Speak clearly now, we don't want you to have to do an encore, do we?' He looked the businessman in the eyes then repeated his own line.

'You've ruined me,' Drake said, unable to disguise the anger in his voice.

Bodkin looked towards the Amy again. Amy checked behind the screen, then shook her head.

'Thank you, Mr Drake,' Bodkin said with more than a hint of sarcasm in his voice. He clapped his hands as he looked around the room. 'Next up... Oh, it's you, Mr Derby.'

'Me?' Terrence squirmed in his chair. 'But I thought I was... I haven't done anything... No, I'm not going to take part in this.'

'Constable,' Bodkin said, looking at the officer standing a few feet behind Derby.

Terrence looked over his shoulder and pushed himself quickly out of the chair as the constable walked towards him. He shuffled across the room wringing his gloved hands. By the time he reached Bodkin he was sweating from every pore.

'Right, Mr Derby,' Bodkin said, fixing him with a stern eye. 'Let's hear your audition.'

Derby tried to speak but all his vocal cords could manage was a high-pitched squeak. He cleared his throat, then whispered croakily. 'Could I have a glass of water, please?'

Bodkin walked to the drink's table and poured water into a crystal glass.

'Ice?' he asked.

Derby nodded frantically and Bodkin picked up the silver tongs and dropped a large chuck of ice into the glass.

'Here you are, Mr Derby,' Bodkin said as he handed the drink over. 'Let's see if that helps.'

Derby took a sip, then a longer one.

'Are you ready for the prompt?' Bodkin asked.

Derby shook his head slowly.

'I'm sorry, I'm so sorry,' he said, then he burst into tears.

Amy walked away from the screen as Bodkin dragged Derby's chair into the centre of the room.

'Sit down, Terrence,' he ordered.

Terrence did as he was told and stared down at his knees, his tears dripping onto his trousers.

'We've done with the screen now, could you fold it away please?' Amy asked the uniformed officer.

As he folded the sections of the antique screen together, there was an audible gasp from the assembled guests. The only thing hiding behind it, was an empty chair.

'What was the point of that little performance?' Drake asked, angrily.

'If you sit down for a moment, I'll explain,' Amy said, sweetly.

'Inspector Bodkin and I had pretty much worked out who the killer was, and the reasons behind the murder, but to be certain, we had to put the last piece of the jigsaw in place. My, 'little performance' enabled us to find that last, but vitally important piece.'

'It was rather theatrical,' Laws said, waving his whisky glass in front of him.

'It was meant to be, Chief Inspector,' Amy replied with a smile. 'You see, I got the idea from Hercule Poirot, who used a similar ruse to crack a case.'

'Hercules who?' Laws asked.

'Poirot. The world's finest detective,' Amy replied.

'Ah, you mean the French chappie in the books. Mrs Laws is always going on about him.'

'He's Belgian,' Amy said, curtly, 'and the idea came to me in a dream last night.' She paused and picked up her glass of water from the table. 'You see, in Peril At End House, Poirot needs to flush out a couple called the Crofts, who have forged the will of the late Nick Buckley. Unfortunately for them, Nick Buckley is alive and well and she plays the part of her own ghost at a séance, set up by Poirot. He is successful of course and the Crofts are proved to have forged the will.'

Amy sipped her water again and tucked a few strands of wayward hair behind her ear.

'I didn't have a Nick Buckley at hand, so I invented my own ghost, and sat her behind the screen. She performed her task brilliantly, at least, I think she did. There is not a shred of a doubt in my mind as to who killed Nelson Kelly.'

'Isn't she marvellous,' Shirley said, excitedly, clutching her husband's arm.

'Quite remarkable,' Robert replied. 'But what made you suspect him in the first place, Amy?'

'He was right down at the bottom of our list of suspects at the start, if I'm honest,' Amy replied. 'But there was always something troubling us when it came to the matter of the open fire door. I have to admit that Mr Derby did send us scurrying off in completely the wrong direction with his description of the man he claimed to have seen, arguing with Nelson that night. That was his plan of course, he had to do something to try to throw us off the scent and we did have two suspects, Mr Kitson and Mr Kelly who fitted that description to a remarkable degree, and both of them were high on our list. The problem for Mr Derby was, there were only two suspects who came anywhere close to the man he described and once they had been eliminated from our inquiry, his evidence was seen for what it was, a tissue of lies.'

'But... Kitson... when was he proved innocent? There's no hint of it in your notes, Bodkin,' Laws said with a puzzled look on his face.

'I went to see the owner of the Barwood club yesterday evening, sir. He told me that Mr Kitson was drunk and disorderly at the club on the night of the murder, and had assaulted one of the security staff. The security guard in question gave back much more than he received, and Mr Kitson was given a punch on the nose which bled so badly that the blood almost covered the front of his shirt. By the time he staggered down the road from the club and hailed a taxi, Nelson was already dead.'

Amy turned towards Kitson and held out her hands.

'You burned a thirty-five-pound suit for nothing,' she said.

She turned to face the Kellys.

'Helen was telling us the truth, Horatio was with her all

evening, but he was passed out in bed at the time the murder took place.'

Amy spun on her heel and looked down at Derby as he sat shaking in his chair.

'As soon as we realised that this fair-haired man didn't actually exist, the rest of the clues fell into place. As I said before, this investigation was all about gloves, and doors, one closed, one open. I'll start with the gloves, because as you can see, Terrence is wearing a pair now. He has to, because his hands were so badly burned when the ship he was serving on was sunk in the war. Mr Derby has to cover his hands with a specially made cream to keep out infection. The chemicals he used on a daily basis for cleaning the offices would do immeasurable harm to his hands if they came in contact. We know he was wearing gloves on the night of the murder because he took them off to light a cigarette when he first spoke to us. Next, we come to the two doors.'

Amy paused for a moment. 'Zena O'Keefe was working with the team of caterers during the presentation, and she was ordered to take the boxes and packaging that the buffet had arrived in, out to the bins which are situated at the back of the building. To get to the bins she had to open the door at the end of the corridor that runs alongside the kitchen. Unfortunately for her, the door was locked and no one could find anyone with a key, so she had to pile the boxes up at the side of the corridor. When Bodkin and I went around to the rear of the building a few minutes after the body was found, we discovered that the door was now unlocked. Someone with a key had obviously entered the building via that route. Derby was the only person to be holding a copy of the key that night. He's the person responsible for locking the building up after his team have finished cleaning.'

Amy ran her hand down the back of her hair, then continued.

'Here's what I believe happened. Mr Derby and his team have finished cleaning at the Register Office and have moved on to the library, skipping the Town Hall because they knew there was an event on. As the cleaning progressed, Derby thought he'd nip into the Town Hall to see if the evening was winding up. He let himself in with his key and dropped it into his pocket, leaving the door unlocked for his staff. He walks along the corridor until he's passed the open kitchen door, then to his astonishment, he sees the man who is about to bankrupt him. You see, Terrence had borrowed fifteen hundred pounds from the bank to buy the Ebenezer Street houses from Drake. As he would only be paid thirty pounds per dwelling by the council, he was looking at a loss of some nine hundred pounds, plus interest. He was relying on the rents from the tenants to pay back the loan. Without that income he was left with a thousand-pound debt and no means to pay it off. He was a ruined man. Anyway, back to the night in question. He sees Nelson walking towards him and he tries to convince him, beg him even, to reconsider his plan. Nelson says something like, it's not personal, it's just business, but he's not in the best of moods after just hearing his wife is about to leave him, so the words may not have come out quite as politely as they might have. Terrence is incensed, he knows he's finished, he notices the knife on the trolley right at the side of him and in a rush of anger, he picks it up and sticks it in Nelson's chest.'

Amy ran her palms down her hips as she collected her thoughts.

'So, Terrence is now in a quandary. He turns to run back the way he came, but there are voices coming from the kitchen and he thinks if he runs past the open door he might be spotted. Then he hears the clicking of Lorna Wetherby's heels coming from the direction of the cloakroom, and he looks around in panic. The only escape route left to him, is via the fire exit door, so he dashes towards it, pushes down the bar and he's out in the cool night air. But which way to go? If he turns right, he'll run straight out onto the main road and any number of witnesses might spot him. The obvious answer is to run directly across to the library's side door, but then he's in a direct line of sight from the corridor he just came out of. So, he turns left and runs to the back of the building, where he crashes into one of the dustbins, tipping it over and landing so heavily on top of it, that he created a huge dent in the side. The collision also causes him to injure either his knee or his ankle, and he is suddenly in a lot of pain, so he hobbles with as much speed as he can muster, to the Register Office, where he knows he can hide for a while and possibly wrap a bandage around his ankle to support it, and maybe change his gloves for a clean pair.'

'That's why he was limping,' Bodkin said. 'I thought he limped because of his war injuries.'

'I thought the same, Bodkin, until I saw him dash across Ebenezer Street just before I paid him a visit the other day.' She walked slowly across to the drinks table. 'How close was that to the truth, Mr Derby?' she said as she added ice to a fresh glass of water.

'I didn't mean to kill him,' Derby said in a husky voice. 'He was just there and I couldn't stop myself.' He looked at Bodkin with teary eyes. 'Honestly, Inspector, I didn't go in there planning to kill him. I wish I'd never gone to check on the progress of the blooming event.' Derby wiped his eyes on his sleeve. 'He smirked at me; he spoke so condescendingly. "It's just business." I couldn't stop myself, he'd ruined me, put me in debt for the rest of my life. I felt this rage inside, I can't even remember picking up the knife... but then I saw him lying on the floor with blood pumping out of him and he's looking up at me... I panicked and ran for it.'

'And, what did you do next?' Bodkin asked.

'Well, I got outside... and it was like you said, Miss, I wasn't sure what to do. There was a man with fair hair leaning on the wall at the end of the alley... It might have been Mr Kitson, he looked like he was crying, or maybe having a pee... anyway I couldn't run that way, and just as you said, Miss, I couldn't risk being seen running straight across into the side door of the library, so I went around the back. I hit that bin at about ninety miles an hour, landed on top of it and twisted my ankle. I knew I had to get out of sight quickly, so I let myself into the Register Office. I've got a cleaning cupboard in there where I keep a couple of pairs of gloves and a change of clothes if I need them. I gave it a few minutes, then I looked out of the side window and saw you and Miss Rowlings standing by the bins. I waited for you to go back inside, then I sneaked into the library by the back door. One of the girls noticed my limp and I told her I'd gone over on my ankle; in case you questioned them later. When we arrived at the fire exit door, I might have looked calm and collected, but I was churning up inside. I threw in the bit about the fair-haired man to try to throw you off the scent. It almost worked; didn't it?'

Derby's head dropped to his knees and he began to weep.

'Don't let them hang me, Mr Bodkin. I didn't mean to do it.'

FORTY-SEVEN

By lunchtime the next day, news had begun to filter out that the murderer of Nelson Kelly had been arrested. The details were sketchy but that didn't stop Big Nose Beryl giving her take on things.

'They haven't said who it was yet, but my money is on his wife. It's obvious really, she stands to get everything.'

'Maybe she can give you some tips on how to kill your husband and walk away scot-free then, Beryl because she hasn't been arrested.' Amy picked up her mug, blew into the steam, then took a sip.

'Oh, here she goes again, little Miss know-all. Who was it then? Come on, you claim to be on the inside of the investigation.'

Amy shrugged. 'I'm not saying anything, Beryl. I suggest you wait for the evening edition of the Post to come out. Sandy Miles will tell you all about it. Are you and he related by the way? He seems to come up with just as much nonsense as you do.'

As Amy left the factory at five-thirty she was surprised to see Bodkin's little black Morris parked outside. Bodkin himself was in the front seat, reading the evening paper. His head jerked up as she banged on the car window.

'Are you famous again, Bodkin?' she asked.

Bodkin motioned to the passenger seat and Amy walked around the back of the car under the watchful eye of Big Nose Beryl and a few of her cronies.

'I wonder where those two are off to,' Beryl said snidely. 'He doesn't buy her all those port and lemons for nothing.'

'Keep it up, Beryl,' Amy said as she climbed into her seat. 'We'll see who comes out on top.' She reached out for the handle to close the door. 'Was your old man at home on Saturday night? Only you were seen arm in arm with that bloke from the iron-monger's as you walked through your back gate. Did you and your old fellow have a card school going or something?'

Amy slammed the door as a scarlet faced Beryl stormed up the hill towards the Old Bull.

'She'll learn one of these days,' Bodkin said with a laugh. He closed the paper and handed it to Amy. 'Front page,' he said.

'Nelson Killer, Sunk,' she read aloud. 'Post Exclusive. Reporter, Sandy Miles. Oh my goodness, Miles is on top form tonight,' she said.

'Just wait until you see who is claiming to have cracked the case,' Bodkin replied.

Amy read a bit further down the column.

'LAWS! Oh my goodness, Bodkin, Laws is claiming to have solved the case... do you get a mention at all?'

Bodkin shook his head. 'You know how these things work. He does mention, 'officers from the Spinton police' but that's it, the rest is all about him.'

'And yet he turned up demanding you arrest the wrong man,' Amy said with a note of disbelief in her voice.

'You handed it to him on a plate, Amy. Your Poirot moment gave him everything he needed to know about the investigation. I bet he was in his element boasting to Sandy bloody Miles this lunchtime.'

'It's such a shame though, Bodkin, he'll get all the credit for this with Grayson and the chief constable.'

'That I doubt,' Bodkin said. 'I think that your big reveal last night will be the subject of conversation at many a future dinner party at the McKenzie residence. And both Grayson and the chief constable will be invited on a regular basis, unlike Mr Laws. Shirley took an instant dislike to him.'

'That's good then, Bodkin, the truth will out, it always does.'

'And you will be the talk of the town, Amy Rowlings,' Bodkin said with a big smile on his face. 'That was some performance. Old Poirot couldn't have done it better himself.'

Two weeks later, after finishing work for the day, Amy caught the bus at the Old Bull and took a ride to the station where she got off and walked through the Haxley estate until she got to Ebenezer Street. In her bag was a birthday card and a carefully wrapped bundle of doll's clothes.

As she turned the corner at the top of the street, she bumped into Helen and Horatio Nelson who were just coming out of the door of number twenty-one, Terrence Derby's former home.

She stopped as Helen turned towards her, not wanting to speak first in case the Kelly's were still angry.

'Hello, Amy,' Helen said brightly. 'What are you doing all the way out here?'

'Visiting a birthday girl,' Amy replied. She hesitated a moment, then went on. 'Could I, erm, ask you the same question?'

'I'm happy to answer,' Helen replied. 'We are here to take a last look at the houses we've agreed to buy from the bank. We can't take charge of them yet, not until after the trial anyway, but we will get ownership of them. We've agreed to pay the bank a bit of compensation. We obviously won't pay them the full amount they lent to Derby, but as they tried to help Drake get the houses back, they don't deserve to get all the money they laid out.'

'What are you going to do with them?' Amy asked.

'We're going to flatten them,' Horatio said. 'Then we're going to build the factory. At the same time, we'll be knocking down the rest of the estate and putting up some decent houses, just as Nelson and Mayor McKenzie had planned to do.'

'But what about the people on Ebenezer? Where are they supposed to go?'

'They'll be the first in the new builds,' Helen said. 'We're going to use Derby's place and the two houses attached to it as temporary dwellings for the families living in the ones we knock down. So, we demolish three, build three, then rehouse three. We reckon the whole process should take about a year to complete, for Ebenezer Street, that is. The families living in numbers nineteen and twenty will get the first of the new houses, then we'll use them as temporary dwellings for the next people in line. There will be jobs in the factory for those with the skills.'

'That sounds wonderful,' Amy said. 'Which end will you be starting at? You couldn't do number one first, could you? I know it's a lot to ask, and I know you won't feel like doing me any favours, but they are living a terrible life down there. The mother works fourteen hours a day, seven days a week and her little girl has to miss school so she can help her do the washing they take in. She's been really poorly recently and—'

'We haven't worked out which end to start at yet, Amy. We were thinking of starting with numbers sixteen to eighteen if I'm honest.'

'Well, could you at least find her a job in the factory? She's an intelligent woman and such a hard worker, I'm sure she'd be an asset to you.'

Helen shook her head. 'I can't make any promises on that score, Amy. We have to take on people with the skills we need.'

'But surely there'll be jobs in the canteen, you'll want cleaning staff, will there be a training program?'

'The answer is yes to all of those things, Amy, but I can't guarantee anything.'

Amy grabbed Helen's sleeve.

'Helen, could you just spare me a couple of minutes. If you still feel the same way after that, then I'll stop nagging you.'

Helen looked at her watch and sighed.

'Five minutes. Then I really do have to get on. We've got a meeting with the mayor this evening.' She turned to Horatio. 'Could you wait in the car for me? I won't be long.'

Amy led Helen towards the bottom end of Ebenezer Street, then turned into the alley before the final block of houses. When she pushed open the creaking gate, she could hear voices coming from Karen's open kitchen door.

'You're about to meet Karen and Beth,' Amy said, quietly. She pointed to the roof with its missing slates. 'Karen's husband fell off that roof and died as he was trying to fix it in the middle of winter. A couple of weeks later, her baby died of Scarlet Fever. She makes a living by taking in washing. Beth is only seven and she's been suffering with scurvy and a host of other illnesses that little girls shouldn't ever be coming into contact with. The thing is, Helen, despite all that, they just keep carrying on, never daring to hope that something better might come along. A job in your factory would mean shorter hours and a regular income for Karen, and it would mean Beth could go to school every day. A new house would mean the world to them, anything is better than this rat-infested hovel, but if she has no job to go to, then she's going to have to keep taking in the washing, and Beth is still going to have to take time out of school to help.'

Amy brushed away the stray strands of hair from her face, and looked up the yard towards the house.

'As I said, Helen. I respect your decision, it's up to you who you employ.'

The two women walked up the yard and climbed the steps leading to the back door. Amy stepped inside first, then stood back so that Helen could enter the scullery. They found the Hamiltons hard at work. Karen feeding a sopping, heavy sheet into the mangle and Beth, keeping a careful hold as she tried to fold it without dropping it onto the filthy floor.

Helen looked around at the dripping light socket, the black, mouldy walls and the puddles of water that littered the floor. Turning, she looked into the living room, at the rodent traps on the floor, the sodden plaster walls and the quarry tiled floor that had lifted in several places showing the wet brown earth underneath.

'Amy!' Beth screamed when she heard Amy clear her throat to get her attention. 'I can't hug you yet. I need to get this sheet through.'

Helen stepped forward and took the end of the wet sheet from Beth's hands. Beth immediately ran towards Amy and threw herself into her arms.

'Happy Birthday, Beth,' Amy said after she had managed to prise the young girl off her.

'I got a doll for my birthday!' Beth shouted. 'Hang on, I'll get her... I called her Polly.'

When she returned with the doll, Amy pulled out her present from her bag and handed it to the young girl along with the birthday card.

'Dolls' dresses,' Beth squealed with delight.

'I hope they fit her,' Amy said, as Beth gave her another big hug.

Helen carefully continued to fold the wet double sheet that

Karen had been feeding into the rollers of the mangle. When it was all through, she held it in her arms looking for somewhere to put it.

Karen pulled a battered, wicker basket from under her ironing table and Helen gratefully dropped the sheet into it.

'It's hot in here,' she said, wiping her brow.

'It gets hotter,' Karen said. 'And steamier too.' She picked up the burnt-black kettle and held it under the tap.

'Time for a tea break, I think.' She carried the kettle through to the living room and placed it on the grid above the fire, then she turned around with a worried look on her face.

'You're not from the welfare, are you?'

Amy shook her head.

'She's not from the welfare, Karen. I wouldn't do that to you.'

Helen looked around the filthy room, taking in the dense, black patches of mould and the strips of wallpaper that contained so much moisture they were peeling from the walls. She shuddered as she saw a slug inch its way out of the earth and onto one of the floor tiles. She turned to Amy with tears in her eyes and after trying, but failing to find her voice, she just nodded to her.

Amy threw her arms around Helen's neck and after whispering a broken, 'thank you' into her ear, she turned towards a confused-looking Karen.

'Karen... Beth... This is Helen Kelly; she's got something she wants to tell you.'

FORTY-EIGHT

THE MILTON COCKTAIL BAR WAS ALMOST FULL AS FERRIS STEPPED UP TO the stage to begin his act.

At the back of the room, Amy, Alice, Shirley McKenzie and Bodkin sat at their table and applauded wildly.

'Do your Groucho Marx, Ferris,' Amy shouted.

'Come on, Amy, drink up, it's my round,' Shirley said. 'What are you having this time?'

'I'll have another Pimm's number one, with lots of ice,' Amy replied, swaying a little in her seat. 'And Alice will have another Martina.'

Alice waved her glass and grinned at Amy.

'How many have I had now?' she asked.

'Four, I think,' Amy replied, trying to count on her fingers.

'It feels like more,' Alice giggled.

Bodkin sipped at his whisky and shook his head when Shirley offered to buy him another.

'Someone has to be sober enough to see this pair home,' he said.

Amy laid her head on his shoulder and smiled happily.

'You do look after me, don't you, Bodkin?'

'Someone has to save you from yourself,' Bodkin said with a wide smile.

'You know... I wish I could do police work with you every day,' she said. 'Imagine the fun we'd have? It's not fair that they won't let me be an inspector, just because I'm a woman.'

'I'm glad you're not in the police force, Amy. I wouldn't like it and neither would you.'

Amy lifted her head and looked him in the face.

'That's mean of you, Bodkin. Why don't you want me in the police?'

'Because you wouldn't be happy,' Bodkin replied. 'It's not all murder and mayhem you know? A lot of the work involves hunting down people like Back Door Billy and there are worse than him around. Anyway, with people like Laws in charge he'd have you out in all weathers, chasing up broken windows and finding the owners of stray dogs. You'd never see the inside of a murder case. You're far too good to have that done to you.'

Amy smiled and put her head on his shoulder again.

'We're all right as we are, aren't we, Bodkin?'

Bodkin kissed the top of her head and put his arm around her.

'Perfectly all right.'

The End

397

ACKNOWLEDGMENTS

Thank you to my editor Maureen Vincent-Northam
    Many thanks to my eagle eyed proof reader and fact checker,
Paul Lautman

ALSO BY T.A. BELSHAW

AMY ROWLING'S SERIES IN ORDER

❧

MURDER AT THE MILL

DEATH AT THE LYCHGATE

Printed in Great Britain
by Amazon